# Crooked Foot

## Evans Bissonette

# DEDICATION

Dedicated to my wife, Sue: I fell in love with you on a blind date over 45 years ago. You have always, and in all things, certainly been my biggest cheerleader.

# ACKNOWLEDGMENTS

*Crooked Foot* would not be the book it is, had it not been for the support I received from all the members of both the *Troy-Birmingham Writers* and *The Writers Connection*. Special recognition goes to Martha Hale (*Russ and Holly: A Midwest Country Odyssey*), Martha Shoopman (*Dancing with Devils*), and Maria Taormina (*Divine Plates, Three Lives in One*) for having freely provided their feedback and encouragement. It is my belief that if everyone had the support of friends like these we would live in a much better world.

# TABLE OF CONTENTS

# Chapter 1: Fresh Tracks

Crooked Foot watched as his paternal grandfather, Howling Wolf, crouch down for a closer look at the footprints. Though he tried to hide it, concern showed on his grandfather's face as he examined the tracks.

"Is it fresh?" the boy asked. Even from this distance, they were the largest prints the boy had ever seen, but then he hadn't seen much.

Boys his age started getting their experience by the time one-hand's[1] worth of summers had come and gone. Their fathers took them hunting where they were taught how to read animal signs, follow game and find their way in the woods. Because he was an orphan, many summers—nearly two-hand's worth—had come and gone and he hadn't been taken out.

However, Crooked Foot was not completely inexperienced. Even though he hadn't been included in hunts, he had listened carefully when the hunters and would-be hunters gathered around campfires and told of their adventures.

From their stories, he learned to make a pouch sling by attaching leather cords to a square of animal hide. After loading fist-sized stones into his sling, trees and rocks became his first targets. Flat rocks—stacked one on top of the other—sometimes three or four such piles in a row were a favorite. He practiced all day, every day.

It was while at practice he was befriended by Red Deer. After setting his targets in place, Crooked Foot retreated to a line a respectable distance away. Before he

---

[1] Counting - In this culture, the people count on their fingers and it is done in sets of five. One hand is a count of five; two hands are a count of ten. Individual numbers are: Da (1); Jar (2); Cha (3); Tug (4); and Mux (5). For numbers six through ten, Pra plus the count, as Pra-Da (6), Pra-Jar (7), etc.

could use his sling, a rock whizzed overhead, knocking over the first target. Angry, he turned to see who played this joke and found Red Deer's smiling face. Crooked Foot had no idea how long the chief's son—at nearly one-hand older than himself—had been behind him, watching him practice. The older boy walked up and playfully tousled Crooked Foot's hair. Laughing, Crooked Foot forgot his anger.

The pair set up the targets again and went back to the starting line. Without a word, Red Deer handed the younger boy one of the two fist-sized rocks he had picked up and took the youngster's sling.

Looking at his new companion, Red Deer said, "Left stack, outside edge." He twirled the sling overhead and let the rock fly. The missile shot through the air and smashed into the target. Pieces scattered, some taking out the stack to the right of the goal. Red Deer stepped to one side and turned to face Crooked Foot. Still smiling, he held out the sling and said, "Your turn."

Accepting the challenge, Crooked Foot nodded and pointed to the remaining stacks. "Far right edge," he said. Then, hefting the rock, he sized up the target and sent the weapon in motion. The stack scattered from the impact. Crooked Foot turned to Red Deer. The older lad laughed and he started forward. "Come on," he said, "let's set 'em up and try it again."

In the beginning, the game that began as a contest using slings and stones expanded to include bolas,[2] throwing sticks, and spears. The games between the two of them began the start of a close friendship. It was during this time that Red Deer showed Crooked Foot how to make a knife and they began making the younger lad's first spear.

Then, three summers ago, Red Deer went off on his

---

[2] Bola - A strong cord with weights attached to the ends. It is used for catching animals, large or small, by twirling the cord overhead and then releasing the revolving weapon to entangle the animal's legs.

sojourn.[3] Most lads were back after one summer's time, but Red Deer had yet to return. Many in the tribe had given up hope and spoke openly of not seeing him again. Not ready to concede that possibility, Red Deer's father, Howling Wolf, remained silent.

Like his grandfather, Crooked Foot knew Red Deer would return. He was certain of this because he had overheard his maternal grandmother, Bright Moon, talking with Howling Wolf when they thought he was asleep. He could not make out all the conversation, but he definitely heard his grandmother scold their chief:

*I told you when Red Deer left on his sojourn that it would be five summers before he returned.*

*You are Shaman[4] and I have never known you to be wrong, but can you be sure? Howling Wolf asked.*

*Bright Moon gave him a sharp reply. I have no reason to change my mind. Even if I did, it wouldn't change what was destined to happen.*

Crooked Foot remained silent, gathered berries, and used their juice to color the spear he and Red Deer had made together. When questioned, he said it was so he could tell his spear from any others. He didn't tell them he did it to

---

[3] Sojourn - A period of time when a person may stay in a place as a traveler or guest. They become a temporary inhabitant, a newcomer lacking inherited rights. In many primitive tribes, this is a traditional rite of passage marking transition from childhood to adult. The candidate's survival proved that they could live in the world outside their village. It also taught them that the world is bigger than their village and there is value in tribal membership. An individual on a sojourn goes out into the world to learn; the greatest achievement is that they find out they don't know everything.

[4] Shaman - A "medicine elder" (not always a male) who uses naturally occurring products, such as herbs, to treat ailments/illness. In order to attend to the tribes' physical, spiritual, and mental needs, they had to be adept at reading body language and using primitive psychology. They were often required by situations to think and act quickly. To become a Shaman, a person would apprentice themselves to a teacher for 20-30 years.

remember his friend.

As tribal leader, Howling Wolf had little time to spend with his grandson. Now, with his son, Red Deer, gone, Howling Wolf began taking Crooked Foot on short outings. It gave him the chance to test what the lad knew, how he performed, and how willing he was to learn.

For Crooked Foot, it was critical for him to learn as much as he could from whomever he could. More importantly, it was time he now could spend with his grandfather.

From his place near the river's edge, his grandfather motioned for the lad to join him. Reacting to that invitation, Crooked Foot used the shaft of his cherished red spear to steady himself as he carefully picked his way along the slippery riverbank to his grandfather's side.

Howling Wolf replied to the boy's question in a quiet tone, "It rained before we started." He pointed to the edges of the imprint in the soft mud. "See here, the mud is still soft. Mamuta, the sun, came to chase away the darkness and the rain, but look, there is no sign of rain in the print. It was made after the rain stopped."

He paused to let the boy take it all in and then patiently continued. "At the edges, the mud is still soft. The sun brought warmth but hasn't had time to make the edges dry." He poked a finger into the soft mud around the print's border and held it out for Crooked Foot to examine. Satisfied the boy understood, he continued, "The cold tongue of Wawakin, the wind which blows off the Great Ice,[5] hasn't made it solid." He looked at the lad for confirmation. Did he understand?

"The rain came and made the ground soft and wet," Crooked Foot acknowledged. "The animal that made this came here after the rain stopped. There hasn't been enough time pass for the warmth of sun or the cold breath of the

---

[5] The Great Ice - The glacial ice-sheet. An area that the people saw as seemingly going on forever.

wind to change things."

The boy aptly demonstrated that he listened and understood. Satisfied, Howling Wolf nodded in agreement. *So far, the boy had done well, but what lay ahead would be a shock.*

Howling Wolf spread his fingers wide, palms down, leaned in close, and used both hands to measure across the paw print.

"It's wider than your hands," Crooked Foot gasped. "What kind of animal made this?"

"Look here." Howling Wolf pointed to the ground in front of them. "Front feet." He stood up and pointed at another set of tracks further away. "Over there. Hind feet … tell me, what kind of animal do you think made this?"

Crooked Foot looked down at the print in front of him and then at the other tracks more than twice his grandfather's height away. Memories flooded his young mind. Memories of nights gathered around the campfires, old men—hunters from long ago—who loudly told many other hunting stories spoke only in hushed voices of this creature lest the animal would hear and come after them.

To Crooked Foot, it seemed like his heart stopped and then began beating again … fast … and in his throat. His mouth went dry. Finally, able to speak, he managed to squeak out one word, hardly more than a whisper, "Tawasiki.[6]"

Howling Wolf nodded. "When you were a baby strapped to the carry board, Tawasiki, the great bear who roams the hills along the Great Ice, came upon our hunting party. Your other grandfather, Kaliska[7]—Bright Moon's mate—and your father fought bravely while your mother put you up in a tree. Before the rest of the hunting party could come to their aid, the great bear took your grandfather and both your parents, but left you."

Howling Wolf fell silent for a moment. His gaze

---

[6] Tawasiki - The Great Bear, the one who roams along the Great Ice.
[7] Kaliksa - Miwok name meaning "coyote chasing deer." Bright Moon's mate.

wandered out over the horizon as if he watched something. Finally, he continued, "Tawasiki has been gone such a long time ... we thought he had gone away ... we thought we were safe." His gaze dropped back toward the paw prints. "It looks like he has returned."

"What should we do?"

Howling Wolf directed his attention back to the boy. "We must go back and warn the people. The council will have to decide whether the Narwikin[8] should stay or leave."

He scanned their surroundings again for any signs of trouble. If they had to run, he knew the boy's lame foot[9] would slow them down. All seemed quiet. For the most part, clumps of low brush, scrub trees, and foxtail pines dotted the slopes of the grassy meadow that bordered the river. The trail followed along the river's edge, skirted around a tall old tree, and turned to climb uphill. The hill, a major outcropping, forced a bend in the river. A mound of debris—brush, stumps, and whole trees all carried off by the annual spring floods—lay jammed into the bend.

Farther inland, away from the river's edge, the meadow and the scrub gave way to tree-covered hills. Snowcapped mountains rose up beyond the hills. From the high valleys between the mountains, glacial ice flowed outward and threatened to swallow the land. Nothing seemed out of place. "Come, we must go now."

"Grandfather, the Narwikin are hungry," the boy protested, "the Long Cold[10] has left them with pains in their bellies. So far this morning we've only managed to slay two rabbits." He held up the animal carcasses. "This won't be enough to feed everyone."

Howling Wolf smiled shyly at the boy's words. Early in their hunt, they had come across a rabbit. By hand-signals,

---

8 Narwikin - 'The People'. The manner in which many primitive tribes simply referred to themselves.

9 A lame foot - Crooked Foot was born with what would eventually become known as a club foot.

10 The Long Cold - Winter. Seasons occurred even in the Ice Age.

Howling Wolf encouraged his grandson to use his sling, then watched quietly, patiently as the lad selected a smooth rock from his pack and loaded it into the pouch. Twirling the sling over his head, Crooked Foot aimed and let the missile fly. Struck, the rabbit lay stunned while the lad rushed up and dispatched it.

In their wanderings, they found a scant few additional rabbits and repeated the process each time, but not always with the same success. Still, Crooked Foot was elated with his efforts and his chest swelled with pride. Howling Wolf, proud of the lad, did his best to suppress his own delight.

The boy watched as ice floated by on the river then turned to face his grandfather. "The sun has returned to warm us. Soon we will see the spring floods and then the giant fish will return to the river. Flowers will appear on the plains and the grasses will grow green and tender. When that happens, we will see the great wandering herds return. Then, there will be plenty to eat, but not yet."

Howling Wolf put a tender hand on the boy's shoulder. Like his father before him, Crooked Foot already showed signs of being a great leader. The sun was near the midpoint, but clouds gathered and would once again cover it. The smell of rain was back in the air. Crooked Foot waited for an answer. Howling Wolf looked into his grandson's eager face and knew the answer he had to give wouldn't be as a grandfather but as a tribal leader. "We're not the only hunters. The Narwikin sent out many hunting parties since the sun returned to chase away the darkness."

The boy was dejected. It wasn't the answer he had hoped to hear.

Howling Wolf tried to soften the blow. "Before they left, each group agreed to return by the time the sun reached the midpoint. Perhaps the others did better."

He watched as the lad scanned the skies in hopes he could wring out just a little more time for them to be together. As young as he was, the lad realized the elements weren't on their side, and they should return.

Howling Wolf offered another reason, "It looks like the rain will soon be on us. Game is seeking cover and will become even harder to find." To add more emphasis, he added, "Tawasiki has also been hunting. We should have seen more rabbits, but he has driven game away from the area. We need to get back and tell the others Tawasiki has returned and he is hungry." Howling Wolf turned and started up the animal trail toward their encampment. His action cut off further discussion.

Crooked Foot fell in step behind him and tried to match Howling Wolf's long strides with his own bouncy quick ones. Being born with a clubfoot made movement awkward, but he hadn't allowed this to keep him from trying to do what others did. What he lacked in speed he made up for in other ways.

The trail they followed paralleled the river before turning to coil uphill. It started to rain, lightly at first and then heavier as the wind picked up. Cautiously, Howling Wolf peered through the rain and scanned the barren bush with wary eyes. Game attracted by the water should be plentiful in the area along the river. The only movement came from the cold wind as it stirred the bushes and trees.

Rain, interspersed with snow, picked up as they reached the crest of the hill. Rounding a bend found them walking directly into the storm.

They hadn't gotten far from the river when Howling Wolf froze in mid-step. Crooked Foot almost ran into him. He looked up at his grandfather and then peered through the driving rain to see what caused him to stop.

He too froze in his steps. Ahead, a few stones' throw away, Tawasiki, his winter white coat just beginning to turn to the browns of spring, stood on his hind feet, and sniffed the air. He looked as tall as three men. Upwind and slightly turned away, the bear hadn't seen them. It would only be a matter of time before he did.

Howling Wolf whispered through clenched teeth, "Don't make a sound ... just back up."

Following his grandfather's instructions, Crooked Foot moved slowly ... quietly ... backward. If they could back around the bend without being discovered, they would turn and move faster, possibly making good their escape.

Fate wouldn't allow that. From somewhere behind them a long-dead tree surrendered to the wind's cold breath. It collapsed with a crash. The sudden noise launched a covey of startled birds into the air.

The sound caught Tawasiki's attention and his head snapped around. Their eyes locked. Howling Wolf and Crooked Foot stood frozen hoping they wouldn't be noticed.

This would not happen. The bear dropped to all fours, turned, and started lumbering toward them, head lolling side to side with each step.

"RUN!" Grandfather yelled, "Quickly ... to the tree by the river."

# Chapter 2: Tawasiki

Tawasiki stood on his hind feet and sniffed the air. It was raining. Hunting hadn't been good. He was hungry. Suddenly, behind him, a noise and birds took flight. Something must have startled them. The noise caught Tawasiki's attention and he turned to face the sound.

Even before he was injured, he had learned that he would never have been able to catch a bird, but he might be able to catch whatever caused them to take flight. Because of his old injuries and the bothersome rain, it took a few moments for Tawasiki to see the two humans, one large one and one small one, frozen in their steps.

He remembered humans. Sometime ago, when he was a lot younger, he fought a trio of them. The fight left him with a spear point buried in his shoulder. It reminded him of its presence every time he moved. The conflict had also left him blind in one eye. The humans had given him these injuries before he killed them. Would this time be different? He didn't know. He only knew he was hungry and they were food.

Tawasiki dropped to all fours. With heavy, graceless steps the great bear started lumbering down the trail toward the humans as swiftly as the pain of his years would allow. As he did, the larger of the two humans made a sharp sound and the pair turned and started running back down the trail. The larger one moved smoothly and swiftly; the smaller one moved slower and with a bobbing motion.

Neither as fast, nor as agile as it once was, the great bear waddled after them as quick as his old injuries would allow. If he couldn't catch the larger one, perhaps he could catch the smaller one. That would be good. He was hungry.

### ###

"RUN!" Grandfather yelled, "Quickly … to the tree

by the river." He turned and ran down the trail the way they came.

Crooked Foot bobbed along after him. He could hear the bear crash through the brush as it lurched along behind them. The boy ran as fast as he could, but with each step he took, the sound got closer.

Realizing he still clutched the dead rabbits, Crooked Foot dropped one and a few steps later, the other. If the bear were hungry and not just ornery, maybe it would stop long enough to gulp down the rabbits. Stopping it even for a few moments would help.

Crash … Bang … Pop … Snap. Like a boulder on a downhill roll, the bear continued to close the gap. The rabbits didn't slow it down. It allowed nothing to stand in its way. Crooked Foot's grandfather was ahead of him and headed for the safety of the old tree, but the boy knew he was too far away from that sanctuary. Another place, one that might offer refuge, was closer, and he went for it.

The rocky outcropping that made up the hill also created a bend in the river. For more years than anyone could remember, when the sun's warmth returned to melt the white rain,[11] the river got new life and energy. It became a wild thing, unleashing devastating floods. Whole trees, dead or alive, big and small were ripped out and swept down the river to be pushed, pulled, jammed, and piled here in the curve by this unstoppable force. Caught in the bend between the river and this stony wall, the debris lay in disarray: tree jammed onto tree, a mix of trunks, brush, roots, and branches.

Crooked Foot scampered out onto this jumbled pile. He hoped the bear wouldn't follow, couldn't follow. Either way, he was wrong.

Grunt … Snort … Crash. Crooked Foot could tell from the sounds that the bear was close, very close. The trunk he was on shook under its thunderous weight and

---

[11] White Rain - Snow was called 'white rain' to distinguish it from regular rain.

confirmed his worst fear. The boy sprang from one tree to another, then another. With each move, he hoped to lose his pursuer. It only seemed to make the bear angry, more determined.

The bear followed every leap the boy made and closed the gap between them. The tree trunk under Crooked Foot's feet all but ran out. He thought he could feel the bear's hot breath on his back. He knew he would have to do something different and do so quickly.

Abruptly, he halted and turned around. If he was to die, he would die as a Narwikin brave. His red spear clenched in both hands, point held menacingly high, he yelled as loud as he could and charged down the trunk toward the bear.

### ###

Tawasiki lumbered down the trail after the pair of humans. When he was younger, he would have had no trouble catching the pair, but now he knew the larger one, with his smooth, swift movements may get away. The chase wouldn't be a loss, however, as the smaller one, the one with the bobbing movements, was slower and should prove to be an easy catch.

The great bear crashed through the brush, ignoring the rabbits tossed in his path. He'd come back for them later if he was still hungry. Right now, he was intent on closing the gap between him and his quarry.

Suddenly, the pair split up. The larger one, the one in the lead, continued down the path while the younger turned and scampered onto the pile of debris. No matter. The smaller one could run, but not hide, and this new place would provide no cover. Tawasiki followed his prey onto the pile. He continued to chase the smaller one from log to log until there was no place left to go. On a timber that ended in open air, his quarry stopped suddenly and wheeled around. Raising the shaft he carried, his prey let out a yell and started toward the surprised bear. It wasn't the way quarry was supposed to act! To meet this mystery, this new challenge, the great bear rose up on his hind legs and let out a bellow of its own.

### 

Grabbed by a crazy idea, Crooked Foot gripped his spear in both hands and then turned around to march steadily back down the trunk yelling as loud as he could.

The bear came to a sudden stop and appeared bewildered by this unorthodox behavior. In a heartbeat the confusion was gone. It rose up on its hind feet and roared its own challenge. The blast of hot stinking breath mixed with slobber coated Crooked Foot. The bear, now towering over him, was right where the lad wanted. Spear clutched firmly in hand, the boy set his face firm and lunged forward. The tip buried itself in the bear's exposed midsection.

Injured, Tawasiki bellowed and swung his paws, catching the spear. The shaft shattered and Crooked Foot, fighting to keep his balance, stumbled backward from the force of the blow. The bear lowered itself to all fours and started forward.

The log Crooked Foot was on shifted and shook under the bear's weight. Unarmed, the lad lost his battle to keep his balance. He stumbled and started to fall. Off to the side, a limb from another tree stuck out. If he could grab it, Crooked Foot knew he'd be able to swing over to a different part of the pile and put a little room between him and his pursuer. His feet slipped out from under him as he leaped for the branch. Stretching out as far as he could, hands clawing at the air, he desperately reached for his goal.

His fingertips closed around the limb and he was greeted by the welcome feel of rough, wet bark beneath them. Then there was a dull pop as the limb, a victim of weather, age, rot, and the sudden impact of his weight, gave way and he fell.

Below him, brush covered logs stuck out of the pile in all directions. He hit their trunks with a solid thump and bounced over onto the brush. The blow knocked the wind out of him, and he went limp. Crooked Foot felt the branches of the brush bend and part under his weight. Like a living thing, the debris pile swallowed him in one gulp. He fell down a shaft between tree trunks. Sharp, broken branches stuck out all over jabbing at him as he bounced off another tree. Before he could recover, he slid off and fell still farther, finally coming to a halt at a lower level. There he laid, an unconscious lump at the bottom of the pile of debris.

### 

"Gonna lie around all day?"

Crooked Foot blinked. His head hurt. Everything seemed fuzzy. Squinting, he tried to focus. "Wh …. What?"

Red Deer leaned over him. "Aren't you listening? There's work to do. You can't lie around all day."

Something wasn't right; Crooked Foot struggled to focus. Finally, he said, "How did you get here? You're on your sojourn."

Red Deer ignored the question. "Where's your knife?"

"Knife?"

Impatiently Red Deer asked, "You got the knife we made together?"

"Knife?" Still trying to get his mind around it, Crooked Foot asked, "How did you get here?"

"The knife," Red Deer straightened as he repeated himself. "The knife we made. You'll need it." He seemed to take a step backwards into the shadows. "Remember, your knife. Get your knife…." That was the last thing he said as he faded into the dim surroundings.

Crooked Foot raised his aching head and tried to see where Red Deer had gone. He searched his surroundings. Nothing! His head spun. The low light changed to darkness, expanded, and engulfed him completely once again.

### 

Pain! That was the next thing Crooked Foot understood. He was dizzy and his aching head spun. He was vaguely aware of a scurrying sound from somewhere nearby, but he couldn't focus his thoughts. His body hurt all over from the bangs and thumps he had taken in making the descent, but even in his dazed condition, he knew enough to lie still.

Overhead, the tree trunks shifted under the Tawasiki's weight as the great bear continued to search for him. *Frustrated,* it pushed, shoved, or batted, to no avail, anything in his path. The debris pile quivered and shook under the assault. At times, debris—twigs, broken branches, dirt—rained down, but little else occurred.

Grunt … Snort … Grunt … The search went on. More *frustrations followed by more* pushing, shoving, or batting. The rain of broken branches continued with each assault. Grunt … Snort … The bear wasn't about to give up.

Slowly, Crooked Foot raised his head and tried to look around. Past floods had piled timbers against the cliff face. It left a small bowl shaped hollow in the midst of this shaky jumble of debris. Light—very little, but some—filtered down to his level, but it was so dim that it was difficult to make out details.

Nearby, in the darkness, something moved. What was that? He pressed himself closer to the rock wall behind him.

"Red Deer?" Crooked Foot whispered hopefully. No answer. Red Deer was not here, had never been here except as a hallucination. Crestfallen, his hopes dashed, he was stirred into action by more scurrying. These sounds were close by.

Crooked Foot's heart began racing. "Time to pull yourself together," he whispered. "Red Deer is not here—has not been here, all that was a dream." He blinked and rubbed his eyes. "Am I seriously hurt? I must look myself over. "

Banged up but alive, his head and most of his body hurt. A scalp wound, maybe more than one, covered him in blood. Dirt, scratches, bruises—plenty of those—covered his body. A broken branch protruded from the fleshy part of his left arm.

It hurt when he tried to move, but he managed to get into a crouching position. His wounds bled profusely. He took a few deep breaths to compose himself. He knew it was important to remain calm. Remembering what his grandmother, Bright Moon, taught him, he scraped some moss from the trunks and used that to stem the flow of blood. He cut off a piece of his tunic and wrapped the worse wounds.

Leaning back against the rocks, he surveyed his surroundings again. He knew he was near river level because the trees he rested on were covered with cold water that lapped at his toes. Somewhere overhead, snorting, and sniffing, Tawasiki continued his search. The surrounding timbers vibrated from the bear's hefty weight. It didn't know where he was, but Crooked Foot figured the bear was determined to find him. To keep that from happening, the boy knew he would have to stay quiet. It wasn't over yet.

Movement from a dark corner caused Crooked Foot's heart to race faster. He looked around frantically, searching for something he could use as a club.

### 

The tall old tree that rose up near the crest of the hill stretched dead branches high into the sky. Howling Wolf reached it ahead of Crooked Foot. Leaping up, he grabbed the lowest branch and pulled himself up into the tree and safety. Turning to help the boy, he was surprised to find his grandson wasn't there. Had the great bear gotten him?

In near panic, Howling Wolf peered through the rain. It took a moment for him to spot his grandson scampering through the mound of trees and brush piled in the curve of the river. Tawasiki was right behind and closing the gap between them. Howling Wolf watched his grandson leap from trunk to trunk in an effort to escape. Still, the bear followed relentlessly until the boy ended up on the end of a timber. Then the lad turned quickly, charged his pursuer, and buried the spear in the bear's midriff. Tawasiki struck out, breaking the spear.

Crooked Foot retreated and then vanished from sight. Faced with the sudden disappearance, the bear stopped short and began to sniff around as it tried to locate his prey. Hoping to distract Tawasiki in his search, Howling Wolf called out loudly, "Crooked Foot, stay hidden!"

At the sound of Howling Wolf's voice, the bear's head snapped around. The heavy rains had subsided, and the sun's rays started to break through the cloud cover. Through the lingering mists, their eyes locked together. Even from this distance, Howling Wolf could see the pure animal hatred in those eyes. Tawasiki broke off his search, left the debris, and started for the tree.

# Chapter 3: Searching

Precariously, Tawasiki had stood on the jumble of logs and bushes that were once growing things while he sniffed, snorted, and clawed at the pile of dead wood. He had chased his prey, the smaller of the two humans here, but it jabbed him with a spear and opened a wound. Even though he had lashed out and easily broke the spear, the damage was done. Part of it was still lodged in him; the pain aggravated his every move.

By the time he recovered from the surprise, his quarry had disappeared. The longer he searched, the more his anger grew. From time-to-time, he would vent his rage on anything in his way. Through it all, he continued to search. He was intent on finding where his prey had gone.

From behind him came another sound. It was that barking noise humans often made. Tawasiki stopped his search, lifted his head, and looked around to discover that the taller one had climbed a nearby tree. Now perched on a high limb, it continued barking. In the heat of the chase, the great bear had all but forgotten about that one.

His eyes, burning with anger, hatred, and frustration, locked on the human's. As the rain diminished, the sun began to shine through the clouds. Despite his bothersome new wound, this could be a good day. He was determined to find prey. He was hungry.

Turning around, he gave up his search, temporarily, and traced his steps back, stopping when he reached the tree on the hillside. This human would make as good a meal as the other one, however, getting to this one wasn't going to be any easier.

The bear found that even rising up on his hind feet and stretching to his full height didn't put the human within reach. In an effort to pull himself higher, he dug his claws into the tree trunk. In spite of his labors, Tawasiki was only able to climb a short distance before his finger-length claws—meant for digging and not for climbing—lost their grip and he slid back to ground level. He tried several times with the same result, but his efforts only caused the quarry to climb higher in the tree.

On the ground again, having decided he was too big to climb far, he tried pushing the tree, even bouncing his full weight against it. The tree rocked under the force of each blow. This caused the branches the human embraced to sway and shake.

From somewhere in the tree's trunk, there was a popping, cracking noise. The tree started to lean. Tawasiki continued to push and bounce. The noise grew louder; the tree leaned a little more with every blow. Unaware of this new development, the bear continued his attack hoping to shake the human loose. Even though the human appeared undisturbed, the great bear did manage to upset something else.

### 

Howling Wolf's message to him was clear. "Crooked Foot! Stay hidden!" So he remained still, scarcely breathing, while he listened to the sounds from above. He could hear the bear as it sniffed around. He could feel the vibrations of the bear's unwieldy movements. Then both sound and footsteps faded away and he was aware only of the water lapping softly over the logs.

There was more movement in the darker parts of the brush pile. He found a short branch, about the length of his forearm, to use as a club and he tightened his grip on it.

What had happened to his spear? He didn't have it. Then he remembered charging the bear. He recalled how it felt when the point sank into the bear's midriff. And then the bear shattered the shaft in one angry blow.

That's right! Now he remembered. He stumbled when he made his retreat. That's when he lost his balance and ended up here at the bottom of the pile.

Maybe if he hadn't attacked, the bear would have ….
He shut the thought of what might have happened out of his
mind. It didn't happen that way. He was alive and safe at least
for the time being. Too bad about the spear though. Red
Deer had shown him how to make both his knife and his
spear. They were his most prized possessions.

Time passed. Slowly, quietly, he tried to stand up
bumping his head as he did. There wasn't much room. He
stopped again to listen. No sounds came from above. Dim
light filtered through the debris. The shaft he had just fallen
through dumped him in the middle of this bowl-shaped
hollow. He just missed being impaled on a limb as big around
as his arm, rising upward from the tree trunk, it tapered off
into a broken point about chest high. Had his fall carried him
a hand's length to the side … he shuddered to think about it.

Complete and utter chaos, the debris pile was made
up of whole trees, fallen logs, and bushes of all sizes. Untold
numbers of spring floods had pushed and piled them against
the rocky face of the bluff, creating this cove.[12]

He looked around for a way out. Unable to stand up,
he was forced to search bent over, not that it made a
difference. He couldn't find an opening large enough to
squeeze through. To get out he would have to clamber up the
way he came down. Around him, the walls of the chamber, a
chaotic tangle of different sized moss-coated trees, sloped up
and away. To torment him further, branches big enough, long
enough, to aid his climb were beyond his reach. The wound
in his arm wouldn't stand too great a strain. It looked like
trying to escape this way was out of the question.

Overhead, there was no noise, no movement. If
Tawasiki still lurked about, climbing up would mean running
into him. What to do? From somewhere else he could hear
muffled drumming sounds. He was unaware the great bear
bounced his mighty bulk against the tree where Howling

---

[12] Cove - A sheltered place. A narrow cavern formed in the sides of cliffs,
mountains, etc., usually by erosion.

Wolf had taken refuge.

Suddenly there was movement in several places around him. While the bear was overhead, whatever caused this commotion lay hidden, lest it also become victim. Now, with the bear gone, the activity began again. At first just a little, but now more, and all around him. Crooked Foot tried to focus his thoughts and determine what kind of threats might face him.

It wasn't warm enough yet to be a snake. It wouldn't be the big cat with curved tusks. There wasn't enough space here even for a small young one. His head spun from the effort. Crooked Foot tried to concentrate. What could it be?

The brush in front of him stirred and parted. He suddenly had the answer. It stared him in the face. It was a rat! Its beady little eyes shone in the dim light … and he brought friends. The smell of Crooked Foot's blood had attracted them.

In a flash, he jabbed his club and knocked the rat off the branch. Whirling around, he bent even lower and swept the branches along the log that lay behind him, catching another rat solid in the ribs. Straightening up, his heart racing, Crooked Foot banged his club against a limb. With the sudden movement and noise, all the rats withdrew to safer areas. He knew their retreat was only temporary. They would wait until he was weaker or needed sleep and then they would return to try again.

Crooked Foot took off the leather rope he used as a belt and used it to fasten his knife to the club. In doing so, he fashioned a makeshift short-handled spear. He didn't know how much time this would give him. He knew the water was cold, and he suddenly realized it was now up to his ankles and getting deeper.

His grandmother had explained that somewhere upriver, pools of water from rain and melted snow formed behind walls of ice. For several days now, the sun's warm rays had been melting snows left by the Long Cold. Leaks develop as the walls weaken. Before long, the ice walls would give way under the pressure of the backed up melt.

Crooked Foot was sure that this was about to happen here. This torrent of water and mud would rush down the river. It would carry away anything in its path … and bury anything it couldn't carry away. That would include him, assuming the rats didn't get to him first. The thought hit Crooked Foot like lightning. In a panic, he screamed, "Grandfather, the great waters are coming!"

### 

Awakened earlier by the warm rays from the sun, Tawasiki's actions stirred They-That-Make-Honey[13] to action, and they took the attack on the tree personally. The first warning began with a low buzzing sound, but it grew quickly. The hum came from a hollow spot near the base of the tree. Shortly, the bear found the air filled with flying, stinging insects willing to protect their home even in rain and mist.

At first, there were just a few. Tawasiki hardly noticed them even after repeated stings. His continued efforts stirred up the rest of the nest. The colony rose like a cloud and soon interrupted his work. Luckily, their attack concentrated on the bear and left Howling Wolf alone. Even better, their attack caused Tawasiki to stop bouncing on the badly leaning tree and retreat to a safer place.

While he considered his next plan of action, Tawasiki heard a muffled bark came from somewhere within the debris pile. The noise was made by the smaller of the two. Maybe that would be the better target after all. Having made the decision, he turned and headed for the spot where he had last seen the smaller human.

### 

Even if he could hold off the rats, Crooked Foot

---

[13] They-That-Make-Honey - Bees. From ancient times, Bees were known for their ability to produce honey and through the ages, many cultures used honey not only as a sweetener, but in many other home remedies.

knew he couldn't stay where he was because of the rising water. To seal his fate, the sound of sniffing and vibrations from ponderous feet on the logs returned to the area over his head. Now, he couldn't leave because Tawasiki had returned. Movement in the dark corners and recesses of the debris pile began again. He had to do something. The bear was overhead. The rats were restless. The water was cold and deeper. He had to do something … but what?

# Chapter 4: Treed

Howling Wolf's loud command, *Crooked Foot! Stay hidden,* had caught the bear's attention. When their eyes locked, Howling Wolf could see the pure animal hatred that burned within the bear. Tawasiki left the debris pile and came over to the tree. Howling Wolf's plan had worked. He had put himself in danger, but for the time being, Crooked Foot would be safe.

Reaching the tree's base the bear rose up on its hind legs and stretched to its full length, but this only succeeded in forcing Howling Wolf to climb higher. The bear tried to follow him, but only managed to claw its way up a short distance before sliding back. Undeterred, it made several more attempts, but was unable to scale the tree. Howling Wolf climbed a little higher, and then scornfully spit at his pursuer.

His scorn for the bear's attempts was short-lived. Below him, loud clomps sounded as the bear began bouncing against the trunk, which rocked under the force of each blow. The branches swayed, shaking the place where he had taken refuge.

Thump! The next blow rocked the tree even more. Caught off-guard, Howling Wolf lost his grip on the wet branches. He thrashed about as he fell, grabbing for branch after branch until he was finally able to regain his grip. He quickly climbed higher and found a more secure perch. Safe and back to reality, he looked down in time to see the bear bounce his considerable weight against the tree trunk once again.

Thump! Thump! Thump! The tree continued to sway with each blow. Howling Wolf heard a popping, cracking noise, and the tree began to lean. Below him, the bear, unaware of the damage he had already caused, continued to bounce against the tree. The popping, cracking noise grew louder. With every blow, the tree leaned a little further. Aware the tree could topple at any time, Howling Wolf continued to hold on tightly as he searched for an escape if the tree hit the ground. He needn't have been concerned. Help was on its way from an unsuspected source.

Roused by the warm rays from the sun and the bear's actions, They-That-Make-Honey took to flight. The air filled with flying, stinging insects. At first sight, Howling Wolf hugged the tree closely and remained motionless. He was left alone while the swarm attacked the bear and forced it to beat a hasty retreat.

Then, from the depths of the debris came Crooked Foot's panicked voice, "Grandfather, the great waters are coming!"

Hearing that voice, Tawasiki turned and went back to the log pile. Howling Wolf's shoulders slumped as he watched the great beast resume its search of the debris. Unless things changed, his grandson was in peril once again. As if the weather was as moody as the bear, the rain returned. He peered through the downpour, studying the horizon for some sign of hope and found what he was looking for— coming down the hill toward him were more hunting parties. When Howling Wolf didn't return, they came searching for him. Waving, he hollered to the others as he began climbing down from the tree.

### 

Driven back to the log pile by They-That-Make-Honey, Tawasiki began to sniff, snort, and claw at this heap of driftwood. Behind him, the taller one made more barking noises, but he paid it no mind. The prey he had chased, the smaller of the two humans, had disappeared here before his eyes. Despite the fact that everything was wet and the scent was colder, he was intent on finding where his prey had gone. Following the trail, the great bear worked his way over the path where the quarry disappeared. Though lessened by the rain, the scent hadn't yet completely washed away.

As he moved further along the log, he felt it quiver under his weight, but was unconcerned, that is, unconcerned until the log tipped downward. By the time he tried to back up, the tree had tipped too low, and he slid down along the wet surface. Alarmed, Tawasiki made a noise—half-squeal half-roar—as he dropped head first through bushes and into a shaft between tree trunks. Due to his size, he didn't fall far, just far enough.

Looking down, it took a moment for his eyes to adjust to the dim light; he saw a blood covered face and a pair of large eyes over an open mouth. He had finally found what he looked for; right in front of him and looking up was his next meal. Tawasiki was wedged between tree trunks, and he'd have to pry himself loose but he was sure his quarry wouldn't get away this time. That was good. He was hungry.

### 

Crooked Foot crouched low and froze in place. Once again timbers creaked and groaned under the weight of the great bear as he prowled around overhead tracing the boy's scent. Suddenly, the bear let out a noise that could only be described as surprise mixed with fear and anger. A crashing sound accompanied this as logs shifted and gave way. Pieces of tree limbs and other debris rained down around Crooked Foot. He looked up to stare into the open mouth of the great bear just an arm's length away. Tawasiki's head, temporarily pinned between logs, filled the shaft above him.

Crooked Foot shrank back. There was no place for

him to go. He ducked down behind the broken tree limb and tried to make himself as small as possible.

Bracing himself, the great bear managed to draw back far enough to pull its head out of the opening. The bear's pushing and shoving caused the logs under Crooked Foot's feet to move. The boy lost his footing, and one leg slipped into the water before they shifted again and pinned him there. Frantically he struggled to free himself. The logs would have to shift again before he could do that and by then it might be too late.

With a triumphant roar, Tawasiki reached one large paw into the shaft and took a swipe at Crooked Foot. The boy dodged as the bear's paw smashed at trees and branches around him. Unhappy with the results, the bear shifted his position and tried again. This time, he not only hit trunk and branches, but also hit Crooked Foot a glancing blow alongside the head. Crooked Foot saw stars for a moment while the bear's claws opened wounds, old and new, on his head and shoulders.

Encouraged by the smell of fresh blood, Tawasiki strained to reach further down into the shaft. Crooked Foot tried desperately to free himself. The great bear pushed harder against the surrounding timbers. The bear felt the timbers move, a little at first and then a little more. Below him, the logs pinning Crooked Foot moved, releasing him from their hold. Scrambling free, he threw himself into a prone position near the upright limb.

Under the force of the bear's efforts, the logs shifted again creating an opening wide enough for it to reach further down. Triumphantly, Tawasiki roared with delight and then with terror as it felt its entire body slip down the shaft.

Crooked Foot looked up in wide-eyed terror as the great bear, mouth wide open, bellowed loudly, and fell toward him. Expecting this to be his end, the lad closed his eyes and clenched his teeth. He clutched the upright limb and flattened himself on the wet timbers and waited. Tawasiki's thundering roar filled his ears. There was a tremendous jar from the bear's impact and the roar quickly died off leaving a soft gurgling noise, then quiet. The boy opened his eyes, just a crack at first, then wider in his disbelief. Nose-to-nose with the bear, he was covered in its blood.

Not a finger's width away, Tawasiki hung above him, partly in, partly out of the shaft. Crooked Foot didn't know, not for sure at least, but he believed the bear was dead. What he knew was the broken tree limb, now covered in blood, disappeared into the beast's open mouth. Jammed in this cramped position, with little room for him to see above the bear's head, he was unable to see where it exited. He was cold—freezing cold. The water, deeper now, lapped around him and he could not stay here.

He wiggled and inched his way around the chamber until he could find enough room to crouch. Tawasiki didn't move. There were no signs of life.

Tentatively Crooked Foot forced himself to reach a hand out and lightly touched the bear. Nothing. No sounds. No response. Shaking, as much from what he had just gone through as from the cold, he closed his fingers around strands of the bear's fur and pulled. No reaction of any kind.

Light shone down from above and Crooked Foot realized the only way out was the way the bear came in. He grabbed larger hands full of fur and began to climb. The wound in his arm began bleeding again. He would have to hurry to tell the Narwikin so they could prevent the rats from feasting on Tawasiki's remains.

To help himself along, he thought about the great bear's death and what it would mean to his people. Its fur would become clothing, shelter, and a reason for merriment. Tawasiki would help fill the Narwikin's hungry bellies until the big fish came back to the river and the wandering herds returned to the plains. Tonight, the Narwikin would sing and dance. Crooked Foot climbed until he reached the point where he could go no further. The rest of Tawasiki's body blocked the way leaving only a small portal … too small for him to get through.

### ###

Howling Wolf and other hunters gathered near the logjam.[14] Before their eyes, they had watched as the great bear slipped into the shaft. They saw it thrashing around and heard the bear's roars. Now it lay still. Only the call of birds broke the silence.

The people, weapons ready, cautiously approached Tawasiki from behind. The bear, back end in the air, lay motionless. Taking a spear, Howling Wolf jabbed its foot, but there was no reaction. Slowly, carefully, the group approached the open shaft and peered down.

From within the shaft—peering up between branches and bear—shone a tired, muddy, blood-covered face. Teeth chattering from cold, Crooked Foot said, "Grandfather, Tawasiki is dead. I need your help."

---

[14] logjam - A pileup or tangle of logs and like debris, as in a river, causing a blockage.

# Chapter 5: Help

"Bright Moon," Howling Wolf called loudly. "Bright Moon, I need you."

Alerted by a runner, a crowd had gathered at the gate. They parted as the men carrying Crooked Foot reached the village. Here and there, dogs barked, adding to the commotion. Eagerly, Howling Wolf scanned the crowd. He spotted Bright Moon by the entrance to her shelter, leaning on her walking stick.

Told by the runner of the events, the old woman put aside her concerns as a grandmother to focus on her role as Shaman.

"Bring the boy in and lay him on the sleeping couch," she commanded. "My medicines are ready." Limping and wheezing, she started to follow the men when Howling Wolf grabbed her arm. Startled, she stopped short, looked him in the eye, and managed to rasp an asthmatic, "What?"

With Howling Wolf's mate, Yellow Flower, sleeping the-sleep-from-which-no-one-wakes,[15] he tried to act on both their behalf. As he spoke, his thoughts were not only of Crooked Foot, but also of his son, Red Deer. The lad had gone on his sojourn and had not yet returned. Many had thought he would never return and had given up hope.

Howling Wolf believed in Bright Moon's prophecy. Spoken on the day of Red Deer's departure, she told her chief that the lad would be gone longer than any of the other boys and when he returned, others would be with him. They would need help. One of them would become his new mate. At the

---

[15] Sleeps the-sleep-from-which-no-one-wakes - Death was associated with sleep, and is referred to as "the-sleep-from-which-no-one-wakes" as well as "the-long-sleep."

moment however, Howling Wolf's concern, bordering on panic, was focused elsewhere. "He's my grandson .... He's .... He's all I have ...."

He looked at her, his eyes pleading his case. It struck him that her eyes, set deep in her wrinkled, weathered face, were still the blackest of blacks he had ever seen. Many summers ago, when he was a lad, hardly older than his grandson is now, he survived a fight with a pair of lions. She was there to clean his wounds and look after him. He still bore the scars from the encounter ... and the memory of her dark eyes hovering over him.

She replied harshly, "He is my grandson, too! I will take care of him ... I will look after him for as long as it takes." As if she read his mind, her tone softened and she added, "Like you, like Red Deer, the boy is brave ... and strong." Trying to reassure her friend, she continued, "So leave him with us. Go now. Let me do my job."

Her features wrinkled with the wisdom of years, her body bent with age, he wanted to trust her. Years before he had trusted her with his own life, but this was different, this was his grandson! Finally, he let go of her arm as he hung his head in acceptance. She hobbled into the shelter to join the young girl already waiting there. Together, they leaned over the boy, and began to examine his wounds.

When they were told the news, she and Abeytu[16]— her sometimes apprentice—had prepared bowls of water and herbs and sat them close at hand. Several small pieces of hides, made soft by hours of pounding, now soaked in this mix. The old woman and the young girl knelt beside Crooked Foot and began to clean up his wounds.

---

[16] Abeytu - Omaha word meaning "Greenleaf". Abeytu is the oldest child of White Bird and Little Rabbit, and is a part-time apprentice to Bright Moon.

When they rolled him over, he cried out. Bright
Moon motioned for a short, rawhide-wrapped stick. "Abeytu!
Quickly! Slide it between his teeth," she commanded.

Calmly the young girl slipped the stick in place and
said, "Great hunter, take this and bite on it to ease your
pain."

Before he lost consciousness, Crooked-Foot felt
skilled hands run over his body, dabbing each wound with a
soft, wet hide. It was a quick and thorough exam during
which he sank into the soft darkness of unconsciousness.

He drifted in and out of a dream world, one that was
filled with memories of charging the great bear; of hopping
from tree trunk to tree trunk; the bear's hot breath on his
neck. But, he also remembered concerned faces: Bright
Moon's or Abeytu's, hovering over him; a light touch, a damp
cloth; warm broth crossing his lips; the sound of voices, at
times cooing softly to him.

Bright Moon did everything she could to keep her
promise to Howling Wolf. Her efforts worked. Under their
care, Crooked Foot, though weak, remained conscious for
longer periods at a time. As he grew stronger, Bright Moon
encouraged him to sit up for short intervals, but she also
encouraged Abeytu to look after him and make sure he didn't
overdo it.

Before Bright Moon sent him away, Howling Wolf
camped outside her doorway and waited for any sign of
change in his grandson's condition. Now, satisfied with the
improvements in the boy's condition, she sent Abeytu to
fetch their chief. Howling Wolf stopped by to see his
grandson and brought Crooked Foot a present.

"A bone? Grandfather, I don't understand."

"Not just any bone. This is special," Howling Wolf
explained. "It is from Tawasiki."

Crooked Foot gave him a puzzled look.

"A hunter must create something useful to honor the animal he slew," Howling Wolf said. "In this manner, the animal is remembered ... and respected. It will know it didn't give its life in vain."

"What should I create?"

"That's up to you. Keep this close, and the bear's spirit will come, maybe in a dream, to tell you what it thinks."

Standing, Howling Wolf said, "Get some rest now." Then he turned and left.

### 

"I need firewood," Bright Moon's statement, as always, was abrupt.

Crooked Foot looked up from his carving. Mallet in hand, she knelt in front of her grinding stone. Looking back at his work he finally said, "I am busy with my carving."

"Put it aside. It will wait." Her voice carried a little spark of irritation. Fire danced in her eyes. "You need to get out, take a walk, and get some fresh air."

He turned the piece over in his fingers and traced the marks he'd made. In protest, Crooked Foot picked up his knife again. "Gathering firewood is a job they give girls to shepherd the little ones. Abeytu is here. Send her. I am making something special." That remark earned him a scornful look from Bright Moon's assistant.

"You'll find some firewood in the forest." Relentless, Bright Moon ignored his comments. "Go now. Take your time bringing it back."

### 

Silver Fox and his friends watched as Crooked Foot, carrying a load of firewood, staggered down the path toward them. "Give the great hunter some room," Silver Fox sneered and motioned for the others to stand aside. They followed the lanky youth's lead and moved off to either side of the path.

Crooked Foot spotted the boys, bigger and older than he, they lined the path ahead. He knew he couldn't turn away; he couldn't flinch. To turn and run from them would be to show signs of weakness. It would bring shame to his family and more torment to him. As Crooked Foot made his way between the rows, Silver Fox stuck out his foot.

Crooked Foot went sprawling. Firewood scattered everywhere as he fell.

Guffaws filled the air and Silver Fox jeered, "Tripping over your own feet. Is that how the great hunter killed the bear?"

A piece of firewood in hand, Crooked Foot jumped to his feet. "You want to see how it's done? Watch this." He swung the wood. Silver Fox put up an arm to deflect the blow, and it caught him just above the elbow. Yowling, Silver Fox leaped on Crooked Foot, and the two hit the ground intertwined. Focused on the scuffle in front of them, none of the boys noticed that a girl walking their way suddenly turned around and started back the other direction. The two boys rolled around, raining blows on each other, while the rest of the on-lookers, dancing about and shouting, formed a circle around the pair of combatants.

The sting of a leather rope rained down on the ring of onlookers. They stepped back, leaving the two on the ground to suffer any additional blows from Bright Moon.

Leaning on her walking stick, leather rope in one hand, she surveyed the situation. A bloodied Silver Fox lay on his back. Crooked Foot sat firmly across his chest, one hand locked in his oppressor's long hair, the other still clutching a piece of firewood. Silver Fox had obviously underestimated his opponent.

"Where's my firewood?" Her voice low, her tone cold

and steady, fire blazing [38] in her eyes, she directed her question at Crooked Foot.

Waving the wood about like a pointer, he spat out, "There's your firewood."

Letting go of Silver Fox, he stood up and kicked a stray piece of wood. "And there … and over there …."

She glared at the firewood scattered around, then at Silver Fox and the group of boys with him. Under the scorching heat of her gaze, everyone tried to make themselves smaller, even wishing they could disappear completely.

"I need firewood, lots of firewood," she hissed. "Since you boys have so much time and energy, you can all bring me firewood."

Getting to his feet, Silver Fox ventured, "How … how much do you want?"

"Just bring it and be quick about it. I'll tell you when I've got enough."

She turned to shuffle away and then looked back over her shoulder to add, "Remember, I know each of you, so don't try to sneak off or I'll hunt you down … and you don't want that. Now go!"

Not needing further encouragement, the youngsters scattered.

Foraging for firewood over the next couple of days quelled any further thoughts of fighting. While there were no open threats or violence against Crooked Foot, it didn't stop their whispered comments.

While they worked, if they had taken the time to notice, they might have been aware that Howling Wolf found a number of reasons to make extra trips to Bright Moon's shelter. If they noticed him, they didn't realize he was there to check on them.

Standing next to Bright Moon, Howling Wolf gave her a sidewise glance and asked, "I am curious. How did you happen onto the fracas?"

Bright Moon smiled. "Ask anyone. They will tell you that I have eyes everywhere and see things others can't."

Howling Wolf shrugged. "No one would argue with that."

Bright Moon chuckled. "When Crooked Foot didn't come back right away, I sent Abeytu out to check on him."

He nodded and eyed the growing pile of firewood. "Since the nights are still cold," he said, "it's nice all these boys want to help you out." A smile played around the corners of his mouth.

Bright Moon twirled the end of a rope lazily, "Just have to ask nicely and apply some persuasion." She glanced Howling Wolf's way before she continued, "This isn't going to change things. Crooked Foot held his own this time. I had to rescue Silver Fox, but he and his friends will find some other way to torment the boy."

Howling Wolf let out a long sigh as he hung his head in resignation. "Some of our boys are ready to start their sojourn and the time is growing close. When Tigal and his caravan arrive, maybe he will need to take on help." He shrugged. "It would be valuable if Crooked Foot had an edge, some unique talent and the training to go with it, but it would have to be a skill that Tigal needed."

Bright Moon could see her friend needed some encouragement, and she reached out to him. "I am getting old and could use more help. I have been training Abeytu, but her mother has her hands full with so many children at home. I felt that Crooked Foot is old enough to understand, so while he was recuperating, Abeytu and I put him to work. We found him to be a quick learner. As it turns out, not only has he become a big help to me, it gave Abeytu more time to help at home. The two of them get along well and there is more than enough work for them, so I have already began training him as an apprentice. By the time the caravan arrives, the lad will be closer to the age they seek and he should have some skills that Tigal could use."

Howling Wolf looked over at her. "Thank you," he said. "A caravan like Tigal's can always use additional help, especially if the helper has some training as a shaman. If you're willing to continue with his training, I will speak to Tigal when he comes."

### 

Bright Moon poked at the pile of animal skins with her foot. Somewhere underneath this heap of skins, a boy lay asleep. "What?" She wheezed, "Are you going to sleep all day? Get up! You're well now and there's work to be done."

Goaded by the woman's prodding, Crooked Foot stirred and finally sat up, but remained wrapped in the animal skins as he looked around. The cooking fire created little warmth. Even inside the shelter, the morning air was crisp enough for him to see his breath.

Bright Moon, wrapped in a heavy hide, had returned to her position near the fire. Sitting back on her haunches, the old woman watched her apprentice go through a well-practiced routine.

Using a pair of sticks as pinchers, Abeytu picked rocks from the middle of this small blaze and dropped them into a pouch slung between nearby posts. The older woman listened to the hiss and watched to see if a small curl of steam rose. Periodically, Abeytu placed a capable hand against the pouch before deciding when to add more rocks. Finally, she was heard to mumble a satisfied, "Good."

A nod from Bright Moon and the young girl poured its contents into a wooden bowl and handed it to Crooked Foot. His mouth watered at the delicious smell and he took it from her eagerly, recognizing that under Bright Moon's guidance, Abeytu had prepared his favorite breakfast: a steaming mix of pemmican[17] broth, parched grain and vegetables.

Having lived with Bright Moon since he was a toddler, Crooked Foot knew she was a good cook. He now understood she was honing this trait in Abeytu. While living with his grandmother, he had also learned the old woman could be crotchety, especially if he didn't move fast enough to suit her. He hoped this was not a trait she was passing on to the girl at her elbow.

Bright Moon watched him for a moment then sat down and began to sort through a collection of dried plants and mushrooms. "When you're finished, we're going for a walk."

"Where are we going?"

While recuperating, he had spent very little time out of the shelter. Only lately had she begun sending him on short errands. After the encounter with Silver Fox, she decided he was well enough for longer, more vigorous ventures.

"Does it matter?" Glancing up, she saw the boy huddled gloomily over his bowl. She never got used to answering so many questions and it showed. Regretting the

---

[17] Pemmican - A concentrated mixture of fat and protein (usually meat) used as a nutritious food was a mainstay while on the trail. It could also be used as a supplement when other food was available. Traditionally pemmican was prepared from the lean meat of large game such as buffalo, elk, or deer. The meat was cut in thin slices and dried over a slow fire or in the hot sun until it was hard and brittle. Then, using stones, it was pounded into very small pieces, almost powder-like in consistency. This was mixed with an equal amount of fat. When available, nuts and dried fruits were pounded into powder and then added to the meat/fat mixture. The resulting mix could be packed into rawhide pouches for storage until needed.

tone of her response, she quickly added, "I thought it would be good for you to get out again. By helping me, you'll learn what things to look for and the walk and fresh air will be good for you."

"When do we go?" He brightened at the prospect of getting out for something more than a simple errand.

"If you'd ask fewer questions, we'd be gone by now."

Biting her lip, Abeytu quickly turned to hide her laughter, but Bright Moon made no pretense and laughed heartily at her own joke. Finally, she got to her feet and added, "When you finish eating we can leave." Still chuckling, she crossed the room, pausing long enough to pat him on the shoulder as she passed.

Crooked Foot continued to sip his broth as he watched her flit about. Humming quietly, the old woman shook out a hide, folded it neatly, and placed it on a pile near the door. One-by-one, Abeytu handed her mentor a selection of pouches and tools—naming each and describing its purpose as she did—and receiving a confirming nod from Bright Moon.

Deep in thought, lost in her planning, she began inventorying aloud additional items she needed. "A clutch of ropes, the two big hides, two poles." Turning to face Crooked Foot, she said, "Bring your ax and knife along. We'll need it for our work."

Looking up, she saw the boy sitting open-mouthed staring at the growing pile. Chuckling, she said, "Abeytu is coming too. When we get back, you can take a rest." Nodding to a bundle in the corner, she concluded, "and then you can get back to your carving."

Crooked Foot eagerly downed his broth. This promised to be a full day. He was anxious to escape his confinement. Today he would be doing something more useful than gathering firewood.

### ###

"Finish tying the sticks to the cross pieces. Keep the sticks about a finger's width apart. The fence is almost done." Bright Moon urged the boy on.

Glancing up from his labors, Crooked Foot questioned her, "What is this I'm making?"

Unaware of how little training Crooked Foot had, his question surprised Abeytu and she replied automatically. "Why, it's a fish weir.[18]"

Crooked Foot was bewildered. "What's a fish weir?"

Bright Moon smiled at the boy. "It's a trap for fish."

Crooked Foot wrinkled his nose. "A ... a ... trap for fish? How do you trap fish?" He was puzzled.

"You'll understand after we're done." Ignoring his questioning look, she motioned him toward the river and continued, "You're going to make a stockade for the fish. Get into the stream and start setting the fences upright in a square."

It was early spring. Crooked Foot knew the water would be cold. He also knew that he could choose to tip-toe in, like a child, or charge in like a brave. A running leap landed him hip-deep in the icy cold water. It took his breath away.

"Be careful," Bright Moon said, "or you'll scare the fish." At the river's edge, Abeytu didn't say anything. She

---

[18] Fish Weir - A fishing weir, or fish garth, is an obstruction placed in tidal waters, or wholly or partially across a river, to direct the passage of fish. For example, a weir can be used to trap salmon and other fish when they attempt to swim upstream, or to trap eels as they migrate downstream. Alternatively, fish weirs can be used to redirect fish elsewhere, such as to a fish ladder. Weirs were traditionally built from wood or stones. The use of fishing weirs as fish traps dates back prior to the emergence of modern humans, and weirs have since been used by many societies across the world.

quickly turned her back again, but not fast enough to hide her grin.

As she issued directions, Bright Moon watched Abeytu hand sections of the enclosure to Crooked Foot as he scurried through the water to accomplish the tasks. "Push the ends down in the mud so they'll stand up by themselves."

Crooked Foot positioned the first section. "Do you want them like this?"

Before Bright Moon could answer, Abeytu spoke up. "No. Make sure the tops are above water. You don't want the fish swimming over them." She watched closely, making sure he understood, before she went on. "Don't leave any spaces between the sections."

Bright Moon sat quietly and let her apprentice take charge. As oldest of a large family, Abeytu would have had many opportunities to take the lead and issue orders. It was a trait Bright Moon knew a shaman needed, so it was what she looked for in her apprentice.

Crooked Foot repositioned the sections, looked at the girl and asked, "Is this better?"

Abeytu nodded. "Yes. Now make a path of two rows side-by-side, but wider at the mouth—the end pointing down river where the fish will come from—and narrower at the end where it meets the square."

Not satisfied with what Crooked Foot was doing, Abeytu waded into the river. "Go in on the side, not the middle." Exasperation evident in her voice, she pulled up two adjacent sections.

"Hey! Stop that!" Crooked Foot ordered. "You never said where they were to meet." He lunged forward intending to grab the sections back, but tripped falling into her. Both ended up under water.

Sputtering, Abeytu sat up, caught sight of Crooked Foot and gave him a dark look. "You did that on purpose," she claimed. Skimming a hand, palm up, through the water, she shot a stream of water at him. It caught him square in the face and she broke into a hardy laugh.

"Think that's funny?" Crooked Foot asked. "How about this?" The question hardly left his lips when he leaped forward. The force of the impact knocked her backward and under water. Sitting up again, she was greeted by Crooked Foot's smiling face and vowed that she would not be outdone by him. Accepting the challenge, she smiled as she started forward to seek her revenge. He was ready and anticipated her next move.

Bright Moon, sitting comfortably on the hill overlooking the river, called a halt to their fun. "When the two of you are finished with the fish weir, we'll leave the hides and ropes here while we go into the woods. I need to find medicines to add to my collection."

Something in the tone of the old woman's voice brought the contest in the water to a temporary halt and the pair went back to work. Abeytu repositioned the sections while Crooked Foot watched.

Back on shore, Crooked Foot turned to study the device from this new vantage point. He was still puzzled. "How is this going to trap fish?"

"It does," Bright Moon said and tossed him a satchel. "Less talk now, more work."

### 

Bright Moon led the way through the trees. "Now pay attention. It's spring and too early to find berries and leaves."

Several parfleche[19] over each shoulder, Crooked Foot

---

[19] Parfleche - A Native American rawhide bag. It is similar in construction to an envelope, but can be as large as a suitcase. They were often painted, decorated and used to carry personal and ceremonial objects. In everyday

hurried along behind her; Abeytu, equally laden, behind him. For an old woman in need of a walking stick she moved swiftly along the path. Neither of the youths complained. After splashing around in the cold river, the briskness of this activity helped warm them.

"Then what is there to collect?" Nothing on this trip was making sense to him.

Bright Moon smiled. The boy was not just following along; he was practical and showed interest in the tasks. The old woman nodded to Abeytu. "You and I covered this before. It is time for you to show what you know."

Abeytu smiled at the recognition. "This is a good time to collect young willow branches, mushrooms, plants like skunk cabbage, and dried plants like snakeroot and foxglove. Also, bugs ... there're fewer places for them to hide. When it's cold like this, bugs, lizards, snakes, toads are slower and easier to catch."

This wasn't an idle stroll. When she wasn't pointing things out, one or the other would quiz him on things they had discussed. If Bright Moon didn't like his reply, if he wasn't fast enough with the answer, she drilled him on the subject until she was sure he knew it well.

"When we get done here, we'll go back to the river," the old woman told the pair, "and see how many fish we've caught. Then we can build some racks to dry and smoke them."

"How will the trap we built catch fish?" Still lost, Crooked Foot's curiosity drove him forward.

Bright Moon stopped and pointed toward some bushes. "Look there, between the branches and tell me what you see?"

---

use, they were typically used for holding objects such as dried meats, jerky and pemmican.

Mystified, the boy looked at the bushes. Finally, he shrugged and said, "I see only more bushes."

Abeytu giggled, and this time she did not try to hide it. She had been through this before. "That's all you see because you haven't trained yourself to see other things." Abeytu said. "I was the same as you."

Bright Moon motioned for them to follow and took a few steps forward. One gnarled finger pointed at a place between branches. "My sister, the spider, weaves her web across this path like Gray Wolf sets his snares." She paused to give him time to look at the web before she continued. "His snares and her web are both traps. They set them in places where they expect their quarry and wait for the prey to come to them." As if prompted by some outside force, a bug flew into the web. Detecting its struggles, the spider began to crawl toward its victim.

Watching this, Crooked Foot's face brightened. "Our trap is like the web. We plant it where we expect fish to swim and then we wait."

Bright Moon smiled quietly. "Good lad, now you've got the idea. Now, train yourself to look at things around you." She watched the boy as he carefully observed the web. "As you look, think about how you can adapt what you see and put it to use."

"Did you teach Gray Wolf how to set snares?"

"No ... your father did."

"My father?"

"Yes, he did. Before you were born, your father taught him how to do that and more."

"Like what?"

"Well," she said. "How to make axes, spear points, arrow heads, scrapers...."

"Good skills to learn. I would know how to do all those things now if my father were here."

The old woman cocked her head to one side. "Would you like to learn?" She asked.

"Yes, a good hunter will need to know all of that," the boy answered. "Would you teach me?"

"No," she replied flatly. The boy looked crestfallen and Abeytu's jaw dropped.

"But, I will speak with your grandfather and Gray Wolf," she smiled, "I'm sure something can be arranged."

Crooked Foot perked up. He grabbed Abeytu and they began jumping and dancing around. He let out a couple of whoops punctuated by a stream of "Yes! Yes! Yes!"

She let them celebrate for a short time and then said, "Come. We must go now."

Pleased, she hummed to herself as she turned back to the trail they had been following. Within a few steps, she picked up where she left off and continued her lectures without letting up. Crooked Foot did his best to take in all she said as he followed along. Singing, Abeytu skipped along behind them.

### 

Crooked Foot waded into the murky river water, Bright Moon's walking stick held tightly in his grip. Quietly, slowly, he moved toward the square that marked the fish weir. Glancing over his shoulder, he saw Bright Moon and Abeytu sitting in the sun watching him. "How does the trap work?" He asked.

"Downstream, the path is wide but here where it joins the square, it's narrower. Fish swim in at that end and follow the path."

Crooked Foot shook his head. "I don't understand. Why couldn't they just turn around and swim back out?"

"They're swimming upstream to spawn ... to have their young. They can't think of anything else. Once in, they can't find their way out. "

Crooked Foot was astounded. "You mean, just like that they're trapped?"

Abeytu shrugged and added, "Even when they're not spawning, they're not too smart."

Eyeing the row of sticks making up the weir, Crooked Foot nodded. "I'm glad I'm smarter than that."

Bright Moon stifled a laugh. "Your day will come."

Crooked Foot eyed the pair on the hillside. "Was it that way for you?"

Abeytu snorted while she tried to hide her laugh. It earned her a scowl from Bright Moon who ignored his question and went on with her instructions, "When you get to the square, run the walking stick slowly through the water inside."

Crooked Foot looked back quizzically. "What's that supposed to do?"

Abeytu, attempting to regain her position of favor, spoke up. "If there are fish in the trap, you will feel them bump the shaft. Lots of bumps mean lots of fish."

"You didn't answer my question. Was it that way for you?" Crooked Foot persisted.

Her eyes downcast, a coy smile on her face, Bright Moon waved a dismissive hand saying, "Pay attention to what you're doing."

Abeytu, trying to hide a poorly suppressed snicker, pretended to find something interesting in the grass.

Following instructions, Crooked Foot ran the shaft slowly through water. He smiled as he felt the fish bump it. "There are lots of bumps," he told her.

"Good. Now come out here, and we will build a drying tent before you start harvesting our catch." With a wave of a hand, she pointed out a couple of trees. "You two, take the poles we brought along. Suspend them, one over the other, in the branches between these two trees."

"What's this for?" he asked Abeytu as they positioned the shafts between the trees.

"After we clean the fish," she said, "we'll hang them over the lower pole." Pointing to the hides they had carried out earlier. "We'll spread the big hide over the top pole like a tent. We have to be sure to hang it with the small holes at the top." She looked at him to make sure he understood.

"How come it has small holes at the top?"

"These hides are made for smoking fish and meat." Abeytu said. "When we get them in place, we'll gather some wood. We'll need both green wood and dry wood to create a good fire with lots of smoke."

Still puzzled, Crooked Foot was about to ask a question when she cut him off. "Along the bottom, we'll build small fires—more smoke than heat—the tent will keep most of that in and quicken the drying time. The holes at the top and bottom are to let in air so the fire can breathe."

He held the hide up to get a better look at it. Satisfied he understood they began assembling the racks.

Pleased with herself, Bright Moon leaned on her walking stick as she watched the pair scurrying about. Everything she had planned was working out.

# Chapter 6: Schooling

With one swift blow, Tawasiki had destroyed Crooked Foot's spear. The one he and Red Deer had made together. The one he had used against the bear.

"The great bear came to me in my dreams last night." Crooked Foot said, "He spoke to me."

Bright Moon stopped puttering in the fire and turned to listen as the boy spoke with Howling Wolf. His grandfather pursed his lips thoughtfully and finally asked, "What did the great bear have to say?"

Crooked Foot spoke slowly, carefully as he recalled the details of the dream. "He said it was right we met; it had been a good fight. He was tired and in pain, but he died honorably." Pausing, he added, "He also said he was sorry he broke my spear. He'd be happy if I'd make a new one."

He looked at the faces of his audience. Both Howling Wolf and Bright Moon listened without comment.

"Does that sound … right?" he asked.

"A dream belongs to the one who dreams it," Bright Moon explained.

"That's right," Howling Wolf added. "The animal's spirit speaks meaning to one person. Does it sound right to you?"

Crooked Foot thought about it for a moment and then nodded agreement. "Yes … the great bear spoke clearly."

"Then it is right," Howling Wolf said. "The bear's spirit message is clear."

Hearing that, Crooked Foot brightened. "Then I will make a new one like Red Deer showed me," he said. "I remember how we did it, so I'll make a new one." Beaming with approval at his decision, Crooked Foot tucked his knife and ax in the rope sash at his waist. "I will go and find a tree to use."

Howling Wolf smiled and playfully mussed the boy's hair. "Yes, the hunter needs a spear. When you return, show me what you've found. Take your time." He watched as the boy, new task in mind, marched off with confidence.

### 

As the day wore on, Crooked Foot's hike became a trudge. His search for the perfect tree proved to be more difficult than he imagined. He went from trail to trail, eventually finding himself slogging along through territory new to him. He had wandered far, but was not lost.

Crooked Foot eyed each clump of trees as he looked for the right type. At a shallow stream, one not more than knee deep, he crouched to get a drink. Animals had also stopped to drink here. The soft dirt at his feet bore evidence of their visits. He recognized some prints while others were new to him. None looked like they were from animals large enough to be a threat.

Wary of his vulnerability, he kept his eyes on his surroundings as he dipped a cupped hand into the water and brought it to his mouth. It was cold and tasted good. It also reminded him he was hungry. Reaching for a second drink, he glanced down at the water. A fish lay motionless in the current near the edge of a streak of gravel, its speckled side sparkling in the sun. Beyond it, the slim silhouettes of other fish danced under the surface. Once caught, any one of them would make a good meal.

He slipped a hand quietly into the water and tried to edge toward the closest one, but it darted away. Waiting, he watched as it drifted back. *Come to me* he crooned under his breath, *come just a little closer* ... Crooked Foot tried again, but he got the same result. *I guess this means I'll need to try a different method or go hungry … and I don't want to go hungry.*

Standing, stretching his legs, he looked around. Beyond this spot, to the left, the creek widened out. Red willows and bulrushes lined the shore. "Perfect," he said aloud, and started for that area.

*I can make a fence to keep the fish in one location.* His thoughts came as rapidly as his movements. Swiftly, he cut willows and rushes, sorting them by size and type as he went. *I will use the thinner sticks to make a basket that I can use to scoop the fish out of the water.*

Not all ideas work exactly as planned. It took some experimenting to get things right. By braiding a mix of rushes and thinner willows among the thicker uprights, he was able to create some fencing. Placing two pieces across the creek—upstream and downstream—he was able to block their escape in either direction.

Stepping into the water, he used an additional section to herd the fish into a smaller pocket where he set up another barrier, reducing the space in which the fish had to roam. By repeating the process, he managed to crowd his prey into one small area. This allowed him to slip his basket, hardly more than a rolled up mat with a lip, in under a fish. Once it was in place, he gently raised it until he was able to flip the fish out of the water.

Working with the basket he made another discovery. Something shiny, near the edge of a stretch of gravel, caught his eye. The light was golden like the sun. Putting his basket aside he reached out and touched the source, tentatively at first. It was a rock, partially moss covered, with one face colored by a mix of gold flecked with green. Using sticks, Crooked Foot dislodged the stone and carried it up on the bank for closer examination.

On shore, he warmed his feet by the fire while he

watched his catch cook on a spit, and studied the shiny stone while he waited. It was unique and he might be able to use it to make a gift for Bright Moon or Howling Wolf. Unsure of his next move, he tucked it away in his haversack and stretched out to relax. Things had worked out well for him this day. Life was good.

Fish, penned up where he left them, splashed around interrupting his thoughts. Later, before releasing them, he'd select a few to take back to Bright Moon and Howling Wolf for their supper, but for now, they could stay there. He had a tree to search for—the beginnings of a spear to find—before he could go back.

### ###

Belly full, Crooked Foot was on the move again. Here, the trees grew straight but most were either too large or too small. Leaving the animal trail, he followed the stream past where he had cut the willows. Deer and other herd animals grazed nearby. The area, an open meadow now, was populated by the charred remains of trees.

Some time ago, a wild fire had passed through leaving stumps as evidence of its passing. Scattered about here and there were clumps of young trees where the forest tried to regain its dominance.

These clumps interested him. He went from one to the next checking and rejecting the trees at each grove. The herd animals watched him, but made no move toward or away. He kept his distance, and they remained undisturbed by his presence.

He found the wood he needed. It turned out to be the limb of a tree toppled in a storm. When the tree stood upright, the limb had stretched out toward the horizon. Toppled, the tree now reached toward the horizon and the limb toward the sky. Taking it all in, Crooked Foot circled his prize, checking it from every angle. It had to be the right wood, straight and tall—but not too tall—and just the right diameter. He and Red Deer had spent a lot of time in the forest looking for just the right specimen. If he were here now, Red Deer would be proud of the selection Crooked Foot made.

A few ax blows separated the limb from the tree. Sitting cross-legged, back against a trunk, he carefully stripped the branches from the shaft. Surveying his work, he hefted the rough trimmed piece in his hand, testing the balance. "Yes," he said aloud. "Red Deer would be proud."

Gathering up his things, he started back the way he came. The herds did not bother to watch him as he crossed the meadow. Reaching the stream, he found the fish still trapped in the corral he made earlier. After selecting a few— enough for Howling Wolf, Bright Moon and himself, Crooked Foot removed the fence. Released, the fish darted off. Fashioning a tether from rawhide, Crooked Foot passed it through each of the fishes' gills and mouths, slung the batch over the spear's shaft, and continued his journey home.

### 

Returning to the village, Crooked Foot found Howling Moon talking with Bright Moon outside her shelter.

"I see you found a tree to make your spear." Howling Wolf remarked, "but what's that you have decorating it?"

"Fish, Grandfather," holding up his catch, Crooked Foot said with pride. "Eat with us tonight, and I will tell you all about the things I found."

Crooked Foot cleaned the fish and stuffed them with mushrooms, wild onions, and herbs. Bright Moon wrapped the fish in a hide. Nearby, Crooked Foot scraped back enough sand to create a shallow depression. Bright Moon eyed the boy's work. Satisfied, she placed the hide-wrapped fish in the depression and Crooked Foot covered it with a thin layer of sand. He placed tinder and twigs on top of the sand and built a small fire, adding larger branches as needed. Crooked Foot sat back and faced Bright Moon and Howling Wolf as they took in the late afternoon sun. All the trio had to do now was to wait for the fish to bake.

Bright Moon chuckled, "Tell us young hunter, what did you find today?"

"There were many things to see," Crooked Foot said. "I kept my eyes open and I observed all I could just as you taught me. I followed an animal trail through the forest but didn't find a tree to meet my needs. I reached a clearing in the forest near a stream. It was shallow, and there were many fish."

He grew more excited as he continued with his story. "I made a fence like grandmother showed me and used it to keep the fish from getting away. Then I made a basket to slide under the fish and flip them out of the water."

"Wait!" Bright Moon, said, "Did I teach you that? I don't remember."

"Well … you showed me the spider's web and told me to observe and to adapt what I saw. You showed me how to build a fish trap so I just adapted it for this …. Is that okay?"

She smiled slyly, "Did it work? If it worked, it must be okay. Let's dig up our supper and see. Get one of the mud-lined baskets for the coals from the hut so we can use them later."

When the lad disappeared into the shelter, Howling Wolf leaned closer to Bright Moon and said, "You showed him how to make a fence for the fish?" It was more a statement than a question.

"No." She replied, "I showed him how to make a fish trap. What he did is new to me."

"And using a basket for a scoop?"

"New."

"What do you think?" Howling Wolf looked at her inquisitively.

"I think I could use more of his help. I think I should keep him around longer. If he gets some more training, I think he will be ready by the time Tigal arrives ...." A small smile played at the corners of her mouth.

Maybe it was a trick played by the fading daylight, but there was a twinkle, possible smugness—mixed with a little pride—in her eyes. Howling Wolf hadn't seen that in a long time.

The pair put additional discussion aside when Crooked Foot returned. Using a slab of shale, Bright Moon scooped the coals into the mud-lined basket. Carefully pushing the sand away she uncovered and handed out the hide wrapped fish.

"So," she said between bites, "where did you go after you found the fish?"

"The stream sits on the edge of the forest ... near a place where a fire had taken the trees. It's now a meadow. Herds graze there. I walked past the herds to find the wood I needed. I found it on a tree that fell during a storm."

"It's from a place that died," Howling Wolf said. "Are you sure you want it?"

Crooked Foot shrugged. "Where there had once been trees, now there's a meadow. Herds graze there, but trees are returning." Studying the hide where the remains of his meal lay, he busied himself picking up the last of the morsels. "Life goes in cycles. Isn't that what you've said?"

Unnoticed by Crooked Foot, Howling Wolf suppressed a smile as he nodded and gave an understanding grunt.

Chattering as he worked, they watched him use a

sharp flint to skin the bark from the limb. The sun went down. Bright Moon started a fire. Gray Wolf, and others, began to gather around. They came to trade gossip, relive past hunts, and tell stories.

Gray Wolf turned to Crooked Foot. "Tell me, my lad," he asked, "did your other spear have a flint point, or had you just hardened the end in the fire?"

"It had a point. Red Deer made it before he left." Crooked Foot paused and then added, "I want this one to have a flint point, but...."

"Would this be something that you would like to learn?"

Crooked Foot's heart stopped and he looked across the fire from one face to another. Was this a joke? If he knew how to make his own points, he would be the equal of the other boys. Because of what he had learned from Bright Moon, he would be even better than most. He wanted to answer in a firm voice, but he only managed to croak, "Yes ... yes, I would."

Gray Wolf smiled. "Bright Moon told me that you would like to learn these things. I agreed with her that it's time you did. When you finish roughing out the shaft, come see me. I will tell you what to look for and send you out to collect different stones. From them we can make skinning stones, flints, knives, arrow tips ...."

Excited, Crooked Foot bounced on his haunches. "Will we make spear points, too?"

"Yes, we will make spear points, and I will show you how to fasten them. We'll need some cord, sinew from shredded animal tendon makes the best, and some of Bright Moon's glue."

"Glue?" Bright Moon laughed. "That's the first time I've heard it called that."

Crooked Foot looked puzzled. *What did they mean, glue?*

Seeing he was perplexed, she explained, "You remember that sticky stuff we mixed up the other day. I had you collect ochre, deer droppings, and pine gum. Then we stirred in some animal fat …."

Crooked Foot's face lit up in recognition. "That stuff you had me use to patch the hole in your shelter. We mixed it up and poured it over a hide before we slapped it in place over the hole."

"Yes, that's right. That's just one of it uses. The sinew is coated with it to help hold arrow heads and spear points in place." Sitting back, she smiled at him.

"When we finish your spear," Gray Wolf added, "we can make an atlatl.[20]" Savoring that idea, he added, "Yes, an atlatl … a proper throwing stick, that would be a good idea."

"Yes," Crooked Foot agreed, "throwing sticks for spears are good; they are useful." He could almost feel an atlatl in his hands; he could picture the smooth motion, the

---

[20]Atlatl - This is a spear-thrower tool that uses leverage to achieve greater velocity when throwing a spear. It may consist of a supporting shaft with a cup or a spur at the end used to support and propel the butt of the dart. The device is held in one hand, gripped near the end farthest from the cup. The spear is thrown by the action of the upper arm and wrist. The throwing arm together with the atlatl acts as a lever. The atlatl is a low-mass, fast-moving extension of the throwing arm, increasing the length of the lever. This extra length allows the thrower to impart force to the spear over a longer distance, thus imparting more energy and ultimately higher speeds. Such a device is a long-range weapon and can readily impart to a projectile speeds of over 150 km/h (93 mph). Spear-throwers appear very early in human history in several parts of the world, and have survived in use in traditional societies until the present day, as well as being revived in recent years for sporting purposes. The ancient Greeks and Romans used a leather thong or loop, known as an *ankule* or *amentum*, as a spear throwing device.

flight of the spear.

"Yes, they are very useful," Gray Wolf said nodding enthusiastically, his words interrupting the boy's daydream.

Crooked Foot went back to work honing the tree branch into a spear shaft. He had been waiting for Red Deer to return. Time passed with no sign of that happening. Now, he would use this time to get his spear ready ... to make it perfect. Red Deer would be pleased.

To remove lumps, ridges, slivers, he would rub a piece of bark in wet sand and swab it up and down the pole until it was smooth and the little imperfections were gone. Working in this manner, he would continue until it was like the perfectly balanced one he remembered making with Red Deer. Gray Wolf would show him how to make a spear point and get it mounted. For decoration, he could carve small designs, animals, fish, and stars into the shaft. Then he could coat it with a mixture of berry juice and ashes. That would give it a distinctive dark red color like his old one wore. If anyone asked, he would say that it was to protect the wood and make the spear stand out. What he wouldn't say was that it was like the one he and Red Deer had made together ... and he wanted to make it like that to remind him of his friend.

### 

Sitting quietly in the brush, Crooked Foot and Abeytu watched as the chickens began strutting across the clearing. Here and there, they stopped to peck at bugs and other edibles.

Crooked Foot knew that the other hunters had always thought of him as a burden during hunts, but they were starting to change their minds. Crooked Foot leaned close to Abeytu and whispered, "I've spent many days carefully watching these birds and learned their characteristics and their habits."

Abeytu shrugged. "Why would you do that?"

"Learning their traits helped me learn what they might do. Knowing this, I believe I can match even the best hunter."

Having watched this ballet so many times before, he had given each bird a name. *Big Man, Speckled, Fancy, Digger.* He repeated their names under his breath as he waited for the last one, the one he called *Plump*, to show. She was not there. *Maybe she was sitting on a nest somewhere*, he thought. *I'll just backtrack along the way they came and see if I can find her.*

He motioned for Abeytu to follow and quietly crawled off leaving the parade undisturbed.

Abeytu gave him a puzzled look. "What are we doing?"

"One of the birds is missing," Crooked Foot explained, "I need to find out why. We'll circle around and find the tracks the others left."

Abeytu gave him a look that said she needed him to continue.

Crooked Foot smiled. "Come on," he said, "let's backtrack and see where they go."

The pair followed the birds' footprints to a tree-lined, dry-creek, its bed a mass of gravel and rocks. There was no tracking them from here. Standing, hands on hips, he surveyed the ground. At his side, Abeytu waited for him to figure their next move.

Crooked Foot scratched his head and thought aloud for her benefit, "No tracks on the other side of the creek, so their nests have to be near here." Scanning the trees, he located a lump of leaves and grasses high in the branches. Pointing, he said, "Look! There's a nest! It must be *Plump*'s."

Abeytu picked up his excitement. "What are you going to do now that you found it?"

Smiling, Crooked Foot sized up the tree. He located a branch low enough to grab and used it to start his climb.

Not happy to see him, *Plump* sat on her nest emitting warning squawks as he carefully stretched a hand toward her. Cooing softly, he tried slowly sliding his hand between her body and her nest. Upset by this action, the bird went from warning squawks to aggressive pecks. Her beak was sharp. Crooked Foot took action of his own: Quickly forcing his hand under the hen, he flipped her off her nest. Startled, she filled the air with surprised-bird noises and feathers. With the nest vacated, he pulled a leather pouch from his belt and quickly collected the eggs.

### 

"... so when I didn't see the hen come with the other chickens," Crooked Foot explained to Bright Moon, "I told Abeytu that either a critter got her or she was on her nest."

Slapping her leg noisily, Bright Moon laughed. "So ... what did you do then?"

"We followed their tracks and found the tree where they nest. Then I climbed up," As he spoke, he waved his arms around imitating the actions he had taken.

"Then he chased the hen away so he could collect her eggs," Abeytu gleefully finished the story.

"Well, my hunters, what should we do with them now?"

"We could eat them ... or see if we could get them to hatch." Crooked Foot fell silent. While he paused, as if to ponder the idea, he looked over at Abeytu. "I think that might be a good idea, don't you?"

Straight-faced, the pair looked at Bright Moon, measuring her reaction. She was stunned. Abeytu, by her side, sat stone faced and waited.

Crooked Foot couldn't keep from laughing. "But, I

think eating them would be a better idea."

Realizing they had played a joke on her, Bright Moon joined the other two in their merriment.

### ###

"See," dumping the contents of his pouch, Crooked Foot danced with excitement, "Here's a stone like the kind you said to look for, and here's another."

Another stone drew Gray Wolf's attention away from the one the boy held. The color—golden orange mixed with green flecks—piqued his interest. "What's this?"

"Something I found when I was looking for wood for my spear. I thought I could make something for Bright Moon."

Gray Wolf handed the rock back to Crooked Foot. "Good idea. I think she will be pleased."

"I hope so. I want to make something nice for her … and a spear point, maybe some arrow heads for Howling Wolf …."

"Good," Gray Wolf said, chuckling at the boy's enthusiasm. "Now, the first thing is to decide what kind of tool you're going to make."

Wrinkling his nose, Crooked Foot questioned his new mentor. "What do you mean?"

Chuckling again, Gray Wolf pulled a pouch around in front of him and then patted the mat next to where he sat. "Sit here and we can start working. I forgot your grandfather said you hadn't done this before." Gray Wolf playfully mussed Crooked Foot's hair. "Don't worry. Bright Moon said you're a quick learner. Soon you will be showing Howling Wolf arrow heads, spear points, scrapers … tools of all types that you made."

Crooked Foot smiled at those words. Eager to get started, he carefully watched Gray Wolf's every move.

"I brought some things to show you because the stone you work with is important." Gray Wolf opened the pouch in front of him, picked out a sample, and passed it to Crooked Foot. "Because it breaks easily into long flat sections, you can use shale or sandstone to make scrapers." He gave the boy time to examine the piece before continuing.

"Use limestone to make grinders because it's harder than sandstone." He handed Crooked Foot two pieces: A round stone flattened on one side and a long flat piece.

The boy brightened. "I've seen Bright Moon use something like this."

"Yes. Tell me how she uses it."

"She puts the long piece on the ground in front of her and covers the top with a thin layer of grain. Then she puts the round part, flat side down, on the grain, and leans on it while sliding it around. Caught between the two, the grain gets crushed into the powder she uses to make bread."

"That's right. Now, have you seen her use one of these?" He handed the lad a bowl shaped piece and a stone spindle.

"Yes, she uses one like that when she grinds herbs and medicines into powder."

"Good. Now here is something different. Obsidian breaks easily, but in small pieces, it's good if you want to make a tool for cutting."

"I've seen this. Bright Moon has a curved stick. It has pieces of this embedded in the shaft. She uses it to cut grain stalks and other grasses."

"Right again. A person can use small pieces of obsidian to cut hides, fish, and meat or fasten chips to a stick, as Bright Moon did, to cut grain."

Gray Wolf paused before he handed over the last piece. "Do you know what this is?"

"Yes, we use flint chips as fire starters," Crooked

Foot replied

"Right," Gray Wolf agreed. "Smaller flakes are used as fire starters. By hitting a larger piece in a certain way, we cut away at the edges to make spear points or arrowheads. It takes a special technique. You want to try?"

Crooked Foot nodded eagerly.

"Okay. Watch carefully how I do it and then you try. Hold the big piece in one hand, and then tap along the edge with the smaller stone. Go back and forth like this until …."

# Chapter 7: Lost Sheep

There! Crooked Foot heard it again. Bleating sounds. Weak, muffled, almost imperceptible, the pitiful noises drifted through the air. Crooked Foot stood still and slowly turned his head. The sounds came from his left, from behind a mass of grapevines that hung from trees. Somewhere behind this veil, something struggled, but its struggles grew weaker.

With his red spear—the one he and Gray Wolf made last summer—at the ready, Crooked Foot dropped his pack and cautiously crept forward. Parting the creepers, he peered in and, when his eyes adjusted to the dim light, he stepped through.

Inside this curtain, the ground was covered with rocks, making walking difficult. This middle-of-the-night blackness was punctuated by dancing spots of sunlight seeping down through the drape of vines. Inside the veil, the bleating was louder and that sound excited him, pulling him forward. Carefully feeling his way, Crooked Foot took another step over the rough ground, and then another, suddenly finding himself putting his foot down on air.

A sinkhole! His arms flayed as he grabbed frantically for something solid. Snatching at the vines surrounding him, he let go of his spear and heard it clatter across the stones behind him.

The vines slipped through his fingers before breaking under his weight. Backpedaling, he landed on his butt as he struggled to regain his footing. Thrashing about, he flipped over on his belly as he slipped over the lip of the abyss, a fist-full of vines in one hand. The action left him dangling over the edge while he searched to find another solid hold and pull himself to safety. Back on solid ground and with increased caution, he lay there and waited until his heart returned to a normal beat.

### 

The vines covered the area. The darkness they created hid the fissure that nearly swallowed him. Crooked Foot leaned over the lip and stared down into the cool blackness. The hollow before him had steep, slanted sidewalls covered in loose sand and gravel. It backed against the rocky mound that made the hillside.

Trapped at the bottom were a sheep and her young. The two lambs were unable to climb through the soft sand, and their mother wouldn't abandon them. He had no idea how long they had been there, but they looked near exhaustion. Vegetation at the bottom of the pit was sparse. The animals had devoured most of what was there. The few stalks that remained hadn't given up easily. Remnants of the animals' wool coats, like trophy flags, fluttered in the breeze. In their search for food, the lambs had uncovered bones, evidence of animals that had previously fallen into the same trap, but had not escaped.

The task Bright Moon had given him—gathering plants and samples for her—would have to wait. In front of him were provisions–food and hides–for the taking. He began cutting down vines, stretching them out, binding them together to fashion a vine-rope long enough to reach the bottom. Not wanting to join the sheep in this trap, he secured one end before throwing the other into the pit. It landed with a thump among the animals creating a short-lived panic.

Satisfied that testing proved it would hold his weight and more, he began his descent, sinking into the loose sands as he went. Wading through it, he was not surprised the animals were trapped and had to suppress concerns for his own ability to escape.

His presence threw the sheep into a short-lived frenzy of running and jumping about. Taking the leather cords from his waist, the ones used to cinch his tunic closed, he cut them into lengths while he waited for the animals to wear themselves out.

Exhausted as they were, it was easy to seize them and to tie the feet of each animal— front feet to front feet, back feet to back feet—as he caught it. Task completed, he looked around and was suddenly hit with a question. Hit as hard as if he had been struck with a club. *How am I going to get them out of here and back to the village?*

He plopped down on the sand to think. A trickle of the soft silt, disturbed by his action, seeped past reminding him that the trip back up would a difficult one. Next to him, a breeze stirred the remains of a thorny bush, one decorated with strands of wool. It tickled his leg, distracting him. He plucked a handful and began to roll it back and forth between his fingers while he thought about his choices.

He'd used all the cords he had to tie the sheep and her lambs. How could he get them back to the village? He couldn't leave bound animals lying around while he traveled back and forth. His prizes could become victims of some other predator.

It was a puzzle. He looked at the wool in his hands. Without thinking about it, he had rolled it into a strand. It was interesting, but it didn't help him now. Deciding to look at it later, he slipped the wool into a pouch at his waist.

As their anxiety grew, the lambs' cries increased and the mother responded. Kicking, scraping, flopping around, parent and offspring tried to reach each other and a plan started to form in the lad's thoughts. *The lambs and mother would stick together. That's probably how they got in trouble in the first place.*

He jumped to his feet and carried the closest lamb

over to the mother. The pair nuzzled each other and quieted down. Going back to the other lamb, Crooked Foot carried it to the end of his vine-rope. Untying the animal's front legs, he passed the cord through the vine in order to secure the animal to the end. Leaving it there to struggle, he used the vine-rope to climb out.

Reaching the top, he began slowly, gently pulling the vine and attached lamb up the steep, soft banks. After the animal cleared the rim, Crooked Foot pinned it to the ground with one knee. It was too weak to struggle and was unable to slip out from under his grip. Happy with the results, he untied the lamb from the vine and made a loop in the cord. This he slipped around the lamb's neck and tied the other end to a tree.

Crooked Foot stood back, hands on hips, and watched to make sure the animal had settled down. Attracted to nearby vegetation, it began grazing contentedly, blissfully ignoring the fact that, while its front legs were free, its hind legs were still tied together. Quietly, the lad picked up his vine-rope and began lowering himself into the pit to repeat the process.

It took two more trips, but he managed to carry each of the animals up and tie them to nearby trees. Like the first, cord around the neck, front feet free, each one ignored the fact their hind legs were bound and began grazing.

Satisfied that his plan had worked, he leaned against a tree to take a rest and give the animals a moment's peace and the opportunity to fill their empty bellies. They would need the food for the trip back to the village. He was less confident of the plan's next part.

It would depend on letting them feed long enough to have strength to make the trip, but not so long they would have the strength to bolt and run off. Singularly, he would untie each lamb from its tree, lead it over to the mother, and tie it to her cord. Once he had the three of them strung together, he would untie their hind legs and lead the group back to the village.

Ready to follow through, he bent over the first one. Noises—rocks scraping on rocks, the clatter of pebbles falling—behind him, interrupted his work. He reached for his spear and turned toward the sound.

A young cougar eyed him steadily as it eased out of the undergrowth and into the open. Attracted by the sheep's bleating it came expecting an easy meal but found a challenger stood in the way. The cougar moved slowly around the clearing as it sized up the situation but never took its eyes off the human.

Like himself, the cougar was young and inexperienced and Crooked Foot knew that the big cat would also be quick and strong. He had survived the great bear. That knowledge gave him the courage to face this beast—to look it in the eye and never flinch. Spear in hand, he brought the sharp flint point slowly around to meet the animal. Whenever the cat decided to make its move, the boy knew he'd be ready. Their eyes remained locked on each other.

To the cougar, the only thing between it and its next meal was this boy—and he could be dessert. But the feline wouldn't win the field by intimidation because the boy showed no fear, no sign that he would run away.

The big cat came to a halt, lowered into a crouch, waving tail steadied, muscles tensed as he prepared himself. Crooked Foot watched the animal's feet make almost imperceptible adjustments prior to launch.

The cougar sprang! Its movement a blur, but having anticipated this action, the boy tipped his spear up and its raised point impaled the animal midair. Crooked Foot staggered back under the impact and allowed the butt of the weapon to bury itself in the ground, absorbing the force of the attack.

The cougar's gyrations, violent at first, lessened after a bit and then finally stopped. Lowering the animal to the ground, Crooked Foot stepped forward to put his foot across its neck, pulled his spear free but kept the point close. The animal didn't move. It was dead. *My new spear and point worked well*, he thought, *Gray Wolf will be proud. The spear we made did its job well.*

A lamb's bleating caught his attention. Work—field dress the cougar's carcass, cut poles to make a travois[21] he could use to haul its  body back, and add the animals to the string—still needed to be done.

### 

He finally had his little group together, but it had taken longer than he thought. With a string of sheep in tow and the travois carrying the cougar, he started for the village with his trophies. On his way, he thought about the next step.

*Gray Wolf was the one who had shown me how to make the spear point. The cougar will make a nice present for him. He will be*

---

[21] Travois - A frame structure that was used by indigenous peoples to drag loads over land, ice, or snow. The basic construction consists of a platform or netting mounted on two long poles, lashed in the shape of an elongated triangle. Sometimes additional poles, bound across the two main poles, were used to stabilize the frame and support the load being carried. When dragged by hand, the travois was sometimes fitted with a shoulder harness to ease the work. A travois could either be loaded by piling goods atop the bare frame and tying them in place or by first stretching leather over the frame to hold the load being dragged. It is considered more primitive than wheel-based forms of transport. Wheeled vehicles excel on roadways, however, a travoise is superior when used on forest floors, soft soil, snow, etc., where wheels would have encountered difficulties. It is possible for a person to transport more weight on a travois than can be carried on the back.

*pleased.*

The sheep were a different story. He would have to put up some stakes to secure them, provide food and water, and a pen for their protection at night.

This would have to come after he explained to Bright Moon why he hadn't collected more samples, but it would work out okay. Today was a good day. He was pleased.

### ###

Taking a break, Bright Moon leaned on her grinding stone and watched her grandson. Sitting with his back to a post, a pile of wool, and a pile of string in front of him, he was intent on rolling the wool into strings. It had been like this since he returned with the sheep, three days ago. "What are you going to do with all this string you've been making?"

Lost in thought, her question startled Crooked Foot. "Don't know... but it's interesting."

Still leaning on her grinding stone, she thought about it a little more, finally adding, "Better get a stick to wind it on before it turns out to be a pile of knots."

Without waiting for an answer, she began dragging her stone over the grain in the slow easy rhythm needed to turn it into flour.

Selecting a stick from the firewood pile, he began wrapping the cord around it. After a few turns, he stopped to ask, "Remember the spider's web?"

Stopping, she shrugged, "I've seen many spider webs ...." Then she went back to work.

"Do you think I could try to make a web like a spider's?"

Without looking up she replied, "I'm sure you could make anything you set your mind to. I'm not sure why you would want to make such a web ... are you planning on eating bugs?"

Crooked Foot laughed. "No, I don't want to eat bugs. Anyway, if I am going to try to catch something bigger, the cord will need to be stronger."

Stopping again for a short breather, she questioned, "Do you know how to make a rope from hide?"

He was puzzled at her question. He could make rope from hide, she knew that. Her look was one of expectation which meant that she knew the answer to her question, but wanted to prompt him in order to make him think about it without giving him the answer. "You can plait thin pieces together like a mother braids her children's hair," he ventured.

Bright Moon nodded, "Yes, and are there other ways?"

He stopped winding to consider her question. "You can twist them together!"

"Yes," Bright Moon nodded. "That is right."

"Which should I use?"

"Use the one that works best." She led him along in his thinking and now, lesson over, Bright Moon went back to her work. He would have to figure the rest out by himself.

### 

"I heard you've been busy since you brought me the cougar." Gray Wolf and Silver Fox eyed the contraption in front of Crooked Foot. "What have you there?"

"Wool from the sheep I've penned up out back. I've rolled it into long strands, but it was too weak to work with, so I came up with a way of winding the strands together to make ...."

Interrupting, Silver Fox said, "This is nothing but a few pieces of sticks and bones with your string wrapped around them."

Crooked Foot was insulted. "No," he said, "it's more

than that. I drilled holes in both pieces of bone so they could be slipped on a branch and turn freely." He looked from Silver Fox to Gray Wolf and back. "Now, when I wind them together, I can sit here and easily draw string from the two. It makes the strand stronger."

"Then what?" Gray Wolf questioned.

"Yeah, then what?" Silver Fox parroted.

"Well ... uh ... I can take the stronger strands and wind them together to make one that's even stronger." Embarrassment burned on Crooked Foot's cheeks. No one had asked that question before. He wasn't ready to talk about the spider web idea just yet, but he hadn't thought about any other answer.

"Hmmm ... a stronger strand ... and then what?" Gray Wolf persisted. Just out of reach, Silver Fox stood safely behind the older man and made faces at Crooked Foot.

Trying to ignore his rivals' actions, Crooked Foot focused on Gray Wolf as he replied, "I've a few ideas, but they need more work right now ...." He let his voice trail off hoping this explanation was enough to satisfy his mentor.

Gray Wolf squatted near the device to inspect it. Satisfied, he got to his feet. "Whatever you come up with should be interesting," he said, and turned to leave.

Hearing these words, Silver Fox's jaw dropped. Gray Wolf, his own father, clearly rewarded Crooked Foot. Recovering from his surprise, the lad hastened to follow Gray Wolf.

Alone again, Crooked Foot breathed a sigh of relief as he began twisting the strands together. *I'll have to come up with something important*, he thought, *something that would impress Gray Wolf and continue to make Silver Fox envious*. If anything was certain, he had his work cut out. He knew this for sure. Lucky for him, the great cold was coming and he would have more time to think about this, to work on an idea when the white rain came. By the time Tigal's caravan arrived next summer, he would have something new to show. He must have something new.

# Chapter 8: Romnog Attacks

The greenery of early spring covered the underbrush where Romnog lay as he watched the village below. It was the perfect hiding spot. For the last time, he parted the branches and looked over the edge of the cliff so he could run a practiced eye over his next set of victims.

For two days and nights, he and his army lay hidden on the hilltop overlooking this riverside village. It proved to be time well spent. From his position, he studied the layout of the encampment and the activities of the village. He watched the tribe exhaust itself by cutting, trimming, and carrying the timbers needed to make rafts. They'll be tired tonight and sleep soundly ... their last good sleep before they wake up as prisoners. He smiled to himself. They'll never benefit from their efforts ... but I will.

Now it was dusk, and he watched the villagers settle into their evening routines. Tools were stowed. Small groups gathered to gossip. Children played games and chased one another. Flavors of the night's meal curled up through the smoke holes in the thatched roofs. Night fires—their protection against wandering predators—flared up in fire-pits. Romnog could find no sign he and his army had been discovered.

His scout's return interrupted his gloating. Crawling back from the edge, he reached a spot where he could stand without being seen from below. Getting to his feet, he confidently strode to where his lieutenants and the scout waited.

Anxious, the scout shifted his weight from one foot to the other until, seeing his leader approach, he quickly prostrated himself. The commander was known to dispose of anyone who failed to provide complete reports, as well as those who reported things he didn't wish to hear. The scout, not knowing how his words would be received, wanted to appear submissive while he waited uneasily for a signal.

Romnog let the boy lie in the dirt and fidget under his cold stare while his dressers, anticipating orders to move out, helped their leader into his battle gear. Finally, he ordered, "Report."

The scout began speaking without looking up. "The stockade surrounding the encampment was built to keep predators out. It'll provide little problem for your men to slip through."

"You checked the places I asked?" Romnog knew the answer. Given an order, or even a suggestion, no man in his army would risk not carrying it out.

"They proved to be as you observed," came the scout's quick answer.

Previously, Romnog had selected, evaluated, and discarded various entry points and plans until he came up with a set he liked, but it was still good to have the scout's first-hand observation to confirm his decisions. Satisfied they'd be able to gain entry, he turned his attention to the shelters. These were the dwelling places of the clans; the places where families and extended families lived.

A central set of buildings—tribal council houses and common storehouses—were surrounded by family dwellings. Totems marked the entrances of each of these houses and each looked out on the buildings in the center. More than decoration, they identified the animals and ancestors of the clan's heritage as well as providing support for the buildings' center roof beam.

"Tell me about the shelters," he commanded.

"The shelters looked to be about two-hands thick, man-lengths long and maybe two or three wide. Their walls, shoulder high at best, are made of stacked rocks held in place with dried river clay."

Romnog nodded his understanding as he asked, "The roofs. Tell me about the roofs."

The scout was excited. He knew the answers to all the questions. This interrogation was going well. "Thatching, made of woven reeds and grasses in overlapping layers. They lay across the support poles that extend from the walls to the roof beam."

*Thatching*, Romnog thought, *will make nice fires.* "Good! Anything else to report?"

"Each shelter rests on a small mound. My guess is it keeps water out during wetter parts of the year." The scout hesitated. It was a mistake.

Impatient, Romnog drove the blunt end of his spear in the ground near the scout's head. "What?" He commanded.

Startled, the scout cringed before he started. "An observation ...."

"Well?"

"The larger shelters at the center of the encampment ...."

"What about them?"

"The large round one appears to be a common meeting house ...."

Cutting off the scout's reply, Romnog asked, "What about the rest of them?"

The scout's words came out almost as one, "The next smaller one is a sweat lodge; the others appear to be storehouses."

The scout was relieved when Romnog grunted an acceptance. Out of the corner of his eye, he watched Romnog turn and walk away, his lieutenants close behind. Even though it was over, some time passed before the scout collected himself enough to get to his feet.

Lost in thought, Romnog pondered the situation's potential. *Looks like this is a permanent settlement,* he mused. *That would be good. As slaves, these people have skills which can be put to use for Kam Udo the Magnificent. He'll be happy when I present him with this gift.* Turning to his lieutenants, he said, "We attack tonight. Prepare the men to move out."

### 

"I can finish getting ready by myself," White Owl said. Mentally checking each detail, he looked around the Spirit House. "The drum has sounded, calling everyone to join us. Go help the others finish lighting the lamps."

Little Fawn made a face. "Father, Mother's sisters have everything in place. Let me help you or you'll be the last one ready." Pretending to watch the women light the animal fat in the clay lamps, she turned her head so he wouldn't see the tears in her eye.

Some moons ago, before the tribe had returned to this encampment, her mother, like others in the tribe, had grown hot with fever. With wide, glassy-eyes they babbled incoherently, at times speaking to those who had died long ago. Even though White Owl, as tribal Shaman, visited them often, all those afflicted grew weaker, finally falling victim to the-sleep-from-which-no-one-wakes. The memory of their passing still stung.

She felt her father's strong arms surround her. "Daughter, my delight," he said, "We have come far. We have shared happiness and loss, but ...."

The doors to the celebration house swung open and tribe members began flooding in to take their places. Interrupting him, Little Fawn said, "Oh, everyone is here! Father, are you ready?"

Sitting on mats decorated with clan colors, the groups

spread out in a semicircle around a central platform. Each clan sat together in the traditional fashion of the Attikamekey: Men and women sat together. Unmarried youths sat behind them, followed by the younger children in the back. As Chief of the Attikamekey,[22] Running Buffalo, along with White Owl, the Shaman, sat flanked by council members—one from each clan—on the platform facing the clans.

Assuming his role as Shaman, White Owl got to his feet. Little Fawn stepped forward and held out an ermine-skin pouch. Reaching in, White Owl withdrew the ceremonial knife. Cradling it in the open palms of both hands, he turned so everyone could see it. No one remembered its origins, but everyone recognized its black obsidian blade set in a carved handle made of animal horn. It had been handed down from generation to generation and was now only brought out at special occasions. Having completed the circle, he turned back to Little Fawn and placed the knife in the folds of the pouch. She stepped away, returning to a place off to the side.

White Owl turned to the crowd. "Attikamekey, we've sacrificed much, endured many hardships, in order to return here as our ancestors returned here. We do this knowing Jaleti, the great fish, will soon return."

At the completion of these words, Chief Running Buffalo stood and White Owl sat. The chief looked around at the gathered tribe members before speaking. "The Attikamekey have worked hard to be ready for the return of the great fish. Before coming here, I walked along the river and saw the sturdy rafts you built to work from as you stretch out your nets." He paused and looked over the people gathered there before continuing, "Everything we need is ready and stockpiled near the rafts."

---

[22] Attikamekey - The Attikamekey (Whitefish People) are Little Fawn's and Waving Grass's tribe.

Running Buffalo's thoughts raced past his words. *We are ready and only have to wait for spring floods and the return of the great fish. When they come, we will let out rafts, float along the river, spreading our nets as we go. The nets will encircle the fish. We can bring our catch ashore and separate the catch: big fish from little fish, right fish from wrong fish. Small fish would be returned to the river to grow. Some mature ones would be returned as well, but most would be kept. Those not set aside to be eaten within a day or two would be sliced into thin strips, salted, or smoked over drying racks to preserve them for future use. To keep things in balance, a few junk fish were also returned to the river. The rest were sliced up for animal food, bait, or would be used as fertilizer when planting.*

Stone-faced, the chief paused again to look at the gathered tribe. "You've worked hard to be ready … Now we wait." Pausing, his face an expressionless mask, he scanned the crowd again. Suddenly, smiling, he clapped his hands and added, "While we wait, we should celebrate."

Several young men carried a table through the doors and sat it before the council. On a bed of cedar branches lay a mock fish, its giant, overstuffed belly distorting its shape. Pulling his own knife from his belt, White Owl stepped forward and cut the cords which bound the belly of this bloated fish caricature.

Turning to the audience he called, "Clans, send your representatives to collect your share of the bounty." The adults broke into song, and the children screamed with glee as the oldest youngsters among them raced up, baskets in hand, to collect gift bags that had spilled out of the fish. Left behind, the young ones, arms outstretched, crowded around the basket carriers when they returned. Each would walk away with a handful of treats—parcels made of a mixture of dried fruit and nuts coated with honey. Relaxing, the clans gathered in small mixed groups filling the air with laughter and chatter as the evening progressed.

Running Buffalo stood with White Owl as they took in the activities. Addressing While Owl, the chief said, "You were right. The people have been through much, have worked hard, and they need a break."

White Owl accepted this recognition, adding, "When the fish arrive, they'll be working day and night. This time offers a lull between getting ready and working."

### 

Romnog and his lieutenants lead his assembly of men down the mountain. Although it was a long twisted route through heavy brush and forest, coming down from their perch was easier than the climb up had been.

To get up the hill and do so without being discovered, meant crawling—mostly at night—over rocks and through brush and brambles. Because carrying their food and water with them limited how much they had to eat the men grew hungry. Romnog knew this. If asked, he would say that it is what made his men tough … and aggressive.

Nearing the stockade, he posted a man outside to act as lookout and then split the remaining men into three groups, one for each of the entry points he had selected.

When Romnog lay on the cliff's edge, the stockade had been his primary focus. The scout reported it wouldn't be a problem. Now, it stood before him. He was finally able to examine it up close. Simple in form, it consisted of two rows of uprights, set side-by-side, with brambles woven through the outer row and willows through the inner. Neither one provided an obstacle for his army to sneak through. He and his lieutenants would each lead a group.

His plans changed in a flash when the doors of the Attikamekey's Central House opened and tribe members strolled out. At his signal, his army hit the ground and lay still. Weapons clutched in their hands, their muscles tensed, they were ready to go into battle at the slightest command.

Holding his breath, Romnog raised his head slightly and watched the unsuspecting tribe members inside the stockade stroll away. Some walked toward their shelters while others stood around in small groups, mixing gossip and chit-chat.

He waited while stragglers meandered to their shelters. When this chaos faded and things fell quiet enough to be safe, he got to his feet and surveyed the area. Satisfied, he signaled the troops to get up and sent them on their assigned tasks.

### 

The night was cold, the sky overcast. In each shelter, fires flickered in the cooking pits and drove the chill away for now. By morning, these fires would be nothing but glowing coals and frost would hang thick in the air. The rest of her clan already tucked in, Little Fawn snuggled under her sleep robe as she settled down for the night. Her plan for sleep would have been successful had it not been interrupted by barking camp dogs. First one started, then another. *Probably some animal, sniffing around the perimeter fence,* she thought. Dismissing the incident, she rolled over ready for a good night's sleep.

The barking grew frantic. Try as she might she couldn't hide under her covers. Rousing herself, she threw back the sleep robe and swung her feet off her cedar packed sleeping couch. Her father, White Owl, and other clan members were already up and moving about.

A yelp, followed by screams, filled the air. Horns sounded and then a deep rhythmic drumming began. Jerking awake, she saw everyone flood out of their shelters. Little Fawn grabbed her fish spear, the first weapon she saw, and ran out behind them, ready to ward off an animal attack.

What she found wasn't what she expected.

### ###

Inside the stockade, Romnog and his men started toward the area containing the storehouses. Close by, a dog began barking ... then another. A man, torch in hand, stumbled out of an adjacent hut to check out the ruckus and spotted them. He cried out before he could be silenced. A woman, following her man into the night, stumbled out of the same doorway, spotted the intruders, and filled the air with screams. Suddenly, people flowed out of every shelter, and the battle was on.

"Call for the pincher movement,[23]" Romnog told his trumpeter. "Beat these peasants back into a corner and hold them there."

The trumpeter put his ram's horn to his lips and played a set of long and short blasts. Even over the din of battle, it echoed through the night, rebounding from the cliff face behind them.

Quickly, Romnog's army formed three rows. The first row consisted of soldiers carrying clubs and shields; the second, carried spears; archers in the third carried short bows. Across the encampment, he knew the other groups were acting likewise and would begin moving this way.

Until now, Romnog had operated in darkness. With their discovery, there was no need to be secretive. "Make fire!" he commanded. Archers struck flint to tinder, and torches flared. Once the formation was arrayed in front of him, he ordered, "Proceed!"

Hearing that command, those in lead row began a rhythmic drumming of their weapons across the face of their

---

[23] The pincher movement – A military movement, used to surround the opposing group.

shields. Designed to intimidate their enemy, it also worked to drown out any commands enemy forces might give. Spears, held by those in the second row, pointed outward between the shields of those in front of them. Archers took aim and let loose against the first targets they saw.

Little Fawn's tribe fought back valiantly. Surprised, outnumbered, and disorganized they were no match for these well-armed, well-organized men. Caught in the pincher between the groups, most of her tribe was pushed back into a corner and forced to surrender or face extermination.

### 

These invaders had broken through the stockade and were looting and carrying off children and young females, as well as anything else they could pick up. Smoke from burning huts filled the air and added to the chaos. Craning her neck and turning in circles, Little Fawn looked for her family members, but they were nowhere to be seen.

In shock, she trotted aimlessly around. As she looked for a familiar face, she came upon two strangers, war club tossed aside, grappled with a young woman.

She fought them fiercely, but in vain. The older, bearded one, held the woman down while the younger one worked at tying her hands. To enhance their ferociousness, animal skulls decorated the helmets and their garb included heavy leather chest pieces and tunics. Their attire provided protection from the woman's blows and their laughter mocked her as she struck at them.

Little Fawn mused, *you fools stand there smug, wrapped in your leathers, but you forgot about your bare legs*. Taking aim at the older assailant's thigh, she sent her fish spear flying and was rewarded when a pained howl confirmed her accuracy. Shoving their half-bound victim to the ground, both men spun around to face their assailant. Shock crossed their faces when they realized they had been attacked by a mere girl of no more than three-hands' worth of summers. Grinning broadly, they forgot about the female they had been harassing and started toward Little Fawn. Recognizing fortune had turned against her, Little Fawn beat a quick retreat.

While the invaders' tunics provided protection against arrows and spears, it was heavy and restricted their movements—she easily slip through the spaces where two buildings came together, but they could not and often had to turn around and run back. The wearers tired quickly. Realizing this, Little Fawn led the two men on a chase around several shelters. Unable to extract the barbed spearhead, the wounded man broke the shaft and limped along after her and his younger partner.

Winding around another shelter, she found herself back where she had started. In their absence, the woman left behind had crawled over to a night fire-pit and was trying to burn through the cords around her wrists.

Little Fawn dropped to her knees next to her, found a sharp rock that she could use like a saw and worked at the cords until they frayed enough to break.

Alerted by gasping and wheezing, Little Fawn knew her pursuers were coming up behind her. "Finish freeing yourself," she instructed the woman, "then gather others to escape!" Grabbing a firebrand from the night fire, Little Fawn turned to meet her attackers. Over her shoulder, she added, "It's your only chance."

# Chapter 9: Little Fawn

Romnog, satisfied that the tribe—now cornered and wounded—had given up and thrown down their weapons, set a guard over them and started the next phase: Rounding up stragglers and looting.

Once they were out of Romnog's sight, pillaging became the guards' focus. Moving from hut to hut, they grabbed anything they thought to be of value. Small items were tucked away in belt pouches or places even more secret. Large items, anyone found hiding, and the wounded were taken back to be presented to Romnog.

After each shelter was stripped of its valuables, it was set ablaze. With each new fire, wails of despair rose from the captives. These cries went on until they were too hoarse to cry out and too despondent to care.

Romnog stood, hands on his hips, and watched the pile of loot at his feet grow. Along with the collection of clay pots, bowls, prime animal pelts, soft, thin mats, it also contained the biggest prizes of all. While other tribes commonly made needles, knives, arrowheads and spear tips from bone or stone, this tribe went farther by wrapping their knife blades, arrow heads, and spear tips with a thin layer of a golden-orange covering. A material his leader, Kam Udo the

Magnificent, had named *kop*.[24] Any spear tip or knife blade covered with kop, had a sharper point and a keener edge. Yes, Kam Udo would be pleased, very pleased.

### 

Needing to get a barrier between herself and her approaching pursuers, Little Fawn looked around quickly. The nearby night-fire, meant to keep predators at bay, offered her only defense. She moved to keep the flames between her and her attackers. The younger one came to a halt on the opposite side, using this as an opportunity to catch his breath and wait for his companion to limp up.

With her pursuers this close Little Fawn was able to size up her opponents. Covered with sweat, both men were shorter and stockier than the men in her tribe. Of the two, the younger one was in better shape, but neither looked like they had ever done any hard work. They looked tired. A streak of blood from the broken spear trailed down the wounded man's leg. His every move seemed to bring more pain. Sometime during the chase, the two had discarded their heavy war clubs and would have to depend on their hands to subdue her. This did not appear to concern them; after all, she was a mere girl. It would be their greatest mistake.

---

[24] Kop - Their word for copper. With the discovery of copper and the ability to applying it over the top of stone or bone tools, tribes are beginning to transition out of the Stone Age. Eventually (meaning, maybe 1,000 or 2,000 years down the road), copper being too soft, tribes would find that adding a little tin to the molten metal would create bronze which was much tougher and it would usher in the Bronze Age. This, in turn (maybe another couple of thousand years), would be replaced by the Iron Age, once the Hittites discovered iron (or conquered the people who had).

From her side of the fire-pit, Little Fawn watched as the older one joined his partner. At his signal, each of the men started around opposite sides of the pit. Turning to meet the older one as he limped toward her, she rolled the burning stick gently in her fingers to insure the flame continued to burn aggressively.

The older one shuffled forward, arms spread out, fingers flexing and his maniacal gaze fixed on her. She started his way, watching his eyes closely for a sign of his reaction. He stopped, grateful for the chance to rest his leg and watched as the distance between them shrank. Unblinking, his eyes stayed focused on her until she was almost within arm's length and then they flickered to the man behind her. An involuntary break for one brief moment, but she knew it was a signal for his partner to make a move. Footsteps behind her confirmed the young one, in his eagerness, had fallen into her trap.

Turning quickly, she left the older one mouth agape, and empty-handed, as she ran toward the youth. Her tactics caught both of the men off guard for a moment.

"Algard," the older one called, "the rabbit's taken flight. She now comes your way." Hampered by his wound, he was content to stand and watch the young one capture the girl. Then he'd have time to make her squirm.

"She won't get away, Sagarld," was the quick reply.

Checking the wound on his leg, Sagarld muttered. *That would be good. She should pay for this insult.*

Attempting to confuse the youth, Little Fawn feinted movements left and then right. Algard halted his forward rush and opened his arms to grab her if she tried to run by. Raising the flame at the last minute, she stuck it in his face. Screaming, he swung wildly at the torch, but she pulled it away and delivered a hard kick to his knee. A loud crunch rewarded her efforts. Yelling and cursing filled the air;

clutching his injury, he went down hard.

Whirling around, Little Fawn ran toward the older man near the fire pit. Wounded, he was still dangerous, probably more so than the youth. He had learned to survive by being wily. He took a swing at her. She leaned away, but the blow caught her enough to knock her on her backside.

Pouncing on her, Sagarld pinned her torch hand to the ground. Frantically she felt around with her free hand for a weapon of some kind. He was about to deliver a blow when she flung a wad of sand in his face. Sputtering, he tried to hang onto the girl and clear the grit from his eyes. Little Fawn grabbed the torch from her other hand, brought it up and set his beard on fire. Screaming and flailing his arms, he rolled quickly away.

Free, she grabbed a rock from the border of the fire-pit, jumped up and began bashing him on the head. Under her efforts, he fell backward and lay still. Breathing heavily, she glanced over her shoulder to make sure his partner had not recovered from their earlier encounter. The young woman, the one Little Fawn freed earlier, held a club, and stood over the inert youth.

"I am Waving Grass," she said.

Surprised, Little Fawn had not realized that the woman she had tried helped was the chief's daughter.

"The enemy is everywhere," Waving Grass said. "I came back to see if you needed help. We must go now." Satisfied these two culprits were temporarily out of commission, the girls trotted off to find their people and join the battle.

### 

Corralled like animals, those who survived the attack—men, women, and children of all ages—were herded into a group near the perimeter fence. A few guards, spears at the ready, stood in front of them. The rest of the invading mob went casually about their looting. Smoke and embers filled the air.

The two girls almost blundered into the midst of this chaos, but were able to duck back into the shadows without being seen. From there, they paused to size up the situation, retreating deeper into the background whenever the enemy started searching nearby. Before long, they found themselves crouching in the darkness, hemmed in by the looters on one side and the perimeter fence on the other.

"Help me," Waving Grass commanded as she started stripping away the willow branches making up the inner fence. They used these to clear the thorny outer cover and create a small hole in the fence. Waving Grass crawled through, looked around, and then motioned for Little Fawn to follow.

Outside the encampment, Little Fawn cautiously looked around. Light from the burning shelters flickered eerily in the darkness. Sounds of conflict still punctuated the night, but it was dying along with the tribe's ability to resist.

With Waving Grass in the lead, the pair moved silently along the outside of the fence until she suddenly came to a halt. Squatting, she motioned Little Fawn down. Ahead a single guard stood near the fence peering in at the melee. Posted as a lookout, he was more concerned with the progress of the looting than in guarding against a surprise attack.

Gesturing toward the village, Waving Grass said, "The noise from inside will cover your approach. Circle around through the brush and come up on the other side of him. When I see you draw near and get his attention, I'll come up from this side and deal with him." She patted the club in the palm of her hand.

Nodding, Little Fawn disappeared quietly in the

darkness. Holding her breath, Waving Grass crept forward as she quietly waited for the girl to show. She nearly missed Little Fawn's reappearance until, over the din, she heard the girl yawn loudly and ask the guard, "What's going on?"

Startled, the guard almost dropped his spear as he turned to face her. It provided Waving Grass the perfect target. A few quick steps followed by the swift movement of her club and he was laid out quietly in the grass.

"It will be sunrise soon," Waving Grass whispered. "If there is any chance of anyone escaping, it will have to happen before then."

Without further discussion, she turned and began moving along the fence once again. Not knowing what else to do, Little Fawn followed until they came to a spot near where their people were held.

"Keep a lookout," Waving Grass commanded as she got down on all fours and quietly burrowed through the fence. Finished, she looked up at Little Fawn and commanded, "Stick your head through and tell me what you think. I'll keep an eye out here."

Little Fawn saw her people, herded like animals, huddled in a small space between the perimeter fence and smoldering remnants of their huts. Smug in their victory, the guards paid little attention to their captives.

Signaling to Waving Grass to join her, both girls peered through the hole. "We might have a chance to free some people," Little Fawn said.

"Yes," Waving Grass agreed. "Most of the intruders are busy looting. They left three spear-toting men to guard our people."

Taking a pebble, Little Fawn tossed it at a woman who huddled nearby, comforting a small child. It took a couple of tries before she got her attention. The woman's eyes bugged out and her mouth flew open. As the woman was about to exclaim, Little Fawn made the sign for quiet. Through more hand signs, she instructed the woman to find her father.

White Owl limped over to squat near the hole in the fence. His back to the two girls, he cradled one arm close to his chest. Matted hair framed his weary face. He did not look directly at her, but she could see enough of him to know he had put up a valiant, but losing, fight. Face covered with a mixture of dried blood and dirt, he looked tired and worn.

"We're lost," he said. "Escape while you can." He hung his head down in defeat.

"The guards aren't watching closely," Waving Grass replied. "Have the others come over in small groups and crawl through the fence."

"It's no use … they'd have nowhere to go … and are in no shape to travel far or fast. They'd be caught when the guards realize they're gone."

"We can escape. We have the rafts," Waving Grass said. "Little Fawn will stay here and help the people out. I will lead them down to the river."

Spirits lifted, White Owl nodded agreement. "We'll send out the women and children first. As they leave, those remaining can shuffle around to confuse the guards so they won't notice. The night is filled with smoke … it's getting thicker and hangs low in the air. It will help cover our escape."

Getting to his feet, he shuffled over to a small group gathered nearby. During the short conversation that followed his arrival, a few members stole cautious glances toward them. When the group broke up, some moved off to spread the message. To cover this activity, others milled around aimlessly; and the guards, intent on the looting, remained unaware.

In ones and twos, women and children gathered in

front of the hole where Little Fawn and Waving Grass waited. There, they faced outward toward the guards, and blocked anyone's view of their escape route. Confirming these changes had gone unnoticed, the people in the rear ducked down and scrambled through the enclosure.

When a group slipped out, those left in front stepped back to take a place near the exit and become the next to escape. Milling about increased with each departure in order to cover their thinning ranks. More of her tribe sauntered over to join the ones at the fence until there were just a few men left and then they too made good their getaway. The guards, busy watching the looters, did not realize they had no one left to guard.

### 

White Owl was the last to crawl through the fence. So far, no one was aware they were gone. Little Fawn had waited anxiously outside the enclosure for him to emerge. Her worried face turned to smiles when she finally saw him.

He returned her smiled. "Daughter, my delight," he said quietly. "We must follow the others quickly before we're discovered."

She helped him to his feet and threw his good arm over her shoulder. Luckily, it wasn't a long trip from the compound to the river. Smoke drifted down from the village.

Clearly, those who had arrived earlier had met no resistance. Men and women worked together to put the rafts in the water while the children scavenged the area looking for anything useful they could bring along. As each vessel filled, the occupants shoved off. Working in teams, one team on either side, members poled their way toward the middle of the river where the current would carry them downstream.

The last craft was already in the water when Little Fawn and her father arrived at the river's edge. Fog hung over the river. She caught a glimpse of the other rafts as they disappeared into its gray shroud. Back in the village, a horn sounded.

"We should hurry." White Owl grinned at Little Fawn. "I think someone has discovered our absence."

### 

Across the compound, the last of the shelters blazed. In front of them, three guards stood rigid, wishing they could disappear into the smoke filled air. As witness to their punishment, the closest of Romnog's army, massed in stiff orderly ranks, and stood facing the trio. Towering above the others, Romnog paced back and forth between the two groups, stopping now and then to give the trio a cold stare.

Earlier, he had strolled over expecting to inspect the prisoners and take inventory: Men, women, and children, young, old, wounded, non-wounded. He found no one. The guards, intent on watching the looting, were as surprised as he. It didn't help their cause.

Finally, his voice a hoarse whisper, he asked, "Where are the captives?"

Standing rigid before their leader, the three guards offered no answer. They had none to give.

"Where are the captives?" Romnog roared.

Sweating, the guards remained speechless. They wouldn't be able to offer an explanation that could satisfy their commander. Anything said by them at this point would only worsen their situation.

"Sound recall!" he bellowed to his trumpeter. The youngster, slow to act, caught the first blows of Romnog's wrath. Prodded to action, he quickly put the horn to his lips and sounded the call. Immediately, his men came running from all corners of the encampment and fell into formation in front of him.

Romnog bellowed for his two lieutenants, "Gachald! Paxtald!" Knowing they dared not be there, he had shouted their names even though he never bothered to look their direction. "Our prisoners have escaped," he fumed. "They were to be presented to Kam Udo the Magnificent ... as slaves ... Bring them back ... or select which of your men will join these three to be presented in their place." He pointed to the pile of captured bows and arrows. "Arm some of your men with these and take the prisoners with their own weapons. It will teach them a lesson."

The formation broke into two groups, and the search of the encampment began. The effort of checking every dark corner and every blazing shelter, stopped abruptly almost as soon as it started with the arrival of the two guards.

Sagarld, the older one, beardless, bleeding from a leg wound, and covered with blisters; while Algard, the younger one, also bleeding, shuffled along using a tree branch as a crutch.

"What happened to you?" Paxtald growled his question. Gachald looked on suspiciously.

"At ... at ... attacked ..." The younger guard stammered.

"We engaged the enemy." The older one spoke up, cutting off his younger comrade, "and before we could subdue them a mob came out of nowhere to attack us." Pausing, he held his side and winced before adding, "We fought valiantly but were outnumbered and our position was overrun ... that's the last I remember."

Not sure they should believe his story, the two leaders looked at each other and then at the pair in front of them. Both Sagarld and the younger man with him appeared to have had some kind of mishap. Even still, they were leery. Past dealings with Sagarld had taught them that he was capable of twisting the facts to his own benefit.

Deciding that continued questioning would be a waste of time, Paxtald decided to put it aside for now. "Where did this happen?" His words were more of a sneer than a question.

Giving a vague wave of the hand, the older guard said, "That way … in the back." Taking a few tentative steps, he added, "Follow me, I'll show you." Stumbling, he caught himself.

"Never mind," Paxtald growled, "We'll find it ourselves." Signaling their troops, they cautiously moved out leaving the pair behind.

Sagarld, the old guard, watched Romnog's lieutenants lead their troops away. When they were out of earshot, he whispered hoarsely, "Go you little flunkies. Go and find everything I fixed up for you to find." His disdain obvious, he spat in their direction.

"Sagarld, what happens when they find out…?" Algard questioned.

Glaring, the older one turned and cut him off, "If they knew we were beaten by two girls, we'd be dead … or worse, slaves." Calming a little, he put a fatherly hand on the boy's shoulder and said, "We cut ourselves, enlarged the fight area back there, and made the hole in the fence bigger to make it look like a large group attacked us and then slipped out. Understand? They won't find out if you keep to the story. Never tell anyone anything else Algard. Are you up to that?"

Hanging his head, Algard mumbled, "Okay."

"Good lad," Sagarld said, clapping him on the back and smiling warmly. Inwardly, he doubted his young partner would be able to keep the secret and he began thinking of ways to get rid of the boy. It would have to look like an accident, but it would be his safer choice.

Shouts arose from the back of the encampment.

Hearing this, a smile crossed Sagarld's face as he thought, *Good, they found the hole I made.* Confirming this, a parade of torches appeared outside the stockade, milled around and then flowed down the fence to gather near the front gate.

### 

Splashing through the water, Little Fawn and her father reached the raft. Behind them, a parade of torches accompanied by shouts and curses, surged out of the encampment, and descended toward the river. The last of the escapees to reach the river, she and her father scrambled aboard and grabbed poles to help push the raft out.

*It would be nice if dawn would come later today,* thought Little Fawn. *It would be nice if the clouds darkened the sky. It would be nice if the thick fog lingered longer.*

Nevertheless, before they reached the middle of the river, before they reached the protection of the fog bank, dawn crept over the horizon … the sky began to clear … and the river's edge filled with armed guards, angry their prisoners had escaped.

"Everybody push!" White Owl shouted, "We need to get to the middle …."

"Down!" A shout from behind cut him off.

White Owl turned and pushed Little Fawn to the deck as the air filled with arrows. On the raft, people screamed and fell, some toppling into the water.

Prone, heart in her throat, Little Fawn shivered with fear while clutching the timbers under her. The vessel, lurching into the current, jarred her into action. Getting to her feet, she grabbed the nearest pole and turned to shove the craft forward only to freeze in place. She was the only one not a casualty. Her father, sprawled across the raft, lay bleeding. Dropping to her knees next to him, Little Fawn took his hand.

"Father …."

He squeezed her hand as he said, "My daughter, my delight …." He coughed, once … twice … wheezed hoarsely, and then closed his eyes … forever.

Even as the current pulled the raft deeper into the thin, gray bank that would be their hiding place, she heard the twang of bowstrings. Those onshore were firing blind into the fog hoping to inflict further punishment.

"Stop …." She yelled frantically. "We're all hurt. Stop shooting."

Her plea came too late. Arrows rained down around her once again filling the air with screams from the wounded. Pain, red-hot pain, jabbed at her arm another at her legs. Surprised, she looked down to see her own wounds, even as she crumpled to the deck. The raft, pulled by the current, disappeared deeper into the fog as the twang of bowstrings sounded again.

# Chapter 10: Returning to the Sea People

Sprawled lazily across a bench near the foremast, Red Deer idly watched the small white clouds drift across the blue sky. He knew they promised good weather. The trip back from Naacal[25] had not always been this way.

"My queen," the ship's captain explained, "the one you called Abooksigun,[26] said you were anxious to get back quickly." He shrugged then added, "This time of year, the northern route is stormy, but it is these storms that propel us the quickest."

Quick it was. Although it meant enduring hardships: a constant dousing with freezing cold rain, waves that often covered the decks, and driving winds that required them to spend many days and nights at the sweeps in order to keep the ship on course. But, they were successful! A trip through calmer waters with more accommodating weather would normally take nearly one-hand's worth of moons. By following the northern route, little more than two moons

---

[25] Naacal - This is the place where Red Deer and Great Buffalo had sailed to during Red Deer's sojourn. This is the name of an ancient people and civilization first claimed to have existed by Augustus Le Plongeon and later by James Churchward. Though there is no scientific or archaeological evidence for the existence of the Naacals, various later fictional works have made use of them. In Andre Norton's Central Asia novels, two main characters are Nacaals. She identifies Draupadi from the Mahabharata and the Hindu deity Ganesha as Nacaal survivors who advise humanity. She describes two warring factions among the Nacaals who have different aims and pursuits. Her Nacaal civilization existed on islands in an inner Asian sea and eventually perished.

[26] Abooksigun - Algonquin word meaning "wildcat."

passed before they arrived at this point.

The vessel's bow rose and fell as it cut its way through the waves. This gentle, rocking motion provided the weary crew with a welcome relief and a pleasant change from what they had experienced most of their journey.

Asleep nearby, Great Buffalo snorted noisily then rolled over. Three summers ago, Tigal encouraged Red Deer and his comrades to build their own craft. They used it to sail away from the village of the Sea People and into a great adventure. But, more than that, it was: a chance to experience new people, a chance to travel across the great waters, to see what lay over the horizon, and a chance to collect new stories. Of their friends that joined them on that trip, Red Deer and Great Buffalo were the only ones who had elected to return.

Great Buffalo was an orphan adopted by Tigal and made a member of his traveling caravan. The wily caravan master sent him and Red Deer on a spy mission to the village of Chief Running Wolf of the Sea People. When the pair reached the village, they found the Sea People in a crisis, and they bent to resolve the challenges the villagers faced. In doing so, they were not only successful in the task Tigal assigned them, they also found themselves accepted by these people and built many close friendships, particularly with the chief's son, Little Wolf.

However, it was not Little Wolf that Great Buffalo longed to see. There was a young woman named Appanoose, daughter of the Running Wolf and Little Wolf's younger sister. He was not surprised to find himself thinking about her more and more each day.

Red Deer had joined the caravan as a part of his sojourn. Normally, boys were away for one summer or maybe two. He had been away nearly five summers. Having grown taller, more muscular, he was definitely not the same in looks or attitude as when he left. He looked forward to seeing his family and to witness the looks on their faces when they saw him again. Then he would know that the changes he felt were not imaginary.

"Sail!" The ship's lookout broke through his reverie.

Early that morning the captain pointed out the mouth of the great river, a familiar landmark even after all this time. He knew then they were close, and they grew closer with each passing wave.

"Sail!" the ship's lookout repeated his call.

Red Deer looked over the rail. In the fading light of late afternoon, a small fishing vessel had dropped its sail, and the crew had manned paddles as they began to thread their way past a rocky point. Smiling, Red Deer poked his friend, Great Buffalo.

Recovering from time spent on the oars during last night's stormy ride, the young man rolled over and squinted, half-asleep yet. "What's going on?"

Red Deer pointed over the rail's edge. "I think you'll find that craft looks familiar; if I'm right, we'll be ashore before night fall."

Great Buffalo sat up, the depths of sleep all but a fading memory. More than two moons' time had passed since they left their friends Aditsan[27] and Abooksigun standing on the beach in Naacal. It was an emotion-filled departure followed by a difficult voyage back.

The captain Abooksigun picked as their guide sailed to the far north where they were able to witness great mountains of ice floating in the sea. From there, propelled by high winds and almost constant storms, they traveled east, and then south, standing just off the wall of white that was

---

[27] Aditsan - Navajo word meaning "Listener".

the Great Ice. Eventually, this white landscape gave way to scrub trees and brush. Since then, the scenery and landscape improved, and both of these young men looked forward to this voyage coming to a close.

Seeing this small fishing vessel was a most welcome sight. From somewhere beyond the beach, a horn sounded. Their ship had been sighted, and the horn trumpeted their arrival.

### 

Villagers had gathered on the crest of the hill to watch the craft approach. When the vessel crunched into the sand, the villagers flooded down the beach to run their hands over the hulls of this sleek craft and marvel at its construction.

Banging drums led a small procession through the crowd, allowing the approach of village dignitaries followed by a sedan chair. The bearers came to a halt and sat the chair down, letting their passenger, a frail, old man, get to his feet.

The old man held his hands up, and the crowd quieted. "I, Chief Running Wolf, greet you and ask if you've brought word of our friends?" Not many strange ships stop here, but he always greeted those that arrived with the same request. Usually they stopped only to resupply or do repairs. Having heard a negative answer so many times, he had grown to expect it, but he would never give up asking.

The ship's captain laughed, "Better than that sir, I believe I've brought you your friends."

### 

Chief Running Wolf called for a feast. Soon tribe members carried out trays loaded with food and everyone began singing and dancing in welcome.

As guests of honor, Red Deer and Great Buffalo sat

across the campfire from Chief Running Wolf. Looking around, Red Deer could not help but marvel at how everything had changed during their absence. On their previous visit, these people who had been lifeless and on the verge of starvation, now were well fed and energetic. When they first met, White Hawk and Running Wolf were older, wrinkled, and frail looking. Little Wolf, the chief's son, was a skinny youth, barely three hands old. His sister, Appanoose was just fleshing out into womanhood.

Now, over the crackling flames of the campfire, though it seemed impossible, both Running Wolf and White Hawk appeared even older. Little Wolf, the chief's son, every bit as tall and muscular as Great Buffalo or himself, sat at Running Wolf's right hand and saw to it that the two old men were well looked after. Appanoose, now a young woman, directed the other women, young and old. She flitted about making sure all the guests had their fill of food and drink.

While Appanoose made sure Red Deer's plate and cup were never empty, she punished Great Buffalo for having sailed away all those summers ago and skirted around him as if he weren't there. In spite of herself, she could not leave him dangling in the wind. From the corner of his eye, Red Deer noticed that Great Buffalo did not starve because Appanoose made sure one of the other servers made casual stops, appearing more like afterthoughts: a task performed when all the others were served.

After serving, the women re-grouped near the food preparation area. They laughed and chattered in low tones, now and then shooting hidden glances toward the men, particularly Great Buffalo. Of all of them, Appanoose was the guiltiest.

Running Wolf studied the boys' faces for a moment. "Yes, the two of you have entertained the council and me with the stories about your adventure, the things you saw and what you learned. I know you speak the truth because you've previously demonstrated your knowledge and your resourcefulness and you brought gifts the likes of which none of us have ever seen." Both the boys blushed at his words, but Running Wolf went on. "Tell us, what are your plans now?

"Well," Red Deer said, "when Tigal's caravan comes this way, I ...."

Interrupting him, Great Buffalo put a hand on his comrade's shoulder and said, "Well, we have no ties here and don't want to be underfoot, so we would like to rejoin Tigal's caravan when he comes this way. He still comes this way doesn't ...."

At close range, a clay bowl dropped from about waist-height makes enough noise to attract momentary attention. At close range, thrown against the ground with force, a clay bowl makes enough noise to interrupt any conversation. All eyes quickly turned to the source.

The food servers, previously clustered together, stood back revealing Appanoose. Hands on her hips, fire in her eyes, she glared directly at Great Buffalo, who calmly sat there smiling.

### 

It had been three summers since Red Deer last saw the village of the Sea People; it would soon be five summers since he saw his own village. Ashore now, armed with the knowledge that this place was a crossroads, and a frequent stop for Tigal, Red Deer waited for the caravan's arrival. He was not disappointed. In less than one hand's days after they landed, Tigal's runner arrived bearing the good news. Red Deer knew he would be starting for home soon and he went to tell his comrade.

Great Buffalo sat on the ridge overlooking the sea.

His back to a tree, he worked on a spear. Red Deer plopped down on the sand next to him and began to tease his friend. It would be his last opportunity. "The ship that brought us is still here if you want to return to Aditsan and Abooksigun in Naacal."

Great Buffalo looked up from his work and made a face. "Our last voyage was enough for me, so I won't be going anywhere soon."

Red Deer, his brow furrowed, faked disbelief. "Tigal's runner arrived. The caravan should be here in a day or two. Does that mean you won't be joining us?"

Great Buffalo smirked. "No, I think I've found a home here. Little Wolf and I had a talk. One day, both Running Wolf and White Hawk will sleep-the-sleep-from-which-no-one-wakes. Little Wolf will become chief, and he will need someone to replace White Hawk."

A chant drew Red Deer's attention. The fishing boat had returned, dropped its sail, and the crew worked the paddles in unison with the chant: *Ooh-dah. Ooh-dah. Ooh-dah.*

"That sounds like a good plan," Red Deer said, "in the meantime, you did such a good job on rebuilding their fishing vessel, maybe you could talk them into letting you build another one for them."

Great Buffalo looked at him. "Why would we need another one?" *Where was his friend going with this?*

Red Deer grinned. "You have the skills to build a vessel," he said. "On top of that, we've been to sea, so you know how to handle your craft. Finally, Abooksigun taught you how to read the waves, the weather, and to navigate. You could voyage to new lands—I don't think you want to go as far as Abooksigun's Naacal—but go to the places that Tigal's caravan cannot reach. You could trade salt for hides and other goods." Red Deer gave his friend time to think about what he had just said.

Great Buffalo looked unconvinced. "Well, I don't know. Tigal will be here in a day or two ...."

Red Deer couldn't contain his excitement, "Tigal is always looking for new trading partners." He paused, but just for a moment, and then went on with, "That gives you time to sell Running Wolf on the benefits to him and when he agrees, then you sell Tigal on the same idea. Myself, I think Tigal will jump at it."

Great Buffalo looked up at the ship nearing shore and gave a dismissive snort. "I think there'll be somebody else I have to convince first."

Red Deer cast a glance toward the vessel. Most of the women had hopped out and were wading ashore. Appanoose, still aboard, directed the securing of the vessel and the distribution of the catch. In between, she could be seen giving worried glances toward the pair of men on the beach. Red Deer was painfully aware that she did not let Great Buffalo out of her sight for long and seldom let him and Red Deer have much time alone lest they cook up another trip.

He gave Great Buffalo a knowing look. "Appanoose and her crew are experienced. Give them a chance to go along on the trading voyages. Her excitement will be endless ... and so will her rewards," Red Deer said. "In between trips, they can train new crews for the second ... and the third ships."

# Chapter 11: Leaving the Caravan

Before the caravan left the village of the Sea People, Red Deer sat down with Tigal to discuss his plan. "I intend to leave the caravan when it reaches the boundary between savanna and forest."

Tigal did not object, he just nodded and puffed on his pipe. "You are welcome to travel with us. Think about it, and let me know your decision when we reach the place where the forest and the grasslands meet."

Red Deer continued to enjoy the hospitality of the Sea People while the caravan stayed on. The trading went on for a few days and then they packed up and left. Before the procession disappeared into the forest, the one that had first sheltered Great Buffalo and himself three adventurous summers ago, Red Deer turned to look back. Great Buffalo stood with Appanoose and Little Wolf and gave him a final farewell wave good-bye.

### ###

After almost two hands' worth of travel, they reached the place where forest and grasslands met. Red Deer thought about his decision and the conversation with Tigal and decided it was time for him to leave the caravan.

With all the animals fed and bedded down for the night, the men not on guard retired to their family campfires. Families visited with families, traded stories, talked over the day's events, or to enjoy a pipe. Now and then boisterous laughter would erupt. Eventually a game of some kind might break out, in which case everyone's attention would be focused there.

Red Deer listened to their talk while he worked on his new idea: a device that could be used as a travois or a sled. To do this, he replaced the lightweight frame normally hung from the user's shoulders with a scaffold equipped with runners. In this manner, Red Deer felt he could drag the device like a sled or shoulder it like a travois.

Red Deer spotted Tigal, pipe in hand, strolling through the camp and stopping to chat at each campfire. It was the Caravan Master's way of keeping in touch with each family, but it was also his way of making a nightly inspection tour.

Red Deer knew it was time for him to remind Tigal of his plan. He continued to work on his sled and waited for the caravan leader to stop by.

### 

Sitting across the fire from the caravan master, Red Deer asked, "Is it true, Sir, tomorrow you'll start your travels through the sea of grass?" He searched Tigal's face for some sign, but saw none.

Gathering his thoughts Tigal took a long puff on his pipe and expelled a cloud of smoke as he spoke. Red Deer learned some time ago that a cloud of smoke accompanied Tigal wherever he went. *It keeps the pesky bugs at bay,* was the explanation gave.

"It's true, my son," Tigal replied. He took another long drag on the pipe and then added, "My animals work very hard. The sea of grass is good grazing, and they need time to forage. We all need time to rest. Along the way, there are many villages waiting for our visit, many places where we can relax and the animals can feed."

"I believe we're near the land of the Narwikin are we not?" Red Deer knew the answer to his own question.

"You know this how?" Tigal expelled more smoke.

"The stars! Abooksigun taught us how to read the stars, the Sun and the Moon. They tell me we're near." Red Deer paused before going on. "I believe it will take your caravan two-hands worth of travel, maybe longer, before you get to the village of the Narwikin."

Tigal knew the youth was correct. He also knew the young man had been away a long time and wanted to get home. He had braved many hardships to get this far. "You're welcome to continue with us if you wish." Even as he made the statement, Tigal knew the answer he would get in return.

"If I follow a more direct route through the forest, across the ridge and then along the Great Ice," Red Deer laid out his plan, "I can follow the melt water and find the river which will take me to my people." He knew Tigal's group would continue to follow the longer, slower route, but his plan could mean he'd be home in a few days.

Tigal sat thoughtfully for a moment while he considered the lad's words. The trip, explained simply enough in a few words, hid many hazards. Things the youth in his zeal would willingly minimize or overlook completely.

"Your trip will take more than just a few days," pausing to adjust his pipe, he blew more smoke as he added, "How will you carry the supplies you'll need?"

"I will take some of my provisions in my backpack," Red Deer said, but, since I'll need more than I can carry, I came up with another solution." Standing, Red Deer propped the device he created against a tree to steady it. "Because it combines both a travois and a sled into one device, I call it a travois-sled."

Getting to his feet, Tigal eyed the device, and the youth's work carefully. "So this is what you've been working on." He had seen a travois before, but this was different than usual. The most obvious difference was the two poles, thicker, heavier than usual, and a little longer than he was tall, these ran almost parallel to each other. Willow canes, fitted into holes at intervals along the length of the poles, held these shafts an arm's length apart.

Red Deer laid his creation back on the ground and pantomimed pulling it behind him like a sled carrying his supplies. "Instead of having the tail ends drag along the ground like a regular travois, I made this to allow the full runners to glide along the ground when I want, or I can shoulder the front end and let the tail drag." Red Deer paused to get the old man's reaction and give him time to comment if he wanted. Tigal squatted down and eyed the device carefully before nodding.

It was then Red Deer confessed, "I am returning with many gifts for my family, more than I can take on my trip. Rather than take them with me, I'd like you to carry most of my goods with you."

Tigal nodded agreement but seemed puzzled. If his caravan was to carry these gifts for Red Deer, why did the lad need this strange device?

Recognizing Tigal's unspoken question, Red Deer said, "While I expect my trip over the mountains to take less time than the caravan, it is as you said, I can't carry enough in my backpack to last for the whole trip. I built this to carry the additional provisions."

The Caravan Master nodded, but said nothing, taciturn recognition that Red Deer had thought through his plan.

Satisfied that the caravan chief approved Red Deer continued with his explanation, "It will be heavy in the beginning, but I'll use the supplies on the travois-sled first. I've curled the ends up so they won't snag as they slide over the ground. When it's empty, I'll use it for my campfire and use the stores I have in my backpack."

"So, you're still going to strike out on your own. I can't talk you into staying on with the caravan?"

"My time away has been an adventure. I've learned much, but I've been away a long time. I feel the need to get home."

Tigal clapped the youth on the back. Holding the pipe in one hand, he smiled warmly, "Well said, my boy. We'll join you at your village by the time the moon is new."

# Chapter 12: Cross Country Trek

They parted company early the next morning with Tigal's caravan stepping out across the rolling, grassy hills. Pack animals, mastodons and camels alike, stopped here and there to enjoy the grasses until prodded to move on by a drover.

While he loaded his travois-sled, Red Deer took time to glance toward this migrating mass until he could no longer make out individual details. Their departure left him on his own once again and with a sinking feeling in his stomach. Had he made the right decision? He shook himself. *How long am I going to let myself stand here? If I'm going to beat Tigal to my village, I had better strike out through the forest for home.*

Towing the travois-sled behind, he made good time in the lowlands by following an animal trail through the forest. The travois-sled was heavy but the path was wide and free of obstacles so he did not have to fight it. Reaching the foothills changed everything. The path became narrower and rock strewn as it circled upward out of the forest and skirted around the cliff face.

He found that the additional obstacles and travel uphill took greater effort. His creation no longer worked well as a sled, so he shouldered the front-end and dragged it along. As a travois, it worked better, but progress was still slow and the hillside still steep. The day wore on. As night approached, he heard wolves howl in the distance. A chill ran up his spine. How far away were they? He listened intently as he tried to gauge the distance, but the sound echoed off canyon walls making them impossible to locate.

As he climbed, he found that trees became scant so he started collecting dry wood for his nightly campfires. A good thought, but it added an unplanned burden to his load.

Exhausted, Red Deer found a spot on the leeside of a rocky ice-covered mound. With a blazing fire at his feet, he chewed on a piece of pemmican while he examined the travois-sled and thought about ways to improve it. *It worked well through the forest where the track was smooth, but kept snagging on rocks and roots when the ground became rough.*

Unloading his creation, he leaned it upright against the wall, closed his eyes, and ran bare hands up and down over the runners. He hoped his fingers would tell him things that his eyes hadn't.

When he first put the device together, he thought the runners were smooth, but now his touch proved different. *I can fix that*, he vowed, and began running his knife up and down the runners, smoothing nicks, scraping off nubs and the remaining bark. This gave the shafts flatter, smoother blades, leaving nothing to snag obstacles along his path. The changes should allow the sled to ride easier across rough ground, broken ice, or deep snow. If it worked as well as he hoped, he could go farther before tiring, quickly covering a greater distance. That would help make up for the time he lost while struggling to climb uphill. Satisfied he had done as much as he could; he wrapped up in his sleep-robe and settled in for the night.

Morning came. Red Deer stirred the dying coals into life long enough to give him some warmth while he checked out his travois-sled. Dragging it behind him, Red Deer walked back-and-forth around the area. The shafts thumped and bumped over rocks but didn't snag, confirming its smoother surface meant improved progress. Chewing on another piece of pemmican, he loaded everything back on the sled and started his journey.

By nightfall, he reached the Great Ice and looked down across the expanse of crumpled mounds of snow and ice. A cold wind swept off this sea of ice and chilled him to the bone. This mass of white was bigger than he remembered and not flat, but tilted from side-to-side, peppered with outcroppings, drops, pinnacles, crags, and buckled, broken bands of ice. It flowed outward through the pass between the mountain peaks. Shoulders of heavy snow clung to overhangs. Worse, the icy mass spread out and flowed downhill disappearing over the horizon.

Backtracking a little, Red Deer made his camp for the night in a crevasse. He wrapped up in his sleep-robe with his back against the rock wall, downed some pemmican, and settled in for the night in front of his small fire.

A wolf's howl split the night air waking him. It was near dawn. His fire was but glowing coals. He debated about throwing more wood on it, a nice blaze would certainly warm him, but his thoughts were interrupted by another wolf's howl ... then another ... then a full chorus. He had heard them last night, but these were closer. They were on his trail. He suspected the smell of smoke had attracted them. A blazing fire now would hold them off until he ran out of wood and then it would be another story. Ending the debate, he packed his travois-sled and broke camp.

Before striking out toward the ice field, he stirred the embers and arranged the remaining firewood to kindle a new flame. As a last item, he placed dried meat near the back wall and at the edge of the fire. The smell of cooking meat would attract the wolves, but if they wanted it, they would have to cross the fire. This might hold them at bay and the delay would give him time to get away. That was the plan. The howls grew louder, closer.

He started off at a quick pace, but with each step he took, the wolves took two. A quick glance over his shoulder at the closing pack confirmed there were enough to count on the fingers of one hand. In the open and by himself, there would be too many for him to fight and win.

He reached the ice field and started across before the wolves arrived. It had a crusty glaze caused by constant thawing and freezing. It was strong enough to hold his weight. The travois-sled slid smoothly along behind sometimes hitting his heels. With the wolves continuing to close, he broke into a gentle lope,[28] unable to go faster across the slippery surface.

The wolves fared no better and had to slow their pace, but they still managed to narrow the gap. The travois-sled clipped his heels with increasing frequency forcing Red Deer to quicken his stride. If he had planned ahead, he would have fastened a longer cord to the sled and it would not have been constantly at his heels. As it was, with it following so close he risked tripping over the sled and falling. Maybe it didn't matter because he wouldn't be able to keep this gait up for long. He hoped the wolves would tire before he did and look for other prey, but he needed to find another solution in case that didn't happen.

The field in front of him curved away in a series of ice-covered slopes. If he reached them, he could ride the sled downhill. It would give him a chance to rest while the wolves gave chase. But, to get there, he would have to skirt around a couple of drops. The first of these looked to be at least the height of two men. About ten man lengths below that drop lay the second. The pair provided the answer he needed!

He slipped the travois-sled in front of him and pointed it at the first drop. It gained speed as he jumped aboard. The bow of his craft dipped down. The wolves were nearly at his heels, their snarls, and barks filling his ears. The

---

[28] Lope - run or move with a long bounding stride

mound of new snow on the front edge of the drop began to crumble and then collapse under him. His travois-sled picked up speed as it flew off the ledge and landed on the apex of this fresh mini-avalanche. This sea of snow rumbled after him, leaving the air behind filled with a fog of snow particles. Behind him, the wolves skidded to a stop just short of the first drop, their prey having suddenly disappeared, his image gone, his scent swallowed by this cloud of white now dissipating in the wind.

For Red Deer, it was a different story. Had he traded pursuit by wolves for pursuit by the smothering white blanket now giving chase? The sled cleared the second drop before he could form an answer. Like an arrow, it flew through the air before slamming back onto the icy surface. His new pursuer reached the edge of the second drop, trickled over like a frozen waterfall, and then quit. Unaffected by the landing, the sled continued to pick up speed as it zipped down the hill. Red Deer let out a hearty warhoop. Near the edge of the first drop, the wolf pack stopped their attempt at locating the prey that had been so close and stared after him as he disappeared down the hill. Recognizing that he was too far away to give chase, they turned and started back, hoping to find other prey the way they came.

The pace of his descent didn't provide time for Red Deer to watch anything but what lay ahead. He had no way to control the speed of his plunge and the only way to control his direction was by leaning left or right. An endless wall of snow appeared before him. He had reached the other side of the glacier and needed to kill off his speed. Clinging to the webbing, he leaned away from his direction of travel. A runner on his sled hit a rock hidden in the snow. The impact tore the runner loose. His ride, now lopsided, was jerked and spun around as it crossed the ice toward a pinnacle of rocks. Having little time to think about it, he let go of the webbing, grabbed his pack and spear as he rolled off this makeshift toboggan.

The travois-sled disintegrated on impact when it smashed into the rocks. The blow scattered the sled's contents everywhere. Overhead, a shoulder of snow collapsed, burying the wreckage.

Red Deer rode his pack to a halt near the opposite wall. He lay there for a minute and then started laughing. Thanks to the wolves, he made it across the ice field in record time with little more than a few scrapes and bruises. When he recovered his senses, Red Deer searched the area and found one runner still useable. Picking it up, he tossed it from hand to hand, as he reflected on his find: *My creation served me well. The provisions on the sled are gone, buried under the snow, or spread all over and I am not going to take the time to hunt them down. The contents of my pack will provide the items I will need until I can go hunting, and now I have a walking stick to help me make the descent.*

The river, a thin silver band spawned by the ice field, crossed the distant terrain. From where he stood, he could also see where it broadened out to cover lowland marshes and where it sometimes disappeared into canyons only to emerge again further away.

Nearby, melt water from the glacier collected in pools around its base before spilling out to form rivulets. These joined streams which flowed downward to eventually merge with the river. He would use these small waterways as a guide, knowing that the place where they joined the river would mark his path home. He also knew that where there was water, there would be game for him to hunt and he would not go hungry.

He made his way down from the heights to the forest. This was the easy part, made easier by walking downhill and not having to drag a travois-sled. He was happy he no longer had to deal with it since this part of his trip was across rock-strewn moraines.[29] Eventually, these yielded to rolling hills sparsely covered with stunted trees and underbrush.

As he neared the forest, the rockiness of the ground diminished. Tall trees replaced scrubby woods. Animal trails became more distinct. Finding his way would not be a problem. Running into a predator could be. Red Deer kept both his walking stick and spear nearby. Ready if needed.

---

[29] Moraines - Moraines may be composed of debris ranging in size from silt-sized glacial flour to large boulders. The debris is typically sub-angular to round in shape. Moraines may be on the glacier's surface or deposited as piles or sheets of debris where the glacier has melted. Moraines may also occur when glacier or iceberg-transported rocks fall into a body of water as the ice melts.

# Chapter 13: A Parade of Prisoners

From his lair in the treetops, Crooked Foot watched each animal as it came to the water hole below him. With his back against the tree's trunk, he straddled the heavy set of limbs he had used as his home for the last few days. High above this oasis, he made mental notes about the habits of each animal: which ones came together and drank when others drank, or fled at any new arrival; which animals came in the morning; which in the evening; which at night. He also learned which animals came to lie in wait, not for water, but food, and when they might show up.

This was the last haven available before leaving the forest and savanna and entering the adjoining desert. This lone stand of trees decorated the leading edge of a ridge, the one that led backward into the foothills. It also led forward to the spring that fed the oasis. The water bubbled out from around the rocks and collected in a pool nestled in the shade.

His grandfather, Howling Wolf, told him *a good hunter carefully watches the animals to learn their habits. To do this it would be best to make a nest in a place where he would be unseen so that he could study each animal as it comes and goes.*

Following Howling Wolf's suggestions, Crooked Foot found the oasis and picked a spot among the treetops. It gave him a good view of the pool of water below and the rolling meadow that was the border between forest and desert.

He did not spend all of his time in the trees, but climbed down now and then to stretch his legs and explore nearby areas. The adjacent foothills had many animal trails, mostly from goats. It gave him a new set of animals to study and he learned to separate one set of tracks from another.

Back in the trees, he thought about what he had learned. He could look at an animal's footprint and tell what kind it was, how big it was, whether it was young or old, male or female, whether by itself or a member of a group, and if it was a predator, whether it was a wolf, a cat, or a bear. All talents he did not possess when he first arrived. It had been worth the effort, but it was time for him to think about getting back to the village.

From his position high in the tree, Crooked Foot looked out over the meadow where a couple small herds grazed quietly or lazed in the shade of a clump of trees. With nothing happening, his mind drifted.

The herds reminded him of Tigal's caravan. It should be arriving soon. Perhaps this time, his friend Red Deer would be with it. Once again, he mentally repeated the conversation between Bright Moon and Howling Wolf: *Red Deer was on his sojourn and would be gone for one-hand's worth of summers,* she had said. At the time, he was almost asleep, but he was sure he had heard her correctly. He held onto that little bit of knowledge, reciting the phrase, and counting the seasons.

The tribe marked the passage of time by recording the movements of the sun and the moon. When the dark, coldness of night swallowed most of the warmth and the light of day, they held a Shortest-Day ceremony to mark the beginning of the Long Cold. When warmth returned, when the light began swallowing the dark, the tribe held a Spring Awakening celebration; later when there was more light than dark, the tribe celebrated the Longest-Day; and when day and night were equal again, the Autumn Harvest celebration. As a part of each celebration, a man carved symbols on a set of totems. In this way, each member of the tribe could track the passage of time.

One-by-one, the summers came and went, one, two, three, four. Crooked Foot waited and counted. He knew that any day now, the caravan would arrive. He knew this was the summer Red Deer would return.

An afternoon breeze wafted through his leafy nest and set the branches gently rocking. The breeze was a cool change from the stifling heat he had experienced. The motion lulled Crooked Foot into a light sleep.

### ###

Noises—moans, screams, wails, cries, intermixed with shouted orders and cracking whips—rolled over the meadow. They jarred Crooked Foot awake. He froze for a second while he looked around, moving only his eyes. When he knew he was safe in his tree nest, he leaned forward, parted the foliage, and scanned the world beyond.

Guards—he did not know if they were well-armed soldiers or marauding thugs—toting spears, clubs, and whips, walked on either side of a mob of captives.

The prisoners, mostly women and children, each had their hands tied behind them; a rope around their necks joined each one to the person behind them. While they moaned and wept, the guards laughed, shouted to each other and at the crowd of people they herded. At times, the guards used their whips.

A slow, sad parade, it took some time to pass. It did not stop at the oasis, although the captives needed the respite. Instead, the guards—either alone or in pairs—satiated themselves noisily, adding considerably to the misery of their captives.

In his treetop nest, Crooked Foot, held his breath and sat motionless lest he be found and made a prisoner. When the last of the cavalcade of misery finally disappeared, absorbed by the desert vegetation, Crooked Foot relaxed, but bided his time not wanting to risk meeting additional groups or stragglers.

Satisfied those entering the desert would not return; that they left no one behind to watch their back; and that other groups would not come from where they did, Crooked Foot grabbed his pack, climbed down and went over to examine the tracks they left.

### 

Kam Udo looked with pleasure at the treasures Romnog presented. "I see you reaped more magnificent tribute from these primitive villagers." Perhaps the most valuable item was the collection of bows and arrows. This design, made in three pieces, was fastened together to make the bow longer. To hold the pieces, the joints were bound with gut-string and covered with an unknown substance. The arrows had feathers attached to the end. He did not know how either device was made, but he recognized this as the weapon he needed to increase his empire. Romnog would find out the secret of their design. He had prisoners and one of them would tell how to make the bow and arrows. "The most interesting is these unique bows and arrows. Have you tested them? How do they work?"

"Yes, Excellency, my lead lieutenant, Gachald, tried the bow. The arrow travels farther and he was able to hit his target each time."

Kam Udo suppressed his immediate urge to celebrate. That would have to wait until after he heard the answers to his next questions. "Did you capture enough bows and arrows to arm all our archers?"

Knowing that his answer would not go over well, Romnog stiffened at the question. "No, Excellency, these are the only ones we captured; most of the rest were destroyed in the attack."

His short pudgy leader looked up at his general and gave the man a long, cold stare. "Tell me, Romnog, did you take slaves? What do these people call themselves?"

"Yes, Excellency, we have a number of slaves. They call themselves the Clam Shell People. They will be invaluable in helping to build your city." Romnog replied. He was relieved, but suspicious about the change in conversation.

Kam Udo's response was a simple grunt. "Do any of the captives have the ability to make these bows and arrows?"

"We questioned the slaves, but have not found any that can."

Another long, cold, silent stare, and then Kam Udo said, "Your previous raid, the one where the slaves covered their tools in kop, did you find out their names? What did they call themselves?"

Romnog squirmed. "We got their name from one of their dying. They were called the Whitefish People or Attikamekey."

His leader looked bored. "You got their name from one of their dying? Why is that? Why didn't you question one of the living?"

"They escaped."

Kam Udo gave Romnog a look, the same type of look that a predator would give his prey. "That's right, they escaped. Right under your nose, they picked up and walked away." His demeanor changed and his voice rose as he shouted, "Now, I want you to understand that I am building a city here. I need to protect the city and expand my empire. In order to do that I need just three things: I need to know how to work with kop; and, I need to know how to make these excellent bows and arrows; and I need workers. Your task is to find slaves who can provide these. Your task is not to kill everyone you conquer, nor is your task to let them escape!"

### ###

Crooked Foot could see that the trail originated from somewhere deep within the forest. It crossed the meadow and then entered the great, dry desert. It was an easy trail to read. Two hands' worth of guards, split between the two sides, walked alongside the captives. Their tracks were uncountable, but he knew that there were many and they were bound for a life of slavery.

*Following the trail into the desert,* he reasoned, would *be a good way for a youth less than three-hands old to be caught; but, if I cautiously followed the trail into the forest, I might find out where it started and learn more about these people.* Taking advantage of any cover, Crooked Foot started backtracking along the path the procession left.

### ###

The sun was setting. It would be dark soon. Crooked Foot had not found the headwaters—the place that was the origin of the prisoners—of the trail yet. He would have to put that off until the next day. Right now, he would look for a place, off trail, to shelter for the night.

Parting the brush that marked the edge of the path, Crooked Foot stepped through, careful to leave no trace behind. Not far off the trail, but far enough that he would be out of sight from passers-by, Crooked Foot found a group of fallen trees. He could tuck in among the trunks and branches and safely stay the night. Before bedding down, Crooked Foot returned to the trail and walked back the direction he had come. Arriving at a bend in the trail, he found a branch he could use as a whisk and wiped out a section of the tracks. If anyone passed this way through the night, the fresh ground would record their steps. Returning to his camp, he settled in for the night.

Morning, and a light fog, came. He crept back to the trail. The prints at that point remained unchanged; the spot at the bend also remained undisturbed. He breathed a little easier, but remained cautious. Returning to his camp, he wiped out the signs of his overnight stay, collected his pack, and returned to the previous day's quest.

### 

By mid-afternoon, he found his trip led him to a burnt-out clearing. At one time, it had been a village. This presented him with new signs to interpret. These told him the attack had been a surprise where the men were killed, the women and children taken prisoner then bound, and forced to march away from all they knew.

Looking closer, Crooked Foot also found signs of people trying to escape; some were successful. Their tracks disappeared into the forest, but then they seemed to reappear. He could tell because the new prints were on top of the old as well as on top of the burnt debris. The people that left the tracks were in a hurry and had not attempted to cover their activities. Apparently the survivors returned to salvage anything they could before they ran away again.

Crooked Foot circled the burnt-out encampment and finally found what he was looking for: tracks leading away into the forest. They attempted to conceal them, but in their haste they failed. These were the ones he wanted! These would be the tracks he would follow.

### 

A shout and then a scream came from up ahead. Crooked Foot stopped mid-stride, his attention focused on the trail in front of him. The path jogged to the left around the base of a butte. This brush covered mound, not more than a man's length in height, jutted out like a foot. Not

133

wanting to blunder headlong into an unknown situation, he climbed the knoll and parted the bushes. Looking out over a clearing, he saw the last thing anyone would want to see.

Harp shaped horns angled forward and waved in the air above a big, black body. Agitated, the bovine turned a tight circle. Crooked Foot could hear the solid clomp, clomp, clomp as it pawed the ground, raising dust with each pounding hoof. The pale stripe down its spine, clearly visible, confirmed Crooked Foot's worst fear. It was an auroch, and a bull at that. Lifting its head, the animal snorted fiercely.

A fully-grown bull stood taller than most men did. His people knew that aurochs were very aggressive and unpredictable—the males are the worst because they had the shorter tempers. Killing such an animal is seen as a great act of courage, but it was a task usually carried out by a group.

He heard voices. The speakers were below the edge of the mound where he crouched. Their voices were too low to be understood, but loud enough to grab his interest and they caught his attention. He dropped his pack to creep forward, spear in hand, and get a better view at the ones who had upset the animal.

Beneath the lip, two worried youths crouched over a semiconscious, bloody body. Too large for them to carry, they were trying to get him to his feet so they could back away before the bull attacked again. The young man stirred and tried to sit up, only to clutch his side, and moan. Blood, caked with dirt, covered the hand still clutching the shaft of a broken spear. Using it as a prop, he tried to stand but was unable to get to his feet.

Crooked Foot could guess at the events preceding this. The three had been out hunting and came upon the bull. It must have charged. The young man on the ground, armed with a spear, stood his ground and speared the auroch, but was unable to sidestep its charge. Smashing into him, it lifted the youth with a flip of its horns and sent him flying. Keeping an eye on the auroch, the other two vacillated between trying to help him and wanting to beat a quick retreat. Injured and upset, the animal would not give them much time to decide.

Crooked Foot quickly untangled his bolo. A simple device, it was made of three cords, one long and two shorter ones. One end of each cord contained a leather pouch weighted with gravel or small rocks. The ends opposite the pouches were tied together. The pouch on the longer cord was the lightest while the other two were of a similar, heavier weight, but never the same weight. The difference was so they would separate when thrown.

Holding the bolo by the pouch on the longest cord, Crooked Foot began to swing it overhead in a flat circle. If the trio on the ground heard the noise, they ignored it to concentrate on the greater danger in front of them. The bull swung its head back and forth. It would be ready to charge anytime. Crooked Foot released the weapon and watched it fly towards its target. It made a smooth whirring sound as it cut through the air. Weights on the shorter cords went on either side of the bull's front legs while the longer cord wrapped around them. Legs bound together, the startled animal tried to take a step, but it came crashing down.

Surprised, the trio on the ground looked up to see Crooked Foot standing over them. Selecting the more forceful of the two uninjured lads, he tossed his spear to him. Pointing to the struggling auroch he ordered, "Here's your chance! Finish him while he is down!"

Catching the spear, the youngster ran forward to plunge it home before the bovine could get to his feet. Recovering his senses, the second youth, in order to also lay claim to the kill, found the remains of the broken spear and ran forward. Crooked Foot collected his pack and went to aid the wounded man.

Older than he had suspected, Crooked Foot was surprised by how gaunt, almost frail this stranger appeared. Kneeling next to him, Crooked Foot lifted the man's head and put his water pouch to the man's lips. The stranger winced, let out a low moan, and held his side.

Unable to give him water, Crooked Foot checked his wounds. A number of minor bruises and cuts, but they paled in comparison to the gash covering his chest. It was not deep, just long. Crooked Foot looked to the others for some assistance. He was surprised to find only one individual, the one who held his spear, standing guard over the downed animal. Crooked Foot motioned for the young man to join him, but was surprised to find the individual unwilling to leave the carcass.

Perplexed, Crooked Foot got to his feet and looked around for the other—the third—youth. Where could he have gone? His question was answered when the youth returned leading a party of men toward them. Some of the men were armed and they all looked threatening.

They were followed by another group—women and children, armed with knives and axes—who fell on the carcass with great zeal. It would be butchered on the spot, cut into manageable pieces, and carried back to their village for processing.

The armed men, weapons ready, quickly surrounded Crooked Foot. "Who are you and why are you here?" They demanded.

"I am Crooked Foot of the Narwikin. I am returning to my village from the sea of grass which lies near the great, dry desert."

"He ...." The wounded man raised his head to speak, "he is not one of them ... he came to our aid. It's because of him we live and have fresh meat." Following his labored comment, the man dropped his head back.

# Chapter 14: The Clam Shell People

After the run-in with the auroch, Crooked Foot accompanied those who helped carry the wounded man back to their village. Pitifully small, this makeshift village sat near a river in a notch between two hills.

Even though everyone seemed to go through their normal tasks—women tended cooking fires, wove baskets, looked after toddlers, sat in front of the few crude huts that now was their village—he detected an underlying uneasiness.

The women went about their business but kept a cautious eye on him. Even though he should be recognized as a respected ally, one who sits at the campfire with their chief, he was still a stranger in their midst: an unknown. Crooked Foot understood their wariness; he had seen it before, at times, he even experienced the same feelings.

Under the conditions, they were hospitable. From a set of common clay cooking pots, they fed him from their meager supplies—simple meals of parched grain, a thin, bland broth, and a few vegetables—and they gave him shelter for the night. Now it was time for him to leave this wretchedly small village.

When he first arrived at the oasis, Crooked Foot had traveled on foot from his village. He could return that way, but the best route, the quickest route, would be by water. This meant he would have to barter with their chief for a boat.

White Badger, a tired old man, leader of a people who had little to offer, tried to remain calm as he pointed out the features of the vessel in front of them. Nodding toward a group of youngsters, the old man wheezed, "From when I was their size, my people called these *bullboats*. Back then, each one was made from the hide of a single bull." His shoulders slumped, and he got a far-off look in his eyes. "Back then, there were many of us ...." His voice trailed off.

Crooked Foot picked the craft up to check its durability and weight. Much lighter than a dugout, this sturdy vessel weighed about as much as a toddler. Its framework, willow branches bent into the shape of a huge, elongated bowl nearly knee-deep. Its keel was almost two man's length long. Leather ties held the assembly together wherever the branches crossed. A patchwork of carefully stitched hides, the edges of which were sealed by pitch to make them waterproof, was stretched over the frame.

These features would be good for getting the vessel in and out of the river, but once in the water, Crooked Foot knew its lightness would let it bobble around like a leaf. It would probably not handle well in rough water nor would it stand up to rapids, but it was serviceable for short trips and calm waters. If necessary, it would be easy to carry and easy to repair. He put the craft down, patted the sides, and asked, "How come you left the fur on?"

White Badger chuckled at the question. "My people found leaving the hair on stops the craft from spinning, and it helps keep water out."

As if rejecting their offering, Crooked Foot waved his hand and looked away saying, "A dugout would hold up much better where the water is filled with rocks."

Hiding his disappointment, the old man spat, "A dugout would be heavy, too heavy for a single man to handle. It would sit low in the water, be hard to steer and even harder to carry between rivers."

White Badger, having pointed out the many faults of the dugout and the many attributes of his craft, had nothing more to say. He stood quietly, both arms folded across his chest, while he waited for the lad's decision.

Crooked Foot bided his time, as if considering the differences between the two vessels, but it was a ruse. He had made up his mind before the negotiations started. It was not just the bullboat he wanted, but an additional treasure as well.

Shortly after his arrival at the village, Crooked Foot saw a man with a bow and arrow. During his brief stay, he saw several other men with similar equipment. These tools were not new to him, but their design was radically different.

Bows that he was familiar with were one piece and barely reached from his feet to his waist. The ones these people used were as long as a man was tall. They had two additional pieces—one at the top, the other at the bottom—held in place with sinew and tree sap. He did not get a chance to look at them closely, but knew they would be something of interest to his people. The arrow shafts were unusual not just because of their length, but because they had feathers on one end. He had not seen them perform, but he felt this practical people did not put them there as a decoration.

The negotiations had now reached a point where Crooked Foot would have to make an offer or back away. It was time for him to spring his trap. Looking the old man in the eye, Crooked Foot turned and motioned toward the pile of goods he had laid out on the mat at the beginning of the deliberations—some dried meat, a couple of hides, and a few small blocks of salt. This last item, he originally brought along on his trip just in case he needed to lure the animals closer for him to observe.

The dried meat and the hides were of little value to this decimated people. However, the blandness of the food told Crooked Foot that the Clam Shell people had found little, perhaps no, salt in the ruins of their village. Without this valuable substance, they would not be able to cure enough meat and fish to survive the Long Cold. Smiling warmly, he turned back to the old man, held out his hand, and said, "The boat, a bow, and some arrows. Done?"

Extending his hand to grasp Crooked Foot's, his counterpart stopped midway, surprised by the lad's counter offer. He did not want to give up their secret for the bow and arrows, but his people did not find salt in the rubble and they needed the salt. What was he to do? Sadly, White Badger nodded agreement and clutched the lad's extended hand. "Done," he said.

Crooked Foot sensed more resignation than warmth showing through. "Is something wrong?" he asked.

White Badger glanced back toward the huts and the people around them. Head hung in despair, he explained, "Before we had been many, but then, after the Long Cold when some of us were on a hunt, the village was attacked. Those who survived told us the attackers came out of nowhere and carried off everyone they did not kill. They took everything they could carry and then put our village to the torch. We could see the smoke from where we lay waiting to pounce on the herd."

He paused for a moment before going on, "When we returned from the hunt, we found smoldering ruins ... and dead ... some struck down in their tracks as they tried to flee."

He gestured toward the huts before continuing, "A few managed to hide ... there wasn't much left of the village, but we took what we could find and left quickly for fear that they'd come back and find us. We traveled day and night before we could relax and set up camp here. Hoping we were finally safe, we tried to start over. Some, still worried another attack would come, picked up and moved on. The rest of us, those too young or too old to travel farther, stayed." He swept a hand toward the mat. "We hunt now, but have to eat our kill right away before it spoils and have no way to preserve the hides. This salt will let us cure game and set it aside, but the Long Cold will be here again, and many won't survive." He sighed. "Your trade goods will help ... but I don't know how much longer we can go on like this before we're all gone...."

Crooked Foot nodded. This old man, his people, reminded him of his own people. "I understand, and I think there is a solution."

"What's that?" White Badger gave him a puzzled look.

"Come join with the Narwikin," Crooked Foot offered. "You will find a home there."

"How can you say this?" White Badger asked. "How can you make this offer without your chief's knowledge?"

"The Narwikin are open to every peaceful tribe, especially those with new ideas," Crooked Foot said. "Howling Wolf, the Chief of the Narwikin, is my grandfather. He will look with pleasure on your gift of the bow and arrows."

Stunned, White Badger was silent for a moment. The youth's words were not what he expected, but were very welcome. The tired old man broke into a big smile. "My people will be happy to hear your words."

White Badger called the Clam Shell people together and told them of the offer. It was greeted with loud cheers and whoops.

"Tell me the best way to reach the Narwikin village," White Badger said. "It will take us a few days to pack."

"The quickest way would be by the river," Crooked Food answered.

White Badger dropped his gaze and let out a long sigh. "Alas, we may not have enough boats."

Crooked Foot shrugged. "The next best way, would

be the way I came—over land. You would have to cross some hills. It will be longer, but not too difficult."

"We are nearly starving now and I expect we will lose many more on a trip on foot like you just describe." White Badger could see the future of his tribe: if they stayed, they could be doomed; if they attempted the trip, they could be doomed.

Crooked Foot understood the problem. "I will stay and go hunting with your people. Fresh meat should help."

"Oh yes, that could help!" White Badger smiled broadly. "Yes, that could help a lot! We should get started now!"

Crooked Foot led the men of the Clam Shell tribe back to the oasis where they bagged three large deer and two goats. Overjoyed at the extra meat, White Badger and his people presented the youth with presents to take back to Howling Wolf: a tunic decorated with beautiful shells and several beaded necklaces. They were the only items they had managed to save from the raiders.

# Chapter 15: Standing in Front of the Council

The bullboat ground into the beach, and Crooked Foot climbed out, happy to be on solid ground once again.

His vessel was a little tricky to handle. It worked well in shallow water; it worked okay in deep water as long as the water was smooth. In spite of these difficulties, he made good time on the river and knew he arrived before the Clam Shell people.

Crooked Foot gathered his pack, the bundle of gifts the Clam Shell people had provided, and then turned to head up the path that led to the village.

A familiar voice stopped him. "You have been gone a long time. What did you learn?" Bright Moon, leading a group of women and small children, paraded down from the village to the women's bathing area. She eyed the bullboat carefully.

"I bring gifts from White Badger, Chief of the Clam Shell people," he explained, "and I have information of interest to Grandfather."

Bright Moon waved the others on and said, "Tell me more."

### ###

Called together by Bright Moon, council members sat on either side of Howling Wolf. Crooked Foot, alone, sat across from them. He glanced at Bright Moon, sitting next to Howling Wolf. She signaled him to stand and start his story. He took a deep breath, rose to his feet, and tried to focus on the idea that the people in front of him for the time being were no longer parents of friends, or grandmother, grandfather, but tribal leaders.

Crooked Foot looked over his audience. As long as Bright Moon and Howling Wolf kept his secret, what they were about to see and hear would come as a surprise. "While I was studying animals, I witnessed a group of people being taken away as captives. Afterward, I followed their tracks to where their village had stood. It had been burnt. Looking around, I found that a few villagers had survived and I followed their tracks until I came to their new village. I was able to help them, first by hunting and then, because they were so few, I invited them to join the Narwikin." Crooked Foot paused to see if the council had any reaction. They did not, so he continued. "Because of the offer, Chief White Badger sends gifts to show his appreciation." Crooked Foot stepped forward and handed the necklaces to Howling Wolf, who examined them and passed them over to other members. Crooked Foot brought out the tunic and handed it to Howling Wolf. The chief examined it and passed it on, but appreciation could be read on his face.

"When I left here, I walked through the forest until I arrived at the oasis. That is where I set up my camp in the treetops. When I returned, I traveled by water using the vessel White Badger's people had supplied. They call it a bullboat. It is sturdy but lightweight, making it easy to move from one river to another. I brought it up here from the river so you could examine it for yourselves. Its design makes it special, but it is not the only special item they have designed."

Crooked Foot unfolded a robe and produced the bow and arrows he had brought back. The unique design of these two common items caught council members' attention. "What do you have there?" They chorused.

Crooked Foot couldn't help but smile. He certainly had their attention now. "The Clam Shell People made this.

They took a bow like ours and added a piece to the top and to the bottom. The arrows have longer shafts. They told me they attached feathers to the end to help them fly straight."

While he continued speaking, Crooked Foot passed the bow and then the arrows over to Howling Wolf for his inspection. "The hunters of the Clam Shell people used these when we went hunting. Their arrows flew farther, faster, straighter, and hit harder than mine."

The low buzz of whispered conversations developed while council members discussed this new device. Finally, they grew quiet and one turned to face Crooked Foot. "How do we know these changes make a difference?"

Before Crooked Foot could open his mouth in reply, Howling Wolf said, "On his return, Crooked Foot told me what he found. I invite everyone to join me at a place in the forest where he demonstrated these tools for me. I found that they are even better than he described. Turmoil seems to be growing in the countryside. I think it better that we invite the Clam Shell people here to join us before they join another tribe and someone else discovers their secrets."

# Chapter 16: Tigal's Caravan Arrives

Crooked Foot stirred in his bed. Something jarred him out of a deep sleep. Except for a thin collar of light, the first announcement of a rising sun, darkness lay everywhere. The sounds of Bright Moon's even breathing came to him from across the room. He heard her turn over and then snuggle deeper into her covers. Nothing had disturbed her sleep. Not wanting to leave the warmth of his bed, Crooked Foot pulled the hides closer and settled back into a comfortable spot. He closed his eyes and began what he hoped was a short trip into deep sleep. A low rumbling noise, followed by a series of snorts, grabbed his attention.

These were not normal sounds. Awake now, his curiosity got the best of him. There would be no sleep until he knew what was making the noise. Cautiously, he threw back his covers, crept to the shelter door and peered out.

Here and there around the encampment night fires flickered in the darkness. They provided just enough light to see that the gate, usually closed at night, stood open. Through the opening, he could see the outline of several animals. Men, strangers to him, moved around them or stood nearby in small groups. Seeing his grandfather and some council members talking with these strangers, Crooked Foot donned his tunic and prepared to venture out.

From behind him came Bright Moon's familiar voice. "Where are you going so early?"

"There are new people and animals here," he said. "I think the caravan has arrived. Maybe this is the one that will bring Red Deer back. I want to go out and see."

Struggling, the old woman propped herself up on one elbow and looked at him closely. "What makes you think Red Deer will be here now?"

Crooked Foot shrugged. "When he left on his sojourn, he joined Tigal's caravan. I heard you tell grandfather that he would be gone one-hand's worth of summers. The totem, the one the tribe uses to mark the passage of seasons, shows that this is the summer he will return."

Bright Moon grunted an acknowledgement, but neither confirmed nor denied his statements. "Go ahead," she said. "Tell Chief Howling Wolf that I will join him shortly."

### 

"Tigal, my friend, it's good to see you." Smiling broadly, Howling Wolf clasped his friend's hand. "Did you have a good trip?"

"I am happy to be here and see friendly faces." Accepting Howling Wolf's warm grasp, Tigal smiled broadly before continuing, "My clans have journeyed far." Waving his hand, he indicated the group of men and women gathered with him. "They are ready to go on, but the animals are tired."

Howling Wolf nodded. "Ah yes, the clans are always eager to travel further, to meet new people, to find new adventures, but your animals have grown tired and need rest. I understand …." Smiling, he let his voice trail off, pausing for just a moment before adding, "But, since the animals need rest, you know you can stay with us for as long as you like. Everybody can relax." Laughing he added, "It will put you in a better mood to trade."

Tigal shrugged. "If we stay that long, everyone will be too old to do business."

One of his men chimed in with, "Still, we could give

it a try." Then he and his crew broke into sidesplitting laughter.

Tigal grew serious as he went on, "We could use a rest where we know we're safe. There are many new dangers in the countryside these days."

Howling Wolf shook his head in disbelief. "Runners from other villages have been here. None had good news." The Council members grunted their agreement. "The runners tell of one who sets himself above everyone; his tribe above all others. He directs his people to attack, to pillage, and plunder." Shaking his head, he paused as he looked at Tigal for confirmation. "What have you heard?"

After taking a long draw on his pipe, Tigal leaned close. "What you heard is true, but it's much worse." Pausing to add emphasis, Tigal looked his friend in the eye. "Much worse ...."

Before Howling Wolf could form a question, Tigal went on. "*Kam Udo* leads his tribe, the *Kam Na Udo*, in conquest. No one knows for sure where they came from, but it is said they are from beyond the mountains on the other side of the great, dry desert. I have heard he has a brother. Their father sleeps-the-sleep-from-which-no-one-wakes, so the two brothers fought for control. Kam Udo and his followers were forced to flee."

Looking Howling Wolf in the eyes, he added. "They roam across the rich plateau to the north. They raid where they please and take what they want. Those who resist are killed and the rest are forced into slavery. I heard they are forcing the slaves to build a great, walled village. Wherever his raiders go, there are few left behind. Those who are left—the very old, the very young, the sick, and the lame—go hungry."

Howling Wolf was apprehensive. "In the old days we sometimes posted a night watch to guard against animals. As the reports grew worse, we've gone to posting guards to keep watch day and night."

Tigal nodded. "We've always had guards … against animal attacks mostly. From time-to-time we see raiders, but usually they're smart and stay clear." Thoughtfully, he added, "Now and then, we've caught a few bandits sneaking around at night, but the examples we made of them limits such encounters." Shrugging, he switched his pipe from one hand to the other, "As the news got worse, I've increased the guard. Lately, half the tribe is on guard-duty each night. My people are worn out. Being here among friends will give them a much needed rest."

Howling Wolf smiled warmly. "You're welcome to stay with us for as long as you need. In anticipation of your arrival, my people cleared ground for your camp not too far from here. A valley nearby will provide water and grazing for your animals. They have also cleared the trading ground. When you're rested and ready to do business, we can send runners to other villages and let them know."

Sighing, Tigal said, "This place has been good for both of us. The plains and river provide food, the hills protection, and so far they have hidden us away from all the other turmoil."

Howling Wolf nodded, "We wish only to live free and enjoy the benefits of trading with our neighbors."

"But it's possible you may not be safe even here much longer," Tigal said. "From what I've heard, their raids have already stripped the plateau, and they are starting to venture further out. Sooner or later, they may be here."

Howling Wolf nodded. "Yes, so we've heard. I had sent my grandson, Crooked Foot, out to study the animals. When he returned to us, he spoke about finding the remains of a burnt-out village and the remnants of another tribe. They were the few that managed to escape death or captivity. He invited them to come join with us here."

Tigal pursed his lips. "Do you think that was a good idea?"

"Even if they could make it through the summer, they probably would not be able to survive the Long Cold that will follow."

Tigal shook his head in dismay. "These are troubled times."

"Yes, but there is another reason we saw fit to make the invitation." Howling Wolf explained. "My grandson brought back one of their bows and some arrows."

Tigal raised an eyebrow. "You already have bows and arrow. What makes these special?"

"Both the bow and the arrows are longer which improves their abilities. These are tools that could help us and we decided we didn't want it helping our enemies."

Tigal nodded. "I know other tribes have tried to make bows that would shoot farther, but they break easily or the arrows go wild."

"Yes, I've seen the same happen," Howling Wolf said. "But this new design is made in three pieces fastened together to make the bow longer," Howling Wolf explained, "and the arrows, like birds, have feathers."

Silent for a moment, Tigal thought about what he had heard and then sighed, "Every day I hear about changes."

Howling Wolf shrugged. "It seems changes are coming fast, maybe too fast."

"Yes they are. Either that or we're getting old."

"You? Me? Old? How could that be?" The two men broke into hearty laughter.

### 

The mastodon shuffled its feet quietly, trunk gently swinging in response to those movements. From the corner of its eye, it watched the boy coming his way. Crooked Foot,

150

wide-eyed, mouth agape, approached slowly so as not to alarm the great beast. He had not seen mastodons or camels in a long time and never up close. The animal, always wary of its surroundings, turned its head toward the approaching youth and extended an inquiring trunk. The lad stretched a hand toward it. Small talk among the groups of men was interrupted now and then by quiet, good-natured laughter. His actions had gone unnoticed so far. Hand and trunk touched. Carefully, they examined each other.

A camel, crouched nearby, bellowed. The noise caught the attention of the strangers. Startled by the camel's alarm, Crooked Foot stumbled backward. Laughter stopped. Conversations quickly broke off.

At the camel's alarm, a man—dark, portly, bearded—whirled around and said, "You boy! What do you think you're doing?" He quickly covered the space between them grabbing Crooked Foot by the arm.

"Wait!" Howling Wolf shouted and turned back to the caravan chief. "Tigal, this is my grandson, the one I was telling you about."

Tigal, a scowl slowly leaving his face looked at Howling Wolf and then nodded to his man. Crooked Foot felt the pincher-like grip that held him relax.

"We can't be too careful," Tigal explained, "the animals can spook easily." He laughed and changed the subject. "Is this the first time you've seen these animals?"

"This is the first time I've seen them this close," Crooked Foot responded.

"Really? The way you made contact with Makata, it looked like you were old friends. You've quite a way with her."

Howling Wolf responded before Crooked Foot could answer, "Our Shaman has been working with him. She said he's a quick learner."

"Well, a quick learner … and good with animals." Tigal stroked his chin thoughtfully, "Those are good traits." If he was going to say anything more, the thought was lost when the mastodon intervened. It seemed to be searching Crooked Foot.

Tigal laughed. "Well, boy, it looks like you and Makata are friends. Would you like a job today?"

Awestruck, Crooked Foot could only stand there open-mouthed and nod.

Tigal smiled. "Let's see how long this friendship lasts. Get something that holds water, lots of water. She is thirsty and if you bring her something to drink, she will like that. Bring some for the other animals, too. They're all thirsty." Laughing, he added, "Try not to get stepped on."

Turning back to Howling Wolf, he said, "It seems that I've had a hand in returning your son and may end up taking your grandson away. What do you think about that?"

His statement surprised Howling Wolf who found himself without words for a moment. "I don't understand, what do you mean, *returning my son*?"

"Why, Red Deer! He joined us at the Village of the Sea People, but not wanting to travel slowly with the caravan, he left to cross the mountains and arrive here sooner. Has he not joined you?"

"No," Howling Wolf said, hanging his head, "we have not seen him."

"It is as I told you when he left, he is on his way," Bright Moon interjected. "He will be here in a few days and he brings many who will need our help, as I predicted."

Howling Wolf nodded. Her prophecy had laid this out for him. He had held on to that idea, but was shocked speechless when Tigal brought Red Deer's name to his attention. Now, he struggled to pull himself together.

Tigal decided it was time to change the mood. "Now,

let's go see what your people have arranged for us."

Satisfied, the two men, and Bright Moon joined three of Tigal's clan chiefs and walked away. Left alone, Crooked Foot watched the group, talking and laughing as they left, disappear into the crowd. Sniffing, the mastodon curled her trunk around him. He did not mind. He stood still and let the animal explore.

### 

"The places you have prepared look so good I don't know if I'll ever get my people to leave again." Slapping his friend on the back Tigal laughed heartily as did everyone around them.

When the laughter died down, Howling Wolf waved to the crowd, "Everyone, come with me. We will sit together and enjoy some refreshments and a pipe while we talk about your travels."

A series of blasts from a ram's horn interrupted the proceedings. Laughter stopped as the Narwikin took up arms.

Howling Wolf turned to Tigal. "Best you see to your men and animals. We may be under attack."

### 

Even before these difficult vessels reached the beach, blasts from a ram's horn signaled their arrival. Undeterred, White Badger's people grounded their crafts and waded ashore.

It had been a long trip. This small flotilla of bullboats and rafts, constructed in a rush, were overloaded with people and possessions. In calm water, the boats often wallowed about like sick buffalos and could easily flounder. If the wind stirred the river, there was the risk of being swamped. During these times people bailed frantically to keep from sinking. Each night they camped and each morning the leaders struggled to get a growing number of reluctant passengers aboard so they could resume the trip.

This arrangement, while able to carry more people and their possessions, moved sluggishly, but the people were able to hold the vessels together. Everyone hoped the directions they followed were good and their journey was near its end.

Disembarking, they formed groups. The few young men in the bunch stood respectfully to either side of the older man. The rest of the gathering, women and children, clustered behind them. The older man started up the path, a signal to the rest to follow. They needed no prompting. Each member of the troupe hoped the path led to the village of the Narwikin and their salvation.

Reaching the crest of the hill, they came to a halt. In front of them, topping the next hill stood a village surrounded by a stockade. The once open gate now stood closed.

Staying where they were, they waited for a sign, some indication they would be accepted or turned away.

Peering through openings in the stockade, Howling Wolf inspected the assembly. Plainly visible, these strangers made no attempt at stealth. Indeed, they wanted to be seen and evaluated. Still, he considered, they may be bait for a trap. With raids and rumors of raids, he needed to act carefully. The new group, an unknown, waited patiently for the results while he deliberated. To Howling Wolf, these people were too few to be a threat by themselves. Certainly, they didn't act like a war party.

Making a decision, Howling Wolf issued commands. A welcoming honor guard was formed and the gate opened, but just enough to allow this committee to slip through. Left ajar, it gave a warm, confident appearance; however, unseen men stationed nearby would snap it shut if necessary.

Seeing the Narwikin assembly approach, the stranger turned both palms up to show he was unarmed. Then, alone, he walked forward to meet them, stopping about half way between the two groups.

Not wanting to overwhelm his lone counterpart, Howling Wolf halted his group. Then, by himself, he walked forward, palms up, advancing to within two man-lengths of the other man so the two of them could look each other over.

Howling Wolf could see the tiredness and the weight of never ending concern in the other man's eyes. Even still, dignity and purpose burned within. He spoke the traditional greeting. "I am Howling Wolf, Chief of the Narwikin. In peace I welcome you."

Seemingly relieved, his counterpart let out a sigh and responded, "I am White Badger, Chief of the Clam Shell people. At the invitation of Crooked Foot, the Great Narwikin Hunter who visited us, we come in peace and seek refuge."

Howling Wolf nodded. "Come, let our people sit together, share a meal, and smoke a pipe ... then we can discuss how we could benefit each other."

He led the group to the council hut where they joined other tribe members, and Tigal and his clan chiefs. Bowls of stew and dishes of vegetables were brought out along with drinking gourds and pouches of fermented chicha[30]. When they had their fill, pipes were brought out. Everyone lit up and sat back. Bellies full, they were now ready to trade stories and gossip.

---

[30] Chicha - A term used for several varieties of fermented beverages, most commonly made from maize, grapes or apples, but which also describes similar non-alcoholic beverages. Chicha may also be made from manioc root (also called yucca or cassava), or fruits, and other ingredients. The drink is often consumed during festivals or provided to visiting guests.

###

Deep in thought, Crooked Foot waded into the river. The wooden yoke, a water-filled leather pouch at each end, lay heavy on his shoulders. His only break had been when White Badger's people arrived. Afterward, he went back to hauling water from the river for the animals at the encampment. How many trips had he made? He had lost count. He knew the animals drank a lot and he wasn't keeping up, something they reminded him of every time he returned. Makata became even more demanding as the sun rose higher in the sky. He needed a different solution.

The sound of water splashing behind him jarred him out of his deliberation. He jerked around to find the mastodon had followed him, anxious to drink her fill. Dropping the yoke, he began yelling and waving his hands while splashing toward her.

Undeterred, Makata continued forward, her head swinging back and forth as she lumbered along. She was right in front of him when he realized she wasn't going to stop. He needed to back up in a hurry or be run over. There was no other choice. Suddenly, he felt Makata's trunk wrap around his waist. He was lifted in the air almost clear of the water. She carried him, cradled between her long curving tusks, into deeper water.

Panic! That was his first reaction, but then he realized her grip, firm but gentle, meant she chose to pick him up rather than run him over. Reaching deep water, she went into a crouch, gently unwrapped her trunk, releasing him to float free. He bobbed in the water in front of her then moved in close and, laughing, climbed on her back. Dipping her trunk in the water, she lifted it and showered them both.

Playing in the river with Makata, Crooked Foot didn't notice Silver Fox and his friends returning from a hunt. His back to them, the group saw him splashing and laughing. To Silver Fox and his friends, it looked like Crooked Foot sat on a moss-covered boulder. As one, they started yelling and jeering and a few threw rocks. To their surprise, the boulder rose and jerked around. On shore, mouths dropped. Then, almost as one, the boys dropped everything they carried, turned and ran. Makata lumbered after them trumpeting as she did. Crooked Foot, still on her back, held on to her long fur with both hands. By the time Silver Fox reached the village, everyone had come out to see the cause of the commotion. The crowd included Bright Moon, Howling Wolf, and Tigal. None of them looked happy.

# Chapter 17: Giving Chase

Pulling back on Makata's hair, Crooked Foot called, "Hup, hup, hup." The mastodon, trumpeting loudly and in hot pursuit of Silver Fox and his friends, slowed to a halt just short of Tigal and the tribal leaders. The villagers, who had gathered at the sound of the commotion, quickly retreated. Those who stayed positioned themselves behind the council members. Silver Fox and his friends also cowered behind them.

Tigal, holding out a hand for the mastodon to inspect, stepped forward and spoke softly to her. After he got her calmed down, he looked up at Crooked Foot. "What's this all about? How did you get up there?"

"We were in the river. I swam over and climbed up."

"In the river? Did I ask you to take her to the river?"

"But ... but I didn't take her ... she followed me ... she carried me into the water."

Tigal nodded. "What happened next?"

Crooked Foot could not tell if Tigal believed him or not. Waving a hand toward Silver Fox, he explained, "Makata got upset when they came by and she chased them."

Tigal gave him a long look before turning his attention back to the mastodon. Laying a hand on her trunk, he gave a command. She crouched down into a kneeling position. "Slide down, boy ... stand over there."

Now that the threat seemed to have disappeared, villagers began to trickle back and gather with the others. Tigal, ignoring the growing crowd, summoned Silver Fox and his friends forward. "You boys, come here."

A guilty-looking bunch of youths stumbled out of their hiding places and lined up next to Crooked Foot.

After giving the boys a long cold stare, he began, "Makata isn't just any animal. She is mine! Makata and I were both young when my father found her. She had wandered into a bog, sank into the mud, and became trapped. The rest of the herd, her mother, and her mother's sisters had also become trapped while trying to rescue her. They are very loyal animals."

Each boy shrank under Tigal's gaze as he paused to look them over. He wanted to be sure he had everyone's attention. "No one knew how long the animals had been trapped, but lack of food and water made them weak. Buzzards and wolves were already gathering when my father's caravan arrived. The men cut timbers to create a path so they could carry food and water to each animal. Between men pulling on ropes, and more timbers, one-by-one the animals were freed. My father thought they would run off as each was freed, but their loyalty would not let them. The first ones freed helped the men free the others. Even after all were freed, they stayed on with us, carrying our burdens, and traveling where we traveled."

Howling Wolf joined in on the story. "My grandfather told stories about the herds that roamed the area when he was young. It has been many summers since anyone saw more than one or two of the animals. Makata may be the last of her kind."

No one said anything. The boys, heads hung, scuffled their feet nervously. This was a lecture they would not soon forget. They would have liked to be elsewhere or to be on the receiving end of a beating rather than be forced to listen to this harsh public reprimand. The worst part was they knew they deserved it.

Breaking the silence, Tigal went on. "Makata remembers those who treat her well and those who abuse her. My men and I take good care of our animals, and they

159

take care of us. They are faithful, hard workers that do not demand much. At every stop, we ask the same respect for our animals that we want for ourselves otherwise we do not stay and will never return. Is that what you want?"

After a time, probably a short time, but to the boys standing there it seemed longer, he said, "Let me confer with your chief and see if we can agree on a solution." He turned his back on them as if they did not exist.

The group of boys stood in a silent knot wondering what would come next. Tigal, Howling Wolf, and Bright Moon huddled together discussing the situation in low tones. Those that dared peek saw a lot of head-nodding and thoughtful chin stroking. Finally, the trio turned their attention back to the boys.

Tigal let the boys squirm a few moments before he spoke. "After my caravan has time to rest, we will be resuming our travels. For our first few trips, we will travel to those villages within one moon's journey, returning here after each venture. It will give us an opportunity to test our equipment. After that, we will leave, not to return for two, maybe three springs. I need new people." No longer staring at the ground, the group of youths had excitement written all over their faces as they listened to the news. "I can only take one or two. The ones I take will have to show that they can fit in with my people. That means they will have to work well with my men and my animals."

Howling Wolf interrupted, "We will pair you up. You will need to demonstrate you can work together."

Bright Moon leaned on her walking stick as she spoke. "There'll be many tests. Many will be everyday things. We will be watching your performance and weeding out those who do not pass. Those who do pass will have another challenge. On his short trips, Tigal agreed to take a couple candidates, a different pair each time, so he can evaluate you among his people before he has to decide who to take on the longer journey."

Excitement grew, fed by the chatter within the group, as the youngsters started pairing up on their own. Howling Wolf let it continue for a few moments and then clapped his hands twice. The chatter died, and the boys gave him their full attention again. "If this were a part of the test, all of you would have failed!" He looked at them solemnly. Their eyes bugged out and their jaws dropped.

*Failed? No one realized the test had already started. How did they fail?*

Howling Wolf said, "I said 'WE will pair you up.' You failed because you did not listen. Listening and following directions are always important, but even more so when you're on the trail."

Tigal looked over the crowd, he knew they had the boys' attention now. "Each pair will build and live in a shelter. This is to demonstrate that you can take care of yourselves. You also need to demonstrate that you can bring something to the caravan, something that'll be of benefit not just to yourself, but to others."

Somber faces looked back at him waiting for whatever was next. "Form a line here, and we'll look you over and give you a partner. When we've given you a match, you and your partner stand over there out of the way."

A line of eager faces formed immediately. Tigal looked on while Howling Wolf walked along the line matching pairs until there was no one left to match except Silver Fox and Crooked Foot. He ignored the barbs these two shot at each other. Pairing them would force this duo to work together and solve their differences.

Tigal told all of them, "Whether you win a place in the caravan or not is up to you and no one else. Good luck."

Dancing around merrily, the other pairs disappeared

into the village, chattering happily as they went. Silver Fox and Crooked Foot, still shooting barbs at each other, stood their ground. Tigal interrupted their standoff with a few words. "You had better make your peace if you want to win a place in the caravan. It's up to you and no one else." Feeling that he had given them enough to think about, he turned and walked off, leaving the boys to decide.

# Chapter 18: Refugees

Although it had only been a couple of days, it seemed like many moons had passed since Red Deer left Tigal's caravan. He let his raft, pulled by the current, glide along the river while he analyzed some of his recent adventures: what went right; what went wrong; and what he would do differently next time. The trip through the forest had its own set of problems, but he finally reached the river. There, he built a simple raft, nothing fancy, it only needed to carry him and he was ready to relax.

The sky was clear when he started, but clouds gathered as the morning wore on. In the distance lightning flashed. The breeze was replaced by a heavy, gusting wind, and the calm river became rough chop. He needed to find a place to go ashore. He began looking for a good landing site.

The storm, a cold rain propelled by a driving wind, broke before he could find a spot. The wind blew clouds of rain over him. The chop increased. Whitecaps broke over the bow of the raft. Red Deer fought to keep it moving forward into the storm. A beach! Through the blowing rain, he spotted what looked like a beach. He hoped it wasn't his imagination. Would it be a good landing spot? He didn't know but he didn't have many choices and he poled hard to get there.

Close to shore, his raft was driven up on a tree branch hidden just under the surface. It ripped at the water-soaked vines he had used to hold the logs together. They began to spread apart, and it began to disintegrate. It was all he could do to get to shallow water before it was completely gone. Grabbing his gear, he jumped into the waist deep water and fought the waves to wade ashore. Throwing his pack up on the bank, he turned to see if he could salvage his raft. It was lost in the waves and rain. Finding shelter was more important now. Once the storm broke, he would look for logs and build a new raft.

He knew he couldn't rest without first checking the area even in the middle of a storm. Who knew what kind of critter might be lurking about? His search proved he had landed in a small cove. Nothing skulked about. Its beach, a rocky stretch of ground with a slight uphill tilt, was littered with driftwood. On the high end, it backed up to a chest-high bank topped with brush and trees. Luckily, the bank had an overhang, probably caused by floods undercutting it. It could provide refuge from the wind and rain.

Satisfied there was nothing presenting an immediate threat, he went back to where he landed and picked up his belongings, dumping them in the shelter of the overhang to shield them from the storm. *Little good that will do*, he thought, as *the rain has probably soaked everything.*

Away from the protection offered by this overhang, the wood was too wet for a fire, but he collected enough of it to construct a simple lean-to. After completing the task, he searched the area closest to the bank and gathered several armloads of driftwood. Protected from the weather, it was dry and suitable as firewood. He built a small fire near the back wall and piled rocks along both sides. This arrangement · reflected the heat, but remained out of danger from gusts of rain. Maybe it was just his imagination, but the glow of this fire seemed to make his shelter warmer already. The setting sun drew a pale line at the base of the horizon, signaling the end of the workday but not the end of the storm. He was exhausted.

Secured for the night, with no signs of the storm letting up, Red Deer crawled into his shelter, stripped off his wet tunic, and dug out some pemmican. *If nothing else*, he mused, *at least I can be warm and dry tonight. Tomorrow will be another day! It will be soon enough to hunt and to build a raft and then I can think about continuing my trip.*

His thoughts were interrupted by a low wail carried by the winds. It sent a shiver up his spine. Listening again, he heard nothing. Just as he dismissed it as a trick of the wind, the sound, something like a death chant, split the air again. Taking a piece of wood from the fire to light his way, he emerged from his shelter and took a few steps up the beach in the dark. The wind and rain beat at him, but he did not hear the sound again. Returning to his shelter, he climbed in and began an uneasy night.

### 

Red Deer spread mud over his face and neck. It was cold, but it was early spring and to be expected. Not the way he wanted to wake up, but his stay with the Sea People taught him that it was the only way to get protection against the constant mosquito attacks. *A small price to pay if I can get away from these pesky bugs,* he thought. The mud would also hide his scent and provide camouflage. Red Deer peered at his reflection in the creek to make sure he hadn't missed any crucial areas.

Donning a headpiece—a hood with makeshift antlers attached—he smiled at his new look. *Looks great, even if I do say so myself! Now I just have to see if it's good enough to fool the animals.*

Smiling over the idea, it occurred to him, though alone, he had been talking aloud a lot lately. He missed the company of others. This would all change when he got home. Home. He had been gone, how long? Five summers? He forgot, but it wouldn't matter as long as home was still there. Had the Narwikin moved on since he left? He didn't know, but he would soon find out.

Setting these thoughts aside, he got to his feet,

notched an arrow in his bow, and started his hunt. Animals would be coming to the river's edge. He needed another hide to make rope in order to build a raft, and some fresh meat wouldn't hurt either. It would mean a longer delay ....

*Put that thought away*, he chided himself. *No one could have seen the branch under the water. It couldn't be helped.*

It was as if his thoughts had issued a challenge to that pesky internal voice: *You should have come off the river sooner. You should have gotten off when you first saw the clouds ....*

*There was no good place to land my craft*, he responded. *The results would have probably been the same.*

*You don't know that and now you have to spend a couple of days curing the skin, and then cutting it into strips to bind the logs together. You should have used them instead of vines in the first place.*

*No, I'll use one of my hides for the raft and save the hide from my fresh kill. I just need the meat. Now be quiet and let me hunt in peace.*

He hated arguing with himself. He always felt he lost ... and that feeling left him empty. However, no matter what his inner voice said, one thing was certainly true: he needed the meat and would enjoy it while he built his raft and complete his trip.

Hoping for a larger animal, a deer or antelope, he scanned the underbrush as he crept through the shallow puddles left by yesterday's rains. Nothing was afoot and there was little sign that animals had been around. A cold wind blew across the river hitting him in the face. Animals downwind would pick up his scent before he could get close. If he moved quietly upwind, an animal would be unaware of his approach.

Barely cracking the horizon, the sun filtered by clouds, left the land along the river in sullen darkness. Low hills, peppered with scrub brush and small trees, peered out of the gloom and fog. Looking for animal signs, he kept a close eye on the ground as he marched along.

His concentration was broken by a low wail—a sound similar to the one he heard last night—weaker this time, but close by. Freezing, allowing only his eyes to move, he scanned the area in front of him. No movement, no sign of trouble. Turning slowly, he checked the area around him. All quiet.

Then, he heard that sound again; carried on the wind; it came from some place ahead, beyond the next ridge.

Staying low, he crept forward to peer over the crest of the hill. The sun was not high enough to eliminate the darkness between these knolls. Long shafts of golden light were intermixed with the shadows which continued to grip the area. Through the fog, bushes, small trees, and tall grasses all seemed to return his searching stare, but nothing appeared to be out of the ordinary.

Slipping over the crest, he landed noiselessly in a crouch and remained still. After making sure nothing stirred around him, he moved forward to peer over the next ridge.

The sun was a little higher, the fog a little thinner. A quick scan of the area beyond the rim found bushes and trees filled the area to the river's edge. Light glistened on the water. The wail, close by, sounded again but weaker.

Squinting, Red Deer scanned the brush. He missed it on the first pass. Looking again, through the brush this time, he spotted something bobbing idly in the water. The wail, more a moan, came again. Having found that the source did not appear to be a threat, he slid over the top of the ridge and crept toward the water.

# Chapter 19: Rescued

Unconscious most of the time, Little Fawn was barely aware of her surroundings. She remembered that her raft was the last one to escape, but their escape had been discovered before they reached the edge of the fogbank and arrows came raining down. Luckily, their craft had been caught in the current and it carried its wounded passengers downriver away from their pursuers. Drifting aimlessly through day and night, rain and shine, the vessel finally ran aground.

Hunger gnawed at her insides. Wet and cold, her aching body was racked by fever and fits of shivering. Delirious, Little Fawn called out as she relived events in her life. Feeling the end was near she began the death chant of her people.

A jolt, different than those that had occurred, caught her attention. Rolling her head in that direction she saw a figure moving along the raft, stopping here and there, to examine those who it came across.

Moaning in protest, she lifted a hand and tried to sit up but barely managed to raise her head off the deck. Eventually, the figure reached her, stopped, and leaned over to take a closer look.

Straining, she tried to size up this creature. A head topped with antlers. Its skin was grey, and cracked. Its dark eyes stared down at her. Shrieking in alarm, she tried to crawl away. Grabbing her by her wrists, the beast pulled her back. She fought and screamed until it finally knocked her out.

### ###

Still in his hunting disguise, although hunting was the last thing on his mind now, Red Deer looked around. A raft, caught on some obstruction, was covered with bodies. The sound he had heard through the night was a death chant. Cautiously, he boarded the vessel and moved along its length, stopping at each victim to examine them until he reached the end. There he found an older man, deep in the-sleep-from-which-no-one-wakes, and a young girl. Was she dead or alive? He leaned over to take a closer look. Her eyes fluttered opened. She took one long look at him, shrieked, and tried to crawl away. There was no place for her to go but off the end of the raft. Red Deer grabbed her by her wrists and pulled her back. Panicked beyond reason, she screamed and began kicking and thrashing about. Red Deer wrapped an arm around her shoulders and, voice low, he tried to calm her. When that didn't work, he drew back a fist and clipped her on the jaw, knocking her out.

Of those left alive, everyone suffered wounds, some more than others. Sick, wet, blue from cold, they were in no condition to care for themselves.

As for the raft itself, golden-tipped arrows protruded from the piles of mats and ropes on deck. The end of the raft closest to shore was stuck on rocks, but the far end bobbed freely in the water. *The raft was probably driven here by a spring storm, maybe last night's,* he reflected. *Unless I can figure out how to free it, the raft will remain there. None of the others here are in any condition to help me. Clearly, these people needed my help. Anything I have that might benefit them is back at my temporary camp.*

They were unable to walk and carrying them one-by-one is out of the question. To him there was only one solution: free the raft and float the whole thing there. Turning, he started back toward where he had boarded the raft. "Better get busy," he said aloud, "or it will never get done."

He picked up a long pole that lay across the deck. In his travels, he remembered seeing people use poles to propel similar vessels. Right now, he had a different use in mind. Sticking the end of the staff into the water, he tested its depth as he walked along. The storm had jammed the near-shore end, for almost a man-length, onto a bed of rocks while the remainder floated free. His measurements confirmed that once clear, the water would be deep enough for the craft to float freely.

Moving back to the free end, he stepped off and found himself in waist-deep, ice-cold water. Sweeping the shaft along the vessel's underside as he went, he moved toward the grounded end.

"Good," he muttered, "no other underwater obstructions." This meant there was no other obstacle between him and freeing the craft.

Back at the sandbar, he tried clearing the rocks away, but they were too large and buried too deep. He would not be able to dig them out. Using the pole as a pry, he jammed it between the logs and the rocks and pulled. The raft slid forward slightly. At this rate, he'd never get it moved in time to help the injured. Boarding again, he moved everything, equipment and people to the free end of the raft. Back on the sandbar, he tried the pry again. It moved a little farther this time. Using a different approach, he stuck the pole under the raft and pulled up in an attempt to raise it off the rocks. It did not budge. He went back to shore, picked up a section of driftwood and brought it back. Placing it close to the end of the raft, he positioned the shaft between the raft and the driftwood.

"Let's see how this pry works." Straining against the weight, Red Deer tugged down on the bar. The scow rewarded him by moving. Smiling, he moved the driftwood, positioned the pole, and yanked again.

Caught by the current, the back end swung around and headed for the ridge. He had to move quickly to keep from being hung up again. Red Deer jumped aboard, jammed the end of the pole into the ridge, and shoved. The craft, caught in the current, pivoted off the ridge and into deeper water. Red Deer was able to relax again. It was not long before they were at the cove and his campsite. To keep the raft from floating away he tethered both ends to a clump of trees.

He did not have much to offer, but he would share his meager supplies, scarcely enough to support one man, with those on the raft. Ashore, he added some small pieces of wood to the coals from his campfire and soon had a warm blaze going. Pushing the rocks closer along each side would get them hot faster. Fire burning brightly, he filled his soup pouch with water, threw in the last of his jerky[31] and draped the pouch over the fire. The soup he was making would not be much, but it was the best he could do right now.

It would not be good enough just to feed these people, to care for them he had to keep the warm. While the stones to heat the soup warmed, he began moving people and supplies around, laying them out side-by-side. Using driftwood, he drove stakes vertically between the decking and strung ropes between the upright stakes.

Going ashore, he located the mud hole he had used before he went hunting. Taking off his tunic, he filled it with muck and dragged it back to the raft. It took several trips, but

---

[31] Jerky - A meat that has been cut into strips, trimmed of fat, marinated in a spicy, salty, or sweet rub or liquid, and dried or smoked with low heat (usually under 70°C/160°F) or is occasionally just salted and sun-dried. Depending on the method of preparation, the result is a salty, savory, or semisweet snack that can be stored for a long time without refrigeration. The word "jerky" comes from the Quechua term charqui, which means to burn (meat). Jerked meat was one of the first human-made products and is derived from this crucially important food preservation technique. It was essential for survival.

he was able to build some fire platforms in the center between the rows of bodies.

Rummaging through the supplies aboard the raft, he found a few hides to drape over the ropes and make tents. This makeshift shelter would protect the people from the weather. It would also help contain some of the warmth from the fires. Red Deer sized up his work. *Not a sweat house*, he mumbled, *but it'll have to do.*

After piling dry wood aboard the raft near the fire platforms, he loaded the rest of his gear. Taking burning sticks from his campfire, he started fires at each platform. The wet mud sizzled from the heat, but it was layered thick enough to protect the vessel. Satisfied, the raft would not burst into flames he went ashore one last time.

Pausing near the campfire, he scanned the area to make sure he had not forgotten anything. All was good. Using a stone shard as a scoop, he carefully picked up a stone from the edge of the fire and dropped it into the soup pouch. It created a satisfying hiss as the hot stone hit cold water. Repeating the process several times warmed the contents of the pouch. Satisfied with the results, he put out the campfire and picked up the pouch. Untying the raft, he boarded the craft and shoved off.

All of this activity got the girl stirred up again. Feisty and feverish, he had to tie her down before he could continue. Even then, she kept thrashing around and making incoherent noises until she passed out from exhaustion.

By his reckoning, if he made good time, he had two maybe three days travel on the river before he reached the Narwikin encampment. It had been a long time since he left. He hoped they hadn't moved on since then—not only for his sake but also for the sake of these unknown people.

Propelled by the current, the raft slid smoothly into mid-stream. Pleased it was moving along well by itself, he added more wood to the fires then began checking on the people under the tent. The air there was a little warmer.

Grabbing the soup pouch and a wooded cup, he went from person to person and tried to get each to take some warm broth. It was a slow process, made slower because many were unconscious or too weak to help themselves. Making the situation worse, he had to stop periodically to redirect his craft if it strayed from the calm, deep waters.

The girl was another problem. Delirious, shivering from cold, weak, bound hand and foot, she fought him as best she could. He had to admire her spunk. When he tried to get her to take soup, she turned her head away. Kneeling over her, locking her head between his legs, he held her vise steady while putting the cup to her mouth, but she pressed her lips tightly together. Attempting to force her mouth open, he pinched her nose closed. Squirming, she fought to free herself while slyly sucking a little air between only partially opened lips. Seeing this, he poured the soup in as fast as he could. In the fight, most of the broth ended up on her face, but her coughing and sputtering confirmed he was partially successful. Trying the same tactics, he found she was ready and spit the soup at him as soon as it entered. Leaving her to struggle, he went back to work with the other patients hoping she might come around before their trip was over.

### 

The landing! At last the landing lay in front of him. Through the day, he recognized landmarks along the way. Night fell bringing on his biggest fear—that he'd miss this crucial landing point in the dark—but in the predawn light it lay in front of him.

Bringing the raft close to shore, he grabbed the rope tether, splashed ashore, and tied the end to a tree. It floated freely, ensuring that the people on the raft, except one, would be safe from predators.

The girl continued to be a problem. Out of her head throughout the trip, she had attempted to crawl away in spite of being bound, almost crawling off the raft in the process. The others would stay where he left them, but she was still trouble. He knew he couldn't trust her there unattended.

Going back to the raft, he picked the girl up intending to carry her ashore. She had different ideas and began to fight him. Anger rose in him. He suppressed his first thought, which was to throw her in the river. Instead, he slung her head down over his shoulder. Wading out of the river, he stepped on a well-worn path. Many had walked this trail ... and recently. Excitement now quickened his pace. It drove back the weariness of the last few days travel. Suppressing his hunger pangs, he continued to stagger forward until the encampment stood before him. The gate was still closed for the night. Exhausted from the efforts of the last few days he leaned against the timbers as he peered wearily at the village beyond this last obstacle.

Familiar totems confirmed this was his village. His people, all asleep, waited just beyond. They'd help if he could only get through the gate. Not wanting to delay—knowing the people on the raft and the girl on his shoulder needed help—he looked around for something he could use to attract attention. Picking up a fist-sized rock he began banging on the gate. Somewhere within the compound dogs began barking. Heads popped out of shelters. A group of men, some with weapons, came to the gate and looked out to see a mud-covered young man with a body slung over his shoulder.

Dropping the rock, he stepped back bellowing, "Narwikin. Open your gate. I, Red Deer have returned... and I've brought wounded."

Inside the compound, torchbearers brought their light

close, milling about continued as villagers tried to peek through the gate to catch a glimpse of the speaker. A tall man strode confidently through the crowd and took command. People backed away from the gate, and the bar securing it was lifted away. The villagers crowded around the gate and the torchbearers, but kept a respectful distance from their chief.

The doors swung open and onlookers saw Red Deer, feet apart, girl slung over his shoulder, waiting silently. Howling Wolf, alone in the center of this gathering, had remained quiet until now. After one-hand's worth of summers, this was the moment he had waited for. Composing himself, he broke the silence, "Welcome home, my son. It is good to see you."

# Chapter 20: Home

At a wave of Howling Wolf's hand, men called for a mat, clustered around Red Deer, and gently relieved him of his burden. Laying the girl's inert form on it, they picked the mat up by the edges and started for Bright Moon's shelter. Someone ran ahead to alert her.

Howling Wolf looked into Red Deer's bleary eyes. How many times, during his son's absence had Howling Wolf agonized over the thought that Bright Moon's prediction might be wrong, that the son he knew and loved might never return?

In a way, they were both right. Bright Moon said it would be five summers before his son—a self-centered scrawny kid, one whose impetuous nature often got him in trouble—returned. That lad never came back. Inwardly, Howling Wolf smiled as he recalled his own youthful journey into manhood so many summers before. He had been a lad no different than Red Deer. The journey gave him a chance to grow; a chance to realize the world was much greater than this village and its hunting grounds. The same was true today. The person who stood in front of him now was a wiser, caring young man, tall in stature and sporting a lean, muscular trunk. It was good to see the sojourn still worked.

"You've come far, my son?"

"Yes, but the most trying part was … the last … the last …." He couldn't remember how long it had been since he found the raft … how long it had been since he slept. "The most trying part was the last few days."

Howling Wolf grunted an acknowledgement as he took his son by the arm. "Come. You need to eat and then sleep."

"Wait, Father," Red Deer, eyes wide said, "there is more wounded ... at the river ... there's a raft ...."

Hearing this, Howling Wolf issued more orders. Following his instructions, a young man broke into a run, going ahead to scout the area around the river.

Having faced casualties from animal attacks and hunts that had gone badly, others began a well-practiced drill. Men and women ran to their shelters and returned with hides, robes, mats, and pouches of water. Organized into groups, they started for the river to be met by the returning runner. Yelling confirmation of wounded, he was able to spur them into a quicker pace.

Watching the troupe scurry away, Howling Wolf spoke, "Do you know what happened?"

Red Deer shook his head. "It appears they had been attacked. I came across them upriver. Whatever they faced had already taken place." Wearily, he shrugged. "Maybe days before ... they were too weak, too sick, to tell me anything."

He turned to look directly at Howling Wolf. "I knew the clan would take them in. What I didn't know was if the Narwikin were still here."

"The same summer you and others left on their sojourn, we decided to stay on and wait for everyone to return." A sheepish smile crossed Howling Wolf's face, "It got too late to pick up and move. Staying on, we found the Long Cold that followed was easier than we remembered." He looked intently at Red Deer. "We've stayed ever since." He softened. "Maybe I'm getting too old to move."

Turning together, they walked into the encampment.

### 

While Crooked Foot slept, Red Deer had returned! By the time the lad heard the news, he and Abeytu were deeply involved helping Bright Moon tend to the sick and wounded.

Before anything else, the wounded needed their attention. He would not be free to greet his friend until these duties were completed. But, in spite of this delay, Red Deer's arrival was music to his ears.

Bright Moon made her way from hut to hut, her two assistants, heavily loaded with satchels of medicines, followed. Standing tall, Abeytu remained serious and calm as she waited for Bright Moon's directions; excited, Crooked Foot ignored the odd looks and rolled eyes that Abeytu gave him and danced along behind Bright Moon, who often had to speak sharply to him to get his attention. The sun was long passed the midpoint by the time the Shaman and her two assistants completed their task and she released them.

Overjoyed and free, Crooked Foot grabbed his red spear and went to find his friend, show him how much he had grown, and tell him everything that had happened during his friend's absence, but he could not.

Initially, it was because, being exhausted, Red Deer slept. Crooked Foot paced up and down outside the hut where Red Deer snored noisily away.

Eventually tiring, Crooked Foot settled down under a nearby tree to wait. Leaning his head back against the trunk, his thoughts of their meeting, their conversation ran wild:

"Look at you," Crooked Foot would say, "look at how you have grown! Why, you've become a man!"

Red Deer would look him over and say, "Look at me? Look at how you have grown!"

"How did you like being on Tigal's caravan? I heard that Tigal told the council that you went to the Land of the Sea People and then sailed across a great sea. It took more than two moons before you arrived at a land where you had to slay river-dragons."

"Yes that's true! I could have used a spear like the red one you hold. Where did you get that? I would like one!"

"Remember the spear we made before you left. I colored it red to

*remind me of you and the fun we had. Before I slayed the great bear,
Tawasiki, it chased me and broke that spear. I sat with Gray Wolf to
make this spear and the point. I used this one to slay a young lion after I
found a pair of lambs and their mother. I made friends with Makata,
Tigal's mastodon, and I can ride her."*

*"I've missed so much! What else have you been doing?"*

*"I bested Silver Fox in a fight. Bright Moon is training me. I
caught some fish by building a fence across the creek. The Clam Shell
people joined us and they use a long bow ...."*

The snoring finally ceased, the moment of quiet that
followed was broken by a loud yawn as the sleeper stirred,
stretched, and started to move about inside the hut. Crooked
Foot, alerted by these sounds, jumped to his feet.

From within the darkened hut, a hand pushed aside
the door flap and a young man emerged to blink at the bright
sunlight. Crooked Foot's jaw dropped. This stranger was not
the Red Deer he remembered. This being was tall in stature,
taller than the lad's imagination had painted; and the man in
front of him sported a lean, muscular trunk. This was not the
slim, gawky Red Deer that left five summers ago, nor was it
the Red Deer that Crooked Foot imagined he became. This
stranger had grown into a man.

Fraught with concern, Crooked Foot's stomach
twisted and turned. *Would it be like it was before? Would he want
to spend time with a youngster like Crooked Foot? Would his friend
even remember him?*

The stranger stretched and then looked at an open-
mouthed, skinny lad standing under a tree and holding a red
spear. Red Deer smiled. "Little brother, how you have
changed! What happened while I was gone?"

Crooked Foot, still wide-eyed, stood awestruck at the
changes in Red Deer, replied, "Na ... Na ...Nothing."

### ###

Over the next few days, Bright Moon moved from shelter to shelter as she looked after the wounded. It seemed she was everywhere. It seemed like she never slept. This wasn't true, however, because Bright Moon pressed others into service. When the women of the tribe made bread, they made extra. When they fixed meals, they fixed extra. The Clam Shell people joined in the process.

Tending to the wounded, Bright Moon issued instructions for each one's treatment, and willing hands helped feed and tend to those who couldn't care for themselves. However, she alone looked after their wounds— inspecting, cleaning, applying poultices, packing them with cattail fluff to reduce bleeding and wrapping each one with softened bark or animal skins.

### ###

Little Fawn peered up at the face hovering over her. In a hoarse whisper she asked, "Who ... who ... are ... you?"

Dark, black eyes, darker than the darkest night, set deep in a wrinkled face, peered back at her. "Shhhhh, drink this now," Bright Moon commanded, "questions later." Gently, she slipped a hand under the girl's head and tipped it forward. Placing a wooden cup at her lips, Bright Moon encouraged the girl to swallow.

Dribbling over her lips, Little Fawn felt the liquid bathe her mouth. The taste—vaguely familiar—she struggled to place it. As she sank into mellow blackness, it hit her, and her lips moved ever so slightly as she formed the word. "Heliotrope ...." Her whisper was barely audible.

Having leaned closer, Bright Moon caught the girl's fading response. Giving her a comforting smile, she gently stroked the soft, young cheek saying, "Yes, my little flower, it's heliotrope." As she lowered the girl's head, she crooned, "It will help you sleep. Sleep is good."

Little Fawn, swimming in a sea of blackness, slumped back, unconscious again.

### 

Crooked Foot, a sour look on his face, dropped the bowl of hot gruel on the stone hearth. "Why do I have to do it?"

Bright Moon gave Crooked Foot a stern look. "Because you're well and she's injured." She shoved the bowl back into his hands. "She needs the medicine and food I fixed. You feed it to her. That's your job! I've others to look after. That's my job!" Wheezing, she turned to leave, but turned back scowling, and added, "If she won't take it, figure out how you're going to get it into her, and then do it!" Bright Moon gave him one of those looks that quelled any further objections. Satisfied that he understood, she wheeled around and departed.

Speechless in the wake of her wrath, Crooked Foot was left standing bowl in hand and open mouthed. He stared at the door-flap still aflutter from his grandmother's abrupt departure. A noise, the sound of movement from a dim corner of the hut, jarred him back to the task at hand. He turned to find the girl trying to sit up, perhaps to get up.

"Wait," he said, almost shouting. "You can't get up!"

"Just watch me … and don't get in my way." Little Fawn attempted to swing her feet off her sleeping couch.

A couple of quick strides brought Crooked Foot to her side. Putting his free hand on her head, he pushed her back. Little Fawn didn't give up. Arms flailed at him while she struggled under his grasp. Unable to control her, Crooked Foot threw himself across her until she wore herself out. In her weakened state he didn't have to wait long, but being tired didn't make her docile.

"Hold still. You need to eat this," he said through tight lips.

Swinging a leg over her, Crooked Foot straddled her chest and was able to pin her arms to her sides. This kept her from beating on him, from knocking the bowl from his hands, but did nothing to make her more cooperative. Little Fawn didn't have enough strength to buck him off, and she seethed angrily, teeth clenched, nostrils flaring with each breath, venom in her eyes.

"Eat this! It's good for you." Crooked Foot hoped emphasizing the need would encourage her to cooperate. It didn't. She was in no mood to listen.

Whenever the bowl came close, she turned her head away. Clamping her chin with one hand, he brought the bowl close to her mouth. Her lips became a tight seal, blocking any entry, as Little Fawn tried to wiggle free. Letting go of her chin, Crooked Foot quickly slipped his hand up, grabbed her nose and pinched it closed. Surprised, she opened her mouth to gasp for air. In a swift movement, he poured part of the bowl's contents down the opening provided. Anticipating her next move, he slipped his hand off her nose and over her mouth, sealing it shut. He wasn't about to have her spit it back at him.

Little Fawn shook her head back and forth, trying to shake his grip. Unable to escape his hold, she was forced to swallow, but satisfied herself by sinking her teeth into an available finger. Crooked Foot's howl encouraged her to increase her efforts. Bowl in hand, he drew it back, ready to plant it where he thought it would do the most good when a familiar voice interrupted his actions.

"My young friend, is that the way a Narwikin takes care of the wounded?"

Surprised, both Crooked Foot and the girl stopped

and looked at the newcomer.

Red Deer, having heard the commotion, had stepped inside the shelter to investigate and now strode forward to take the bowl from Crooked Foot's upraised hand.

"I'll take over here," he said, "Bright Moon needs your help in the next shelter. You might want to have your hand looked at too."

Getting to his feet, Crooked Foot looked at his hand. Fingers that barely separated a set of teeth moments earlier were rewarded with an open wound which bled profusely.

Grabbing some items he could use to tend to the cut, he ducked out of the shelter, glaring at the girl as he did. Little Fawn returned his glare with a smug I-won-I'm-better-than-you-and-there's-more-where-that-come-from smile.

Hackles rose on the back of his neck especially when he heard Red Deer ask, "You look hungry. Can I get you something to eat?"

"Oh, yes. I'm starving," came her soft reply.

The door flap dropped into place cutting off further conversation. It was just as well. He wanted to be rid of her, anyway ... but not quite.

With Red Deer's help, Little Fawn was able to sit. It was a task she knew she could've accomplished on her own, but it seemed better to have his help.

He sat on the edge of her sleeping couch, wrapped his strong arms around her and gently lifted her into a sitting position. Turning away he dipped a bowl, similar to the one that earlier had almost become a weapon, into a nearby pouch of hot soup. Turning back to her, he held the steaming bowl between them. There was an awkward silence.

Coyly she eyed his frame. He was tall and lean ... muscular, not skinny. Their eyes met. She had looked into them before. She tried to place the event.

Red Deer held her gaze for a long moment before he

spoke. "It's hot. We should blow on it to cool it off."

Heart thumping wildly, she could feel color rising in her cheeks and was unable to speak lest she reveal the emotional turmoil she felt. Not wanting to give herself away, she could only nod. Still fixed on his eyes, she pursed her lips and blew gently.

Across from her, he puckered and gave short puffs. The hot liquid danced under their combined efforts. In the dim light of the shelter, she finally recalled where she had seen him and smiled.

"What is it?" he questioned, handing her the bowl.

"Your antlers ...," she explained. "When I first saw you, you were wearing antlers." Taking the bowl, she sipped its contents.

Stumped for a moment by her words, he finally remembered their first meeting. "I was hunting when I found your raft. You put up quite a fight ... all the way here."

Breaking the deadlock on their gaze, she dropped her eyes. "Yes. I'm sorry. I thought you were ... one of the slayers of my people."

"No, you're safe here with ... among the Narwikin."

She gave him back the empty bowl. "No. No one is safe while they live." Lying back, she drew her sleeping robes close, tucking them under her chin. "I'll find them. They'll pay for what they've done." Closing her eyes, she said softly, "I must rest now."

# Chapter 21: Recuperation

"Where are your mother and father?" Little Fawn asked. Sitting cross-legged atop her sleeping couch, she watched the boy, a couple of summers younger than she, as he bobbed around the shelter pursuing various tasks. Getting stronger every day, she became curious about these strangers who cared for her and wanted to learn more about them.

Crooked Foot looked up from the fire he was nursing. "They sleep-the-sleep-from-which-no-one-wakes." He went back to staring at the flames, watching them grow because of his handiwork.

Little Fawn stared off into nothingness as if she were watching actions in another time, another place. Wood on the fire popped, bringing her back. When she spoke there was a touch of melancholy in her voice. "A few summers past, my mother began the-long-sleep. Because of the raiders, my father joined her. How about you? Did your parents begin the-long-sleep recently?"

Omitting the details, Crooked Foot gave a brief explanation. "No. When I was a baby still strapped to the carry board, a great bear came and took them."

Little Fawn's curiosity was not satisfied. "How come you drag your foot? Were you injured then?"

"No. I was born this way." He found himself a little ill at ease. Everyone in his village knew him since birth. No one had ever asked that question before.

Unchecked, Little Fawn pressed forward with her questions. "You get around okay?"

Why was she asking such questions? Crooked Foot didn't know, but felt he needed to defend himself. "I can do anything anybody else can do."

"Anything…?"

"I can …." Crooked Foot started to explain, but Bright Moon, Red Deer, and an older man entered the shelter, cutting off his response.

"Good," Bright Moon said, "I see you're awake. Do you feel up to answering questions?"

Little Fawn looked from one to another. They appeared straight faced and solemn, but not threatening. No matter. She could claim weakness and delay, but she could not put off their questions forever. Wishing she had time to make herself presentable, she sat erect and nodded.

The older man, slim and tall, stepped forward. His face was weathered. There were a few wrinkles around his eyes and the corners of his mouth. His hair, dark except for a slight fringe of gray around the temples was neatly braided. His demeanor, the respect the others gave him, indicated his high rank. In a voice deep, firm, confident, the tone of one who is used to speaking commands and having them obeyed, he said, "I am Howling Wolf, Chief of the Narwikin."

A few images stuck with her through her delirium and recovery. She remembered struggling with Red Deer on the raft and fighting with Crooked Foot here in the shelter. There were memories of Bright Moon, her voice cooing as she hovered overhead, but Little Fawn also remembered this unknown face, softened by concern, peering down at her.

Trying to imitate his formal introduction she said, "I am Little Fawn, daughter of White Owl, Shaman of the Attikamekey. Our village…." Her lips quivered a little as memories of the events came flooding back. *Don't cry! You can't cry. You must be strong!* Taking a deep breath, she bit her lip, and then went on. "Our village sits near a place where two great rivers meet and become one." She stopped, waiting for his next question.

He sat silent, giving her a moment to compose herself

before he went on. "You've come far from your village. What brings you here?"

"We were waiting, had prepared everything, for the return of the great fish when we were attacked in the middle of the night. The attackers put our village to the torch. Those not killed would've become their slaves. We managed to escape on rafts." Her eyes grew red-rimmed and swollen as she spoke but she managed to hold back her tears. "My father and I were on the last raft when our escape was discovered. Arrows filled the air again, and again. I begged them to stop … but they wouldn't. My father gave his life protecting me." Unable to continue, she turned her head away. Her shoulders trembled a little, and soft, sniffling sounds penetrated the air.

A shuffling noise followed by a conference of hushed whispers, only partially audible, followed the termination of her story.

"… needs rest …" came Bright Moon's voice.

"… take care … prepare her … when sister moon is full again…:" It sounded like Howling Wolf but lacked the same timbre. Could it be Red Deer's voice?

"… let me … everyone else needs to leave. Now!" That was definitely Bright Moon's voice.

Surprisingly, the shuffling noise came again and then near silence, the only sound being gentle footfalls approaching. Little Fawn felt the sleeping couch move as Bright Moon sat down next to her.

"It's time for you to rest." Bright Moon slipped an arm around the girl's shoulders in an attempt to get her to lie back. Instead, Little Fawn turned and buried her face in Bright Moon's shoulder, her young body racked in sobs. While the girl cried, Bright Moon held her close, softly cooing almost forgotten words as she rocked her.

It had been a long time since Bright Moon had the opportunity—a long time since she let herself have the opportunity—to do anything like this. Not since … not since her daughter had placed her baby's carry board safely out of reach in a tree before she turned to face the great bear … the one called Tawasiki.

Pain, grief, all the emotions she had buried years before and hoped never to face again, came flooding out. Bright Moon's tears mixed with Little Fawn's as she whispered, "It'll be alright … it'll be alright … my daughter."

### 

"Add the mushrooms to the stew," Bright Moon instructed.

Little Fawn eyed the mushrooms that lay on an open hide. "These mushrooms?" She eyed them suspiciously. "Why do you want me to add these?"

Bright Moon shrugged. Busy cutting up some wild onions, she didn't bother to look in the young girl's direction as she replied, "They'll add flavor."

Little Fawn's jaw dropped. Recovering she said, "If I add these, it would be the last meal a person eats. They're poison."

"You know this how?"

"My father, White Owl, is … was … Shaman for the Attikamekey." Her voice cracked at the memory of his loss, and she looked away quickly. "I learned from him."

Cackling gleefully, Bright Moon nodded, "You passed my test. I knew you would. I knew you had knowledge when you recognized heliotrope in the sleeping potion." Wrapping the mushrooms in the hide she threw the parcel in the fire. "Have you given any thought to your future?"

"My future …?" Surprised, Little Fawn found she had no answer. Still recovering from the shock of the attack and its aftermath, she hadn't thought about what would happen the next day let alone anytime beyond.

"Yes, your future. What would you like to do?" Seeing the puzzled look on the girl's face, Bright Moon continued, "I am Shaman for the Narwikin, but I grow old. I could use help. You could stay with me and I'll teach you." She studied the girl as she spoke, looking for some sign of acceptance ... or rejection. All she found was confusion.

"But ... but ... but what about Abeytu and Crooked Foot ...?"

Bright Moon cut her off. "Don't worry about them. There's enough work for all of us. Besides, Abeytu comes from a big family and her mother needs her help. As for Crooked Foot, Red Deer's return will provide more time for the two of them to spend together. He'll need that if...." She stopped mid-sentence. Leaving whatever she was going to say unsaid. Instead, she ended by repeating, "He'll need that."

Little Fawn gave her a puzzled look which Bright Moon chose to ignore. Changing the subject, the old woman picked up her medicine basket. "Feel up to a little walk?" Not waiting for an answer, she shoved the basket toward the girl, "Take this. Follow me. We're going to visit your people. They'll take comfort in knowing you're well and getting around."

Starting for the door, Bright Moon stopped, leaned heavily on her walking stick as she turned to speak to the girl. "The next full moon, the council will meet. Every able-bodied Narwikin will be there. The Attikamekey will be presented then. They'll be asked if they want to stay and join with the Narwikin or remain Attikamekey, move on and set up their own village elsewhere. If the choice is to leave, Narwikin will provide them any items that can be spared." She paused to let the girl assimilate this information. "When the council meets, they'll address your people as a group but would like one person to speak for the Attikamekey." The old woman looked at her as if she expected a response.

Dumbfounded, Little Fawn gave her a blank stare but finally managed, "Why are you telling me this? What do you want from me?"

"I wish to prepare you for what's ahead. From what I've gathered from listening to your people, you and a woman played a key role in their escape. You'll see that many of those who were on the raft with you are still in bad shape. A few are even worse than you were when you were brought here. Your people look to you as a leader."

Her? A leader? Little Fawn was shaken by the thought. She couldn't believe what she was hearing and swallowed hard.

Bright Moon wrapped a comforting arm around her shoulders. "Come, daughter, it's time we visit your people. You can assess their condition yourself. We can take as long as you need ... and when we're done you can come back to rest ... before you make your decision."

Little Fawn's head spun. Which was more over-powering? Finally getting a chance to get out and visit her people? Being asked to be their spokesperson? Or being addressed as 'daughter' by this venerable old woman?

# Chapter 22: Little Fawn in Front of the Council

"Bright Moon left instructions." Failing to reason with Little Fawn, Crooked Foot thought the mention of the Shaman's name would persuade her to slow down. "I'm to see that you don't exert yourself."

Ignoring him, Little Fawn flitted around the shelter, collecting things she thought would be useful. Placing them in a basket over her arm, she told him, "I want to gather some clay. If you're to tag along and look after me, grab a cooking pot and something to dig with."

Puzzled, Crooked Foot picked up a trowel and the cooking pot she indicated. "What are you going to do with the clay?"

"We're going to make a cooking pot."

"Cooking pot?" He waggled the one in his hand. "We have a cooking pot … why would yours be any different?

"It will. You watch and see." A cryptic smile decorated her face. "I want this to be a surprise. You must promise not to tell anyone until we meet at council. Okay?"

Crooked Foot had no idea what she had in mind, but agreeing seemed innocent enough. He also knew the only way she'd let him come along would be to agree, and that was the only way he'd find out what she was going to do.

The pair followed the path down to the river and then along the river's edge until Little Fawn called a halt. Crooked Foot looked around. He didn't see anything that would pass for clay. Rather excited, Little Fawn had dropped her basket and ran into a stand of reeds.

"What's going on? Where is the clay?"

"Haven't found any yet but this is a great find. Look around and help me remember landmarks because we need to come back here and collect some reeds."

Finally, satisfied she'd be able to find the place again, they went on until they reached a place where a small stream dribbled into the river. Crossing the stream, Little Fawn found a good spot and stopped there. Putting her basket down, she dropped to her knees and began digging a basin in the dirt. There, she began mixing water and clay making a thick mud. "Stand in the middle and move your feet up and down like you're walking. It'll keep the mud mixed up while I work with it."

Crooked Foot stepped into the basin. The mud squished between his toes. Throwing in more clay, she watched as he churned the contents into mush. He continued marching around, and she continued adding water and clay. Before long, the mix was knee-deep.

"Okay, we're just about ready." Excited, Little Fawn took a hide from her basket and spread it out nearby. "Come out of there and dig a fire pit over here in the sand. Then gather a bunch of wood."

Crooked Foot clamored out of the mud, happy to be done with the task while she scooped a blob of the mix out of the pit.

Kneading and rolling the clay like bread dough she found herself smiling as it reached the right level of elasticity.

Crooked Foot used his digging tool to scoop out a fire pit, but was curious about the next step. "What are you going to do?"

"I'm going to line the outside of the cooking pot with clay."

"Huh? Why do that?" Caught off guard by her answer, he paused in his digging.

"To get cooking pots and the like." Putting more clay

on the pot, she patted it in place while she continued her explanation. "Narwikin make wicker baskets and cover them with mud. The Attikamekey do the same, but then they bake it over a fire."

Crooked Foot wrinkled his nose. "Baked over a fire? Why would do you do that?" He watched her mold the clay around the inside of the cooking pot.

Absorbed in her work she didn't answer until she was satisfied the clay was evenly layered around the pot. Sitting back, she looked over her work as she explained, "Most of the wicker is burnt away leaving just the clay pot. After cooling, it can be decorated with colors, patterns, even covered with a glaze." Crooked Foot didn't seem impressed until she added, "It doesn't leak!"

At that news, Crooked Foot's face brightened. Their mud-coated wicker baskets always leaked.

"I'll put this in the hole you dug, and you get the fire going. While the pot is baking, we can go cut some reeds, and I'll show you what we do with them. Okay?"

Eager to see what was next, Crooked Foot quickly gathered firewood and kindling.

### 

"We can sit by this fallen tree and use it as a work surface." Little Fawn was excited as she dropped an armful of reeds nearby. "If we had a lot of time, we could soak them in water to soften them. Lay one length-wise along the trunk, and use a rock to pound it." She glanced at Crooked Foot to see if he had questions. Everything looked good so she went on. "We need to break down the outer skin to get at the fibers inside. We'll twist the fibers together to make stronger cords."

Crooked Foot's face brightened. "That's what I'm doing with the fur from my sheep." His enthusiasm faded as he added, "Only it's taking a long time to get enough collected to make anything."

Little Fawn nodded. "Reeds are plentiful and my people were able to get enough to weave some into thin mats. Talk around our campfire was that one day they might be able to weave something to replace hides. Can you imagine wearing reeds instead of leather?"

Crooked Foot laughed. "Were they playing a joke on you?"

She shrugged. "Maybe they were, but they seemed serious. Who knows?"

Crooked Foot nodded. It seemed like a crazy idea, but maybe it would work.

"If you sit here and get started, I'll find a rock and join you. Okay?" Little Fawn went off to find a rock suitable for the job while Crooked Foot started working on a reed. She returned almost as quickly as she left and was even more excited. In her arms were several stones.

"What are you going to do with all those?" Crooked Foot knew she'd only need one to work on the reeds. This had to be something different.

Dumping her load nearby, she dropped to her knees next to him. "Look at this. I found a bunch over in the creek." She held a rock out for his examination. The top half was plain rock but the bottom half was different. It had a golden-reddish tinge flecked with green.

"Oh, I've seen stones like that before." He was surprised to see she was shocked by his revelation. "What are they good for?"

In her excitement, she spoke quickly, the words almost running together as they tumbled out of her mouth. "If we get these really hot and then drop them in cold water, the rock splits and gives us the golden stone. This can be worked into shapes." Pausing to catch her breath, she looked at Crooked Foot to see if he had questions before she went on. "Many things can be made with this wonderful material. The Attikamekey would pound out thin strips and wrap pieces around arrow heads and knife blades to give them sharper points and edges. I am sure the Narwikin can think of more things that can be done."

### 

"... so Howling Wolf talked with the council. Tonight sister moon will be full again. All of your people will sit with the clans. You can become a part of the Narwikin ... or leave and set up your own village elsewhere." Red Deer, excited, smiled encouragingly, adding, "I traded for shells and made something for you to wear. You'll look great."

The necklace in his extended hands flashed in the light, but Little Fawn didn't seem impressed. "I can't go to council. My clothes are dirty and in tatters. I haven't anything to wear. My people can't be any better off."

Speechless, Red Deer was taken aback. This was a great opportunity, why didn't she see that?

Bright Moon, stirring a cooking pot, chuckled at his predicament before finally coming to his rescue. Nodding toward Crooked Foot she told Red Deer, "Take the boy, Silver Fox, and a few others. Go hunting. A nice, plump antelope will make tonight's council a celebration. I'll take care of things here."

"But ... but ..."

Bright Moon turned to Crooked Foot. "Grab your stuff. Red Deer is taking you boys hunting." Turning back, she gave Red Deer a sharp look. "When is the last time you saw an antelope in here? Get moving."

In shock, Red Deer moved toward the door as if in a dream. Crooked Foot, however, was the exact opposite. Dropping his current work, he collected his hunting gear in one swoop and exited the shelter as if it were on fire.

Even though she witnessed the events, Little Fawn couldn't believe the power this old woman wielded … and how effectively she did it.

Digging through a pile in the corner, Bright Moon came up with a length of rawhide. Pointing to a spot on the floor, she commanded, "Stand here. Turn around and hold your arms straight out."

Like the others, Little Fawn found herself following Bright Moon's directions without asking questions. The woman stretched the cord, wrist to wrist, across the girl's back. Grunting she made a knot in the rope and set it aside. Taking another cord, she measured from Little Fawn's neck down. Grunting her satisfaction, she knotted this strand, set it aside and began running her fingers through the girl's hair.

Giving Little Fawn a final look, Bright Moon said, "Relax. I'll be back in a little bit." Taking her walking stick she ducked out of the shelter.

Suddenly left alone Little Fawn was in a state of shock. The contents of the cooking pot started bubbling. It reminded her, she hadn't eaten. Definitely on the mend, Little Fawn had finished her second bowl and was debating about going back for a third by the time Bright Moon returned, a basket over her arm.

Bright Moon motioned to her. "Come. Hurry along." She wheeled around and headed out of the shelter. Little Fawn set the bowl aside and hurried after the old lady.

By the time they reached the village gate, they were joined by others—women, girls, small children—headed the same direction. A number of them, but not all, were strangers to Little Fawn. Intermixed, paired up actually, with each group of Narwikin were Attikamekey survivors from her raft. The Narwikin women, like Bright Moon, all carried baskets.

The group followed a winding path through the bush

to a cove. A sand bar sheltered the mouth of the inlet nearly cutting it off from the river. The water in the cove was only waist deep at best and warmed by the sun. Racing toward the water's edge, the Narwikin children squealed in delight as they threw off their clothes and splashed into the water.

Leaning on her walking stick, Bright Moon dropped her basket and turned to Little Fawn to explain, "This is the women's bath. There's plenty of sand to help clean your skin." She nudged the basket with her toe and said, "When we're done, I've brought along oil, squeezed from flowers and plants, for our hair … also, some fresh clothes for you. Smiling warmly, she added, "This should help you feel better about tonight."

"Oh, thank you for …. for … for everything." In her zeal to hug Bright Moon, Little Fawn pounced on the old woman and nearly sent her sprawling.

"Stop, daughter, stop," laughing, Bright Moon complained. "You're taking away from my bath time," she protested, but they both knew she didn't mean it.

Peeling off her ragged clothes, Little Fawn joined the others and marched into the water. Bright Moon followed right behind her. Cries of delight filled the air as the cool water closed around them.

# Chapter 23: Hunting Antelope and Boars

The plains were home to a number of animals, large and small: prairie chickens, jackrabbits, and coyotes as well as herds of buffalo, deer, and antelope

Luck was with Red Deer and his young hunters. Ahead, antelope grazed on the tall grass. Now and then one would look up to scan their surroundings for trouble. These were jumpy animals, wary of the slightest change. To survive, when the only weapon you had was your speed, you were vigilant ... or you were dead.

Spread out downwind from the herd, hunting party members hid behind the bushes each had cut for their cover. Everyone else hung back as Silver Fox crept nearer to the herd. Getting this close required he move slowly, taking small steps, but only when the animals had their heads down grazing. Whenever any animal raised its head to look around, Silver Fox stopped, becoming rock still.

Believing he would get no closer, he carefully pinned the bush in place with one foot, put an arrow shaft between his teeth, and notched another. An antelope looked up. Once again Silver Fox froze in place. The animal scanned the area again and went back to grazing.

Drawing back, Silver Fox took careful aim and let the arrow fly. Almost before it hit, the second arrow went from mouth to bow. Notched, he drew back, ready to fire again. It was a movement made automatic by need and smooth by practice. Never once did he take his eyes off his mark so he was immediately aware of his success.

On target to the end, the first arrow hit the antelope

in a vulnerable spot. Startled, the herd leapt into action, racing across the grassy steppe, their wounded comrade with them.

The speed at which they reacted made a second shot useless. Silver Fox knew his first shot was good. Though it raced away with the others, it wouldn't last long. Watching the direction the herd took, he relaxed the bow's draw to sit and wait for the creature to exhaust itself. Eventually, it would seek cover; probably lie down. By the time the hunting party found it, the animal would be too weak, and too stiff to get up.

Grunts and squeals from the bush behind him gave warning there would be no sitting around. The shrubs erupted, spewing out a wild boar. It was a male, from the size of his tusks, a mature one. It stopped to sniff the air. Upwind from the beast meant Silver Fox couldn't expect to go unnoticed. Angry by nature, the animal didn't need encouragement to take after anything. It started toward Silver Fox on an unswerving course.

Silver Fox knew he was in a bad position. Nothing nearby offered him protection. A lone tree, one he could climb, stood some distance away. Notching an arrow, he drew back and planted the shaft in the charging beast. A squeal signaled success; however, the shot wasn't fatal. On impact, the creature tumbled head-over-heels in the dirt. Regaining its feet, it turned in circles trying to extract the remains of the broken shaft before it recovered enough to remember its original target. An adult boar is dangerous; a wounded adult boar is all the more dangerous.

As the animal closed the distance, Silver Fox reached for another arrow. It would be a close race to see if he could get off a good shot before the brute struck. He drew back and fired, just missing the boar. There would be no time for another shot. Turning away, he began to run toward the tree.

As he ran, something red flashed over his shoulder. Squeals erupted from behind him. Silver Fox turned in time to see Crooked Foot bob up, atlatl in hand, and grab the end of his red spear. Pinned to the ground, the creature thrashed about until others were able to come finish it off.

Still a little shaken at this close call, Silver Fox walked back to join the rest of the hunting party. His emotions were in turmoil. He was happy to have escaped, but unhappy Crooked Foot had come to his rescue.

Recognizing there could be a problem Red Deer sent the rest of the group out to track the wounded antelope. "It will give you younger ones—especially the first time hunters—some practice in following a blood trail. You older ones keep an eye out in case another hog is around." As an afterthought he added, "Yell when you find his kill. Then cut a couple of carry poles[32] so we can take both carcasses back to camp. Tie the antelope to one and bring the other pole here to carry the boar."

Under the watchful eyes of older members, the younger ones, excited over their first hunt, went tearing off, each trying to be first to point out any sign as they went. When they were out of earshot, Red Deer turned to Silver Fox. "Nice work with the antelope and the pig, but you would never have made it to the tree."

Silver Fox's cheeks burned. He knew Red Deer was right. Crooked Foot would have an opportunity to gloat.

"He knew the wounded animal couldn't think straight," Crooked Foot chimed in, "so he was leading it back to us."

Silver Fox couldn't believe it. Crooked Foot, his rival,

---

[32] Carry Poles - A pole used to carry items of equal weight. For balance, the items are fastened to each end of the pole and balanced across the individual's shoulders.

was defending him. How did this come about? This shouldn't be! He went from humiliation to anger. He raised his hand to strike when Red Deer caught his wrist. "Don't .... Don't make any of us sorry we didn't side with the boar."

### 

Clean! Little Fawn couldn't remember the last time she felt so clean. Rubbed with sand, her skin glowed. Most of the original group had returned to the village. Only a few women and children remained. Her long wet hair, now oiled and perfumed, hung down her back. Little Fawn held up her new outfit and admired her reflection in the water. She looked good! Happy, she started to sing and dance around. Close by, Bright Moon leaned on her walking stick and smiled as she watched the girl.

A child's cry and a woman's terrified scream shattered the mood. Like everyone else, Little Fawn looked for the cause. Near the water's edge, a young mother cradled her child in protective arms. A snake, having swum in off the river, prepared to strike. Without thinking twice, Little Fawn cast her outfit aside. Ripping the staff out of Bright Moon's hands, she bounded toward the snake.

Before it could strike, the girl swung the stick, catching beach-sand, water, and snake in the same blow. Not having a clean swing, the serpent didn't receive a fatal wound, but was knocked aside. It recovered quickly and tried to coil back into striking position. Just as quickly, Little Fawn reached into the twisting loops and grabbed the tip of the snake's tail. Jerking her catch upward, she began to twirl the creature over her head. Gaining momentum with each circle, the serpent was forced to stretch out until, satisfied with the results, the girl it let go. Everyone watched the snake, still cutting a circle in the air, arc over bushes and land in the river.

The women let out a cheer and showered the girl with praise as they crowded around her. Embarrassed by their attention, Little Fawn asked that they see to the comfort of the mother and child while she looked after Bright Moon. Eager to please this new celebrity, the ladies crowded around the pair of all-most victims. Picking up the walking stick, Little Fawn took it back to Bright Moon.

"That was a good thing you did … and quickly thought out." Bright Moon beamed with admiration.

She shrugged. "It really wasn't something I thought about. I just did it." She leaned over and picked up her clothes.

"All the same, it was a good deed." Nodding toward the group of women, she added, "it will increase the stature of the Attikamekey should they choose to stay."

Little Fawn looked over at the gaggle of women, their tongues wagging, and shook her head in disbelief.

Bright Moon chuckled. "Like it or not, you've become the talk of their day."

Shaking the sand off her outfit, Little Fawn commented, "By the time the story reaches the village, the size and number of snakes will have grown."

Interrupting this scene, a parade of returning hunters carrying their prizes on poles came strutting down the path. "There you are," called Red Deer. "We heard a scream and thought you needed our help."

His message was rewarded by a scowl from Bright Moon and a scream from Little Fawn. She clutched her garment in front of her as she screamed, "No! You can't be here." She glowered at him "This is the women's bath!"

Unconcerned, he shrugged off her remarks saying, "I've been here before."

"I don't care. I'm here. You shouldn't be. I have nothing on. Leave!"

"It doesn't make a difference."

"LEAVE!"

Red Deer smirked. "But I took care of you on the raft when you were delirious."

"I'm not delirious now, so leave!"

Red Deer rejected her response. "We heard a scream and wanted to see …."

Bending down, Little Fawn picked up a fist-sized rock and set it flying his way. And then another. Red Deer managed to dodge the first missile. He wasn't as lucky with the second. It grazed his head, breaking the skin and raising a welt, but he wasn't deterred.

Discarding her outfit, Little Fawn began picking and throwing rocks with both hands. The air quickly filled with projectiles—too many to dodge—forcing Red Deer to beat a quick retreat. Reaching a safe distance, he turned to look back. Bright Moon wasn't happy. Little Fawn, naked, a rock in each hand, stood seething at his presence.

Wanting to test her resolve, Red Deer laughed as he took a step forward. "Hey, we just wanted to see if you needed help."

Cocking her arm back, she pitched a rock hard enough Red Deer had to move quickly to avoid being hit. With her mood still as black as night, she readied the next rock.

"If you want to help," Bright Moon said, "take the boughs from everyone's sleeping couch and replace them with freshly cut limbs. Put the old ones in a pile, and we can have a bonfire tonight after the celebration."

### 

A group of elders sat with Gray Wolf, discussing the plans for the night's celebration, when Red Deer and the hunting party reached the village. Seeing them, someone waved and called out, "My friends, I see your hunting trip has been successful."

Red Deer returned the greeting. The procession of hunters, animal carcasses slung on carry poles between them, realized they were under inspection and stood a little taller. Gray Wolf and the others, wishing to inspect the catch and swap hunting tales, quickly gathered around. The older members of the hunting party, hoping to appear seasoned, stood back waiting for recognition. The younger members, for some this was their first hunt, bubbled over with details. For them, the words couldn't come fast enough as they raced each other to give information.

The boldest of this group, was the first to burst out with his description. "We cut bushes to hide behind while we crawled toward the antelope."

Spurred on by this, another quickly said, "Silver Fox got the closest and got off a good shot before the animal bolted."

The older men chuckled and clapped Silver Fox on the back. His chest swelled at the mention of his name, but he said nothing.

Becoming wide-eyed, the storytellers raced on with their tale. "Yeah! And … and, while he waited, a boar—a big male—came out of the brush and charged him."

The group gasped at the event. They knew an encounter like this could end in disaster. Mention of the episode made the hairs on the back of Silver Fox's neck stand up. He tried not to let it show.

The young hunters continued their account. "Silver Fox planted an arrow in the beast as it charged." Admiring murmurs went up from the crowd. "It flipped over but got up again before he could get off another good shot." Anxious after hearing this revelation, the listeners were eager for the next detail.

"Silver Fox turned and led the boar toward us, and Crooked Foot speared it."

A cheer went up from the throng, and they gathered around Silver Fox and Crooked Foot. Everyone laughed. Chatter increased. A lot of back slapping followed as portions of this and other hunts were relived.

Silver Fox felt good about the hunt. He'd have felt better if Crooked Foot hadn't been mentioned. The glory would have been all his.

Crooked Foot's role had been remembered. For him, life was good.

Milling about, one of the elders noticed the wound on Red Deer's head. "Oh, my boy, how did you get that nasty cut?"

Before he could answer, a voice from the crowd replied, "I heard he had a run in with a wildcat!"

Laughter followed. Red Deer knew the story of his encounter with the girl would become known eventually, but he hadn't expected it to precede his arrival. Taking the good-natured ribbing in stride, he replied, "That's a story for another day."

His words produced more laughter, mixed with chattering, as events at the river were retold. Chagrinned, Red Deer sent his hunters to collect boughs as Bright Moon requested, while he arranged to have the meat prepared for the night's celebration.

# Chapter 24: Red Deer's Wound

"There," Red Deer said. "New boughs for your sleeping couches, these are the last ones." He turned to Bright Moon. "Anything else you need?"

"Sit down over here," she said.

Sitting cross-legged in the place she indicated—a mat bathed in sunlight in an otherwise dimly lit shelter—he asked, "What is it you want?"

"Hold still. I want to take a look at that cut." She bent close to peer at the gash.

Singing to herself, Little Fawn entered the shelter. Embarrassed, she stopped her song and glanced his way. Was he wrong or did scorn still smolder in her eyes?

"Daughter, come here and look at this," Bright Moon commanded. "My eyes aren't as good as they used to be."

Reluctantly, Little Fawn crossed the shelter, bent over him, and looked at the cut. "Hmmm. Skin is broken, a nasty cut." She peered at it a long time hoping to make him uncomfortable with her silence and finally asked, "How did you get it?"

"A hunting accident," he replied. "Rumor has it; I had an encounter with a wildcat!"

"A wildcat? A large one with big tusks?"

"No. A scrawny little runt. Mean! Contrary in nature and not at all good looking."

Hearing that, she reached out and poked a fingertip gingerly into the raw wound.

"Ouch!" Red Deer jumped.

"Oh, did that hurt the big hunter?" Her voice sticky

sweet with mock sympathy, she reached toward the wound again. "How about this? Does this hurt?" The sweetness in her voice had melted, leaving only venom in her tone.

He grabbed her by the wrist before she could carry out any more of her mischief.

Bright Moon intervened. "So, daughter, do you see anything? How should it be treated?"

Straightening up, Little Fawn pried her wrist free as she addressed Bright Moon's questions. "The skin is torn and pulled back, but it's still there. I'd clean it, apply a little extract of willow bark and then sew it up."

Bright Moon nodded agreement with each statement until the last. "Sew it up? This is something new. The Attikamekey have learned how to do this? How is that done?"

Nodding, Little Fawn smiled at Bright Moon. At last, she had something to show her teacher. "If you get me a small needle—the smallest you have—I can show you."

While Bright Moon brought out her sewing kit, Little Fawn cleaned the wound and coated the area with the extract.

"Well, here's what I have." Bright Moon held out a rawhide with a selection of carved bone needles tucked in the folds. Looking them over, Little Fawn picked up one then another, testing each for their sharpness and flexibility, until she found one that met her needs.

"Move over this way," she pointing to a slightly different place, "where there is more light. Put your back and head against that post and stay still."

Red Deer moved where he was told and sat cross-legged against the post. The women crowded around him.

"Wait!" he said.

"Wait?" Bright Moon asked. "What's wrong?"

Red Deer gave Bright Moon a sharp look. "You're not going to let *her* do this are you?"

"Well … my eyes aren't as good as they used to be …," she said. "She has done this before, so I'll stand over here and watch."

Having no choice, he pressed himself tight against the pillar. Little Fawn stepped closer, reached out and fingered his hair. Separating one long strand from the rest, she gave it a yank.

"Ouch!" He looked at her angrily. "What was that for?"

"Oh, does the big hunter need a bite-stick?" Turning her attention to Bright Moon she explained, "We've found using a person's own hair as the thread works better. I don't know why, but it does."

Turning back to Red Deer she commanded, "I have to get really close. Sit with your knees tucked up under your chin and slouch down a little."

Little Fawn waited while Red Deer settled into this new position then knelt at his side. Here, she'd be close enough to look directly at the wound. Concentrating on the task, she commanded, "Remain very still!"

Bright Moon stood close by, watching her every move.

Realizing she was the center of attention, Little Fawn suddenly felt embarrassed. A warm flush washed over her. Her nerves flared up twisting her stomach into a knot. She hoped no one noticed how her hand shook. A lot rested on this being successful. For everyone's sake, she wanted to do a good job.

*Breathe*, she told herself, *just remember to keep calm and breathe.*

Stretching to reach a better working position, she swayed gently. Instinctively, Red Deer's arms came up and wrapped around her. Moving forward with the needle, she paused giving him a stern look as she admonished him, "If you want this to turn out okay, remain still … very still!" Composing herself, she leaned close to him for support as she resumed her task.

His hands on her sides, Red Deer was surprised to find the calm exterior she projected shrouded the panicked beating of a wild heart.

Her fingers, gentle now, held his head steady as he felt the first poke of the sewing needle. This girl—no, this young woman—was an intriguing mystery. She could be demure one moment and aggressive the next. Red Deer wanted to know more about her. Such knowledge could be fatal … but he didn't care. He wanted to know more.

Smiling, Bright Moon watched the girl work. It seemed like peace was finally settling between the pair. She hoped this meant they would soon learn to appreciate each other.

### 

The Tribal Council, made up of members from each clan, sat on mats arranged on either side of Howling Wolf and Bright Moon. In front of them in their traditional rankings were Narwikin clan members, divided into two groups: Narwikin men sat in the front; unmarried young men behind them, followed by the women and, finally, the younger children in the back.

Between the two groups sat the surviving members of the Attikamekey, mostly women, children and the elderly. Unlike the Narwikin, their traditional ranking was men and women together, youths, and then children.

Wearing the shell necklace Red Deer had given her, Little Fawn, as spokesperson, sat crossed-leg in front of her group. Just behind her sat a man and woman. Between them, a small mound, contents concealed by a hide, sat undisturbed.

Earlier, as the full moon was breaking the horizon, a

drummer marched through the village. He thumped the ceremonial drum and called all able-bodied members to attend the council meeting, and they accompanied this rhythmic throb. With all collected now, the signal was given, and the drummer ceased.

All grew quiet as Howling Wolf rose to speak. Solemn-faced, arms folded over his chest, he addressed Little Fawn and the Attikamekey with her. "I am Howling Wolf, Chief of the Narwikin. Who speaks for these people in front of me?"

Mimicking his movements, Little Fawn rose smoothly to her feet and crossed her arms over her chest. A murmur arose from the Narwikin. This was a girl … a mere girl. What right does she have to speak?

"I am Little Fawn, daughter of White Owl, Shaman of the Attikamekey. I speak for my people."

Another murmur rippled through the Narwikin. Little Fawn felt a lump in her throat. Her heart seemed to be beating out of her chest. She feared her knees would knock, or worse yet, her legs would grow weak, buckle and she would collapse in a heap.

Howling Wolf came to her rescue. Raising both hands, he called for quiet, and then he went on with his interrogation. "Do the Attikamekey come as friends?"

"The Attikamekey's greatest wish is to be at peace with everyone."

"I would like to meet these people. Smoke the great pipe of friendship with their chief. Where would I go to find them?"

"Our village …" Taking a deep breath, she bit her lip and began again. "Our village is no more." A wail went up from some of the Attikamekey. "It had sat near a place where two great rivers meet and become one."

Murmurs went through the Narwikin.

Howling Wolf waited for the discussion to die before he went on. "You have come far from your village. What brings you here?"

"We were waiting for the return of the great fish when we were attacked in the night. The attackers put our village to the torch. Those not killed would have been made slaves. Some of us managed to escape on rafts."

The air swelled with discussion as the Narwikin talked among themselves. When this died down, she continued.

"Those of us here were on the last raft when our escape was discovered. The arrows of our enemy filled the air again and again."

She paused a moment and looked around. All eyes were on her as they waited to hear more. "My father and others gave their lives trying to protect the rest of us. Even then, we were wounded. Helpless, we drifted for days through all kinds of weather until a Narwikin, the one you call Red Deer, rescued us. With great effort, he brought us here where your people have cared for us."

Many beamed with pride and an approving undercurrent of conversation went around. Those nearest Red Deer gave him the warmest and loudest praise.

When things quieted once again, Howling Wolf continued, "So, what are your wishes?"

All eyes on her, Little Fawn fingered the necklace while she looked over her audience. Taking a deep breath, she started, "We have nothing except that which the Narwikin has generously provided. Still recovering from wounds, we're in no condition to go out on our own. It would please us to be accepted by the Narwikin." Another round of conversations broke out, and Little Fawn waited until it died before she continued.

"Although we have nothing, we don't come empty-handed because we have many ideas, many skills which we are willing to share. Our women work, hunt, fight alongside of our men. The abilities of Attikamekey women in battle have been clearly demonstrated." From the corner of her eye, she could see someone nudge Red Deer. A murmur—accompanied by stifled laughter—rolled through the crowd.

When that died, she continued, "Because of their contributions, women are considered equals and sit with their men at council." A noisy outburst followed. When quiet returned, she continued, "Along with new ideas, we also have many items to share."

Turning, she nodded to the couple behind her. The man parted the hide long enough to allow the woman to reach in, extract a set of arrows. Little Fawn held them out, points down, for all to see. Turning to face Howling Wolf, again, Little Fawn said, "These are offered for your consideration."

Howling Wolf nodded to an attendant, who brought them to him before returning to his post.

Inspecting each arrow, Howling Wolf noted the fine craftsmanship used in their construction, but the more interesting thing was the arrowheads. In the flickering torchlight, everyone noticed the golden-reddish tinge setting them apart. He tested the edge and found it sharper than flint arrows. The other end had been split; feathers inserted, and then bound shut. He passed the arrows to council members for their inspection. The council passed them to the clans. Everyone marveled over their construction.

As soon as the arrows left Howling Wolf's hands, Little Fawn nodded to the couple. They drew out the next piece, a small knife with a carved bone handle. The blade on the knife had the same golden-reddish tinge. Once again the attendant delivered the offering to his chief, but this time he couldn't help sneaking in a quick inspection of his own. The admiration and excitement he felt seemed to grow as the sharp-bladed knife passed from council member to council member.

Next came two bowls. The first, carved out of white alabaster, was polished smooth. The second, made from clay, was unlike any bowl the Narwikin had seen before. A Narwikin bowl was a reed basket covered with clay. This was made solely of clay. Its outside was decorated with a variety of colors and coated with a glaze. Having nothing like either bowl, the Narwikin were clearly impressed.

Finally, the last item was uncovered and the hide cast aside. It appeared to be a simple mat but highly decorated and very colorful. Narwikin mats were made of woven reeds. The Attikamekey soaked reeds in water, beat them to expose the fibers, and then used the fibers to make their mats. As it passed by each council member, those that touched it marveled over its softness, color, and design.

Inspection of each item brought conversations to a peak. Howling Wolf had the drummer beat a sequence on his drum, bringing quiet again. Taking advantage of the lull he said, "The Attikamekey have ideas different from our own. They have shown us many new things. We should take time to consider these and then discuss them." Again, everyone tried to talk at once. Howling Wolf held up his hands for quiet. "I understand you're eager to talk about everything you have seen and heard. The hunting party was successful. I think it a good idea that we talk on a full stomach." With that, he signaled the drummer who played a termination beat as he marched toward the door.

At the mention of food, the assembly—Narwikin, Clam Shell People, and Attikamekey alike—spilled out into the central clearing. Near one side, the antelope was being cooked over a bed of hot coals. Half buried among the coals were clay pots baking portions of boar meat. They would eat well tonight and this would put them in a good mood.

# Chapter 25: Shelter Construction

Feinting deep thought, Red Deer scratched his head. "Let me see if I understand this right." He paused, let them stew a few moments, and then gave them a look that some would say was more smirk than smile. "You're telling me that Tigal created a little contest and the winner gets a place in his caravan. Is that right?"

The boys nodded enthusiastically. They had given him a long story, omitting some of the facts and minimizing others in order to put their needs in the best light. They could have saved themselves the trouble. Red Deer, like everybody else in the village, was well aware of the rivalry between the two. He also knew that the pair of eager faces in front of him mirrored his own and that of his rivals when he was their age.

Red Deer looked from one to the other. "So, after hearing Tigal's challenge, you two decided to pair up and want me to build a shelter Tigal will like?" Red Deer looked at the boys' eager faces and decided he had tormented them long enough. "I guess I can give you some help, but you two have to do the work. Walk with me, okay?"

Silver Fox was ready. "Where should we build it? How about over there?"

Crooked Foot asked the more practical question. "How big do we make it?"

Red Deer laughed. "Well, the answers to your questions are, it depends."

His pair of young students gave him perplexed looks and then each began trying to outtalk the other. Patiently, Red Deer ignored this interplay and went on with his explanation. "It depends on where you are and what materials are available. Those factors determine what you are able to do."

Their chattering came to a standstill and the boys gave him another mystified look. So, Red Deer went deeper into the detail. "There are times when your needs are simple. You might brace your walking stick between something sturdy, like two tree trunks or two boulders. Throw a hide over it and peg down the edges with rocks."

He watched their expression to see if they understood. They mulled it over and then nodded. Satisfied, Red Deer went on. "Use a similar method when you shelter near the Great Ice, but pile snow on the edges to help keep out the cold. In hot, dry desert areas you could bury the edges under …."

Silver Fox interrupted. "Why do you need to keep warm in the desert?"

"Yeah," Crooked Foot chimed in, "it's already hot there."

"For desert areas, that's only partially true. There are two things you need to think about. If you stop midday, you'll need some protection from the sun. Stay overnight and you'll find it can get really cold."

Red Deer watched the boys, giving them time to think about his words before he went on. "To survive, you'll need to change your shelter type to fit your surroundings. Wherever you go you'll need protection, but there's no one shelter that'll fit all your needs. You need to know how to use whatever you find, wherever you stop to build temporary shelters that'll keep you warm and dry."

Silver Fox shook his head. "I've been out to Tigal's camp," he said. "His people have pretty sturdy shelters."

Red Deer explained. "Most of the time you'll only need a place for overnight, but sometimes the caravan has to stay longer so your shelter has to be sturdy."

Silver Fox came back with, "I've got my bedroll to keep me warm."

Crooked Foot gave him a puzzled look.

Silver Fox slapped his swelled chest and reported, "I went out and killed a couple of deer, skinned them, tanned the hides, and sewed them together into a pouch. It's nice and warm."

Red Deer smiled. "That's good; you'll need the bedroll, but you want something to keep the rain and snow off too, right?"

Silver Fox gave him a smug look. "I can wrap up in one of my sleep robes and I'll be nice and warm."

Both boys nodded vigorously. To them it seemed like a good idea and such an easy solution.

Red Deer smiled at their innocence and went on. "As a part of the caravan, you're going to be carrying a large pack of trade goods along with your own equipment. You can't discard the trade goods, but a few days on the trail may find you casting off your own gear, so I'm going to show you how to make a small debris hut. It's fairly easy to construct." He gave the boys a warm smile. "Put your bedroll in it, and you'll have a warm and dry place to spend a night or two."

Serious again, he went on, "The most important thing is the location. Don't build in low spots and stay away from standing dead trees 'cause you don't want anything falling over on you in a wind storm." That got a laugh out of his audience.

When the boys settled down again, Red Deer continued, "Take time to find a spot that feels right, a place that is close to the things you'll need to use to build your shelter and your campfire. A choice spot can save a lot of time and energy, but sometimes you have to adapt to whatever the surroundings provide. Show me what kind of spot you'd pick out around here."

Turning in a circle the pair looked around and finally agreed on a sandy spot on a slope, adjacent to a stand of fir trees and shaded by an oak.

"Yup, that looks like a good spot," Red Deer agreed, "Now, the first thing you'll need is a strong ridgepole. It should be a little longer than you with your arm stretched over your head. You'll also need something for one end of the ridgepole to rest on—a stump, boulder, a fork in a tree—something that'll prop it up in the air. The other end will rest on the ground. At the high end, the ridgepole should only be about waist high. That should give you enough room to crawl in and stretch out. Everybody with me so far?"

Seeing nodding heads, he continued. "Okay, find a ridgepole and get it set up."

The youngsters eagerly scampered off on their quest to return a short time later shouldering a log between the two of them. "We found a good one," they called.

"Good. I think it is bigger than you need, but it will work. Set it up against the tree and brace the base."

They jammed one end of the pole into the ground and forced the other tightly against the trunk of the oak. Satisfied, they stepped back to admire their work.

Red Deer didn't let them bask in their success for long. "Once your ridgepole is in place, you'll need to collect ribbing for the sides. Use short, thin logs and branches; lean them against the ridgepole fairly close together. Make sure you remember the opening—your entrance—will be at the high end. " He looked from one to the other. Neither one had questions. "Okay, go find the ribbing and put it in place."

Off again, the boys retuned after a few minutes, their arms piled high. Dumping their loads nearby, they began putting up the ribbing.

"Once the ribs are in place, crawl inside feet first and

check to see that it's still snug and cozy. If your shelter is too big you'll have trouble staying warm. If it's too small, you could roll over in the middle of the night, knock it down and wake the whole caravan."

The youngsters chuckled at that idea.

Getting serious once again, Red Deer went on, "Okay, after the ridgepole and ribbing is in place you can add a layer of lattice, something to hold debris in place when it's piled. Brush with twiggy branches works well."

"The lattice," Silver Fox interrupted, "how tight should it be?"

Red Deer clapped him on the shoulder. "Good question. The answer is that it depends on the debris available. Small stuff requires a tight lattice while large stuff can use a loose lattice."

The boys nodded and he continued. "The structure is now in place, and it's time to add insulation. Shuffle your feet or use branches to make yourself a rake and then start gathering debris! For good insulation, you'll want material that can trap air. Obviously, it's best to use dry material, but take care to keep your campfire away or you'll end up burning your shelter down." Grinning, he added, "Probably don't want to do that."

Laughing at the idea, the boys began scraping up piles of leaves, ferns, grass and other available debris.

"Keep piling, keep piling, till you have enough to go about the distance from your fingertips to your elbow," Red Deer instructed. "Remember, if you don't want to get rained on, deeper is better."

Smiling broadly, Crooked Foot and Silver Fox chorused, "Don't want to get wet."

"Good. Finish up your insulation by adding some small branches that'll hold the debris in case of wind."

"Is that it? Are we done building our shelter?"

"Not quite. Be sure to close up the door area so you've just enough room to squeeze in without disturbing the structure. Crawl in to see how your cocoon feels. Now with the outer layer complete, it's time to stuff your shelter with dry, soft debris. If you don't have dry leaves, wet ones will do. You may get wet, but you can still be warm. Once your shelter is full of debris, wiggle in to compress a space for your body. Add more debris as needed, and don't forget the foot area! Fill up the spaces if you're concerned about being cold. Before you crawl into the shelter for the night, gather a pile of leaves near the door so you can close yourself in most of the way."

He looked from boy to boy and then at the shelter. They had followed the directions well. It was a good piece of work and he was satisfied. "Working together, you've done well, Narwikin. You've done well ... together."

# Chapter 26: New Arrivals

In the Narwikin village, as in most villages the caravan passed through, the men took time to inspect and repair their equipment. It was different here because of the long-standing bond of friendship that existed between Tigal's people and the Narwikin.

Unlike time spent at other villages, here they felt at home. At least as at home as these vagabonds would ever know. Single men and women looked for suitable mates. The families among Tigal's group took time to visit with friends and relatives in their clans as well as within the Narwikin clans. Tigal's men went hunting with the Narwikin when the tribe went hunting. They went fishing with the Narwikin when the tribe fished. The children of both tribes played together. Even the animals, herded onto a grassy meadow, took time to relax as they foraged.

Interrupting everyone's relaxation, youngsters ran into the village breathlessly shouting news. "Many people … on rafts … up river. We were … hunting … in the swamp … we came 'cross country … ran all the way."

The Narwikin had already taken in a number of refugees and talk of raids was a constant subject around their campfire. The possibility of attack had become foremost in Howling Wolf's mind. He listened carefully to the youngsters, and then held up his hands for quiet. Pointing to the oldest member there he asked, "How many rafts did you see? One hand, two hands, more?"

The youth's face lit up. "More than two hands for sure, but no one stayed long enough to count how many."

Hearing that response, Howling Wolf nodded and asked, "Tell me about the people. Were they men alone, men and women, or men, women and children?" *Men alone could mean a war party*, he reasoned. *Men and women together would mean a hunting party. Men, women and children would more than likely be a tribe on the move.*

"Men and women, I'm sure it was men and women together." The youngster replied confidently.

"I heard a baby's cry …." Everyone turned to this new voice.

The speaker, Bright Moon's apprentice, Abeytu—oldest child of White Bird and Little Rabbit—stood before him covered from head to toe in mud. She didn't cringe under anyone's inspection. Chin out, she stood firm with no remorse for speaking out.

"A baby's cry … you're sure?" Howling Wolf asked. He spoke without inflection in his voice or expression on his face so he wouldn't intimidate the girl. He needed information and didn't want to influence what she was saying.

"Yes sir. I was separated from the others when the rafts came 'round the bend. I had to hide, so I lay flat in the mud behind a muskrat's burrow until they passed. I couldn't see the people, but I heard a baby's cry." Howling Wolf knew this girl would know the sound of a baby's cry. Her mother, Little Rabbit—aptly named—had several children already and was heavy with child again this year.

Howling Wolf nodded. "You've done well, Narwikin." He saw the young girl's chest swell with pride at the praise. Turning to the others, he said, "You have all done well. We now have time to prepare for guests; or to defend ourselves. However they wish to be greeted."

From upriver came muffled shouts, could these be fierce cries or cheers? No one was sure.

More youngsters, stragglers from the original hunting party, exploded out of the brush yelling, "They caught Small Turtle! They caught Small Turtle!"

### ###

Waving Grass and her people had been on the water for two moons now. They searched the rivers for signs that family members had traveled this way, but found nothing. Their efforts drained her and her people of their strength and their will to go on. *Would today be any different? Yes, it would,* she told herself, *and something tells me we're very close. Today will be the day. Her people, as weary as she, were ready to give up, but they knew they owed it to their tribesmen to continue. Today had to be the day!*

Ashore, water splashed near where the river blended into the marsh. More splashing and then a goose exploded from the rushes that grew on the shore side of a small sandbar. Suspicious! Startled waterfowl would have flown away sooner.

She signaled the rafts behind hers to head for shore. They would land above the disturbance blocking escape in that direction. Letting the current carry her vessel past the sandbar, she directed the paddlers to steer for shore below the commotion.

Two men from her raft slipped quietly into the water and waded toward the sandbar as her craft approached the river's edge. As soon as it came to a halt, she leaped onto the sand, club in hand, covering the space to the rushes in a few strides. Others followed behind her; groups from the remaining vessels did the same.

A youth—hardly more than seven or eight summers—bolted from the reeds and made a leap toward the sanctuary offered by the river and deep water. If he made it there, he could disappear under the surface and get away.

Crouching in shallow water, hidden from him by the rushes, the two men from the lead raft sprang up and caught the lad before he reached his goal. Though he struggled to free himself, strong hands held him. He couldn't get away.

The men carried their struggling captive aboard a raft. The next craft in line pulled alongside and a mob gathered.

"What do you want with me?" Small Turtle, although gripped tightly, was defiant.

The throng formed around the boy and his captors parted, allowing a tall, slim woman to pass and then it closed after her. Arriving from another direction, someone produced a couple of geese secured with a rawhide. They were the sum of Little Turtle's catch.

Nodding to the guards, she sat down and they released him. "Sit with me," the woman said. She patted the mat softly for emphasis. "I wish to talk."

Free from their grip, the lad frantically looked around for an escape route, but found himself surrounded by armed warriors. He looked at the woman sitting patiently in front of him. Thin, she looked tired, worn, as if she carried a great weight. Her dark eyes watched his every move. "You fought bravely, honorably, but you cannot escape."

Her quiet voice, her soft words were comforting and carried no note of threat. "We mean you no harm. There is no point in struggling longer." She smiled encouragingly, patted the mat again, and quietly repeated her request. "Sit with me. I wish to talk."

Slowly, he sank into a cross-legged position across from her. She rewarded him with another warm smile.

Mimicking the posture Narwikin elders took when in formal meetings, Small Turtle folded his arms over his chest and attempted to appear confident. Raising his chin, he boldly looked her in the eye and said, "I am Small Turtle, Hunting Brave of the Narwikin."

A tittering of laughter greeted his pronouncement, but it was immediately stifled after a scorching glare from the woman.

She pointed to the birds. "Well, Hunting Brave,

you've done well for yourself." She honored him by using the formal title he had used and not his name. "Tell me, how did you manage to catch so many birds?"

His face lit with pride, Small Turtle explained, "I lay hidden under a mat. When they get close, I slip into the water, swim under them and grabbed their feet." Proudly pointing to the birds on the leash, he added, "Then I tie them up."

That explained the ruckus that attracted their attention earlier. Raising her eyebrows, she exclaimed, "Oh, how interesting. Is this something your people do?"

Nodding, Small Turtle said nothing but watched her closely, trying to read her sincerity.

"I would like to visit your village, trade with your people. We could learn much from each other." She stopped and waited to hear from him, but Little Turtle made no reply.

Knowing he might not give up any information voluntarily, the woman searched his face for some sign of an acknowledgment hiding there. "I ... we," she motioned with one hand to include those who surrounded them. "We come from far away. Our village was at a place where two great rivers meet to become one. Two moons ago, during the night, we were attacked. Those of us here were the first to slip away, reach the river, and escape. These very rafts carried us to safety."

Seeing a glimmer of recognition in the boy's eyes, quickly suppressed, she continued, "Some of our people, the last group to slip away, were separated from us. After a few days, we sent scouts back to the village to search for them. They found only ruins ... and our dead. We don't know if the others managed to escape, or if they did, where they are. They are our people and we have been looking for them ever since." Pausing, she let her words set in before continuing. "Since then, we searched many of the rivers that branch off the great river that provided our escape. It has been a long search. We have grown tired."

Silent now, weariness clearly visible in her face, her tearful eyes pleaded with him as she said, "I am Waving Grass, daughter of Running Buffalo, Chief of the …."

Interrupting her, Small Turtle spoke one word. Almost a whisper, but it caught everyone's attention. "Attikamekey."

Frozen by the sound of that word, a word she had longed to hear, but had almost lost hope in ever hearing again, it took a moment for her to come to her senses.

"Attikamekey." Had she really heard him say it? A gasp, followed by a murmur, rippled through the crowd as those closest repeated the boy's remark to those farther back.

Realizing it was true, Waving Grass dove across the space between them and wrapped Small Turtle in a bear hug. Still holding him close, almost smothering him in her arms, she jumped to her feet and danced around happily screaming, "Attikamekey! Attikamekey!"

Shouts and cheers went up from the crowd, and everyone began dancing. Hearing herself say that word made her giddy. Head spinning, she addressed her people. "At last my friends, we've found our people. Rejoice! We've found our people!"

### 

There wasn't much time to prepare. Howling Wolf sent word to Tigal and then had the Narwikin retreat to the safety of the stockade. Following his instructions, the braves remained there as well. He, council members, and a couple of runners, sat on mats spread under a tree. They didn't have to wait long.

Nosing the rafts onto the sandy beach, the Attikamekey waded ashore and grouped up. There was no one around to greet them, but their presence was no secret. Ram's horns had sounded long before they saw the beach where they came ashore.

Waving Grass, walking hand-in-hand with Small Turtle, followed her advanced scouts along the path up the hill. Her people, except for those left on the rafts with the youngest children, followed closely behind, weapons close but not obvious. Stopping at the top of the hill, they surveyed their surroundings.

A shallow swale lay before them. Cresting the next hill lay the Narwikin village surrounded by a thin stockade. It looked much like her own village had looked.

The village gate, left half-open, sent the message it could be opened for friends but closed to enemies. Alongside the barricade, a mastodon bearing armed men sauntered up. Even though she couldn't see them, she knew that inside the stockade were more armed warriors.

Close by, a group sat calmly in the shade of an old oak tree ready to talk. Another clear message—peace or war—everyone appeared to be waiting for them ... for their next move.

Leaving her side, Small Turtle broke into a run toward the group in the shade, shouting, "Attikamekey ... Attikamekey ...."

Hearing that message, Howling Wolf leaned over and said something to a youth within the group. Hopping to his feet, the youngster ran for the stockade. After a short delay, he returned with a young woman in tow.

Waving Grass watched her cross the space from the stockade to the shade tree, her long, dark hair streaming out behind her as she ran. Even at this distance, there was something familiar about her, something that reminded her of a younger girl, one on the verge of womanhood. The pair took a seat under the tree behind the others.

Howling Wolf stood, held his hands out palms up to show they were empty and then crossed his arms over his chest. Small Turtle beckoned Waving Grass forward. Motioning for her people to stay, she walked toward the shade tree empty hands held out for all to see. When they were a few paces apart, she stopped and they sized each other up.

Waving Grass thought him handsome, dark hair in braids, slightly graying at the temples, dark eyes, tall, muscular; he wore few adornments, almost none of the trappings of rank, except for worry lines.

He found her to be an attractive young woman, aged by the burden of leadership. Long dark hair pulled back and held in place with a rawhide tie.

Howling Wolf greeted her. "I am Howling Wolf, Chief of the Narwikin. In peace I greet you."

Returning his greeting, Waving Grass started, "I am Waving Grass, daughter of …."

Another voice interrupted hers. "Running Buffalo, Chief of the Attikamekey."

Stunned, she looked past Howling Wolf at the group sitting in the shade. The speaker, the young woman, the one summoned from the stockade, was on her feet now and plainly visible. Her heart leaped. It was Little Fawn. "My sister! You live!"

Her voice, cracking from emotion, Little Fawn responded, "Yes, I … we live … because of our Narwikin friends."

# Chapter 27: Attikamekey

For two moons, Waving Grass drove the Attikamekey in their search for their lost people. Now they were finally together again, but they were exhausted from their efforts. Sitting in the shade with the Narwikin council, this young woman was both relieved and drained.

Recognizing this, Howling Wolf invited her and her people to spend time with the Narwikin. "You … your people have been through much," he told her. "Stay with us while you recover. Give yourselves time to think. The Narwikin people are willing to share. We could learn from each other." Council members chorused their agreements.

"I … I don't know what to say," Waving Grass stammered.

Little Fawn spoke up, "My sister, after we escaped, we were wounded and in no condition to care for ourselves. Our raft was adrift. We were dying. Then a Narwikin, the one called Red Deer, found us and brought us here. We would've perished if it weren't for the aid these people provided."

Another voice cut in. "My hunting party returned to find our village sacked," White Badger told her. "My people had been slain or carried off into slavery. A few survived and returned to us, but I knew it would make little difference. We were left to continue by ourselves, but there were so very few of us that we could not. Then a Narwikin, the one called Crooked Foot, came and invited us to come here and join with his people."

"Let me speak what is in my heart." Waving Grass looked at each of those facing her. "Since the night we were attacked, my people have spent day and night searching for lost friends. They are exhausted and need rest, but I fear if we stay too long we won't want to move on."

"Would that be such a bad thing?" Little Fawn asked. "Those of our people who survived with me did so because of the care we received at the hands of the Narwikin. We found comfort here."

Her face showing the turmoil she was feeling, Waving Grass said, "It would mean more mouths to feed."

"We were faced with the same questions you now face," White Badger said, "but we knew we couldn't continue on our own. By ourselves we were few, but by joining the Narwikin there are more hands to plant and gather; more to hunt and fish, and each tribe has a place on the council."

"What has been told is true," Howling Wolf said. "Many generations ago, there were no Narwikin. Then several small clans realized they would be stronger, and could do more, if they banded together. They agreed that each clan provide a member to sit on the council. That gives them a voice and their needs are recognized. Eventually, other clans also joined this group. Today, descendants of these people are the Narwikin."

Fatigue sapped her strength. These stories were overwhelming, and she was at a loss for words.

Howling Wolf came to her rescue again. "You don't have to decide now," he said, "let us sit together and eat. The Narwikin will share their shelters. When you've rested, you can decide. In the meantime, you have a place on the council so you can make known the needs of your people."

She was impressed. He seemed—they all seemed—genuinely concerned, although she wasn't sure if it was her or her people's welfare that concerned him. She decided to set the question aside; food and rest would do them all good. "I agree, my people are tired and need rest."

Howling Wolf nodded. Turning to the council, he said, "Go now. Ask the people to bring food here to share and make room in their homes for our guests."

The meeting ended, the council and on-lookers began the organized chaos of rearrangements necessary to carry out their chief's request.

Bright Moon looked from Waving Grass to Howling Wolf. "My chief, do you remember the prediction I made when Red Deer left on his sojourn?"

Howling Wolf frowned, and then slowly answered. "The one about his return?"

A cryptic smile on her face, Bright Moon nodded, "Yes, that very one." Turning to Waving Grass, she asked, "Tell me, where is your man?"

Caught off-guard, Waving Grass raised her eyebrows. The old woman who had sat beside Howling Wolf was nothing if not abrupt. Recovering her composure, she lowered her eyes and managed to choke out, "He sleeps-the-sleep-from-which-no-one-wakes ... as do our sons."

Bright Moon gave Howling Wolf a sharp look. "So does your woman ... you both have had to shoulder the burden of leadership alone far too long." Getting to her feet, Bright Moon turned to Little Fawn and said, "Go help Waving Grass with the arrangements. Then bring her to our shelter so she can rest. It would be good for you and her to have time together."

### 

"... so with the recent additions to our tribe, we're running out of places for people to stay." Bright Moon paused to gauge Crooked Foot's reaction.

The lad thought about her proposal. "This is just temporary, right?" he asked.

"Yup! Once things get situated, you can move back here if you want. Right now, I need to make room for Waving Grass. I think it will be best if she and Little Fawn are together until I am able to make other arrangements."

Crooked Foot's head spun. He did not know what his grandmother meant about *making other arrangements.* Still puzzled, he knew there was no use arguing so he asked, "Where should I go?"

"How about the shelter you told me about, the one you and Silver Fox built?"

He brightened; that idea changed everything. "I hadn't thought of that. It would be a good place and I could see how it works out before Tigal's caravan leaves."

Bright Moon gave him a broad smile. "Sure. You can still come here to eat. I just need the sleeping space. I've some hides you can use to make yourself a sleeping bag. That should make you more comfortable in your new quarters."

"Yeah, especially since this place is going to be overrun with wimmin[33] ...." Making a face, he let his voice trail off as he gave her a sidewise glance.

Still smiling, she reached out and tousled his hair. "I'll give you wimmin ...."

### ###

Pointing to a sleeping couch Little Fawn explained, "Bright Moon sleeps over there. You can sleep here or over here."

Waving Grass looked at the eager girl through her tired eyes. "Where will you sleep?"

Eager to please, Little Fawn simply said, "Whichever place you choose, I'll sleep in the other."

Warmed by Little Fawn's eagerness, Waving Grass smiled. "I mean, where do you sleep now?"

"Over there."

"Then I'll sleep here."

---

[33] Wimmin - Women. Crooked Foot was teasing his grandmother.

231

"Good," Bright Moon interjected. "That's settled. Now we can eat." She motioned to Little Fawn to dish out some stew from the pot bubbling over the fire and then plopped herself down on a mat. Waving Grass took a place next to her. The stew's aroma reminded Waving Grass she hadn't eaten yet today. She gratefully accepted the steaming bowl Little Fawn handed her. Then Little Fawn, her own bowl in hand, took a seat facing her older idols.

Their first bowls disappeared quickly, but they lingered over the second, enjoying the warm feeling, and taking time to chat. The day had been full of surprises, but Waving Grass didn't know her biggest surprise was yet to come.

A mastodon's trumpeting sounded. Squeals of delight followed.

Little Fawn got up and peeked out the door. Returning to her seat, she said, "Looks like Makata is showing off for the children."

Waving Grass raised an eyebrow. "Is that the mastodon I saw earlier?"

"Tigal, the Caravan Master, and his people use animals—mostly horses, camels, and a few mastodons—to carry their baggage." Pausing, Little Fawn filled her bowl again before continuing. "They've stopped here to rest before moving on."

The Attikamekey were never visited by a caravan and Waving Grass was curious about this routine. "How often do they return?"

Little Fawn shrugged and looked at Bright Moon for an answer.

Thoughtfully, the old woman blew on her stew bowl before she finally replied, "Once every four or five summers … depending on which paths they choose to follow."

Waving Grass shook her head. "Don't know that I

could live that kind of life."

Little Fawn chimed in with a hearty, "Me either!"

"It gets in your blood," Bright Moon replied. "You get so you always want to see what's over the next hill."

Both younger women stopped sipping their stew and gave her all their attention.

Seeing that she had an interested audience, Bright Moon added, "I was born in a caravan like that. We traveled all over, and I got to see many things ... meet many people."

Little Fawn was puzzled. "But you're here ... those who speak of you—Crooked Foot, Red Deer and others—say you've always been here."

Bright Moon patted the girl on the knee. "Except for Howling Wolf, those who would know otherwise have long ago gone into the sleep-from-which-no-one-wakes. Many of the ones you mentioned came along after I decided to linger here. They know nothing else."

"But ... but ... Tigal, the other men, don't they know?" Little Fawn was dumbfounded.

"Know?" Bright Moon scoffed. "What does any man know? They hunt and fish. It's the women who plant and gather ... it's the women who care for things ... it's the women who remember ... it's the women who *know*!" Cackling, she slapped her thigh and said, "What does a man know?"

Mystified, Little Fawn watched as Bright Moon doubled-over with laughter. Turning to Waving Grass for an explanation, she saw tears streaming down the woman's face as she joined in the merriment. Little Fawn stood and waited while they recovered.

Wiping tears from her eyes, Bright Moon said, "Speaking of men, how long has yours been gone?"

Composing herself, Waving Grass said, "It's been two summers. My man ... my two sons ... were on the river when a storm came. There was fire-from-the-sky … and it took them ….” As she spoke, her voice dropped and she became quiet.

“What of his other women?”

“I was his only mate.” When it happened, Waving Grass hoped that the messenger, the bearer of this news, was wrong. She had hoped that what was told her didn't happen to her mate, her children. Now, knowing she would have to face what she had previously hidden away from herself, what she fought to hold back, what she had been unable to release back then. The young woman raised her head and the old woman could see the tears trickle down her cheeks.

An awkward silence followed until Bright Moon roused herself. Leaning close to the sobbing woman, she wrapped an arm around her shoulder and told her, “You have been through so much, but now it is over. I can see that you are tired. Relax here, among friends and get some rest. Two summers! Far too long for you to be alone.”

The old woman motioned to Little Fawn. “I need to make some arrangements. See that our guest gets some rest." Getting to her feet, Bright Moon found her walking stick. “Yellow Flower, Howling Wolf's woman—his only woman— has been gone a long time.” She ignored their looks as she headed for the door. “The burdens of leadership are too great to bear alone. It would bring the two tribes together. I'll arrange it.”

Mouths agape, both Waving Grass and Little Fawn stared after the old woman as she left.

# Chapter 28: Proposal

Stunned, Howling Wolf was speechless. He stared into the old woman's face as if seeing it for the first time.

Waiting for his response, Bright Moon grew impatient and started again. "Yellow Flower is gone—has been gone for some time—leaving you alone to carry the burdens of your position. You need someone you can turn to, someone like yourself, who knows the joys and penalties of being a leader."

Rejecting the idea, Howling Wolf shook his head. "Losing one mate was enough for me."

"Listen to me!" Bright Moon was starting to anger, and it showed. "Yellow Flower is gone! There is nothing you can do about that."

Howling Wolf shrugged. "The Narwikin are a tribe of many clans. I couldn't take a mate from one clan without upsetting the others, and I can't take a mate from each clan just to keep the peace."

She grew exasperated with his slowness. "They arrived when Sister Moon turned her face to us. It was a good sign. Our tribes work well together. Now our Sister turns her face toward us again. The timing is perfect. This woman is perfect. You'll not find a better match or a better time. It will bring the two tribes together without upsetting the clans."

"What about the woman? Is all of this acceptable to her?"

"Her name is Waving Grass! You should get used to calling her that," Bright Moon scolded. "She's tired now, but is considering it. So should you. Then present yourself to her at dinner."

For emphasis, she slammed the tip of her walking

stick into the ground, adding, "Tonight!"

### 

Still shaking his head, Howling Wolf followed in Bright Moon's steps as she shuffled through the woods. A steady stream of thoughts and emotions boiled in his head. *I don't know why we jump when she speaks, but we do. I probably should think about that more, but she has years of wisdom ... more than any of the rest of us ... and no one can remember her being wrong ... ever.*

"My friend," Tigal called warmly, "I am happy to see you ... even happier to see this day come."

Without Howling Wolf realizing it, Bright Moon had led him along an unfamiliar path to Tigal's camp. Surprised by this, he was left nearly speechless and struggled for a reply, finally managing, "This day ...? What is this?" Howling Wolf was mystified.

Everyone laughed. When they settled down again, Tigal answered. "Bright Moon came to me to ask for help with the arrangements. She told me of the opportunity you have and I, that is my people and I, agreed to help."

"Help? Help with what?"

Realizing that Howling Wolf was still lost, Tigal cleared things up by adding, "Your wedding! My wives made a wedding suit for you. We have other gifts for you to present to your bride."

"My ... bride?"

"Yes, if you expect to win Waving Grass over you need to dress for the occasion and have nice gifts for her."

"Come this way and see what my wives have for you?" Pleased with himself, Tigal chuckled as they walked. "I ... my people, have waited a long time for this." Again, he laughed heartily slapping Howling Wolf on the back. "It's finally here."

Still puzzled, Howling Wolf glanced at Bright Moon.

She said nothing but did a bad job of hiding a mischievous smile. *What else has she been up to?*

Smiling warmly at their approach, Tigal's wives sat under awnings near his tent. At a nod from Tigal, his first wife rose and made a show of spreading a sable robe. Sounds of appreciation from his other wives filled the air. Then another wife rose and laid out a string of pearls, jet-black intermixed with ivory. The third presented a turquoise necklace.

Together, they brought out a soft buckskin tunic and breeches, both decorated with colored stones and feathers.

"I don't know, this is all so quick, and I haven't spoken to her, Waving Grass I mean. I haven't made a place for us. Then there's the celebration. I'm unprepared."

"We knew all of this. Our peoples—the Narwikin, the Clam Shell, the Attikamekey, and my clans—have worked to expand the village to provide for all the new people. Bright Moon arranged for a new shelter for you. Our peoples went hunting and fishing. There's plenty of food, and it's ready for this occasion." Pleased with himself, Tigal smiled broadly.

Howling Wolf's head was spinning. He barely managed to stumble through a reply. "My friends, I don't know what to say…"

"Say nothing." Bright Moon prodded him along. "Go make yourself presentable, and then go see Waving Grass. We'll take care of the rest."

### 

"Hold still!" Little Fawn knelt behind the nervous woman seated in front of her. "I can't get the flowers woven in your hair with you fidgeting around all the time."

Sitting up straighter, Waving Grass anxiously smoothed the folds of the new dress Bright Moon had brought her. "What do you think? Is it the right thing to do?"

"Yes, it is. Bright Moon said it will bring the tribes together because it will blend the Attikamekey and Narwikin peoples. She also said it would be good for the both of you."

Worried, Waving Grass began to fret. "Maybe it's too soon. Maybe we should wait until the tribes know each other better ... until we know each other."

Fire in her eyes, Little Fawn lashed out, "Maybe! Maybe! Maybe! Maybe, if you delay, the Attikamekey will become just like all the other clans within the tribe, and you'll lose the opportunity." Her hands flew around Waving Grass's head as she completed the flower weave.

"There!" Little Fawn said triumphantly. "I finished the flowers in spite of you."

Getting to her feet she moved around to face Waving Grass, "Stand up and let me take a look at you."

Meekly, Waving Grass rose and stood inspection, worried some last minute detail would ruin everyone's plans.

Little Fawn looked her over approvingly. "Good! You're freshly bathed. You have a beautiful dress. Your hair is done. The food is ready .... My job is finished! The rest is up to you."

Concern, bordering on panic, flashed in Waving Grass's eyes. "What if ...." She started.

Little Fawn cut her off. "You're beautiful. He is wise and kind. I know him to be a gentle man ... who, like you, is lonely. Relax, everything will be all right." Smiling, she added. "You know I should be jealous. As representative of the Attikamekey, you'll be taking my place on the council ... and Crooked Foot will take your sleeping couch in Bright Moon's lodge."

Waving Grass gave the girl a quizzical look. "Is that a bad thing?"

Little Fawn raised her eyebrows. "He snores."

Laughing they shared a warm embrace. Hearing male

voices nearby, Little Fawn gave her one last squeeze, saying, "They're here. I must go now. Remember, if everything goes okay, you're to drop the door flap. It'll be the start of your new life together. If he leaves before then, everyone will think you rejected him."

### 

Tigal at his side, Howling Wolf, dressed in his new outfit, slowed his step a short distance from the new shelter. He shifted the bundle tucked under his arm. He was told that Waving Grass was inside nervously waiting for him. That knowledge didn't make it any easier. He turned to look at his friend for reassurance.

Day had faded into dusk, but Tigal could still read Howling Wolf's features. He spoke quietly, "Is this not like going on your first hunt?"

Howling Wolf chuckled. "Worse I think! It's been so long, I don't know if I remember what to do."

Tigal nodded, and they started forward again. "Bright Moon has spoken with the woman. She is strong and a good leader. If it was not acceptable, we would have heard before now."

Howling Wolf knew that these were well-meant words of comfort from his close friend, but they did little to still the butterflies he still experienced.

As they neared the shelter, Little Fawn emerged. Her appearance cut off any response Howling Wolf might have made. Looking straight ahead, as if they weren't there, she passed nearby without saying a word, but a poorly suppressed smirk spoke volumes.

Glancing at the open doorway, Tigal said, "I believe everything is ready. Good hunting!" He clapped his friend on the shoulder and then walked away leaving Howling Wolf alone.

Throat dry, Howling Wolf entered.

Lamps of burning animal fat provided a warm glow and softened the near emptiness of this new dwelling. Waving Grass, her back turned to the door, stood on the far side of room. Hoping to get her attention, he announced his presence with a light cough.

At the sound, she turned and smiled softly. "The mighty Narwikin Chief has come to visit me. I am honored."

Howling Wolf looked around as if he were looking for someone else. Returning her gaze, he tipped his head slightly saying, "I see no one else here but you and me."

"Really? And who are you?"

"I am but a man, a Narwikin hunting brave." Holding out the bundle he added, "I come bearing courtship gifts."

She sat down cross-legged on a mat in a pool of lamp-light and pointed to a place opposite her. Smiling shyly, she asked, "Are these things you created? Would you show them to me?"

Sitting down across from her, he laid out each item, watching her reaction as he did. Was she as nervous as he felt? She appeared confident. "They are things of great beauty, things my friends picked out for me to present," he said.

Impressed by the selection, by the fact his friends would provide items of such beauty, her eyebrows went up, and she said, "These are beautiful. Your friends think a lot of you, but what does the Narwikin hunting brave bring?"

Howling Wolf looked down at his hands. He needed time to think. The drumming of his heart seemed to fill the night, muffle other sounds, and impede his thinking.

When he looked up, their eyes met, and he spoke softly, "I bring a promise. I will respect you. Treat you as an equal. We will act together. We will work together. It is all I have."

Swallowing hard, she said nothing, but her eyes seemed to take on a shine. It reminded him of Yellow Flower's eyes when she was too happy to speak. She rose without saying anything, went to the door and lowered the flap.

Night has its own set of voices—crickets chirp, frogs croak, wolves howl at the moon, breezes rustle trees and bushes—but not this night.

Up to this time, everything had been quiet, as if the evening stopped and held its breath … but no longer. As sudden as a lightning strike, general bedlam broke out. The stillness was shattered by the din of rams' horns, cheers, whoops, and the beating of drums.

Holding out a hand to him, Waving Grass said, "My man, you have brought me great happiness. Let us go out and greet our people. They wish to celebrate."

# Chapter 29: Trade Fair

Now rested, Tigal's clans were ready to begin trading. To reach those villages too small or too far off the regular trail to be worthwhile, Howling Wolf and Tigal declared a trade fair to start at the next full moon. Runners went out to spread the word to anyone within three-days' travel. News of the event was something each of these small settlements eagerly anticipated. Hearing this announcement, clans made plans to pack their goods and make the trek to the Narwikin village.

The village of the Narwikin would take on a festive atmosphere for the next three days. The first day would be filled with many dinners as friends and extended families came together. The next day would be filled with games and contests for everyone. Once the festivities concluded, the business of trading would begin.

The afternoon before the fair, Tigal's people put on a special dinner for their Narwikin hosts. Dishes of maize, rabbit, goose and salmon in front of them, they shared the meal and talked. Attendants scurried about, bringing more dishes or filling drinking gourds with fermented chicha. Howling Wolf opened the conversation with a question. "Now that you're rested, what adventures do you look forward to this trip?"

As an answer, Tigal called for a pouch and instructed his man to empty the contents on the mat in front of the group. Council members and clan chiefs were surprised when rocks clattered out. Bright veins in the stones sparkled in the afternoon sun and caught Howling Wolf's attention. He reached for the nearest one, then stopped to look at Tigal to make sure he approved.

Tigal slapped him on the back and laughed, "Go ahead, my friend. Take a closer look."

Picking up the nearest, he noticed it showed tinges of green along exposed gold faces. "Where did you get this?"

"Our travels often take us to the land of the Sea People where we trade for salt." Tigal looked at his friend, and then off in the distance as he recalled the events. "After leaving there, great rains came. The rivers flooded, and we had to go a long way off our usual route. In doing so, we came across a tribe we had never met before. They were on their way to new lands, and they needed to make some trades to keep going." He paused to take a breath and then went on with, "The people, their language and customs were strange to us." He shrugged a little as he went on, "Bargaining, they traded for the usual stuff, but they needed more than they had goods to trade. We were going to take our leave when they reluctantly brought out some special objects they used in their ceremonies. I was able to make a trade for a few of these."

Laughing a little, Howling Wolf looked at his friend. "Traded goods for these? Have you gone soft, or is there more to it than this?"

At Tigal's signal, his attendant stepped forward and laid a bundle on the mat. "As always, my friend, you are chief of the Narwikin because you are wise. As you suspected, there is more involved. This is another part of it."

Carefully unwrapping the bundle, Tigal passed its contents to Howling Wolf for his examination. It was a thin wooden knife with a carved bone handle. The covering on the blade, a layer of golden material, gave it an edge like few had experienced.

Turning away, Howling Wolf called an attendant, issued some instructions and then turned back to face Tigal. "Not long ago this would have been a surprise all of us would have marveled over."

Murmurs of agreement went up from the council members present. "I was saving this demonstration for later," he confessed, "however, it seems like now is a good time to share it with everyone."

At a nod from Howling Wolf, Red Deer brought him a hide-wrapped package and joined them. Opening the bundle, the Narwikin Chief presented the contents, four arrows and a bow, to Tigal.

The caravan master could easily see these were new and unique. Tigal wondered if this could be one of those from the Clam Shell people that his friend had told him about.

The tips on these gleamed with the same golden color as the items Tigal had just shown. Like them, the edges were sharp and barbed. The shaft was longer. Bird feathers were bound to the trailing end. He passed it to one of his clan chiefs and turned back to Howling Wolf. "I have never seen anything like this."

Acknowledging Waving Grass and White Badger, Howling Wolf responded. "Nor had I before I met the Clam Shell people and the Attikamekey. As you know, both groups are victims of the marauders. Some of them managed to escape and ended up here where they joined us. Both tribes brought many new ideas."

Tigal nodded agreement and handed the arrows back. "These are unique, but how do they perform?"

"Wait till you see it in action." Getting to his feet, he said, "This morning, I had a water pouch set up as a target over there," a general wave of his hand pointed the way. "Have your best man try to shoot his arrows into it."

"From here?" Tigal got to his feet to get a better look. A murmur went through his clan members and they also got to their feet.

"The best hunters would not be able to hit it from half the distance." Tigal was incredulous. Others echoed his sentiments as they craned their necks for a better view.

At a signal from Howling Wolf, Red Deer produced a bow almost as long as he was tall. Notching an arrow, he drew back and let it fly. It covered the distance, hitting the target squarely. Stunned silence was followed by gasps and excited chatter.

Red Deer handed the bow to Tigal. "When the Clam Shell people joined the Narwikin, White Badger showed us how to make them. When the Attikamekey joined the Narwikin, they showed us how they used the golden stones. Now that our tribes are one, we have adopted both of their designs."

At these words, attendants brought out more bows and baskets of golden-tipped arrows, enough for Tigal and all the clan chiefs.

Tigal smiled broadly. "The Narwikin have always been quick to recognize good ideas and fashion them to their own need. It's one of the reasons I enjoy coming here. We leave with as many new things as we bring."

One of Tigal's men spoke up, "That's good for business ... and the food, well, that's good for us."

Roaring with laughter, the men spent the rest of the afternoon trying their hand with their new bows.

### 

In answer to her summons, Crooked Foot found Bright Moon and Little Fawn outside their shelter. Abeytu, a toddler balanced on one hip and another playing at her feet, stood there listening to their conversation. None of the women mentioned the dressing down Crooked Foot and the others had received from Tigal. However, he knew they had been there and were aware of everything, including the competition for a place in Tigal's caravan.

"It is customary for the trade fair to begin with a festival. Food and games lead the way to entertain everyone, put them in a good mood," Bright Moon said, "and they help test skills, but more importantly, they build friendships among the tribes." *Have I used the right words to describe the events of the next few days? Did Little Fawn understand the role I want her to play?*

Not familiar with trade fairs, Little Fawn looked bewildered.

Optimistically, Bright Moon added, "Think about the games and how you can help. It will be fun. Abeytu has done this before and she will be there to answer questions or help if you run into a snag."

Little Fawn shrugged. "Okay," she said, and picked up the child at Abeytu's feet. The two girls, each with a toddler perched on a hip, walked away chatting and laughing as they left.

Seeing Crooked Foot waiting, Bright Moon's face brightened. "Good. You're in time." She motioned for him to follow her. Nearby, under the watchful eye of two of Tigal's men, were bricks of white blocks stacked on a hide. "Dig a hole for the center pole," marking a spot on the ground with her walking stick, she added, "right here."

Living with Bright Moon, Crooked Foot knew this was the time to work, not the time to ask questions … and certainly not the time to bring up past events. Grabbing a digging stone, he began quickly scrapping away the sandy topsoil then the heavier clay underneath. He worked steadily.

"Deep enough," Bright Moon observed, "now round it out a little and make the bottom flat." Touching two nearby flat stones with the tip of her walking stick she added, "When it's good, put one of these in the bottom."

*Good?* A little shocked by the shift in attitude Crooked

Foot mused, *Bright Moon left the decision on the details up to me. This has to be a test and the outcome will affect my chance of winning a place in Tigal's caravan.*

### 

Standing at the top of the hill, Silver Fox held the willow hoop in the air for all to see. "Hunters, are you ready to *shoot the deer?*"

A cheer went up from the crowd stretched out down the hillside and they waved their spears in the air. Young and old, male and female, all not occupied with another task or in another game lined up in two rows. These hunters stood a spear's throw on either side of the *deer's* path.

The *deer* was a simple device made up of willow branches bound together to make a circle about waist high. Their target, a rawhide square stretched across the center of the circle, beckoned them.

"Ready," Silver Fox called. Looking around at the eager faces, he set the hoop rolling down the hill.

Picking up speed, sometimes becoming airborne as it hit obstacles along the way, it proved elusive. The air filled with cheers, shouts, and laughter. As it rolled by them, hunters launched their spears in hopes of garnering a hit, or at least a near miss, bringing the thrower bragging-rights around the night's campfire. While the hoop was being retrieved, the hunters found their spears and traded stories. This gave the players another chance at greatness.

Those that tired of this game could wander over to other areas. Some were attracted to the place where the targets were clay-covered baskets dangling from a rope stretched between two trees. Sling-toting youngsters took aim in an attempt to pelt their mark with stones. Others might go to where bolos whipped through the air in an attempt to encircle a pair of log *legs* daggling from a scaffold. It was pulled along this pathway in an attempt to provide an elusive target for all the challengers.

### ###

Too young to participate in other events, the children were paired up—beginner with an experienced partner—to play the part of quarry. Hands covering their eyes, Little Fawn and her cohort chorused, "Hide, rabbits hide." Hearing this command, the pairs of youngsters scattered, ducking into the nearby brush for cover.

"Ready rabbits? Here we come!" Uncovering her eyes, Little Fawn, a *predator*, fingered the bone whistle that dangled from a cord around her neck. She and her partner scanned the area looking for footprints, bent grasses, broken branches or other marks their *prey* may have left when they scurried into their hiding places.

The first ones the *predators* were able to find were those who were inexperienced, inept, careless, or noisy. Unhappy at being found, they consoled themselves with the thought that they would have another chance to become better next time. After a short search, Little Fawn blew a series of short blasts on the bone whistle to let *prey* still hidden know they outlasted their hunters and should return. Regrouped, partners reshuffled, and the game would start again.

### ###

Gesturing to the surrounding area, Abeytu instructed her charges, "We must stay in these sand hills." Pointing to one group, she commanded, "You three will play wolves. The rest have rocks they may choose to hide or carry with them. Their job is to play *Wounded Mother Bird* and lead you away from the hiding spot. Your job is to find their treasures—is it on them or buried in the sand—before I blow my whistle.

We will take turns at each role."

### 

The group of men on mats with a crowd of attendants darting around made Howling Wolf and Tigal easy to find but hard to approach. Their conversation stopped when Crooked Foot arrived.

"Sir," Crooked Foot began, "Bright Moon wants you to know that it's ready." He took a step back and waited for instructions or a signal of dismissal.

Howling Wolf nodded his acknowledgement and Crooked Foot turned to leave.

"Wait!" Tigal commanded.

Startled, Crooked Foot turned back to face them.

"What is it that Bright Moon has ready?" Tigal asked.

Crooked Foot blinked, surprised by his question. "Why, it's the scale. The scale is ready."

"Really? What is a scale? How does it work?" Tigal continued his questioning.

Realizing this could be part of his test, Crooked Foot started his explanation. "A scale is used to measure equal weights of two items."

Tigal nodded in agreement. Crooked Foot understood the scale's purpose. What else did he know?

Confidently, Crooked Foot went on, "The main part of the scale is a vertical pole set in the ground. Bright Moon had me dig a hole and put a stone in the bottom. That stone has a hole in the center. The pole slips into this hole, and then I packed the dirt back around it. I slipped another stone over the top of the shaft and lowered it to the ground. The two stones work together to anchor the pole and keep it from moving. A cross beam, notched at the center to keep it from slipping off, rests on top of the pole. A small weight hangs down from the center of each arm of the crossbeam."

"What are those? Decorations?" Tigal questioned. Howling Wolf, working to cover a smile, turned his head away.

"No, sir," Crooked Foot responded, "not decorations. They show when the two sides of the scale are in balance."

"What good is that?" Tigal raised a questioning eyebrow. "Why would anyone want to know that?"

"A wooden bowl hangs down from each end of the crossbar. When something is put on one side, the scale goes out of balance, lowering the bowl on that end and raising the one on the other. It remains like that until enough items are put on the high side to make it level. When that happens, the weights are even."

"Items? What kind of items would you weigh?"

"Salt, oil, grain, dried fish … the kind of things you would trade with people like the Narwikin."

"Well, if I am to trade with you, how do I know your scale is correct?"

"To make sure the scale and weights were true, your man and Bright Moon put their weights on each side and then traded stones and did the same."

Tigal paused for a moment, it seemed like a lifetime, and then said, "Very good. Go back and tell Bright Moon we will be along shortly." He turned away, dismissing Crooked Foot.

### 

The days of feasting and the games now over, Howling Wolf, his council, along with other chiefs and their councils, sat on one side of the scale. Tigal and his clan chiefs sat on the other. As the ritual began, weights placed in the bowls showed those present that the scale was true. Leaders on both sides gave the scale careful scrutiny, conferred, and then nodded their agreement.

As host, Howling Wolf stood and made the opening speech, addressing Tigal as if the caravan had just arrived. "Tigal, long a friend to all Narwikin, it's good to see you and your people here after your long trip. The Narwikin wish to see what you have brought to trade and what you need from us."

Howling Wolf took his seat. Tigal stood and looked around at those gathered. Spreading his hands wide, he said, "Howling Wolf, we have grown old together. Though I have visited many places, the home of the Narwikin is always my favorite. Because of this what I bring you is special." He paused to let his words sink in and then continued with, "The Narwikin need salt. My men traveled to the land of the Sea People to bring you this." At those words, his men got up and moved forward to place blocks of salt on the mats in front of the scale. Having set a jovial mood among the council members, Tigal also sat down.

Howling Wolf stood. "Tigal, your men have traveled far. You're most generous to the Narwikin. We're pleased to have such friends. The Narwikin hope to honor your efforts with a small token." At his words, people standing off to the side came in carrying stacks of hides and furs and placed these on the mats opposite the salt. Tigal and his men smiled broadly.

This session would last a bit longer before breaking up. Then, small groups would meet with similar sized groups among Tigal's people to barter for individual items.

# Chapter 30: Crooked Foot's Net

When he first started making it, Crooked Foot was concerned the net would be too light causing it to fail the first time he used it. If it did, everyone would laugh, and Tigal might choose someone else.

To prevent that he began interweaving rawhide and sinew strands for strength. It was slow, methodical work, but now the task was finished. Crooked Foot gathered up his homemade net. Straightening up, he staggered under its unexpected weight, but it assured him it was sturdy enough for small game.

When he first came up with the idea Bright Moon had listened as he explained his plan, but there had been little discussion about the value of the task. She didn't comment, encourage nor discourage his efforts, nor did she stop him. Instead, she continued her daily labors while feigning lack-of-interest in his work. Now and then he'd look up and catch her watching. She'd quickly look away still pretending to be uninterested. That was in the early days.

Working steadily the net grew with the passing of days, and so did her curiosity. She no longer bothered hiding her interest, but continued to avoid conversation about his creation and his intentions.

Shouldering his pack, he said, "I guess it's time to test this."

"Where will you go?"

"To the woods between the plain and the river, I've scattered grain there to attract ducks and geese."

A slight smile played along the corners of her mouth.

She lifted the lid of the grain basket and made a show of peering inside. "Oh, so that's where my grain has gone. I'd better use the rest before I have none left."

Kneeling, Bright Moon placed her grinding stones on the hide used to catch 'runaways'—those pieces that broke and flew off—as well as the flour that resulted from her efforts. Pausing, she gave him a scowl. It was one Crooked Foot had come to learn was more show than anything else.

"This better work; your birds grow fat, and I grow hungry." Her smile, now a smirk, began to fade as she went back to her task.

Dipping a wooden ladle into the grain basket, she poured its contents on the long, flat stone. With a practiced hand, she spread the grain in a thin layer before topping it with the grinding stone. Leaning forward to apply her weight, she began moving the rock in a circular motion used to turn the hard kernels into a soft powder.

How many times had he watched her perform this same chore? He couldn't remember. She kept flour in a couple of small sacks made of animal hides. Grain was kept in baskets. "Flour might spoil or bugs could get in it before you use it all," she explained. "It's better to make flour in small amounts." When one bag ran out, the empty sack was turned inside out and placed on a short totem outside the shelter for a night or two as a part of the cleansing ritual.

Made out of an animal skin cut into a square, the inside, like most hides, had been scraped, salted and dried in the sun. The outside had been scoured clean of fur and coated with layers of bees' wax *to make it waterproof*, she told him.

Encouraged by her actions, Crooked Food ventured, "Do you think it'll be worth it?"

"Worth it ...?" Puzzled by his question she stopped, leaned back on her haunches, and put down her grinding stone.

"The time I spent ... do you think it'll be worth it?"

Bright Moon gave him a sharp look. This time she meant it. "It doesn't matter what I think .... It only matters what you think." She gave him a long piercing look and then added, "If you believe in it, you'll make it work."

Picking up her grinding stone, she leaned forward and began again. He watched as the grain, caught between the flat stone and her grinder, cracked open under the pressure of her rhythmic motions to yield the fine powder she used in cooking.

Bright Moon paused to catch her breath and check her work. Satisfied with her progress, she carefully swept the flour onto the waiting hide before she noticed he still stood there watching her.

"Don't be gone all day. There are more mouths to feed since the Clam Shell People and now the Attikamekey have joined us. To help our hunters and fisherman, we'll need to plant more. I want to start planting this afternoon and will need your help to break up the ground." Turning her attention back to her work, she ladled out more grain and started grinding the next batch.

An onlooker might think that her actions were a dismissal, but Crooked Foot saw it as her way of giving him permission to go and try. The discussion was over. It was up to him now. She had given him as much encouragement as he was going to get from her. It was as close to a *blessing and best wishes for your success* as he was going to get. Smiling to himself, he picked up his spear and waddled out under the weight of his burdens.

### 

"... so, there's a clearing not too far from the river, and I've been spreading grain there to attract some birds."

Crooked Foot studied Silver Fox to see if he was showing any interest.

"Why would you do that?" Silver Fox was bored.

"On my first trip with Abeytu and Bright Moon, she showed me a spider's web …."

"So?" Silver Fox's surly reply cut him off. "Everybody's seen spider webs."

"It was her way of explaining things. I was supposed to build a fish weir but didn't know how it worked."

"Humph. No surprise there," Silver Fox couldn't pass up the chance to take a jab at his rival. Boredom was beginning to return to his voice, but curiosity got the best of him. Pointing at the bundle of netting, he asked, "What's that supposed to do?"

Crooked Foot ignored the sourness coating his adversary's remark and went on, "She said the fish weir works like a spider's web."

Wrinkling his nose, Silver Fox looked at Crooked Foot. "Go on …."

Encouraged by what appeared to be hidden curiosity, Crooked Foot perked up. Maybe his competitor was becoming interested. "Abeytu and I started working with the fur from the sheep, rolling it into string. Then Little Fawn showed me how the Attikamekey used fibers from reeds to do the same thing. To give it strength, I added some rawhide and sinew cords."

"Why not just use all rawhide?" To Silver Fox, that was an obvious solution.

Crooked Foot made a face. "All rawhide would be good, maybe even better than mixing it with sinew, but the tribe doesn't kill animals unless we need the meat. Even when we do, you might be surprised at how many uses for hides and sinews there are. I had a hard time getting everything you see here in the amounts I needed."

Silver Fox poked at the clump of netting at his feet. "Then your contraption doesn't use either of them?"

Crooked Foot shook his head. "No, there's some of each, along with a combination of string from the sheep and fibers from reeds. Now I want to test it." He paused and then added, "I thought you might like to go along and help."

"Well, I don't know," Silver Fox said. "It doesn't sound like it'll work."

"We won't know until we test it. When it does work, word will get back to Tigal. It should sit pretty well and improve our chances with him."

Hearing the words, *improve our chances with him,* Silver Fox looked up and gave Crooked Foot his full attention. "When do we start?"

Crooked Foot pointed to the pile with his foot. "I got the net right here. We just need to carry it out, get it hung up and fix a place to wait."

Scooping up the net, Silver Fox said, "What are you waiting for? Lead the way. Let's go!"

### 

Crooked Foot and Silver Fox stood back to look up at their work, moving around in the clearing as they did. A twig snap interrupted their study and they both froze in their tracks. Their weapons leaned against a tree across the clearing. If it were an animal, there could be trouble.

"Hey, my young friends, what are you doing here?"

The boys relaxed and turned toward that familiar greeting. Red Deer, followed closely by Little Fawn and Abeytu, emerged from the brush.

"I had an idea and made a net," Crooked Foot said. "We've been busy setting it up."

His explanation puzzled Little Fawn. "A net? Aren't you a little far from the river?"

Red Deer took a different line of questioning. "A net for what? How does it work?"

Crooked Foot nodded to Abeytu. "On one of the trips Abeytu and I took with Bright Moon, we stopped to take a rest, and she had us watch a spider spin its web."

"Yes...?" Hand on his chin, Red Deer's growing interest was obvious.

"Watching bugs get caught in the spider's web got me wondering: could I build a trap like that? If I did, would it work the same for me? I didn't know, so I put the net together to find out."

Abeytu brightened. "I wondered what you were going to do with all the wool we rolled into string."

Looking up at his creation, Crooked Foot said, "Silver Fox and I hung it up there."

Following his example, they looked up to see a mass of strings and rawhide cords suspended from a framework of sticks. Like a canopy, it draped down from the branches on three sides of the clearing. Red Deer walked around the glade, examining the boys' creation from all angles. Finally he said, "Hmmm .... It looks interesting, but how will your net catch anything?"

Pointing to the grain at their feet, Crooked Foot explained, "Well, a few days ago, I began spreading some of Bright Moon's grain around as bait. You can see that I scattered thinner amounts at the edges leading to this pile in the center. I want to get ducks, geese and other birds trained to come here."

The two girls looked at each other and began to giggle. "I'm sure Bright Moon was happy about the grain," Little Fawn said.

"Yeah," Abeytu agreed. "I can just imagine how happy she was."

"It'll be okay," Crooked Foot said, "as long as it

works." Grinning, he added, "If not, I'll be in trouble."

"How are you going to get yourself out of trouble?" Red Deer persisted.

Crooked Foot gestured toward the far side of the clearing, "Silver Fox and I don't expect anything to come from that direction because there aren't any animal trails on that side ...." He paused to let his audience mull over his words before he went on. "We staked that end and the two sides down, and stretched the rest of the net overhead. The trail from the river leads right into the open mouth." Hands on his hips, he finished with, "Now, all we have to do is climb up in a tree, wait for an animal to wander in, and begin eating the grain we've put out. When they do, we can pull some cords, and the net falls capturing them."

Red Deer pursed his lips thoughtfully and then said, "Where will you wait? We'll wait with you. I want to see how this works."

Smiling, Crooked Foot said, "Follow me. Silver Fox and I fixed a place up in a tree." He turned and led the way to their hiding spot.

### 

Small birds were the first ones to arrive. They were soon joined by water birds, mostly ducks, none of whom wanted to miss a free meal. Red Deer, Little Fawn, and Abeytu quietly watched the activity below while hand signals filled the air between the two boys. Ready, the pair wrapped the trigger cords around their hands and slowly pulled them taut. Watching the birds feed, they waited quietly while the parade gathered closer to the center of the clearing. Everyone held their breath.

The boys yanked the cords in one quick motion. The trap, fringe weighted with rocks, fell. Surprised, the panicked birds scattered but not quick enough to avoid the net as it collapsed around them.

Silver Fox tossed a handful of ties to the others, "Bind their feet. We want to keep them alive if we can." Jumping down, everyone scrambled around to secure their captives before they could escape.

The birds fought back, pecking and flapping around under the net, but in spite of their efforts, they ended up bound and exhausted. Red Deer cut a pole and began stringing the birds over it.

Task completed, the others sat back on their haunches and looked at their work. Little Fawn began laughing, "I ... I think Bright Moon will be happy." The others looked at her, and then everyone broke into laughter.

Abeytu was the first to jump to her feet. Brushing grain from her hands she said, "I think we have enough grain left to set the trap and try again."

Crooked Foot looked around at the ground. "It is scattered around, but if we sweep it up I think we'll have enough grain. The birds we caught may give us away. Someone will have to take the catch back to the village."

Red Deer turned to Little Fawn and Abeytu. "How about taking our catch back? I want to stay here so we can raise the net and try again."

Taken aback by the suggestion, the two girls gave him a cold look. "What? You want us to take them back?"

Red Deer pursed his lips. Thoughtfully, he looked at the girls and said, "The first person to arrive at the gate with a set of birds will be the center of attention. They will also impress both Howling Wolf and Bright Moon." Red Deer shrugged dismissively. "It's a heavy net, and it has to be untangled and hung up. It's going to be a lot of work, but it is Crooked Foot's idea, one that he and Silver Fox put together, so maybe they should take the birds back and get the credit."

Red Deer appealed to the girl's vanity by giving them

choice between work and fame. Though it was the better of the two opportunities, they chafed at being out maneuvered. With a flip of their heads, the scowling pair of females shouldered the pole and marched off toward the village leaving a chill in the air behind them. As the girls moved out of earshot, the last words heard were, "Boys!"

### 

Back in the tree, the net reset, the three young men clung to branches waiting quietly for their next prey. They didn't have long to wait, but what emerged from the brush wasn't what they were expecting.

Large animals, taller at the shoulder than the tallest man in the tribe, a pair of musk oxen moved quietly into the clearing as they grazed. From a distance, these beasts looked formidable. Now, they were close, so close the boys could've reached down and touched their hairy backs. They looked fearsome. If his heart hadn't been pounding so hard Crooked Foot could've heard them chew; he could've heard their feet shuffle as they walked. He looked over at his friends.

Red Deer, a smirk on his face, raised an eyebrow. Safe on a tree limb above them, he whispered softly, "Should I cut a bigger carry pole?"

Red Deer's remark caught the boys off guard. Attempting to suppress their nervous laughter, Silver Fox threw a hand over his mouth, and Crooked Foot choked.

Startled by these strange noises, the musk oxen raised their heads and then bolted from the clearing right into the net. Under the impact of their assault, the stakes holding it in place ripped out of the ground. Continuing their charge, the animals pulled the assembly—net, framework, weights and all—down with a crash that made the oxen more frantic. Bellowing noisily, the net-covered animals continued their flight.

With the trip cords wrapped around their hands and arms, the boys found the lines so tangled they couldn't free themselves. Yanked from the tree, the pair hit the ground at the tail of the net, landing on the remains of the framework. Rushing through meadowlands, the stampeding musk oxen easily dragged them along. Red Deer jumped down from his perch and raced after them. Still caught up in the ropes and netting, the boys struggled to get free but were being buried in the growing collection of brush and logs being picked up. Red Deer realized they were on the path the girls had taken and began shouting as he ran.

### 

Reaching the village with the carry pole of live birds still balanced on their shoulders, Little Fawn and Abeytu stood at the gateway talking with those gathered there. Hunters returning with the results of efforts usually earned momentary attention. Two young girls carrying a pole with live birds was a different event. Just as Red Deer predicted, Little Fawn and Abeytu became the center of the villagers' attention, and they delighted in relating the tale.

A commotion behind them interrupted their conversation. Glancing over her shoulder, Abeytu was able to see the approaching musk oxen. "What's that?"

Little Fawn turned to see the bellowing animals, dragging a mass of brush behind them, being chased by Red Deer.

Turning back, she found the crowd around her had scattered. Agog at this new adventure, the few who remained no longer had interest in the girls' tale.

"Glory grabbing boys!" No longer the center of anyone's attention, Little Fawn spat out this single disparaging comment, and then the pair made their way into the enclave.

In an attempt at turning the animals, those still outside the gate started jumping and yelling while others tried to swing the heavy gate closed. The oxen swerved away from the stockade. Running along the walls, they swerved again and headed toward the area being readied for planting.

Taking a break, Bright Moon sat in the shade of a cluster of trees and directed the women's activities. Seeing the charging animals, she yelled a warning and dove for cover. Following her lead, the others scattered.

Still caught up in the netting, the lads lay buried under the accumulation of debris. Tufts of grass, small bushes, sand, dirt, anything in the way was ripped out as the log-infested net passed by, digging ruts as it went. Bellowing, the oxen drove past the knot of cowering, wide-eyed women before, finally exhausted, the animals slowed and then came to a halt.

Stepping from her hiding place, an angry Bright Moon faced the animals. Shouting something in an unknown language, she raised her walking stick overhead and then brought the tip down, burying the end in the ground in front of them. Unimpressed, the musk oxen mooed softly and began grazing.

Winded from the long run, Red Deer trotted up to find the pair of oxen docilely tugging on the tangled mass of logs and brush that held them back from reaching clumps of grass. Not giving them another thought, Red Deer began digging through the rubble, clearing away debris until Crooked Foot and Silver Fox were able to sit up.

Though still spitting grass and dirt, they gave each other a broad smile. "What a ride!" they exclaimed, "What a ride!"

"I'll give you 'what a ride' ...." Fuming, Bright Moon shuffled toward them, her walking stick held more like a weapon than a cane.

"Honored Shaman," Crooked Foot waved a hand at

the path they had just traversed. "What is wrong? With the help of the great beasts you sent our way, the area you wanted to plant has been cleared and dug up."

Bright Moon stopped in her tracks and looked back at the furrowed path behind the animals. Attempting to suppress their smiles, the trio looked at her expectantly. The path the animals had taken lay clear, no grass or logs in the way, the ground worked up and nearly ready for planting.

Snorting a half-hearted acceptance, Bright Moon said, "Very good." Looking the threesome over, she concluded, "You've done well, Narwikins."

Hearing that coveted phrase, the trio relaxed. Crooked Foot and Silver Fox broke out in big smiles. Red Deer was relieved. They were off the hook.

Their euphoria was short-lived, however, as Bright Moon added, "Having done the job so well and so quickly, there are some rocks that need to be cleared. I hope you do as well with them."

Shaken, the wide-eyed village women began slowly emerging from their hiding places and gathered around the old shaman. Having listened to this exchange between Bright Moon and Red Deer, they looked at the nearby animals, now calmly grazing as if under a spell. Before nightfall, the story of the shaman's powers would make the rounds in the village, growing in detail with each telling.

Standing with Abeytu in the open gateway, Little Fawn also listened to the exchange. Elated at the current turn of events, the girls watched the boys' smugness deflate into defeat and resignation.

"Good," Abeytu said under her breath.

"Yeah, it serves them right," Little Fawn agreed.

Neither of the girls admitted to having even a small pang of guilt. Secretly they recognized, had things been just a little different, both of them would be facing Bright Moon's wrath. In the end, amazement would replace any guilty feelings as they heard the retelling of events and listened as the story grew.

To the villagers, Bright Moon conjured up the musk oxen. Her magic caused them to become tangled in the net and clear the land. Then, shouting magical words she waved her wand and brought the animals to a halt.

It was evident to everyone, Bright Moon, their shaman, possessed magical powers.

# Chapter 31: Corralling a Herd

Tigal and his clan chiefs followed Red Deer up the trail. Nearing the crest of the ridge they arrived at a bare outcropping where they found Howling Wolf and the Council members. Clusters of animals dotted the plain below.

Tigal greeted his friends and then looked from the youth to the man. "Well, my friends, the view up here is beautiful, but is there more to this trip?"

Unconcerned with the answer, Tigal's clan chiefs busied themselves taking in the sights.

Howling Wolf paused to take in the scene again and then turned to Red Deer. "It is as you said, my son. From here we can see across the plain."

Excited, White Badger added, "Knots of animals—buffalo, antelope, and musk oxen—stretch to the horizon. We should go on a hunt."

It was true; the rolling grassland teemed with clumps of grazing animals. An impressive sight, it stirred memories of past hunts. Stories soon filled the air.

Howling Wolf allowed time for conversations to die down before giving Red Deer an approving nod. The young man cleared his throat, "I know this has been a hard climb. I asked you here so you could see the herds on the plain."

As Red Deer spoke, he included the view with one sweep of his hand, "Since the Clam Shell and the Attikamekey have joined the Narwikin there are more mouths to feed and a greater need for hides."

"The plain holds many animals," White Badger said, "enough to feed all of us."

Red Deer nodded, but added, "That they do, but this is only temporary. Each day the meadows grow browner and the vegetation along the river's edge grows thinner. Soon, the dry season will be upon us. The grasses will wither, and the plains will turn to dust. Before that happens, the herds will migrate to greener lands."

He let his words sink in. "They'll leave behind them only the sick, the lame, and the old. When that happens, the Narwikin must choose between staying and following the herds. If we stay, we will be left with little to eat."

White Badger stepped forward. "We've all gone through hard times and have experienced everything you say. Did you bring us here to tell us what we already know, or do you have a plan?"

"A plan …. Yes, I have a plan." His eyes met White Badger's and they stared at each other for a moment before he went on. "You have heard how Crooked Foot and Silver Fox captured live birds and two musk oxen in a net. Now we have to choose between keeping them and eating them."

Quiet until now, Waving Grass chimed in saying, "This is not new. When we arrived, Small Turtle was one of a group that captured live water birds by swimming under water."

Red Deer looked around, allowing time for discussion by those with him. "We've all watched wild dogs position themselves to cut a cow from the herd." He swung an arm around to include the scene as he continued, "They spread themselves out in a long line at the edge of the herd. After separating a single animal, one or two dogs will chase it along that route. When the pursuing dogs tire, fresh members of the pack are close at hand to pick up the chase. By working together, the dogs run their prey to the ground. From the moment it was selected, the cow never had a chance."

Red Deer spoke the truth. It was common knowledge. The group fidgeted while they waited for him to go on. "From the stories of our ancestors, our hunters would separate small groups of animals from the herd and drive them over a cliff. This would provide meat and hides, but their actions only delayed lean times."

The council responded noisily. He waited for the murmur to die down before he continued. "When the herd moves, the Narwikin are forced to move with them or starve."

He paused for a second to let his words sink in. "The Narwikin have long used dogs to guard against predators. Our youngsters capture chickens, ducks and geese and keep them alive until they are needed. Recently, musk oxen were captured and used to clear a new field for planting."

White Badger showed his impatience. "This is not new to us."

Looking around at his audience, Red Deer said, "Tigal, friend of the Narwikin, brings us many new ideas. For as long as any of us can remember, his caravan has made use of animals to carry their trade goods. He tells of tribes along the Great Sea who no longer follow the herd. They capture animals and use them when needed to provide meat and hides. I believe we can do the same."

He had stated the obvious but in such a way that it sounded like something new. His statements stirred the group into active conversation.

Red Deer smiled confidently as he held up his hands to gain control. "You asked if I have a plan. Yes, I have a plan. It combines the hunting traditions of our ancestors, the cunning of the wild dogs, and the news brought by our friend Tigal. For the plan to work, I'll need everyone's help."

All eyes were on him as he continued. "It's a dangerous plan. If anything goes wrong, many could get hurt, even killed." The men were silent as they waited for him to continue.

"Groups of two or three will cover themselves with

animal skins. They'll move slowly, like grazing animals to get behind the herd." A low murmur went up from the men as he described actions already used by hunters. Red Deer stifled the desire to quicken his pace. He wanted to appear confident, not nervous. "Others will wait along the path. It should be wide where the herd grazes and narrow at the other end."

"The other end?" White Badger asked. "What do you mean? Where does the path lead?"

Not wanting to appear arrogant, Red Deer suppressed a smile. "Follow me over here." He waved in the general direction of the summit, and they followed him.

A short climb over the crest brought them to the backside of the ridge. They no longer faced the plain but only tree tops and other ridgelines. He led them along the slope until they reached the lip of a canyon. Red Deer allowed them time to take in the view.

"The other end of the path leads here," he explained. "It lies between this ridge and the next one and has only one way in or out. This place has gone unnoticed because the walls are steep but not high—in most places no higher than the tree tops."

White Badger wasn't convinced. "Once the herd enters the canyon, how are we going to hold them there?"

"A short distance in from the plain, the trail turns left and you enter a narrow pass. It leads to this small valley where there is grass and a spring-fed lake. The Narwikin can build a stockade with a gate, and we can close it after the animals enter. With the herd barricaded in there, they'll be trapped, but they will have food, water, and protection from predators … and with them in there, the Narwikin will have food."

###

A bead of sweat hung from the end of his nose. It had been a mere pinpoint on Red Deer's brow before it gathered with others to form into a drop. After gaining sufficient weight, this collection of sweat made an agonizing trek down his face to the tip of his nose. There it hung suspended, taunting him. A short distance away, groups of animals grazed uneasily on dry grasses. Red Deer ignored the aggravation. The drop of sweat would have to wait. To keep from panicking the animals, he had to remain motionless under the animal skins that camouflaged his companion and himself.

Nearby, other hunters also hidden under animal hides suffered the same fate, while they slowly maneuvered to a place behind the herd. The wind favored them. What little breeze that existed came from the direction of the herd. It was near dusk—the time when the trap would be sprung. In place now, they would wait as the Narwikin have always waited ... patiently.

A drum sounded from atop the canyon. The moment had finally arrived. Nearby, animals stirred nervously at the unfamiliar sound. Musk oxen formed protective circles, adult males—heads down, horns out—on the outside, calves and females on the inside.

Behind the herd, tribe members threw off their disguises. Free of their coverings, the men struck flint and ignited tinder. Torches ablaze, they jumped to their feet, fanned the air with the hides and unleashed a torrent of yells and screams.

Alarmed by this pandemonium, some of the animals in the herd—deer, antelope, buffalo—broke and ran. The startled oxen drew back, tightened their circles, but stood their ground.

Jabbing firebrands at the circled pack, the men forced the animals to back up as they closed in on three sides. Under this pressure the circle broke, and the oxen joined other animals in blind flight along the unblocked fourth side. Close behind the stampeding animals, the men continued to make noise and wave their torches.

Previously, rows of dry grasses and brush were gathered and piled high along the chosen route. With the herd now in motion, these were set afire creating a wall of flame on either side of the path. The animals fled with the clamoring hunters trailing after them. Hemmed in by flames and the noise, they charged forward into the canyon. Stampeding through the pass, they entered the valley and raced around the lake.

When the last of the animals went through, tribe members closed the gate and lifted logs in place to bar the opening.   Blankets of vines and brush were draped over the stockade, further disguising the barricade. Red Deer, along with the rest of the drivers, came running up.

Silver Fox and Crooked Foot greeted them, gleefully. "The herd is barricaded in the valley," the pair sang and danced.

"Did anyone get hurt?" Concerned that his plan brought more harm than benefit, Red Deer looked around.

Still excited, Silver Fox hopped from one foot to the other while he sang, "No injuries, no injuries, no injuries."

Red Deer let out a loud whoop. "Time to celebrate!"

A shout of joy went up from the crowd. Singing and dancing, everyone joined in with Silver Fox.  Their celebration would last far into the night.

### 

Howling Wolf nudged Red Deer. Roused from sleep, the younger man sat up and rubbed his eyes. Having celebrated most of the night, he peered into his father's smiling face through groggy eyes.

"Come," Howling Wolf said, "It's daylight. The Council and I want to see what has been accomplished." Turning on his heel, he started off. Red Deer scrambled to his feet and rushed to trail after his father.

Howling Wolf, the Council, Red Deer, and Tigal climbed to the crest of the ridge where they turned to look out across the plain. Two black streaks tinged with gray ash stretched across the ground and marked the rolling hills. Clusters of grazing animals, undeterred by last night's actions, stretched to the horizon. The success of the Narwikin's efforts had done little to disturb the balance of nature.

Crossing the crest, they came to the canyon and paraded along the rim that marked this side of the pass. Opposite them, another ridge mirrored their own. They scrambled over the rocks until they came to a spot where they could peer into the valley. Below, beyond the barricade, the basin opened into a flat bowl. Rimmed by steep canyon walls a spring-fed lake sat in the center of a grassy meadow. Clumps of animals grazed or rested calmly under shade trees.

"Grass, water," Howling Wolf commented. "It looks like the herd has what it needs, and for now, so do we." Murmurs of ascent came from council members.

Smiling, Tigal clapped Red Deer on the shoulder. "You've done well for the Narwikin. Your plan worked so well that I will be taking this knowledge with me."

His words came as a surprise to Red Deer, although they shouldn't have. Everyone knew and had known for some time that the caravan would be moving on. But, like the rest of his tribe, Red Deer had grown comfortable with their presence and hadn't given it much thought. Tigal planned to have the caravan begin with short trips—probably no more than one or two moons' time—to condition the animals, pack-bearers, and equipment. They would return to the Narwikin village after each trip for rest and repairs. Once he was satisfied, the caravan would begin their long trip. It would be two, perhaps three summers before they returned. Moving from place-to-place, never lingering, this was the life the caravan had chosen.

# Chapter 32: Romnog Plots Another Attack

Following his usual methods, Romnog and his army lay hidden as they watched the village. The villagers had recently expanded their settlement, but otherwise this place was no different than any of the other villages he had attacked. For the past two nights, his scouts quietly probed along the sides and back walls of the stockade. A moonless night now, and under this blanket of darkness he divided his forces into two groups. The first group would feint an assault at the front. The second group would crawl through the brambles that made up the stockade walls and sneak into the village.

They would steal anything they could. There was always a need for more slaves, so kidnapping women and children wasn't out of the question. They could begin their life in servitude by carrying the booty his men had stolen from them. He smiled at the idea. Anything they couldn't carry off, Romnog decided he'd burn. If he couldn't have it, then no one could. He smiled even more at that.

### ###

Barking dogs … one started and then others joined in. The Narwikin used dogs for hunting, and have always kept a few of these staked out at night inside the stockade.

Interwoven with branches from thorn bushes, the stockade and the scent of the dogs were usually enough to discourage predators. The dogs had been acting strangely the last few nights. Tonight was no exception.

Crooked Foot rubbed sleep from his eyes, threw back

his sleeping robes, and rolled out of bed. Somewhere out in the darkness, men were speaking in low voices. He could not hear what was said, but their tone carried the sound of concern.

In her own sleeping spot, Bright Moon sat up and leaned on an elbow. Her hoarse whisper cut through the darkness. "Where are you going?"

"Out to investigate."

She sniffed. "It's not necessary."

"I'm going out to join the other men," he persisted.

Stunned by his words, Bright Moon rearranged her bedding and lay back. He was becoming a man. She realized, even if she wanted to there was no argument she could present that would change that. She understood he needed to do this even though it might not amount to anything.

Little Fawn, her sleep disturbed, stirred and then sat up. "What's going on?"

Bright Moon replied, "The dogs are barking. It is nothing to worry about."

Crooked Foot stumbled out of Bright Moon's shelter and looked around. Men had stirred up the dying coals and put more wood on the night fires near the council house. Others had lit torches and were looking around. Everything seemed in order, yet the dogs wouldn't be quiet.

In the center of the common area, Red Deer, White Badger, and Waving Grass stood with council members and Howling Wolf. Crooked Foot edged closer to Red Deer so he could eavesdrop on the conversation. He felt movement beside him and turned to find Silver Fox.

"... runners told us raiders hit their villages in the middle of the night when there was no moon." Howling Wolf paused to look over his audience.

One hand on Howling Wolf's arm, Waving Grass confided, "My husband, there was no moon the night we were attacked!"

White Badger nodded. "We were off hunting, but it was a moonless night like this when the robbers attacked and burnt my village. The glow from the fires lit up the sky that night. When dawn came, the glow was replaced by a pillar of smoke."

One of the council members spoke up, "Luckily, we have the dogs to give alarm." Others nodded their agreement.

White Badger, as if he was acknowledging a mistake, confessed, "My tribe did not have any dogs."

Waving Grass said, "The Attikamekey had dogs. It didn't help."

A scream arose from the front of the enclave. Turning, craning their necks, they saw a place where a patch of night had suddenly become a patch of day.

Flames blazed from a burning shelter creating a circle of light in the darkness. Near the edge of the circle, Little Rabbit stood with Abeytu. They were surrounded by a handful of smaller, wide-eyed youngsters. A few possessions lay scattered near their feet.

"Fire," yelled Red Deer, "Sound the alarm. Get the gate open! We must get water."

"Wait!" White Badger yelled. "It's a trap. Don't open the gate!"

Red Deer was beside himself. "What? There's a fire. We can't let it spread. Open the gate!"

"Everyone, arm yourselves!" White Badger commanded.

Confused, tribe members looked to Howling Wolf who had remained calm. "Arm yourselves, quickly, and then open the gate! Stay alert!"

The men, following his directions, ran to get their weapons. Turning, Howling Wolf spotted the boys at the edge of the crowd. "You two take the dogs to the back of the village and wait there. Prepare yourselves. Stand alert!"

The men returned, armed with clubs, axes and spears. The gate swung open, and guards stepped through to peer into the night. Everything looked calm outside the stockade. The rest of the men ran through the open gate to the nearby creek. They took any container that would hold water as well as hides that they could soak and use to beat the fire.

### 

The dogs were hard to manage. Something in the nearby woods agitated them. They wanted to track it down. Crooked Foot and Silver Fox had all they could do to pull the dogs away and take them to the back of the stockade. This only seemed to increase the dogs' anxiety. They pranced and pulled at the leather cords holding them. Women and younger children turned out of their shelters to gather in small, worried groups. Reaching the back, Crooked Foot helped stake the dogs and then returned to Bright Moon's shelter to tell her what had transpired.

She mulled his story over for a minute then got to her feet saying, "I think I'll go out and see if I'm needed." Her voice was calm, but her movements were quick and filled with purpose. Before leaving, she turned back to watch Crooked Foot select weapons: Axe, bone knife, sling, bow and arrows, spear. "What are you doing?"

His voice emotionless, he replied, "Chief Howling Wolf said to be prepared and to stand alert."

With mixed feelings, she managed to grunt an acknowledgment. Turning her back, she hid her concern from him and tried to focus on her task. Having gathered his equipment, Crooked Foot followed her out of the shelter.

Throwing back her covers, Little Fawn grumbled, "I can't get any sleep with everybody running around. I might as well get up and see what's going on."

Outside her hut, Bright Moon stopped to scan the area. Several families, women and children mostly, stood around in small groups. Growing concern could be read on their faces. The air should be filled with the sounds of crickets, frogs, and night birds. Except for the barking dogs, the night was still ... too still!

Silver Fox watched Crooked Foot, ladened with weapons, approach with disdain. "Preparing for battle?" he questioned.

"I am following Chief Howling Wolf's instructions ... and you?"

Silver Fox raised a hand and made a threatening step toward Crooked Foot, but his opponent held his ground. Seeing this, Silver Fox hesitated. He had gone up against Crooked Foot before and not fared well. Little Fawn's arrival rescued him from having to decide his next step.

"What stirred up the dogs?" the young girl questioned. Together, the boys filled her, and everybody there, in on the events ending with Howling Wolf's instructions.

Bright Moon leaned on her walking stick and pondered her dilemma. Between the two lads, she knew she could not name one rival as leader without upsetting the other, but the wily old woman had watched Little Fawn as she listened thoughtfully to the boys' narrative, and knew the young girl was the answer she needed. When Little Fawn looked her way, the old woman smiled slightly and nodded.

With that blessing, Little Fawn turned to the other women and children. "Gather rocks, clubs; whatever you can find that can be used as a weapon." Pointing to a nearby spot on the ground, she concluded with, "and line up here."

### 

Attempting to quell the blaze at the front of the

enclave, Narwikin men ran back and forth through the open gate. As they grew tired, they discarded weapons.

Without warning, a rock sailed out of the darkness and hit the guard at the gate knocking him off his feet. It took a few moments for the others, numb from exhaustion, to react. Before they did, the darkness exploded with screaming, weapon-swinging men. They seemed to come from all directions. The Narwikin did their best to grab anything available and fight off their attackers.

Chaos reigned for a time. The battle was not going well for the Narwikin until suddenly, arrows, screams, and yelps filled the air. Howling Wolf glanced quickly behind him to find their source. Near the gate, Waving Grass directed a line of Attikamekey women. Armed with the new, longer bows and kop-tipped, feathered arrows, they let loose yet another barrage.

Surprised, the attackers faltered and started to fall back. From somewhere in the darkness, a horn sounded. As suddenly as it started, the attackers faded into the night taking their wounded with them.

Red Deer, covered in dirt, sweat, and blood, stood club in hand, as he peered into the night. Satisfied the attackers had retreated he turned back and walked through the gate. Fires continued to burn out-of-control, filling the air with thick smoke. The Narwikin had given up on the fires, first to fight off the attack, and now to tend to the wounded. They gratefully worked under the protective eye of armed Attikamekey women.

Howling Wolf joined his son, followed closely by Waving Grass, who was attempting to look at her husband's wounds.

Red Deer was the first to speak. "I asked White Badger to check on everyone and report to the council."

Howling Wolf nodded. "Good. Bright Moon, with

the help of her assistants, will look after the wounded. I ordered the gate closed and some guards posted in case they come back. We need to find out why they attacked and if they'll attack again."

Red Deer let out a long sigh. "What had the runner said? Did his people know anything?"

"Hold still!" Waving Grass commanded. *Perhaps*, she thought, *I will have better luck caring for my mate's wounds if I can tell him something that will hold his attention*. "When the raiders attacked the Attikamekey they were after anything they could carry off easily especially young women and children."

"Women?" That caught Red Deer's attention. "Where's Little Fawn?" He turned and ran toward the back of the village.

In the midst of the turmoil and too busy for thoughts other than survival, no one realized that one group of marauders led the attack at the front while another group snuck in the back to rob and kidnap at will.

# Chapter 33: Attacked

Shouts and sounds of the battle going on at the front gate reached the back of the enclave, Little Fawn, those gathered around her, and the dogs. Their barking grew more frantic, and they strained at their tethers.

Selecting two youngsters, she commanded, "Quickly, put more wood on the night fires." To another two, she ordered, "Light some torches and stick them in the ground over there and down there." She knew the light would expose her little group, but it would also expose everything else. In spite of the sounds of battle, she hoped the dogs' concerns were due to an animal. If this were true, perhaps their activities and the fires would scare it off.

One of the youngsters, flaming torch in hand, ran up the path between shelters but came to an abrupt halt. Surprised, he announced his discovery with a shriek, "In … In … Intruder!"

The culprit grabbed the youngster's free hand, ripped the torch out of the other, and tossed it on the thatched roof of a nearby shelter. The dried material caught immediately, and the blaze lit up the surrounding area. Everyone could make out the man's rough features and his strange garb. He wore a leather chest piece and a helmet decorated with an animal skull. Stunned, Little Fawn realized she had seen the uniform before. These were the same people who had attacked her village.

Intruders, now visible in the light of the burning shelter, darted in and out of lodgings ladened with whatever they could carry. Taking these spoils to the stockade, they passed their loot through a hole in its wall to waiting hands on the outside.

The young Narwikin torchbearer struggled as the raider hoisted him over his shoulder and turned to make a getaway. Crooked Foot loosed an arrow, sending the shaft into the gap in the culprit's armor under his raised arm. Surprised, the man bellowed and dropped the boy. Grabbing the shaft of the arrow, he yanked it out and took a step toward his attacker. Crooked Foot let another arrow fly, not at the villain's protected upper body, but squarely into his meaty thigh. The man yelled again and retreated as quickly as his wounds would allow. Other thugs, armed with clubs, dropped their goods, not to come to his aid, but to threaten their assailants.

Recovering from her shock, Little Fawn commanded, "Let the dogs loose."

Silver Fox swung his ax cutting the leather thongs, but broke his blade in the process. Freed, the frantic animals launched into action, leaving Silver Fox to search for a club.

"Stones! Throw stones!" Little Fawn commanded.

Without further encouragement, the air filled with the swishing sounds as youngsters cut loose with their slings. A sharp snap signaled the end of the winding movement and the launch of their missiles. Without prompting, the youngsters picked up another stone and began the winding motion while they searched for their next target.

The intruders tried to duck and dodge the projectiles, but the arrival of the dogs thwarted their efforts. Their organized attack broken, each intruder attempted to deal with snapping teeth and flying rocks on his own.

Crack! A twig snapped. Invaders had managed to sneak up from behind. Crooked Foot tried to notch an arrow, but he wasn't quick enough to both aim well and give full draw to his bow. The arrow bounced off the leather chest piece. His attacker laughed. Ducking down, Crooked Foot feigned a move to the left, then the right.

The villain swung his club knocking Crooked Foot to the ground. Rolling to the side, the lad scrambled to his feet, fists clutching loose debris. Bent on harming the one who dared attack him, his pursuer lurched forward to grab the boy. Intent on hurling him across the open area, he lifted the struggling youngster off the ground. On reaching eye-level, Crooked Foot delivered his fists full of rubble—first one, then the other—directly in the interloper's face, temporarily blinding him.

Seeing Crooked Foot's plight, Silver Fox joined in the foray. Swinging his club low, he caught the culprit at the knee. A resounding crack followed immediately. Howling, the big man dropped Crooked Foot and went down in a heap. Rolling around on the ground, he clutched his knee.

Another club-swinging attacker saw Bright Moon standing near the group. *She is the one directing the actions of these youngsters and should be easy prey*, he thought, *our attack will fare better if I attack this old woman.* He took a swipe, but she danced backward out of his reach. Pushing forward he swung again, but she continued to dance and weave just out of reach. What should've proven to be an easy mark was turning out to be more of a challenge than he imagined. Unable to back away without losing face, he rushed forward for another swing. Reversing direction, she side-stepped his charge and then inserted the tip of her walking stick between his feet. Tangled up and off balance, her foe went sprawling. Before he could get up, Bright Moon freed her walking stick, swung it hard and caught her attacker beside the head. He went down again, out like yesterday's campfire.

Wheezing and puffing, she turned to find the last intruder standing over Little Fawn. He had clubbed her from behind and sent her sprawling.

Grinning he grabbed the unconscious girl by the collar and began to drag her off. Silver Fox and Crooked

Foot quickly came to her rescue. Using axes, they attacked the prowler driving him off. He and other stragglers left the way they came, setting torches to more shelters as they did.

### 

Armed with spears and clubs, Red Deer and others came running up, looks of panic on their faces. In the light of blazing shelters, he saw two intruders spread-eagle on the ground. Silver Fox and Crooked Foot, axes in hand, stood guard over them. A couple of the camp-dogs pranced around the open area, stopping now and then to sniff at the stockade and then dance back to join the youths standing guard. Cradling her head, Little Fawn sat in the midst of a gathering of youngsters while Bright Moon applied a damp compress.

Red Deer came to a halt and then crouched near Little Fawn. "Are you all right?" he asked quietly.

She nodded and then winced. "Yes," she managed a weak smile as she waved a hand to take in the group surrounding her, "Once again, my Narwikin friends came to my aid."

Trying to jerk her head toward the two captives, she made another pained expression and decided just to point. "They should be so lucky. Their friends left them behind."

Red Deer glanced over at the two thugs. They looked morose now that the two boys were joined by a circle of spear carrying Narwikin. Thoughts of escape were dismissed, and they waited to learn their fate.

"Tie them up to posts … in separate areas so they can't talk to each other," Red Deer ordered, "and post a guard. We'll deal with them later." *Might as well let them stew about their fate for a while.*

# Chapter 34: A New Location

Tigal's night-watch woke him when they saw the fire's glow against the night sky. They were sure it was the Narwikin village. It was in the direction of their next day's travels.

Morning came, and a gray shroud of smoke rose to replace the glow. In other times, Tigal's first thoughts might have been that this was a prairie fire or the result of somebody's careless campfire, but these were troubled times. From the story the sky told, there was an attack on a village; he had already decided that it was Howling Wolf's. Even if this were not the Narwikin village, he knew that the attack had already occurred. No matter how hard he drove his caravan, they would be too late to prevent the assault, and too late to help beat off the marauders. But, if he moved fast enough, his people might be able to help the survivors.

He divided his men into three groups: one to scout the surrounding area and warn of an attack on the caravan; the second one to protect the caravan's baggage train, burdened with the goods of trade. His animals must have time to rest and graze which meant the caravan would move slowly, but with as much speed as caution would allow. Finally, the third group would form an advanced guard. They would take the lead to keep the caravan from blundering into a trap as well as to make a forced-march to the Narwikin village to give aid.

### ###

Bright Moon found Howling Wolf on an inspection tour. "My shelter caught fire, but Crooked Foot ran in and grabbed my medicine kit. He was there so long I thought we had lost him."

Howling Wolf nodded. "He is brave, but sometimes he fails to consider his actions." He sighed. "I am at a loss. I need to chastise him for nearly becoming a casualty, but I know it will fall on deft ears if I recognize his contribution."

It was Bright Moon's turn to scoff. "So says the one who, when he was that age, fought two tigers at the same time."

She had him again! Changing the subject, Howling Wolf asked, "Do you have what you need to care for the wounded?"

"We do not have enough shelters if it rains, and few have sleep-robes, but otherwise we are okay. Our people know where to bring the wounded to get our help. Most of my medicines were lost in the fire, but Crooked Foot's quick action saved a few. He, Abeytu, and Little Fawn have enough knowledge and are willing to help. They were tested overnight when some of our women delivered babies."

Howling Wolf gave an exhausted grunt. "How are they doing?"

"They'll survive," Bright Moon said and then smiled as she added, "the mothers and their babies will, too."

A ram's horn sounded, alerting every one of the potential of an attack. Had the raiders returned to finish what they started?

Hiding her concerns, Bright Moon gave her friend a reassuring pat, "You go now. We will be okay."

### 

To quickly cover the distance between the caravan

and the village, Paytah[34] pushed the men in the advanced party without a break. Leaving Tigal's caravan to follow along behind, the men moved quickly, without complaints. It was mid-morning when he called a halt. They were near the edge of the forest surrounding the Narwikin village.

His men still undercover, Paytah parted the foliage and studied the scene in front of him. The column of smoke was gone, but a thin veil still hung in the air from fires that continued to smolder within the village. He was happy to see the familiar totems visible above remnants of the palisade walls along with their colorful banners, though some of these wore the scars of this recent battle. Sections of the stockade walls had collapsed. It looked like the villagers were busy repairing these breeches under the protective eyes of armed guards who also stood at the gate, now closed.

Was it as it should be? Had the Narwikin managed to survive the night? Were these actually Narwikin guards protecting the villagers or were they somebody else forcing the villagers to work? Tigal had chosen him to lead, find out what happened, and report back. How could he know all was well?

Paytah divided his men into two groups: one to hold back, keep watch, and retreat if necessary; the other, well the other was his job. Taking a deep breath, he gave the signal for his group to move forward. To a drum's beat, his men stepped into the clearing and formed into a block.

The drum sound caught the villagers' attention. They looked up to see armed men approaching and immediately stopped work. One or two of the workers ran into the village shouting. A moment later the alarm sounded. The remaining workers picked up weapons, joined with guards, and formed into armed groups. Facing Paytah's men, these groups were

---

[34] Paytah - Fire (Sioux).

ready to do battle, not as captives, but of their own free will. These actions answered his questions. Paytah brought his group to a halt and unfurled Tigal's banner. A cheer of recognition went up from the Narwikin.

### ###

Late afternoon found the Council seated on mats near the stockade gate. Villagers stood or sat in a circle around the council. Armed men were everywhere.

Howling Wolf stood and spoke, "Last night's attack was unprovoked and without warning. With the help of the Attikamekey, we beat them off. Everyone should be proud." With a sweep of a hand he gestured toward the group of youngsters surrounding a smiling Little Fawn, "Especially those who defended our fallen member."

A rousing cheer went up from the tribe. Howling Wolf paused to let the people celebrate. In the face of everything that had happened, they needed that moment. Finally, he raised a hand to bring quiet and order once again.

"I would like to let our celebration go on but cannot." Everyone grew serious as he paused before continuing. "We don't know if the raiders will be back, but the council agrees that it is highly likely. Under these conditions, we feel we should move our village to a safer place."

A low murmur rose from the villagers. Again, he let it continue briefly before calling for calm. "This has not been an easy decision, but as you can see, the fires they set destroyed most of our shelters." He paused, letting the villagers look around and take in everything before he continued. "We'll rebuild, but we'll rebuild in a new place. Should they come again, they will find us harder to attack."

"Where will we find this place?" a village woman, Red Bird by name, asked.

"Good question," answered Howling Wolf. It was a

good question because he had prepared for it, "Our friend, Tigal returned just after midday. He knows of a place where he believes we will be safe. Right now, Tigal leads a party of Narwikin—White Badger, Waving Grass, Red Deer, and a few others—to scout a new home. We'll know what they've found when they return. If this doesn't work, then we'll find another location … we'll look until we find one." He looked over the crowd and finally said, "Go back and gather your things … prepare to move."

"And if we don't want to move?" Red Bird persisted.

Howling Wolf knew the problem wasn't moving, but security. Being a nomadic people, their ancestors had long followed the herds, making seasonal treks whenever the herds moved or when the weather grew harsh. He answered her patiently, thoughtfully. "We are Narwikin. It would be best if we all stayed together; however, the decision is up to each individual. If you're set against moving, you can stay here or find a new place. Either way, we will provide you with what we can spare, but you will take your chances should they return."

### 

The search party left immediately after Tigal's arrival. They traveled that day until the night grew so dark no one could see their next step then they stopped to rest. When the horizon began to show signs of the approaching morning, they resumed their trek. They had not gone far when they reached a river still cloaked in mist.

Pointing, Tigal said, "There. It's there, just as my scouts reported. See it?"

Through bleary eyes, his companions—Red Deer, White Badger and Waving Grass— looked out over the deceptively calm waters. Squinting as they peered through the early morning fog, the group looked for some sign of what

Tigal was talking about.

"Rocks!" Waving Grass said triumphantly. "I see rocks! Is that the opposite shore?"

"No," Tigal said. "When I first came across this place a few summers ago, it was mid-day. There was no fog then. That's the shore of an island that divides the river in two. The two channels join up below the island and just before the falls."

"Falls?" The others chorused.

"Yes, falls," he said. "Not too high, but really rough. They're at the base of the island. Both channels flow through narrow ravines … fast water and high rock walls on both sides with many rapids throughout. That's why nobody's over there."

White Badger shrugged, "If nobody's been over there … how do we get there?"

Pointing upstream toward the end of the island, Tigal said, "I think there's one spot where you might be able to come ashore. It's near the point and on this side …."

Red Deer grew excited. His thoughts racing his words, he interrupted the caravan leader, "We'll need a long rope. A swimmer starting from a short distance up river will have to swim out, maybe with a log as a float, and let the current carry them downstream."

White Bader was perplexed. "Why not swim across here where the river is narrower?"

To answer his question, Waving Grass threw a stick. It twirled through the air and landed near midstream. They watched as the current swept it downstream.

Red Deer pointed toward the open mouth of the gorge. "See how fast the stick moves? With the current that strong it would carry a swimmer into the ravine before they reached the other side. By starting above the island, the current will carry them downstream as they swim across.

Once over there, the swimmer can tie off the rope. It will be used to guide the rafts." Smiling confidently, he looked at Tigal and White Badger, hoping he could inspire some support.

"Sounds easy enough …," White Badger said, not quite convinced.

Red Deer smiled and said, "It'll be okay, you'll see. Let's go back and bring the others."

### 

It took two days for the villagers to pack their things and make the journey from the old village to the shore overlooking their new home. Howling Wolf gathered the council and gave Red Deer and White Badger time to explain the next step.

"Someone will have to tie a rope around their waist and swim over to the island," Red Deer explained.

"But first, we should assign men to build some rafts," White Badger interjected.

Waving Grass shrugged. "The Attikamekey arrived on rafts. We can start with those and build others as necessary."

Interrupting again, Red Deer volunteered, "It has been a long time since Tigal has been here. I want to lead a party over to make sure the place is uninhabited and the land is good."

Howling Wolf nodded. "Yes, once you can get across, make a quick search. If it appears clear, light two fires; if there are problems, set one fire."

Turning to the Council members, he said, "We should go forward with the idea that others have not settled on the island. We need work parties to gather materials for our new village. Have the clans provide workers for this task."

###

Howling Wolf found Red Deer, Silver Fox, and Crooked Foot in the middle of a mob of youngsters who were busy tying leather ropes together. Nearby, Bright Moon and Waving Grass chatted. Little Fawn, under the pretext of sunning herself, lay on a nearby boulder and watched Red Deer, the center of her attention.

Howling Wolf nodded to Red Deer. "What are you doing?"

"Making ropes long enough to stretch to the island," Red Deer replied.

Howling Wolf looked at the coils of rope piled in front of them. "Don't you think you have enough?"

Red Deer, busily testing each knot, answered, "I don't know … I have to guess, and hope I'm not short." He looked up from his work and added, "I don't want to get half way over there and find it's not enough."

In a low voice, Bright Moon said something to Little Fawn and gave a short nod to Waving Grass. Unnoticed by the men, the trio rose, and the younger women nonchalantly followed the old woman upriver and around the bend, disappearing behind an outcropping.

Once out-of-sight, Bright Moon looked over at Waving Grass. "The men are spending too much time talking and not enough time doing, don't you agree?"

Waving Grass dropped her eyes. A rosy flush came to her face. "Yes."

Bright Moon came to a halt, "I thought so too." She turned to face Little Fawn, "Sometimes women have to move things along." She raised an eyebrow waiting for the girl to make sense of her words.

Waving Grass helped by asking, "The log at your feet, do you think it will float?"

The log in question, grounded there during some earlier flood, was left abandoned when the waters receded. It sat on an incline between the bank and the river. Little Fawn put her foot against it and gave a shove. Rolling down the embankment, it plopped into the river, bobbed to the surface, and began drifting downstream.

"Your log is getting away," Waving Grass observed.

Smirking, Bright Moon added, "If you want to move this along, you'd better get going."

Waving Grass looked at the surprised girl. "We'll bring your clothes over on the first trip. In the meantime, you can lay on the rocks over there and sun yourself."

Grinning at the idea, Little Fawn slipped out of her tunic and entered the water.

### ###

Perplexed, White Badger joined Howling Wolf and Red Deer. "Tell me how this is going to work again," he asked.

"We'll use our rope," Red Deer explained. He pointed to a tree on the bank, "One end is tied to that tree. The other end is tied around the swimmer and a log."

Red Deer looked at the others to make sure they were still with him. "The swimmer uses a log as a float while they cross."

Still doubtful, White Badger looked at the tree then at the island, and the river. Seeing White Badger's concern, Red Deer added, "The log will give the swimmer a place to rest along the way. The rope will let us pull him back if needed; otherwise, it will let the swimmer cross, and he can tie it to a tree on the island."

White Badger's next response was curtailed by splashing water and a yell from Little Fawn, "Hey, somebody throw me a rope."

Everyone turned toward her voice. Little Fawn, clutching a log, splashed water their way as she drifted by.

"Hurry up and throw the rope before the river carries me too far away," she demanded.

Before anyone else could move, Silver Fox flung a rope her way. It was a good throw, falling across the log. He made sure the other end was securely anchored to a tree.

Little Fawn tied a loop in her end of the rope, slipped it around her and over the log. Pushing the log ahead, she began paddling toward the opposite shore as the current carried her downstream.

Over her shoulder, Little Fawn yelled, "Don't forget to bring my clothes ... this water is cold." Turning back, she began paddling in earnest.

"Wait," yelled Red Deer. "Come back here. You can't do that."

Howling Wolf tried to hide his laughter behind a fit of coughing. More direct, White Badger clapped Red Deer on the shoulder and said, "Save your breath. She has a mind of her own, and you're just shouting into the wind."

Red Deer stood open-mouthed, watching the girl paddle across the river. Neither Howling Wolf, seemingly always solemn, nor White Bader was able to contain their laughter.

Even though they saw what had transpired, Silver Fox and Crooked Foot stood there dumbfounded. What was it that brought such merriment to the older men and stopped Red Deer in his tracks? Though they had witnessed it, neither one of the boys understood what occurred.

### 

Pulling on the rope, feet braced against posts, Howling Wolf and the others hauled the raft through the darkness to the safety of the island. The young, the old, the lame, brought across on earlier trips, waited their arrival.

This trip brought supplies, tools, ropes, small animals,

dried food, buffalo robes and hides. Those already there and those yet to arrive would need these items to start rebuilding their new village.

A bump signaled their arrival. Howling Wolf turned to White Badger. "It looks like we're here. What do you think of it?"

White Badger clasped his friend's shoulder, "The scouts told us fresh water is readily available along with trees and meadows. In smaller amounts, it has everything we left. I just don't know ...."

"What?"

"It looks okay so far, but ...." White Badger shrugged. "How long do you think we'll be safe on the island?"

Howling Wolf nodded. "It's hard to say, but I think we're safer here than where we were." He picked up a basket of goods and gave it to the next man in line. Passed hand-over-hand, the goods were shifted from the raft up the embankment to those waiting above.

Not ready to accept his answer, White Badger went on with his questions, "What do you think will happen when they come back?"

Howling Wolf shrugged. "It will take a while before the raiders find us, and even then they will have to figure out how to get at us ... or if it's worth the effort."

Shaking his head White Badger related. "I think they got just about everything ... what they didn't get, they destroyed, but I guess you're right. We could not stay where we were. At least here, we will be harder to get at."

His arms filled with bundles, Howling Wolf nodded his agreement, "They got plenty but they didn't get it all. At any rate, the council is convinced we need to be ready next time."

"I guess you're right my friend," White Badger said.

Perking up, he added, "Given enough time, they could get a big surprise if they decide to come back."

The arrival of a next raft interrupted their conversation, and they scurried to unload the new vessel.

Working through the night, the Narwikin cleared ground and built shelters. By early morning, things were starting to look good. By midday, the animal pens were in place, and the new village looked even better than the one they just left.

### 

Leading Council members to the foot of the island, Red Deer yelled to be heard over the roar of the falls. Pointing out features along this section of the river he told them, "Our rafts landed upriver, on the other end of the island. Just beyond the point where we crossed, before the bend, the river is a little wider, the current a little slower."

He swung an arm around to take in the wild terrain of the island, "Wide there, the island divides the river and forces it into two narrow gorges. As you have seen, these ravines contain many rapids that force the river current to run faster until the waters drop over the falls below us."

Peering over the edge, council members watched the river tumbling over the rocks. The narrow ravine forced its waters to snake along the path it carved. As long as it was like this, no one would dare cross the river here. No boat could navigate it. No warrior, no matter how brave, could survive it.

Howling Wolf nodded. "The rafts worked okay when we had to move in a hurry," he agreed, "but now we need a path that can be secured when danger threatens. What do you propose?"

"A bridge," White Badger suggested. "We could build a bridge here, two bridges actually, that would meet in the middle," he pointed to the pinnacle rising up from the middle of the channel, "at that rock." He summed it up with, "A bridge built there would let us cross, but be easy to defend."

Raising his gaze, he examined the pinnacle standing between the two sides. It gave the appearance of a rocky bone stripped of its soft flesh. At some point in the past, this might have all been a level plain. Then some force had gouged the river channels, leaving the island and the pinnacle here. In his life, he had seen flash floods roll over soft ground leaving gorges where none had been before. Looking at the wild river below, it wasn't hard to imagine the same thing having happened here.

"A bridge would be good," Howling Wolf looked around at the stunted vegetation, "but it would need a lot of big trees."

White Badger was ready for him, "I heard the story about the place where Crooked Foot defeated Tawasiki. In that place, there is a pile of trees of all sizes. We could free some and float them down to the rafts. From there, we'd have to bring them ashore and carry them overland to this place."

Nodding, Howling Wolf listened carefully before he spoke. "A good idea, but it would take more time than we have right now."

Wanting to bolster White Badger's spirits, Howling Wolf said, "We should use the rafts and the timbers you spoke of to build a floating bridge where we crossed. One we can cut loose, if needed. When we are settled, we can consider a bridge like the one you suggest."

Everyone nodded agreement. It would be work, but the Narwikin have always worked and worked hard. That wasn't a problem.

# Chapter 35: Nuts and Berries

Berries! Plenty of plump berries and nuts—acorns, walnuts, chestnuts, and pecans—were in abundance. Early fall had arrived and the forest brought forth its bounty. Little Fawn and the group of youngsters she led were there to take advantage of this gift while the harvest was in its prime. As they worked, Silver Fox and Crooked Foot stood watch. Little Fawn thought their presence unnecessary, but in light of the most recent raid, the council was firm about providing protection for her and the youngsters.

Both of the boys were less than excited about the idea. Tigal's caravan had ventured out on another of their short excursions. The boys would rather have been chosen for that expedition than be here, but they stood watch anyway, wary that this too could be a test. Test or not, they kept a sharp eye out for any signs of intruders. All seemed quiet.

Voices hushed, Little Fawn and her charges busied themselves picking fruit from the bushes or nuts from the ground, dropping their prizes into small baskets attached to cords at their waists. This freed the workers to pick with both hands as they cleared each bush or the ground under each tree. As each basket filled, or when they had to move to another patch, the smaller baskets were dumped into larger containers. Poles through the handles of the larger baskets made them easier to carry from place to place.

Moving from one thicket to another, one nut tree to the next, the group advanced through the forest until, near the crest of a hill, their path through the forest merged with one that came up from the river, forced this way as an alternate to crossing a bog. The combined track followed the ridge before winding down the steep hillside to a meadow which was the boundary between this forest and the next.

Half way across the meadow the path split again. One leg headed toward their goal, the forest beyond the grassland. The other, having skirted around the bog, wove its way through low brush and thin clumps of young trees before it turned back toward the river. To move on, they would have to leave the protection they currently enjoyed, cross an open meadow and enter the shelter of the next forest.

Silver Fox signaled the group to stay back and to remain undercover until he made sure it was safe. Following his directions, everyone crouched down along the animal trail to watch him cautiously exit the trees, move forward down the hill, and enter the meadow. While Little Fawn and Crooked Foot lay hidden, they scanned the meadow area looking for any sign of trouble. Grasses, clumps of bushes, and trees waved innocently in the breeze.

Through the undergrowth, Crooked Foot could make out the silver ribbon that was the river. But wait! Something was different. Long dark shapes, only partially visible through the leaves, bobbed idly on the water. Boats! Intruders!

Silver Fox, beyond the base of the hill, had ventured out into the meadow when he heard a bird call from behind him. Hearing the warning from his friends, Silver Fox turned to retreat, but a group of men erupted from hiding. Surrounded, he made a valiant attempt to fight his way free. This ended with a blow to the side of his head. He went down, and a couple of the thugs, cords in hand, were on top of him. The others gathered in a small group with weapons still at the ready.

Little Fawn had to struggle to keep Crooked Foot from running down there. "Think!" she whispered in his ear. "You'll do him no good, and you'll get caught too. We must protect the children. Listen to what they say and let's make a plan." Reluctantly, he agreed.

From this distance, the two Narwikin youths could hear talking—mostly muffled words—and could only guess at what was said. The gestures these brutes used were easy to interpret, and they didn't make either of the watchers feel good.

Silver Fox's attackers kept looking up the trail he had followed out of the forest unsure if he was alone or if he was the first of a larger force. Both Crooked Foot and Little Fawn knew these goons would come up here to investigate as soon as they worked up the courage.

"We don't have time to run," Crooked Foot said. "We need to hide the children."

Little Fawn nodded but added, "Someone needs to go back to the village and get help, and someone needs to lead those men away from here." Taking White Eagle, the oldest of boys in the group, by the arm she looked him in the eye and asked, "Do you know the way back to our new village from here?"

Speechless, he nodded.

"Good," she said, "then you go now and go quickly. Bring the Narwikin here. We are depending on you."

He turned up the path but stopped short when he heard Crooked Foot's hoarse whisper, "Wait!"

Puzzled, White Eagle and Little Fawn turned to him. She thought he was going to make an argument about her choice. Tossing White Eagle his red spear, Crooked Foot smiled confidently saying, "In case you need it along the way. You can give it back to me when you return."

Awestruck, White Eagle smiled. This was not just *any* spear, it was *the* spear. It was the one Crooked Foot used to slay a cougar and a wild boar. It was made just like the one he had used on Tawasiki. Everyone knew that it was *magic* ... or the closest thing to *magic* a person could hold.

Filled with confidence, he gave Crooked Foot a big smile and started off at a pace that he would be able to keep for a long time. Reaching the split in the trail, he went to the right and was swallowed by the forest.

Satisfied Crooked Foot looked at Little Fawn, "Good choice. He can travel faster than I, and will be back quicker, but are you sure you want to be the bait? We could both take the children and hide."

Crooked Foot could read the concern on her face. Little Fawn shrugged, and quietly admitted what they both knew. "It is not what I want, but what I think is best. If they find someone to chase, they won't take the time to start beating the bushes here."

Not waiting to hear his argument, she turned to her brood. "Listen carefully, children. You're going to play a game of *Hide Rabbit, Hide*. I want you to hide well and leave no trace. I am going to play *Wounded Mother Bird* and lead these people away from you. We've all played these games before, but this time it's not a game. Everyone's life depends on each of you doing your very best. I want everyone to spread out and hide in the fern. Be very careful and don't leave any sign you entered. Don't make a sound. Crooked Foot will be here with you. Stay hidden until the Narwikin come and call you."

She looked down the trail toward the thugs. Silver Fox lay bound hand and foot, and two men were standing over him. Under different conditions, two men guarding him while he was tied up might have been funny. Another group of men, weapons at the ready, were cautiously making their way along the meadow trail toward them. Under these conditions, it was anything but funny.

Turning once again to face the children Little Fawn said, "Go now, my little rabbits. Follow Crooked Foot and hide in the fern. Don't make a sound. Take the berries and nuts with you so you have something to eat. Wait for White Eagle's return with the Narwikin. Everybody understand?" Wide-eyed faces looked her way, and heads nodded. "Good," she said, "While you hide, I am going to play *Wounded Mother Bird* and lead them away. Go now."

Dismissed, her group melted into the undergrowth leaving nothing behind. Not a footprint. Not a twig snapped. Not even a bush was left tremoring from their passing. Swallowed by a patch of ferns, they blended into the forest. Beyond this protective fringe, the trees were bigger, closer together, moss covered. Little sunlight found its way to the forest floor. If she was able to lead her pursuers away, the young ones would be safe until White Eagle returned.

Little Fawn turned and ran up the trail away from her hidden rabbits. She stopped, on the path that paralleled the river about three man lengths beyond the split, and waited for her pursuers. She didn't have to wait long. The group of wary men, looking left and right, came into view. They saw her soon after she spotted them. Not wanting to lose them nor raise their suspicions, she played her role and faked a limp as she ran away, baiting them into giving chase.

Weighted down with weapons, shields, heavy layers of leather armor, and skull decorated helmets the group of brigands came after her, but moved slowly. She was able to lope along easily and still keep some distance between them. Had she wanted to escape she could've kept it up all day. As bait, her intent was to lead them away from the children and wear them down. To make sure they stayed interested, she slowly let the distance between them shrink. Otherwise, they might have grown tired, gone back, searched around, and perhaps discovered Crooked Foot and the children.

Leaving the trail, Little Fawn dodged around trees, through undergrowth, running up and down hills, always circling away from the place where her charges lay hidden.

When she believed she was far enough from her starting point and her pursuers worn down enough they'd be satisfied to look no further, she slowed her pace even more and allowed herself to be captured.

These rogues, older-men, soft from easy living, finally surrounded her. Gasping for breath and barely able to hold their weapons they smiled triumphantly at their accomplishment. Between gasps, their leader managed, "Stick … out … your … hands."

In their defense, she did not carry any weapons. Unlike them, she did not wear heavy body armor made out of hides plaited together restricting her movements. She also did not carry a heavy wooden shield covered with hide. It was no wonder they were tired.

In their present condition, Little Fawn could've made short work of at least a couple of them before being overpowered. But, if she were knocked unconscious, she wouldn't be able to steer them away from her starting point and her hidden rabbits. So while they gloated she did as she was told, trying not to laugh at their triumphant boasting. Laughter would only get them upset. Worse, it might make them suspicious and she didn't want that.

### 

Little Fawn and her captors followed the river back. Luckily, it avoided the path they just traversed. At the cost of her own freedom, her game had worked out as she planned. She paid a price for this subterfuge, but it was no greater than the one paid by Silver Fox who lay in the bottom of a dugout and fought against his restraints. Now and then he received a blow for his efforts from one of his guards who stood waiting for the others to return.

In front of their friends, her captors acted as if her incarceration had been a great accomplishment. Tired of their bragging, the leader used a mixture of cajoling and threats to send Little Fawn's captors back up the hill. They were ordered to search the area where Little Fawn had first been spotted in case others lay in wait. Visibly fearful, the thugs disappeared up the trail.

Reaching the crest, the group's leader called a halt signaling his men to spread out and take a defensive stance while he examined the area. He made a show of reading tracks knowing that if they did exist, they were covered by his men's when they gave chase.

A breeze stirred the ferns along the path. Curious, the leader pushed into the foliage and scanned the area beyond the fern. Blotches of sunlight barely penetrated to the forest floor. He had to wait for his eyes to adjust before he could make out individual moss-covered trees. Small boulders protruded from the uneven ground along with downed trees lost to storms summers before. He took a step forward and was knocked off his feet by a startled buck. He picked himself up amid unsuppressed laughter from the men on guard.

That was enough! He decided that there were no threats hiding here and signaled his men to return. Strutting as his group rejoined the others, he was able to report he made a thorough search, but found no sign of anyone else. Silently, Little Fawn breathed a sigh of relief.

Pushing and shoving, they steered her into the dugout with Silver Fox and began paddling upstream. It was a long, hot ride before they finally came ashore near a village.

From Little Fawn's position, the settlement seemed to be made up of a string of thatched-roofed, wooden huts hugging the steep riverbank. The shelters, built on platforms over the river, lined the river's edge for some distance, making it longer than it was wide. Walkways connected the huts and common areas. Villagers looked up from their work or stood around in small groups apparently to sneak a look at the latest arrivals.

On their arrival, someone left the river's edge in a hurry, disappearing up a ladder and into a cluster of huts. Noise and voices arose from somewhere within. A crowd, the source of this discord, came their way descending on the boat, its crew and their victims. One man, who differed in dress and stature from the villagers, stepped out from the crowd and looked over at the prisoners.

The leader of the captors stepped forward to meet with this newcomer. "Magram, we have two prisoners ...." Further details of their conversation were buried under the chattering of the villagers crowding around.

After loud bantering, an agreement was reached. The thug returned and signaled his men, who promptly pulled Little Fawn and Silver Fox from the dugout and threw them face down on the ground. She attempted to get up, but a spear point stabbed in the ground near her head, and a foot planted squarely in her back quickly changed her mind.

During the trip, neither she nor Silver Fox were given food or water. The thugs wouldn't untie either of them. Now ashore, their guards bound the two prisoners together at the waist. A longer cord, leash-style, was fastened around Silver Fox's neck and a matching one around Little Fawn's. As a final step, each of the prisoners had a short cord tied between their ankles. Secured like cattle, their captors felt safe enough to untie their hands and roll them to their knees.

Stepping forward, Magram looked down at the pair kneeling before him and gruffly asked, "Who are you?"

Not getting an immediate answer, he rained a few blows on each of them with a short, knotted leather rope and then snarled, "Don't ever make me ask the same question twice."

"We're Narwikin," was Silver Fox's reply.

Magram nodded, "Good. You learn quickly." He gave each of them a long, cold stare before going on, "You were found on our lands, so you are ours and will be put to work as we see fit."

"We had no idea these lands belong to you …." Little Fawn started. Her words were cut off by a series of sharp, stinging blows from the knotted rope.

"Silence," ordered Magram. "You speak when spoken to, understand? Now, these are our lands. And everything on them is ours. You were found here, and now you are also ours."

For added emphasis, he completed his tirade by delivering a couple of blows to each of them, then nodding to a couple of his guards. "Take them away. Put them with the others."

A guard prodded them. "On your feet!"

Their captors laughed as the pair struggled clumsily to stand. The Narwikin were separated by little more than an arm's length. Once on their feet, they could move without stepping on each other but wouldn't be able to break and run.

Taking the end of the lead cord, the one around Silver Fox's neck, a ruffian gave it a jerk, saying, "Come on … move."

Little Fawn wasn't surprised to find someone had taken up the cord around her neck. The little procession— one guard in front, one in back—with Silver Fox and Little Fawn between and trussed up like captured fowl, moved forward.

They were led by their handlers up the hillside and away from the river. The sun was setting. She didn't know what Silver Fox was thinking, but she thought things looked pretty bleak.

###

White Eagle crossed the raft-bridge by late afternoon. A ram's horn trumpeted the alarm shortly after his arrival.

"... and then what happened?" Howling Wolf found Waving Grass questioning the boy as she gathered and checked weapons: spear, flint knife, bow and arrows.

"What has happened?" As he spoke, the baritone sound of the log drum filled the air. "Who ordered that?"

"I did." Pointing to the boy, she explained, "Little Fawn sent White Eagle back for help. They were with a group gathering nuts and berries and were attacked by intruders. Silver Fox was captured. We must go to them."

Turning to the boy Howling Wolf motioned toward the shelter's open door. "Go and see Bright Moon. Get some food and drink, and then rest. Go now." The lad quickly disappeared.

Laying a hand softly on her shoulder Howling Wolf said quietly, "My woman, calm yourself!"

She stopped what she was doing and looked at him. Having lost her own children, she knew something of what the mothers must be going through. It was a look of pain mixed with panic. "We must ...." She started.

"We promised each other we would act together. At this time, we must be calm ... think this through and then act. Now, tell me what you know, and then we'll have the boy tell the council."

She knew what he said was the correct action, so she took a deep breath and laid out the story White Eagle had given her.

Howling Wolf listened quietly, and when she was done, he said, "I know the place. It's some distance from here. Whatever mischief these thugs have done has already been accomplished."

Pleading, she interrupted him, "But, we must go ...."

Howling Wolf put a finger to her lips. "The children's

fate lies in Little Fawn's hands. Her cunning and their cleverness will save them. The council will want to hear. We'll go together and stand with the boy when he speaks. Then we'll come up with a plan."

### 

Fire pots, shaded to limit the light, illuminated the way for the Narwikin search party. Arranged in three groups, the armed men and women silently followed White Eagle along the trail. White Eagle stopped and crouched down. The others followed his actions.

Red Deer listened. There were only night sounds: crickets, birds, small animals scurrying in the grass, the rustle of leaves in the breeze. White Eagle leaned close and whispered, "We're near the place where Little Fawn hid everyone."

Red Deer nodded. Putting his hands to his mouth, he made a bird call, waited and then another. Everyone waited, listening. Their patience was rewarded with an answering call in the same pattern. Smiles broke out.

Through hand signs Red Deer signaled the groups to wait there while he and White Eagle crept forward.

They reached the crest of the hill and peered out across the meadow. Bathed in moonlight, it appeared quiet … empty.

Satisfied, he made the bird calls again. The answer came right away and from close by. Moving in the shadows, the pair moved back away from the crest. Pursing his lips, Red Deer whistled a low warble.

From a nearby shadow, a low whisper, "Narwikin, what kind of bird makes a noise like that?" A familiar figure bobbed out of the darkness.

Red Deer greeted his friend. "Crooked Foot! I am glad to see you!" He grabbed the boy's shoulders and hugged him gleefully. Excited, White Eagle jumped up-and-down.

Giving them both a wide smile, Crooked Foot said, "Not as glad as I am to see both of you."

White Eagle waved the spear he carried. "I brought this back to you," he said.

Crooked Foot rewarded the young lad with a big smile and a simple message. "You done well, Narwikin."

"Where are the others?" Red Deer questioned.

"Silver Fox was captured first. Little Fawn led the thugs away, but after sometime I saw them return by another path. They brought her back all tied up and put her with Silver Fox. Then these thugs stood around bragging a while before a few worked up the courage to come back here and search the area. None of them were very brave so they didn't go into the forest very far. When they didn't find anything, they hurried back to join their friends. There's a river the other side of the meadow. The thugs took our people away in dugouts."

At a nod from Red Deer, White Eagle went back and brought two of the groups forward. The first group positioned itself at the crest of the hill and sent scouts into the meadow to check for enemy. The second group waited with Red Deer and the third group stayed where they had first stopped, protection against a surprise attack from behind.

"And the children, where are they?"

Crooked Foot smiled. He whistled softly, waited and then whistled again. From above there was rustling noises, and then baskets of berries and nuts descended. The children followed. Crooked Foot smiled and said, "Nobody thinks to look up."

# Chapter 36: Captives

The sun was yet to make it over the horizon. Darkness and the chill of night filled the air. The quiet was broken by their jailer's barking command, "Wake up! It's time to start work!"

For Silver Fox, who lay protectively next to Little Fawn, his introduction to this new life was a kick planted sharply in his side. The jailer continued to make his way down the line waking sleepers, and roaring commands. "Everyone! Get on your feet and in line! Hurry up, I don't have all day!"

Magram and two others followed closely behind the jailer. They watched him apply the same persuasive manner to the prisoners not already standing. Each time murmurs went through the rest of the slaves in anticipation of what they feared might follow. When there was no response, the jailer gave an extra kick. If there was still no reaction, Magram motioned to the men with him to drag the corpse out. For the captives, it was confirmation that some of their rank had not lived through the night. Wails greeted each of these events, but defenseless the slaves could do little else.

With the survivors on their feet and in a line, Magram began separating captive pairs into the day's workgroups, barking out assignments as he walked down the line. "Mineworkers, wood gatherers, ovens, construction …."

Silver Fox and Little Fawn, no longer bound at the neck, lined up with the others. Whatever abuse they'd be subjected to, they wanted to face it together.

Except for the lack of neck leases, the guards used the same methods that morning they had previously used on Little Fawn and Silver Fox. When the groups were assembled, guard details stepped forward: one set of guards positioned themselves in front and one set behind each pair of workers. They were there to prod the workers into action as they were taken away.

Towering over everyone, Magram looked Silver Fox and Little Fawn over. "Well, here are our newest arrivals. You're strong, so I'll give you to Great Elk, the brickmaker. Since you're new, I'll tell you this once: The guards are armed and always around to make sure you don't escape. Don't dally or take breaks. The guards decide when you get a water break. You get one meal … when you're brought back here."

Finished, Magram motioned to the guards. At his signal, the guard in front casually said, "Follow me." Without warning, the one in back gave a push and commanded, "Get moving! There's work to do!"

### 

On their arrival at the work site, the lead guard called, "Great Elk, I've brought you fresh, willing, young workers today."

Great Elk, a stocky old man, didn't like the invaders. "Why don't you go back to where you belong?"

The guard raised his whip handle close to the brickmaker's face. "Be careful what you say, old man. One day we won't need bricks; then we won't need you. Now, tell these two what you need done and get to work."

Ignoring the guard's glare, Great Elk turned to Silver Fox and Little Fawn. "The main ingredients in bricks are sand, clay and water all mixed in the right proportions. That's my job."

He waved his hand in various directions as he added, "Clay has to be dug out of the river bank and brought here along with sand from the knoll over there and water from the creek. Those are your jobs. I'll tell you what I need, and you bring it."

"From the looks of the excavations, you've been working here for some time," Little Fawn observed.

A guard got her attention with a sharp crack of his whip across her bare arm. He glared at her and said, "No talking! Your job is to work, not to talk."

Turning to the brickmaker, he said, "You got bricks to make. Get the boy a digging tool and the girl a basket so they can get to work!"

"They're bound together. If you want them to do these jobs, you'll need to separate them." After that demand, Great Elk defiantly crossed his arms over his chest.

Bested in this round of verbal battle, the guard smoldered but finally cut the cords at their waists. "Don't get any ideas about escaping. With your ankles still tied, you can't outrun me."

Separated from each other, the Narwikin pair was led to the clay pit to begin work. Silver Fox kept the digging tool busy enough to escape the wrath of their guards. While he dug, Little Fawn scraped loose clay into her basket and lugged it to the brickmaker. She took her time and gave Silver Fox a rest between trips.

"Dump your basket in the pit and then bring water," Great Elk told her as he pointed to a couple of water pouches.

Emptying her basket, she picked up the pouches and headed for the creek where she found another woman. Nearby, a guard dozed in the shade of a tree while this woman, knee deep in the water, filled pouches. Little Fawn quietly entered the water and stood near her counterpart.

The woman whispered, "Who are you?"

"I am called Little Fawn. My friend and I were collecting acorns when these thugs captured us. And you?"

"I am Bending Willow, of the Sabala. This is our village. The invaders fell on us one night, and now we're held hostage."

"Hostage?"

"Yes, we still live in our homes but aren't free to leave. They make us do their bidding by confining our mates and our children. I have to haul water for the guards and the animals."

"Animals? What animals?"

"The ones I've seen are called camels. A few nights ago, a caravan visited us. They went to sleep free men and woke up prisoners."

"Their leader, do you know his name?" Little Fawn asked anxiously, her voice enough above a whisper that it roused the guard.

"You! No talking! More work!" The guard, his nap disturbed, grumpily silenced their conversation and enforced his orders with the bite of his whip. With their pouches filled, the women left the creek and continued their assigned tasks. The guard went back to dozing under the tree.

### 

After each trip, the brickmaker tested the mix. By mid-morning, he sent them to the sand knoll. Soft, it was easier for Silver Fox to dig, but harder for Little Fawn to carry. The sand leaked through the mesh of the wicker basket, leaving a trail behind her. The brickmaker wasn't happy with the amount arriving each trip and said so. "I need more sand, girl. Can't you carry a full basket?"

"It was full, heaped full, when I started, but the basket you gave me leaks so badly this is all that is left." Turning, she pointed to the golden trail behind her. "The rest covers the ground between here and there." Facing Great Elk once again she stuck her chin out defiantly. Startled at her outburst, he blinked and then looked where she pointed.

Having the upper hand, Little Fawn questioned the

312

brickmaker. "How do you keep sand in the mixing pit?"

"Why do you ask?"

"Maybe we can come up with a solution."

Great Elk shrugged. Their guard napped in the shade of a tree. It would do no harm to explain. "The bottom and sides of each mixing pit are lined with brick. This keeps the mixture pure. To add body and keep the bricks from shrinking, dried grasses are chopped into short pieces and put into the mix. Each batch is stirred and kneaded with wooden paddles until it's doughy enough to pass my inspection. These are delivered to the molding area."

"I'd like to see that."

"Find me a solution," Great Elk said, "and I'll take you over there."

Waking from his nap, the guard shouted, "Hey, you! What are you doing standing around here? Get to work, now!"

Great Elk glowered at the guard. "She is working. As soon as we solve this problem, it'll improve our work."

The guard, open-mouthed, stopped. He did not know what went on while he slept which meant he did not know what to do next.

Great Elk looked at Little Fawn. "You'd better come up with something, fast!"

Little Fawn smiled. "The solution is simple and right in front of your eyes."

Frowning, he blinked as he drew back and looked at her in disbelief.

"You lined your mixing pits. If you want to stop the basket from leaking, line it with hides to plug the holes." She arched her eyebrows and smiled sweetly at him.

He glanced from her to the basket and back. "Yes, that'll work."

Leaning closer, he lowered his voice and said, "Let

me warn you: Don't let on how much you know or how quick you are. Magram looks for people such as you. He particularly wants someone who knows how to make the longer bows and how to best use kop. Such knowledge could cause you more problems." Enigmatically, he didn't explain his meaning, but went on to add, "Go back and get more sand. I'll get a hide, and we'll test your suggestion. Then I'll take you to the brick molds."

He turned his back and began examining the contents of the mixing pits. Realizing she had been dismissed, she picked up her basket and shuffled back to the sand knoll.

### 

"The clay-mix gets put into boxes. This is where the boxes are made," Great Elk explained.

A tree trunk lay between boulders. Workers wielding stone hammers pounded wedges into this log. Their efforts split the timber into long, narrow slices that were neatly stacked to one side.

"We split tree trunks to make boards," Great Elk explained. "These are used to make uniform wooden boxes. The boxes are used as brick molds."

Little Fawn already knew the answer but asked, "The clay that passes your inspection is put into the boxes?"

Walking again, they covered the distance to the brick molds while Great Elk explained, "Not right away. First, the boxes are wet down and dusted with sand."

"Why do you do that?"

"Sand is used to prevent the clay from sticking. We use a flat board to scrape off the excess, and then we set the mold in the sun to dry."

Little Fawn looked over the rows of clay-filled boxes sitting in the sun. Next to them, sat clay blocks. "What about the blocks out of the boxes? She asked.

Great Elk pointed out a set of shelter-like huts. "Later on, when they're dry enough to come out of the mold we fire them in an oven to harden."

### 

After sunset, they were led back to their cell where they collapsed onto moldy straw.

The cell door swung open and a pair of women, not slaves though not much better off, entered. Their job was to provide food and water to the slaves. One distributed water, another ladled out a watery stew. The guards gleefully watched slaves scramble to the head of the line.

While they waited their turn, Little Fawn whispered to Silver Fox, "I found out a few things today, none of it good."

"Not good. Not much of a surprise. What did you find?"

"I talked with a few people."

"Talked? The guards didn't mind."

"Oh, they did, and I got a few reminders from their whips. Anyway, the people here, the Sabala, are like us. The villagers are the ones who make the bricks and were here when the invaders came. These thugs overpowered them and now hold their families hostage. Slaves, like us, are required to do the heavy work. We're caged up because we don't have anyone they can hold hostage and control us. The guards are the conquering invaders, called the Kam Na Udo—the People of Kam Udo—their leader."

Grunting, Silver Fox said, "That name has come up before. I believe I heard council members mention it when they were talking about the raids. It sounds like they've made a lot of people's lives miserable."

The concern on Little Fawn's face deepened. "Worse. I heard they took a caravan captive. I suspect it was Tigal's, but a guard woke up from his nap before I could find

315

out for sure."

Shaking his head, Silver Fox stared emptily at the contents of the wooden bowl in his hands. "It's not right. All these people held here against their will. They work us all day, and they bring us this slop when we're too tired to eat."

"It's just as well," Little Fawn consoled him. "It's barely edible."

A rasping voice interrupted their conversation. "I'll eat it if you're not going to."

They turned to look closer at the speaker. A scrawny woman uncurled herself from a dark corner and stretched skeletal hands out for their bowls. Little Fawn took a long look at the speaker and then gasped, "Red Bird!"

Fear painted across her face, the woman jumped as if jabbed and drew back hiding her face.

"Wait, Red Bird. It's me."

Red Bird took a closer look and then broke down in tears. "No … no … no. Narwikin, they caught you, too. Not you … no, we are all lost."

"Red Bird," Little fawn begged, "tell me what happened."

Red Bird sobbed, "When the Narwikin moved their village we struck out on our own. Two nights later, we were attacked. My man and others were slain."

She paused to take a deep breath. "The rest of us were brought here, to this awful place. And now they got you, Narwikin."

Red Bird turned away, burrowing into the darkness; her words punctuated the despair of her sobs. "Not you! No! We are all lost!"

# Chapter 37: Escape

"Wake up! It's time to get to work." The guard's gruff call announced their third day of captivity.

"Everyone, get on your feet! Hurry up, get in line! I don't have all day!" Magram yelled as he followed the guard. A new person, a stranger to all there except Magram and the guard detail, walked next to him. It was obvious to Silver Fox that Magram was showing off for the stranger's benefit.

Wanting to avoid a kick in the ribs, most of the slaves moved without much prompting. A trio of guards quickly covered the cell, ready to jolt slow movers into action.

There was only one person who didn't respond. Magram motioned to a guard who stepped forward and dragged the body out.

Turning to the stranger, Magram said, "We only lost one last night, Romnog, but we lost three the night before. Your men are going to have to find us more replacements if we're going to get the work done."

Looking Magram in the eye, Romnog grunted but said nothing.

As the guard carried the lifeless body out, Little Fawn caught a glimpse. It was Red Bird. She hadn't lived through the night. Suddenly weak in the knees, Little Fawn went limp, grabbing at Silver Fox for support.

Silver Fox didn't see the body and thought Little Fawn was weak from hunger. Hoping for the best, he yelled, "When are we going to get something to eat?"

Glaring, Romnog came down the line. Reaching Silver Fox, he said, "Here boy, eat this!" Raising his whip, he struck Silver Fox a quick blow with the heavy handgrip. Then he laughed, daring Silver Fox to retaliate.

"What's going on here?" A late arrival, a different stranger, interjected. Romnog took a step back. Magram did more than step back; not wanting to get between these two, he edged into the security of a dark corner.

Little Fawn could see Silver Fox slowly relax, waiting to see who this stranger was and what he was doing here.

"Ogdun! What gives you the right to interfere?" Romnog was angry, but he managed to restrain himself.

Silver Fox glanced at Little Fawn. She nodded, only the slightest move of her head, showing she too recognized this new person had power. Each hoped it would mean changes were in store.

"Kam Udo, your leader!" Ogdun looked Romnog straight in the eye, "He wants me to build his city. I can't do it, Romnog, if you insist on beating and starving the workers. Why don't you feed these people something decent at least once a day?"

"Keeping them hungry keeps them working harder. It makes them less likely to escape or revolt and if they do, their efforts are easier to put down." Romnog folded his arms over his chest.

Ogdun's disgust showed on his face. "Escape? Revolt? You've got their feet tied together at the ankles. It's all they can do to shuffle."

"Why am I explaining this to you?" Romnog was on the defensive. "It's none of your business. You don't have the authority to interfere."

"Yes! I do! Check with Kam Udo if you doubt me."

At the mention of that name, Little Fawn noticed Romnog's demeanor change. Turmoil showed on his face, but he could not act and had to back down. "All right, everybody line up." Underneath, Romnog seethed. He could do nothing about his rage but bury it for the time being. "Guards, get them ready."

318

He gave Ogdun one last glaring stare and said, "It won't always be like this. When Kam Udo's city is finished he won't need you. We'll see what happens then."

A slight smile played at the corners of Ogdun's lips. "I'll look forward to that day. Till then, Romnog, I will make the most of the current situation."

Romnog clenched and unclenched his hands in frustration. There was nothing else he could do now but wait for another time.

The guards busied themselves binding the prisoners together, signaling Romnog when they were done.

Romnog took a deep breath and shouted, "All right, let's get moving. There's work to do."

"Wait!" It was Ogdun again.

Romnog, back turned to his adversary, closed his eyes and asked, "What now?"

Ogdun stood with arms folded across his chest. "Where are you taking them?"

"You know where they're being taken." These questions from this meddlesome fool brought Romnog's rage to a boil. "They're being taken to work, to do your work, to build Kam Udo's city."

Ogdun squinted, his lips drawn together in a thin line. "Where?"

Romnog squirmed under Ogdun's interrogation before finally offering, "Some to make bricks and mortar, some to haul wood to feed the fires in the big ovens." He licked his lips nervously before concluding, "The rest to the mines to dig out more ore." He looked away from Ogdun's cold stare.

"I told you not to put people back in the mines until new air shafts were dug."

"People!" Romnog spat. The term seemed to leave a bad taste in his mouth. "These aren't people. They're …

slaves ... not people."

"They are people. The air in the mine is bad. The torches eat it all up, and the workers fall over like flies."

Romnog came close to Ogdun, so close their noses almost touched. "That's why I send the children into the mines. They are smaller and breathe less. What is it with you? Why are you so concerned about these slaves? I don't care about them, why do you? You and me ... we're just alike."

"Take my word for it, Romnog, we're not just alike." Ogdun didn't look away ... didn't even blink as he went on. "Now, set the mine workers to digging an air shaft. Use the brick workers if you need them. It needs to be done before you send anyone back in, unless you want to take a torch and go in yourself."

Romnog drew back, less confrontational now. "The mine workers and the brick workers? Why don't I just use everybody and get it done faster?"

"You know the answer." He gave Romnog an exasperated look. "There wouldn't be enough room for everybody. It would slow the work down. If the work slows down, you'll answer to Kam Udo."

"What about the others?" Romnog asked.

Ogdun raised a questioning eyebrow. "Others? Oh, the wood gatherers. We have more ore to melt. We'll need the wood gatherers. If you don't want to use the brick workers, set them gathering wood. Keeping the ovens going will please Kam Udo."

Romnog, at a loss for words, remained silent, though he continued to seethe on the inside.

With a nonchalant wave of a hand, Ogdun pointed toward the group that included Silver Fox and Little Fawn. "Take the first two groups to work on the air shaft," he suggested, "and use the last group to gather wood."

"I have lost too many workers the last few nights. I

can't spare all of them. I'll send the two new ones to work on the air shaft."

"Fine, just get it done. Don't send anybody back into the mine before the shaft is completed." Smug satisfaction written on his face, Ogdun turned and left, oblivious to the poisonous looks Romnog sent his way.

### 

If yesterday's work had been back breaking, today's was shaping up to be even worse. Silver Fox was lowered into a pit. It was the beginnings of an air shaft being carved downward through the rocky hillside in order to vent the mine shaft running horizontally below it. Like a chimney, it would allow the torch smoke to escape and provide those in the mine with breathable air.

Silver Fox used digging tools when the ground was soft but more often had to use a stone hammer and chisel to break rocks. There was little air movement in the pit. The temperature there climbed with the sun.

Little Fawn knelt at the opening with an empty basket at her side. She waited for Silver Fox to break enough rock and dirt loose. Then they could change places. It would give him a short break while she loaded the basket with the clutter created. When she'd come out Silver Fox would return to digging while she carried away the basket of debris.

It was late afternoon, almost evening, when Romnog, trailed by Magram, two prisoners, and two guards, came around. "You there, in the pit," he bellowed, "come out!"

Even though he didn't know what was going to happen, a tired, sweaty Silver Fox didn't have to be asked twice. Just about anything would be better than staying down there longer.

"Where's the girl?" Romnog demanded.

Before Silver Fox could answer, Little Fawn carrying

her empty basket, returned.

Glaring, Romnog questioned, "Where you been, girl?"

Little Fawn held out her empty basket. "My basket was full. I had to take it up to the building site and empty it."

Romnog glared at her and then shifted his venomous gaze to the other workers. "You two," he spat out, "take over here."

Redirecting his toxic gaze to Little Fawn and Silver Fox, he commanded, "Come with me now! Be quick about it!"

Turning, he started off leaving, Magram to follow. Little Fawn, Silver Fox and the two guards trailed them.

A long walk carried them away from the air shaft and farther uphill into the forest. Cresting the hill, they followed an animal trail until they finally came to a halt at the edge of a grassy bluff overlooking the river. Here and there, other groups scavenged fallen timber under the watchful eyes of armed guards.

Pointing to a fallen tree, Romnog came to a halt, "There. Pick it up and carry it back to the village. Then come back and get more like it. Both the brick and the ore ovens are in need of wood."

Looking at Magram, he sniffed in disdain. "The others you put here, those weaklings couldn't gather enough wood to keep up with our needs. It is lucky for you that I am patient and willing to give you these two." Turning back to look at the two Narwikin, he raised his whip and threatened, "Don't let me down." Grunting his disdain, he turned and left. Magram followed.

From his attitude, Little Fawn guessed the ovens had run out of wood and his glorious leader became upset with the way Romnog had handled it. The rebuke he suffered was doubled by the time he got to vent it on Magram—too bad for him. Not wanting to feel another stroke of this angry man's whip when he returned, she moved forward, urging Silver Fox to do likewise.

Split apart in a storm, the tree had fallen and now its trunk lay partially buried in the ground. Trees grew closer to the work area, but they would have to be chopped down. It would be beneath his soldiers' dignity to actually do any work, and he certainly wouldn't be willing to arm slaves with anything that could be used as a weapon, so Romnog would be soon faced with a dilemma. One with only one answer: they would have to circle farther and farther afield to scavenge for broken branches or fallen trees. Every day, the ovens required more wood, which meant that every day the circle that was their search area had to grow larger. As it grew, so would the demand for more slaves to do the work. Not a good omen for the Narwikin ... or anyone else.

The trunk was a little longer than a man and two or three hand-widths wide. Little Fawn walked to one end and gestured to Silver Fox to go to the other. She eyed the length of the trunk as if she was sizing it up. In reality, she was watching Romnog as he and Magram walked down the hillside. Not wanting to face Kam Udo's wrath again, they were out to check on other projects and make sure none fell behind.

Squatting, Little Fawn and Silver Fox attempted to lift this heavy burden. It didn't move. She stood up and scanned the surrounding area. "Look for something we can put under the edge," she said to Silver Fox, "something to use as a pry." She watched as the guards shuffled nervously, shifting their grip on their spears while they watched their captives.

Silver Fox found a tree limb nearby. Under watchful eyes, he picked it up and wedged it under the tree trunk. Bracing it against a rock, he pulled down. The tree moved slightly.

One of the guards, older and more experienced than the other, gestured to Little Fawn commanding, "You! Get over there and help."

Following his instructions, Little Fawn joined Silver Fox. The pair tugged at the pry. As they did, Little Fawn whispered, "Fox, I have a plan ... this tree is part of it. We need to move the guards closer to the river. When we pick it up, pretend it is too heavy and drop it. Make sure it rolls their way." Silver Fox shot her a glance but said nothing. The end of the log came up and, unaware of their conversation, the guards smiled and relaxed. Little Fawn and Silver Fox moved to the other end and pried it loose from the ground. Having freed the log, the pair stood leaning on the pry bar for a second.

"Don't just stand there," the older guard commanded. "Pick it up. You act like it's going to get to the oven by itself."

"Okay," Little Fawn said, "but you two will have to stand over there out of the way." She motioned to a spot on the far side of the log toward the edge of the bluff. Without question, the two guards moved around to the place she indicated and stood facing them. So confident of their role, they failed to notice that the edge of the bluff was less than two steps behind them.

Little Fawn motioned to Silver Fox to get on the other end, but on the same side of the log as she. Then, squatting, they attempted to pick up the heavy timber.

Making a show of grunting and straining, they raised it about two hand widths from the ground and then, giving it a twist, they let it drop. The log rolled a short distance toward the guards and stopped. The guards watched unaware of their ploy, but they said nothing and didn't appear concerned.

Silver Fox made a show of changing ends with Little Fawn. Grunting and straining they made another attempt, getting it up to about the same height before they dropped it again. The log stopped rolling just short of the guards' toes.

"What's the matter?" the older guard sneered, "Can't you pick it up?"

"We've had nothing to eat," Little Fawn replied. She looked at Silver Fox for support.

He caught on and chimed in with, "I think we could carry it, but we need some help getting it up in the air and onto our shoulders."

"Well … what do you expect us to do about that?"

She shrugged. "If you don't mind feeling the bite of Romnog's whip then do nothing, but if you want to avoid that, help us pick it up."

Little Fawn squatted as if to pick up the log. Following her lead, Silver Fox squatted at the other end. The pair looked expectantly up at their guards, focusing on them and not at the bluff behind.

The older guard spat, "We're here to guard you, not to do your work."

Little Fawn relaxed. "Suit yourself. Enjoy the whip when you get it."

"You're the one who'll get the whip if this doesn't get to the ovens."

"Oh, I'll get a beating anyway, if not for this then for something else," Little Fawn said nonchalantly, "but when Romnog finds out the fires are without wood because you wouldn't help pick this up … well, when I get my beating, I'll know for every stroke I get, you'll get two. Enjoy it."

"We're here to guard you … to keep you from escaping."

Pointing to herself and Silver Fox, she said, "We're a girl and a boy … weak from hunger. What do you think we can do? We have no weapons, and our ankles are tied together. It is all we can do to shuffle, let alone walk or run.

How far do you think we'd get?" She continued to look at him in apparent dumbfounded amazement.

Not having a reply, and certainly no desire to taste the touch of Romnog's whip, the guard lay his spear aside and shifted his shield to his back. The younger guard did the same. The pair approached the far side of the log and squatted opposite Little Fawn and Silver Fox, both of whom tried not to smile at their subterfuge.

"Okay," Little Fawn said, "altogether we lift." Everyone put some effort into lifting the log, and as it reached about chest high, Little Fawn said, "Forward Fox! Now!" They dug their feet in, quickly pushing forward as they did. Surprised by this action, the guards did not yell as they back-stepped and attempted to lean away from the log. The weight of their shields slung across their backs accentuated their backward movement. Little Fawn and Silver Fox kept up their attack, forcing the guards to back up until there was no place for them to go. The solid ground gave way to the open air beyond the edge of the bluff. It was then that both guards found their voices. Their screams filled the air.

Little Fawn knelt on the edge of the bluff and watched as the guards and the tree faded into the dim evening light. Plumes of water blossomed white in the gloom and signaled their entry into the river. The tree, no more than a dark form, bobbed to the surface again. The guards, weighted down by their shields and armor, didn't.

Silver Fox, attempting to free himself of the leather thongs binding his feet, looked at Little Fawn to see if she was doing the same. She wasn't. No, she was taking off her headband. "Fawn, what are you doing? They're going to be after us … we've got to get free and get out of here."

Paying little attention to his remarks, Little Fawn worked to free the headband from her long, now unkempt hair. Freed, she held it up for his inspection and beamed.

Attached to the end dangled a short obsidian knife blade. A part of her attire, it had gone undetected under her mass of hair. She cut through the cords that bound her ankles and then turned to free Silver Fox. As she finished, an arrow landed near her feet, another buried itself in a nearby tree.

Jumping to her feet, Little Fawn yelled, "Let's go," and started running. Silver Fox was right on her heels. They cleared the crest of the hill and started down the opposite side only to encounter a rock wall. Perpendicular to the river, it ran straight toward the sky. Weathered smooth, with few handholds it blocked their way.

Squeezed between the wall and the river, the bluff narrowed before coming to an end. Turning, they saw the guards clear the crest of the hill. Pointing their way, their pursuers shouted and waved weapons. There was no going back that direction and there was no way to climb up.

Silver Fox grabbed Little Fawn by the hand and shouted, "Come on!" He started forward toward the edge of the bluff. Any doubt Little Fawn had about his choice dissolved with the arrival of more arrows. Forward they went, hand-in-hand, right off the edge of the bluff.

Closer to the water than the guards had been, the pair survived the impact. The rock wall that cut off their escape over land also cut off their pursuers following along the bank, insuring, for the time being, their freedom. However, the river entered a narrow ravine spiked with rapids.

After Little Fawn and Silver Fox fought their way to the surface, they had to struggle to stay there and stay together as the current swept them along. Bouncing off rocks and ravine walls and near exhaustion; they were suddenly rescued by the arrival of a tree trunk, probably the one used against the guards. They both struggled to get to the tree. Reaching it, they labored to hang on while traversing the rapids.

Looking back over her shoulder, Little Fawn could see Silver Fox gripping a branch near the end of the trunk. Fighting for breath, she had to yell to make herself heard over the thundering rapids, "Make ... sure," she gasped, "you ... have ... something ... to ... hang ... on ... to."

Equally winded, Silver Fox hollered back, "Do ... you ... think ... we ... could ...drown?"

"No ...," Little Fawn wheezed, "the ...falls ...will get ... us ... before ... then."

Falls? Silver Fox raised his head enough to look ahead of them. It was then he saw the rising cloud of mist and became aware of the dull roar signaling falling water. There was no way out.

# Chapter 38: The Hunt

Gachald and Paxtald stood stiff as a tree before Romnog and listened while he raged. "Gone? What do you mean they're gone?" Romnog was incredulous. "Gone where?" he boomed at his lieutenants, knowing the level of their discomfort would be passed along to their men.

Looking for a way to draw his leader in, to make him part of the problem, Gachald explained, "After you took them out to gather wood, they overpowered their guards. My men gave chase, but the pair jumped into the river and swam to the log they were supposed to carry. My men said it looked like they were clinging to it when they entered the gorge above the falls. We've sent out search parties and they are combing the area between here and the falls, but I don't expect them to find …."

With a dismissive wave, Romnog signaled he had heard enough. He started to turn away but turned back to add, "If you don't find them, expect trouble …."

Romnog started off again, and Gachald looked at Paxtald, but his slow-witted counterpart had no insight on their leader's remarks. *Expect trouble?* Gachald thought. *From whom? Trouble from the missing pair or from Romnog? Would it matter? Oh, well. I managed to escape my leader's wrath for the time. I'm not going to risk stirring it up now by asking questions. Instead, I'll send out more search parties … No; I'll lead these search parties. That would look even better!*

### ###

To Silver Fox it seemed that the log reached the edge of the falls and hung there forever. Then, as if it could hang on no longer, the nose tipped down plunging log and people into the churning waters below. The pool at the base of the falls swallowed the timber and its passengers. The water that plummeted down after them pounded the pair deeper into the pool. They twisted, turned, and tumbled along under the onslaught. The river current finally came to their rescue by carrying them away from the melee.

Escaping the pressure of falling water, the tree and the escapees bobbed to the surface. Exhausted, they drifted for a time, the tree barely in their grasp as they continued their trip downstream. In due course, working together and with great effort, the pair of fugitives managed to paddle into shallow water. To make it look as if they had drowned, they pushed the tree back into the current, and then the pair turned and crawled ashore. Clouds would soon swallow the moon. Silver Fox led them away from the river. Slipping into tall brush away from the river's edge, they collapsed under a clump of trees and fell asleep.

### 

From his position in the front of the dugout, Gachald ordered the torch held higher. He scanned the dark shore looking for a sign, any sign, someone had recently come ashore. He found nothing. Cupping his hands around his mouth he called to the party searching along the river's edge, "Any sign?"

"Nothing … no sign of them … don't think they survived …," came Paxtald's reply.

Gachald grunted in disgust. *No sign, no bodies, nothing … Romnog would not be pleased.* Clouds had gathered and all but covered the moon. Dampness in the air signaled it would rain soon. *The pair are dead or gone,* he thought, *most likely dead. This whole search was a waste of time, but I must stay out longer to look good for Romnog.* Waving a hand toward downriver he told his oarsmen, "Search on." The boat moved forward. *One more*

330

*pass,* he thought, *or until it starts raining and then I'll call off the search for tonight. Start again in the morning … that should satisfy Romnog.*

###

A hand covered her mouth and Silver Fox whispered in her ear, "Fawn, don't make a sound." His body, close to hers, was rigid. Closer to the river, there were voices, the sound of rippling water. Little Fawn couldn't make out what was said, but footfalls along the riverbank confirmed Romnog had searchers in boats and on foot.

From nearby, another voice broke through the darkness, "Nothing … no sign of them … don't think they survived." Then lower, the speaker added, "Don't see how they could."

Peering through the reeds, Little Fawn watched a man holding a torch walk by, his back to them, his attention focused on men in a dugout. A search party, one of several, it moved on to join others on the river. After a short conference, they moved the search downriver. Those walking along shore scurried to keep up.

Little Fawn could feel the tension go out of Silver Fox. They stayed quiet for a time, listening to the night sounds to make sure the hunt here was indeed over. Satisfied they were in the clear; they rose to a crouch and peered around. Darkness had settled in almost everywhere … except downriver.

There, torches danced around the river's edge as the search continued. Just beyond them, campfires outlined a village built on stilts over the water, its shelters hung from the steep sides of the river banks. It was the one they arrived at on their first night of captivity. It would be the one they would have to go through to get to freedom. They had no other choice.

### ###

The water was as cold as the night was black. A light drizzle started, coating everything and muffling sounds. Throughout the village, pitifully small fires burned in protected areas. Few were about. Those who could, remained inside to enjoy the warmth of dry shelters. Those who could not get inside sheltered wherever they could find protection from the weather.

Slowly and with great care, Little Fawn and Silver Fox climbed over the scaffolding under the huts above them. From overhead came the sound of movement—footfalls, light shuffling—as villagers moved about. Night grew late, people settled down and these sounds all but died.

They took turns leading. Silver Fox, in the lead, held up a cautioning hand. Little Fawn froze.

Having reached the end of the village, Silver Fox's next step would be onto the beach where they first came ashore. He peered through the darkness. Figures moved. It was the night watch. They prowled around the shore checking each of the dugouts beached there. Satisfied everything was secure, the guards moved on. Nothing else stirred.

It would be morning soon. The rain, which had provided cover, was beginning to let up. If they stayed longer, Silver Fox knew they'd be caught. Climbing down from his perch, he slipped noiselessly into the river. Little Fawn did likewise. They moved to the dugout farthest away, thinking its absence wouldn't be missed, at least not right away. Slipping ashore, they positioned themselves at either end. Intending to pick it up, they found it too heavy. They had to push it into the water.

"Check for paddles," Little Fawn whispered, "I'll be right back." Before Silver Fox could protest, she was gone.

In the dark, he had to go by feel but was finally able to locate a couple of paddles. Little Fawn returned and said, "I tried to cover our tracks. In the dark, I don't know how well I did, but I found something to eat." Placing a bundle in the bottom of the dugout, she asked, "Are you all set?"

He nodded, and they both climbed aboard and started paddling downriver. The rain increased, but the river was flat, and the dugout cut swiftly through the water. The first signs of light were starting to mark the eastern sky.

### 

The rain finally stopped, but was replaced by a cold wind. People were slow in moving about. It was mid-morning before someone noticed a dugout was missing. It took longer for the fact to reach Gachald, but not much longer for the same message to reach Romnog.

Facing Romnog, Gachald and Paxtald stood together on the beach overlooking the row of dugouts; behind them stood rows of armed guards.

"I told you they'd be trouble," Romnog accused. "Now, what are you going to do about it?"

"Do we know it's them? Can we be sure?" Gachald was defensive. "Maybe it was somebody else. Maybe some of the villagers took the boat and left ...." He watched Romnog carefully, hoping to see some glimmer of acceptance.

"Come with me," Romnog said. He led his young lieutenant, the brighter of the two, over to where the dugout had been beached. Romnog's stoic[35] features did not betray his thoughts: *How do they expect me to run an army, to conquer these primitives, with dimwits that I have to lead around by the hand? When the city is finished, Ogdun is finished. I will see to that. And, I think the little runt, Kam Udo, will have outlived his usefulness, too!*

---

[35] Stoic - free from passion, unmoved by joy or grief.

Pointing to the ground, he demanded, "Tell me what you see?"

Gachald squatted to look closer at the signs left in the wet clay. "The marks where the dugout was beached … drag marks … marks left when somebody tried to wipe out their steps. They missed some footprints in the mud near the water." He stopped and looked at Romnog. "You're right. It was them. No one else would have tried to cover their tracks. Lucky for us they didn't do a better job."

Romnog stopped as if he were considering Gachald's words for a moment and then added, "But, even if it was somebody else," he stopped long enough to give his lieutenant a cold stare, "we can't have anyone just up and leave. So, what are you going to do about it?"

"Go after them!" Gachald hoped this reply, eagerly offered, would help placate the man in front of him.

"Yes, good," Romnog agreed. "Bring them back and make an example out of them. Leave your dimwitted companion, Paxtald, here to handle the local guards, that way the glory will be all yours."

Realizing he was getting off easy, Gachald quickly turned to his aide and ordered, "Ready all the boats and get them in the water. They've got half a day's start." Men scurried around getting equipment together and boats into the water.

Romnog smiled. *Gachald thinks he is getting off easy but he'll be surprised to find out, success or failure, his fiasco will be addressed when he returns eagerly expecting glory.*

Romnog watched Gachald and his men launch the dugouts and head downstream. They were going with the current, but the river was choppy and they were pushing into the wind. Progress would be slow and the men would be near exhaustion by the time they caught up with his two escapees. Turning, he left the beach to check on his other projects.

### ###

Kam Udo paced back and forth, stopping now and then at a table where shiny golden bladed knives, the new bow, and newer arrows lay on display, taunting him. Turning to Romnog he said, "Tell me again what makes these different from what we already have."

Emotionless, Romnog said, "Excellency, as you observed, these are covered in kop."

Relentless, Kam Udo continued, "Tell me again where these came from."

"They were taken from members of the caravan that arrived a few days ago."

Kam Udo persisted, "Where did they get them?"

"They traded for them in an unknown village."

"So an unknown people in an unknown village have weapons that I want, that I need, and that you've yet to provide!"

Romnog clenched his fists and then relaxed them. *This is not the time to get upset*, he thought, *but I so want to strangle the little runt. I will have to wait until the city is built and then it will be a different story.* "The last moonless night, we attacked another village …."

Kam Udo interrupted his general's narration. "That's nothing new."

"This village beat off our attack by using long bows and arrows with kop tips. We went back after a few days and found a couple of our men, captured during the raid, but no one else. The men told us the village had packed up and moved."

Kam Udo shrugged. "What does that mean? It sounds like you don't know where these people are! What good is that?"

Romnog smiled. "These people call themselves the

Narwikin." He paused letting Kam Udo stew a moment before he explained, "The two young captives that just escaped, called themselves the Narwikin. My lieutenant, Gachald, is leading his men in pursuit. When Gachald returns, he will either have captured the runways or he will know the location of their village."

### 

A string of rafts, a welcome sight, bridged the river. Not having any room on the island side, Silver Fox and Little Fawn guided their dugout to the onshore bank. They beached the cumbersome thing and happily started across the bridge. Before they covered half the distance, a ram's horn sounded. On shore, armed men emerged from the brush blocking their return. At the island, more armed men blocked their forward movement. Little Fawn and Silver Fox stopped in their tracks not sure if they had fallen into a trap. The wall of men separated and Waving Grass stepped forward to eye this pair.

Dirty, disheveled, underfed, exhausted, and covered in filthy rags. Little Fawn smiled, "I know we look a mess, but have we been away so long that no one recognizes us?"

Waving Grass did a double take. "My sister!" she yelled. Cheering, everyone relaxed. The men hoisted the pair on their shoulders and carried them into the village.

### 

Late afternoon found Gachald and his men still on the river. Even traveling downriver, it had been a tough slog, and the men were tired. There had been no sign of the missing dugout or the escapees. *After they rounded the next bend,* he thought, *I'll look for a good place to come ashore and make camp for the evening. We can get a fresh start in the morning. The longer I stay away, the less wrath I'll suffer if I return empty handed. On my return, maybe I can come across a couple of villages to sack and bring*

*slaves back as an offering. That should endear me with Kam Udo ...*
*and maybe put an end to Romnog!*

The flotilla rounded the bend. Ahead of him, Gachald could see where the river split into two channels. Which should he take, right or left? Before he could decide, a lookout in the lead craft spotted something in the water. It was a string of rafts spanning the right channel from shore to island. It didn't matter whether this was the home of his escapees or an innocent village; it was an opportunity he could use. From somewhere on the island, a series of blasts from a ram's horn sounded. "Make ready for battle," he ordered. In each boat, every other man put aside his paddle, picked up his weapon and adjusted his shield. The rest kept on paddling toward the island's only landing spot. To Gachald, it seemed everyone's morale, even their energy levels had gone up. He didn't notice the current had picked up as well.

### 

Little Fawn and Silver Fox, a bath, a meal, and now wearing clean clothes, sat in front of council and villagers and told of their ordeal. A ram's horn sounded a series of blasts, interrupting their tale. Little Fawn and Silver Fox were wide-eyed as everyone jumped to their feet. The pair witnessed armed groups dispersing to various points around the island. Following White Badger and Howling Wolf, they arrived at the bluff overlooking the river. Narwikin braves, weapons in hand, crouched behind bushes or lay hidden in the underbrush.

Dugouts, filled with armed men, had rounded the bend upstream. They were coming this way.

"We've lead them here," Little Fawn said. "I'm sorry. We should have never returned."

"It's alright, my sister," Waving Grass comforted her.

"The Council decided we'd have to face them sooner or later."

Howling Wolf nodded in agreement, "We're prepared for them this time … and they're not prepared for us."

### ###

Gachald heard the ram's horn sound a series of blasts then silence. Soon after, two people dashed across the raft-bridge from island to shore and disappeared into the undergrowth. Gachald dismissed them as cowards, but as he watched the pair disappear, his heart skipped a beat. On shore, where the raft-bridge ended, a dugout—their dugout, the one the fugitives had stolen—lay beached. He found their village and he would make it his. On his triumphant return, he would skip reporting to Romnog and present his captives directly to Kam Udo.

The raft-bridge parted midway, and the end of each portion, carried by the current, swung downstream. There was no other activity. His armada made for the place still occupied by a portion of the raft-bridge—the island's narrow beach.

### ###

From their vantage point, Howling Wolf and White Badger could see the group of dugouts closing on the landing beach. Hidden out of sight, a group of archers made ready. Near the same beach were several ropes. Their ends tied to trees, the free ends passed through the bushes and disappeared into the river. They lay hidden beneath the water to all but those who knew where to look. Here and there along their lengths, a few branches were tied to the ropes as markers. The flotilla approached. Quietly, Howling Wolf watched the place where these markers broke the water's surface. Satisfied the attackers had reached the right spot,

Howling Wolf softly spoke one word, "Now!" White Badger passed the signal along. A ram's horn sounded. The archers stood and began shooting.

### 

Gachald's dugout was the first to hit the rope barricades. Other dugouts in the lead formation also hit the same snags. The jar knocked some of the men into the river. Weighted down by their weapons and armor, they disappeared under water, never to surface. Those left in the dugout tried to paddle free, but their boats caught on the ropes, slid sideways and rolled over, dumping everyone.

Seeing the problems the lead dugouts encountered, those trailing behind tried to back paddle, hoping to avoid the same crisis. They were able to slow their approach but found the current too strong to escape. From somewhere on the island, another ram's horn sounded. The men in the dugouts were too busy to give it consideration until the first arrows arrived. They panicked under the onslaught. People fell out, dove out, or cowered behind their shields as arrows rained down and dugouts tipped over. Once in the water, most disappeared under the surface, but some clung to the dugouts even making it past the rope barricades. Their chances of making it through the rapids were questionable. Small consolations since those who made it that far wouldn't make it past the waterfalls that lay beyond. Gachald's attack was over almost as quickly as it started and he had lost.

# Chapter 39: Spies

Crooked Foot stirred the fire outside their small shelter. "That should hold it for a while."

Huddled over their pitiful fire, Bright Moon adjusted her tattered sleep robe around her shoulders. "Do you have enough wood to hold us through the night?"

Staring into the flames, Crooked Foot barely looked at her as he gestured, "Over there, under some hides … in case it rains."

"Good," she grunted. As hard as she tried, it was difficult to keep up her gruff exterior with him. Yes, it is true; she owed him more than her contempt.

When he was a toddler her mate, his parents—her daughter and Howling Wolf's son—were taken by the great bear. He had been in her care ever since. It was not his fault he had been left an orphan.

Having one so young to care for gave her no time to grieve her own loss. It was a little better for Howling Wolf and his mate, Yellow Flower. They consoled each other and rejoiced at having Red Deer, their rowdy youngest son, to deal with. Fate was against them, however, and a pox settled on their community. The Narwikin lost many. Among others, Yellow Flower was taken. Even Bright Moon had been taken ill. Red Deer, already a handful, became even more tumultuous.

Though there were times when she felt Crooked Foot to be underfoot, and she certainly tried to ignore him, she had to admit she had grown used to having him around. Though she would never admit it to anyone, and until now, never to herself, she had grown fond of the lad.

Looking up from the fire, Crooked Foot asked,

"What we're doing, do you think it'll help?"

"You worried?"

He shrugged. "Maybe. I don't know."

"I am," she confessed. "I would feel better if I knew you were too."

Confused, Crooked Foot looked at her.

"If you are not worried, you could act without thinking; forget the role you are to play, the answers we have rehearsed. You might become smug, get trapped, and end up a slave."

After letting her words sink in, Bright Moon added, "If you are worried, you will be more alert, you will think faster, take fewer risks, and have a better chance of getting back home." She shrugged, took a deep breath and said, "That is why I think being worried is better, and it is why I would feel better if I knew you were worried."

Crooked Foot smiled. "You can feel good. You can feel really good!"

Tousling his hair, she smiled back at him and said, "Get some sleep. I will take first watch."

Without further urging the boy climbed into the lean-to and curled up on the pine boughs that made up their bedding. Pulling an animal hide robe over him, he settled in for the night. It wasn't long before she heard the rhythmic sound of his breathing. *Sleep well, young one. We have a busy day ahead of us.*

Shifting her gaze back to her little fire, she watched the flames as they danced in the darkness. How fast things can change. Just a few days ago, she had sat in the long house with council and the tribe and listened to Little Fawn and Silver Fox describe their captivity.

### 

Little Fawn and Silver Fox stood in front of their

audience: the council, clan chief, and tribe members all had gathered to hear the pair tell of their captivity.

"Whenever we could, we spoke with other prisoners," Little Fawn explained, "they said the raiders call themselves the Kam Na Udo, the People of Kam Udo." Her pronouncement of that name created a low rumble of recognition that rippled through the gathering.

Standing next to Little Fawn, Silver Fox joined in on the commentary. "These invaders came from the place where Mamuta, the-sun-in-the-sky, goes at the end of each day. They descended on the village of Sabala, the Protectors of the Great Fish. The Kam Na Udo made everyone in the village their slaves by holding their mates and their children as hostage. They have enslaved others too. Red Bird was captured and held prisoner there, but now she sleeps the-sleep-from-which-no-one-wakes. Everyone, even children are put to work. They are beaten or killed if they refuse. One and all are worked to exhaustion, and they are given very little food and water. It's not good."

The pair stopped their tale while the council and villagers broke into noisy discussions. Howling Wolf let this go on for a few minutes, then stood and held up his hands. The background discussions faded like a wave rolling out to sea. When all was quiet again, he nodded to the pair and sat back down.

Little Fawn looked over the audience and then started her account again. "One of the Sabala women told me the raiders captured a caravan. It is my belief that it is the caravan of Tigal, friend of the Narwikin. If he and his people were captured, he may have been killed by the Kam Na Udo," she said. "These marauders are using camels to drag skids of brick from the ovens to the construction site. I think I recognized some of the drovers as Tigal's people. There were many guards watching them. I could not get close enough to talk with the drovers, but some of their guards carried bows like those given to Tigal and his clan chiefs." She looked around at her audience and added, "They are also using a mastodon to drag large stones. I did not see Tigal, but he would not have allowed this. You understand now why we fear the worst."

The crowd was in turmoil once again. Tigal and his people were well-liked and the assembly voiced their concern. Howling Wolf let it go on longer than before, but even after he rose to speak; it took more time for everyone to quiet down. Finally, turning to Little Fawn and Silver Fox he asked, "Were you able to discover their purpose?"

Silver Fox looked at Little Fawn. "You were able to move around more than I. What did you see?"

Little Fawn nodded, accepting the opportunity, "The Sabala are a peaceful people with many talents. Besides being the Protectors of the Great Fish, they are experts in clay and make many useful items, jugs, bowls, and the like, better than any I have seen."

She stood quietly during the chatter that followed as her audience acknowledged her appraisal of the craftsmanship of the Sabala.

When quiet returned, Little Fawn began again. "They also dig a unique stone out of the earth and use it for decorations. Apparently, Kam Udo believes this is a new material. I brought back a small sample." Little Fawn held up a pebble. In the flickering torchlight its golden surface, flecked with blue-green, sparkled as she turned to give everyone a good look. Murmurs of recognition arose from the gathering. She handed it to Howling Wolf for his examination. He looked it over and then passed it on to the next council member for their assessment.

In silence, Little Fawn and Silver Fox watched the pebble pass from hand-to-hand before she continued. "When these thugs captured the Sabala, they captured their knowledge and the place where this rock is dug from the ground. Unsatisfied with pebbles, the Kam Na Udo forced their slaves to dig deeper, to a place where the air goes bad quickly. Many adults began the sleep-the-sleep-from-which-no-one-wakes and then the Kam Na Udo found children, because of their small size, last longer. Even then some don't survive."

The throng gasped at the idea and then broke out into heated discussions, some with raised voices.

When quiet resumed, Little Fawn continued her description. "The Attikamekey made use of this stone. It is also the same material Tigal showed us when he was last here. The gift he presented to Howling Wolf, the great knife, is covered with this substance. If the Kam Na Udo captured Tigal's caravan, they recognized the benefits of the longer bows and the arrows with the golden tips. They would like more weapons like this, but do not have the skills to make them. Because of this, they search out those who can. I believe they attacked the Attikamekey and the Clam Shell People to capture workers who could make what the Kam Na Udo need."

Silver Fox put a hand on Little Fawn's shoulder. "You can see that Little Fawn speaks the truth. The invaders are using the Sabala's skills to dig in the ground. They also use their skills with clay to make bricks, something the Sabala had not made before. These are being used to build a great walled-city."

Another interruption from their audience as members traded comments. When quiet returned, Little Fawn continued, "The Narwikin combined the Clam Shell People's bow with the Attikamekey's use of the golden stone. The Kam Na Udo wants to do the same thing."

Pausing, she looked around to make certain everyone

had absorbed this information before continuing. "Kam Udo is building a stronghold guarding the pass over the mountains. No one will be able to come or go without their permission. They want to control everything, and everybody. They will be able to do so if they learn how to make the bows and arrows you now enjoy." Not having any more to add, both Silver Fox and Little Fawn sat. It would be some time before this group settled down.

### ###

Crooked Foot turned over in his sleep and mumbled something. *A dream*, Bright Moon thought as she stirred the coals, *hopefully a pleasant one.* Adding another log to the fire, she watched, entranced, as the flames embraced the wood. It reminded her of the fire at the council meeting.

### ###

Long before Little Fawn and Silver Fox completed telling their tale, turmoil erupted, first in small waves, then larger outbreaks, and finally ending in complete chaos. Bright Moon waited for the gathering's energy to dissipate before she stood, pulled her cloak close and began, "Times are changing," she reminded the council. She looked around at her audience. Crooked Foot, also wrapped in a cloak, huddled nearby. She did not wait for a reaction but continued with, "I can remember when disagreements between clans would split a tribe, and factions would go off on their own." Older members, remembering the same thing, nodded their agreement while younger members recalled hearing tales told around campfires.

Catching her breath, Bright Moon continued, "Some families would go one way while others went another. This occurred several times in my life, but never," for emphasis, she jabbed her walking stick in the ground, "never have I experienced battles between tribes. Times are changing ... or I'm just getting old." She sat down after her outburst and put a protective arm around Crooked Foot.

Smiling at her, Howling Wolf waved his hand to include the rest of the council as he addressed her. "Great Shaman, because of your skills and wisdom, we are all able to sit here getting older with you." Changing the tone of his voice a little, he went on, "I have seen strife among the animals we hunt. Wolves fight to become the pack leader. Bulls fight to protect cows. When it comes to greed, are we any different?"

"Yes," White Badger said, "before we were attacked, we lived in peace with our neighbors. We arrived here after we escaped the raiders. The Narwikin are kind and made us a part of their tribe. They have also provided for others who are homeless, but we weren't safe even here. The Kam Na Udo attacked again. From Little Fawn's stories, they will keep at it. What are our choices? It is clear to me. We leave; we face them; or we surrender and become slaves."

"Before we can make a decision," Howling Wolf intervened, "we need to gather more information. We can start by sending runners to other tribes to request aid. This will tell us how much help we can expect. We also need to find out more about what is going on in the city of the Kam Na Udo and what has happened to Tigal."

Perplexed, the members looked at Howling Wolf. White Badger summed up their feelings by saying, "We agree we should seek help from other tribes. We are also in agreement on the need for more information. But, to find out what is going on in their city, in the heart of the Kam Na Udo, I don't know how we would find out more than what we already know."

Howling Wolf was nonchalant. "Somebody needs to go there."

"Go there! Why, they would risk certain capture and slavery. Who would go there?"

"I have a volunteer, well two volunteers, really, to act as spies. Two people the Kam Na Udo would not see as threats nor would they see them as useful slaves."

White Badger shook his head in disbelief, "A person would have to be out of their mind. Who would be crazy enough to go there? The Kam Na Udo would enslave anybody who came near."

Bright Moon nudged Crooked Foot. Together, the pair stood up, threw off the cloaks revealing the ragged, dirty, clothes they wore. She held a hand out in front of her and assumed the stance of a sightless person. "Who would go there to spy on them? How about an old blind woman ..." and putting a hand on Crooked Foot's shoulder, she interjected, "... and a lame beggar boy."

Jaws dropped as the council members all turned to look at her and Crooked Foot.

Howling Wolf smiled. The council had been caught off guard by this pair of spies. If the plan worked out, the Kam Na Udo might also be fooled.

### 

It had been more than two-hands days ago when Bright Moon and Crooked Foot left their village. They had walked a long way since then. As they walked, Bright Moon drilled him with questions he might be asked, listened carefully to his responses and coached him so his answers didn't seem prepared. Between sessions, they made small talk. Hoping to calm the boy's fears, she tried to answer his many questions.

"When will we get to the city?"

"Pretty soon, I think. Remember, I told you we can't just walk straight there. We have to give the Narwikin and

347

their allies time to make arrangements for our departure when we need to leave. We also have to look like we come from far away. By making a big circle we will come in from a different direction. It has taken many days, but doing this solves both of these problems."

"Yes, I remember. It is also why we have to dress in rags and castoff things from those who sought shelter with the Narwikin."

"That's right. We cannot dress like Narwikin or any of the other tribes. We have to look like we scavenged our clothes. I play an old blind woman; you play the part of a lame simpleton. If they think you're not too smart, it might keep them from asking too many questions. Taking time to come round-about makes the trip longer but it also gives you more time to practice walking with a crutch."

This prop was a parting gift to Crooked Foot from Little Fawn and Abeytu. Nothing more than a rough tree limb ending in a distorted wye[36], it fit well with his disguise. The wye end was wrapped in scraps of leather and the whole thing had been soaked in a dye made from wet leaves then rolled in mud to give it an aged appearance.

Abeytu stood just behind Little Fawn when the pair handed their present to him. Expressionless, Little Fawn said, "I hope your appearance will help convince the Kam Na Udo you wouldn't be useful as a slave."

Abeytu pointed to the cushioned-top and added, "I put some stones under the leather padding. They will give it weight in case you need to use it as a club."

Both of the girls knew that if it came to blows, he wouldn't have a chance against these thugs, but since they could not be there to help, the crutch was all they could offer. Perhaps they hoped his knowing of it would bolster his

---

[36] Wye - the letter y; a Y-shaped part or object.

confidence and help him through the ordeal. When either spoke to him, they were emotionless, their faces set as if in stone, but in spite of that, the pair looked at him through red-rimmed eyes and there was a slight quiver to Abeytu's lips. Before Crooked Foot could thank them, they turned away and quickly melted into the crowd of villagers.

Thinking about this made him uneasy. He shifted the crutch under his arm and went on, "I understand that, but the beating our people gave me before we left ...."

A little irritated, Bright Moon cut him off in mid-sentence, "Will be nothing to the one you'll get if the Kam Na Udo discovers who we really are." Giving him a playful cuff, she concluded, "Or the one I might give you just for the fun of it."

"Blind old woman," he teased, "I should run away and leave you to fend for yourself."

Bright Moon laughed at his joke and then grew serious, "The beating the Narwikin gave you was for your own good. It gives you the look of someone who has been driven out of villages along the way. Our people, our friends gave you that beating for a reason—they want to see you return to them."

"I think Silver Fox hit me the hardest and the most. He must really want to see me back."

"That young-one, is truer than you know. Silver Fox has been where you're going. He can't be there with you. He delivered his blows knowing it was all he could do to help. The rest depends on you. You must be strong by playing weak; be smart by playing simple. Our lives," she wagged a bony finger between the two of them, "depend on you."

### 

Before mid-morning, the Narwikin pair reached the top of the last hill. They stood there for a moment to take in the scene before them. The terrain, rough and rocky, sloped down to meet the river as it twisted and curved around. A village on spindly stilts decorated the river's edge. Beyond the village, the river curved as it skirted a dry marsh filled with tall reeds and grasses. A small copse[37] of trees decorated the river's edge near the bend. The marsh seemed to go on forever. From somewhere behind the village, curls of smoke decorated the sky. Dotting a hillside path, a drover was urging his camel to drag a sledge load of bricks uphill. There seemed to be guards everywhere.

"We are here." Bright Moon's statement was unemotional. She took a deep breath and let it out. There was ring of finality to it. Crooked Foot felt a chill run down his spine.

---

[37] Copse - A thicket of small trees or shrubs; a coppice

# Chapter 40: In the Enemy's Camp

Bright Moon and Crooked Foot, wicker packs on their back, leather pouches at their sides entered the Sabala village. Almost immediately they were surrounded by guards, spears at the ready. The Narwikin pair stood in a huddle. Crooked Foot, playing his role, clung to Bright Moon's skirts. The guards glowered at the pair while they waited for someone in authority to arrive. Noisy villagers, remnants of the Sabala tribe not already enslaved, craned their necks to catch a glimpse of this unlucky pair. Time passed before a hush fell over the crowd. Magram had arrived. Crooked Foot knew it was him by the description Silver Fox had given.

Magram enjoyed the power that came with his role and scowled as he approached. "Who are you and what are you doing here?" Blunt and to the point, he gruffly began questioning them.

Bright Moon, in her role as a blind woman, didn't look directly at him but turned her head in the general direction of his voice. Crooked Foot, playing his part, pushed back deeper into the safety of her skirts.

"Well," thundered Magram, "I asked a question."

Bright Moon held out a hand, palm upward, in the general direction of the sound and pleaded, "Please, master, help an old blind woman and her grandson in their time of need."

Magram took great care to look them over. The woman, bowed over under the weight of many years, leaned heavily on a walking stick, every breath wheezing and rasping through her body. *Was she truly blind?* He watched as she

351

twisted her head around, trying to locate him by the sound of his voice, the noise of his footfalls, and the rustle of his clothes. *Yes, that was a good question. Was she blind or was this an act?*

The boy, sporting a crutch and an oversized wicker pack, timidly peered from the folds of her skirts. "Humph[38]," Magram grunted. "Boy, get out here where I can see you."

Crooked Foot emitted a wail and pressed himself closer to Bright Moon, hoping he wasn't overdoing his role.

Magram signaled one of the guards with a jerk of his head. Stepping forward, the guard grabbed Crooked Foot by the wrist, yanked him free, and sent him sprawling. The meager contents of his pack spilled, littering the ground around them as the boy landed hard at Magram's feet and lay cowering.

Magram hooked a toe into his victim's side and flipped him over. Quickly curling into a fetal position, Crooked Foot covered his head with both arms and peeked out at his assailant from under them. He found himself starring directly into the face of his new nemesis as Magram bent over to examine him.

"Tattered rags! Bruises! Dirt! Wretched smell! Lame! Worthless!" Crooked Foot's oppressor pronounced each word with disdain, "What's your name boy? What are you doing here?

"Cr ... Cr ... Crow." sniffed Crooked Foot as he tried to hide from the inspection.

"Crow? Crow what?"

"Ahhh ... ju ... ju ... just Crow. Don't have any other name."

"So, Crow, what are you doing here?"

"Want food and shelter."

---

[38] Humph - used to express doubt or contempt.

"Humph." Magram grunted as he straightened up. Leaving Crooked Foot lying on the ground, he strode over to stand in front of Bright Moon and lean in close. True to her role, her unseeing eyes looked past him.

"Your name?" He demanded.

She jumped as if startled by the closeness of his voice and wheezed as she answered, "I am Bright Star." Leaning heavily on her walking stick, it was as if the effort to speak drained her.

"Where are you from?"

Bright Moon retold a story that she had heard from her childhood. "I was born into Absaroke, the Bird People. Drought brought famine and disease. It took all but the boy and me."

Magram waved a hand before her eyes.

Bright Moon continued to stare straight ahead, but asked, "Why do you make motions in front of me?"

A smirk came across his face; it was one of his snake-like, I-gottcha smirks. "If you're truly blind, how do you know I was making motions?"

"I felt the wind as you moved."

The smirk left his face. "Humph," he grunted. "The boy is covered with bruises. Why?"

"Not all tribes treat us well. Some are afraid. They see us as a bad omen and drive us away."

"Because they believe you're a bad omen or because you are thieves?"

Shocked at the suggestion, she quickly responded, "Not thieves! We are poor wanderers, poor misunderstood wanderers. We are not thieves."

"Humph," his grunt cut her off. Turning to the guards he added, "They are of no value and can't possibly hurt us. Let them go. Send them on their way." Turning, he started to walk away.

"Wanderers, we look for a new home," Bright Moon called after him, "I invoke the *Wanderers' Right*."

Magram was astounded by her demand. "What? What's this you say?"

"The *Wanderers' Right* binds you to provide us with food and shelter for three days before you can turn us out."

Grabbing a spear from the hands of the nearest guard, Magram started back toward Bright Moon, spear at the ready. Unflinching, she stood her ground and moved her head as if to determine what was going on by the crunch of gravel under his feet.

Aware the crowd was watching his every move, Magram came to a stop, spear tip no more than a hand's width away from her. Through clenched teeth he addressed her, "Do not try me, woman." Still glaring, he added, "I will give you your three days, and then if you are still here, I will have my men use the two of you for spear practice." Having said that, he relaxed a little and turned to leave once again. Passing by the guards, he tossed the spear to one of them; they could sort out ownership without him. As a final jab, Magram yelled over his shoulder, "Consider today your first day."

"You are most kind and generous, master," Bright Moon called after him.

"Humph," Magram grunted. This was followed by unidentifiable mutterings which are probably best left unidentified.

With Magram's departure, the crowd and the guards also dispersed, leaving Crooked Foot and Bright Moon alone. In the event anyone was watching from afar, Crooked Foot continued to play his role. Whimpering, he crawled across to Bright Moon. Likewise, she continued to stare aimlessly until he reached her. Feeling a tug at her skirts, she crouched to cradle him in her arms while gently cooing to him. A distant watcher might have found this to be a touching scene. Anyone within earshot of them may have heard her whisper, "You've done well, young-one. We're in their camp. They do not suspect that we are spies. They don't see any value in us as slaves and we do not appear to be a threat. This frees us to look around before we have to get out. Even still, I believe Magram will have someone watch our every move. Don't let your guard down, not even once."

### 

When they felt enough time had gone by, Crooked Foot crawled around picking up his scattered belongings while Bright Moon leaned on her walking stick and waited. When ready, he shouldered his pack, tucked his crutch under his arm and hobbled over to her.

Bright Moon placed a hand on his shoulder.  Having practiced with her in this manner while they were on their way here, he had learned to read her the instructions transmitted by her grip: slow-down, speed-up, turn right, turn left, and stop.

With him in the lead, the pair made slow, steady progress into the village as if seeking food and shelter. Now and then, she'd signal a stop for a short rest period. By observation, he figured out these breaks weren't because she was tired, but because she was looking at layout from different angles.

They passed through without challenge. Most villagers would have nothing to do with them; a few, a very few, darted out to provide small bundles of food sacrificed from what little they had, before darting away again.

Exiting the village, the pair hobbled up the path used by those going back and forth to the construction site. Little Fawn, had carried basket-loads of rubble from the mine and oven areas along this path. She knew it well and was able to

355

describe it to them perfectly. Periodically, all foot-traffic had to move out of the way to let a camel drawn sledge-load of bricks pass.

In many ways a sledge is like a raft except it travels on land. Three or four sturdy logs are laid down lengthwise. Pegs are driven in the sides, at intervals, to hold the logs in place. Spaced along the top surface, smaller logs are secured in a similar fashion across the width. These hold the sledge together and provide a platform for the load being moved.

The passage of a sledge was always accompanied by shouts and whistles from the drovers and guards. Each incident gave slaves a break allowing them to sit or squat by the roadside before having to shoulder their burdens and get under way again.

Bright Moon and Crooked Foot were able to blend in with the others. She took advantage of any opportunity to gather information without raising anyone's suspicions. No one seemed to take note of the way they studied the movement of people or the questions they asked. When a slave-woman with a basket load of rubble dropped down next to her, Bright Moon asked, "Oh, my grandson is so excited by these animals. He has never seen anything like them. Where did they come from?"

"A merchant came through to barter goods, and he was invited to stay on," the woman replied.

"He stayed to help, how nice."

"Humph. Yeah, just like we're staying to help."

"You mean … you're not free to go?"

"Free to go?" She scoffed, "Do you see the guards here? You're not free if you want to keep on living." Her voice dropped and took on a sad tone as she added, "Even if I could escape, they have my children locked away. What would happen to them?"

"Guards? Guards?" Bright Moon clawed helplessly at

the air, searching for her grandson. "Crow, you never said anything about guards. Crow! Where are you?"

The slave waved a hand in front of Bright Moon' face. Getting no reaction, she realized Bright Moon was sightless. "Oh. You can't see. That's why you're not a slave."

By then, the sledge had passed, and the guards would begin rousting everybody not already on their feet and moving. In that manner, Bright Moon was able to collect a small piece of information here, a small piece there, all without arousing suspicion.

### 

When Bright Moon arrived at the construction site, she realized the Kam Na Udo were building more than a city in a mountain pass. They were building a fortress! Even though it was as Little Fawn had described, it was something that had to be seen. The walls butted against the ravine on each side completing the stronghold. They were made of two parallel rows of brick. Rubble from the mine was used as filler between the brick walls.

The entrance, protected by heavy wooden doors, lay at the foot of alley, vee-shaped at both ends. This passageway cut into the interior about midway between the sides of the ravine. The doors stood open to let the constant flow of traffic through.

Bright Moon leaned against one door as if resting. While there, she tried to search out its weak points without being obvious. She sent Crooked Foot across to the other door to size up the distance. To the casual observer, she appeared to be resting in the shade; he appeared to be playing a game, nothing more.

"You there," a guard came running up to challenge the pair. "What are you doing here?"

Bright Moon now leaned heavily on her walking stick

as she voiced her reply, "Your master has been most kind to us." She reached into her leather pouch and extracted a tattered apple. Volunteering it, she held the apple out in the general direction of the guard's voice as a sightless person might. "I wanted to return the favor by sharing my simple fare."

The guard took one look at the offering cradled in her open palm and made a face. "Move out of the gateway, old woman before you get stepped on." He started trying to herd her out of the opening toward the outside of the compound when he spotted Crooked Foot leaning on the other wall, "You too, boy!" he yelled. "Move … now!"

No sooner had he spoken when a shadow, a very large one, fell across them. The earth beneath their feet shook. Bright Moon pressed herself against the alley wall as Makata, Tigal's mastodon, entered. It pulled a sledge bearing a large stone.

Crooked Foot stood frozen in his original position, back still pressed to the wall, mouth open. The animal stopped near where he stood. Turning its head, Makata's trunk snaked out toward him. In the beginning, Crooked Foot did not know if he would ever see the animal again, but now it appeared Makata might reveal his identity. Panic gripped him!

Leaving Bright Moon to fend for herself, the guard started over to grab Crooked Foot bellowing as he went, "You, boy! I told you to move!"

Spurred to action by the guard's command, Crooked Foot started toward the interior of the compound as quickly as he could hobble, howling loudly as he went. The guard started after him, but Makata turned her head. Swinging her trunk around, the mastodon's move intercepted the guard. The impact knocked the man off his feet and gave Crooked Foot time to enter the compound.

Inside, beyond the gate, he took a look at the construction. A platform hugged the interior of the walls. This would be used by defenders. There were several buildings in various stages of construction. These skirted an open courtyard. Beyond the courtyard, shining in the sunlight, sat a large building. Towering over everything around, it backed up to the only thing larger than itself—the ravine wall.

More importantly, the center of the courtyard was divided by a low wall. Adjacent to the wall stood a platform. Mounted on the platform, surrounded by workmen sat the largest bow he had ever seen. It lay on its side, and he didn't recognize it at first glance. It was mounted on a swivel allowing it to be turned. He watched workers load it with a heavy spear. After attaching a line to the bowstring, the guards used whips to force a group of slaves to tug on the line, drawing the bow back. On release, the spear flew forward striking a tree used as a target. The impact split the tree.

A heavy hand fell on Crooked Foot's collar and knocked him down. The guard, a little worse for wear, had managed to scramble away from Makata's feet and then continue his pursuit of Crooked Foot while others worked to calm the beast.

"You're not to be here," the guard said. "I told you to move."

Rising on one elbow, Crooked Foot was in time to see Makata exit the compound, towing the sledge. "I did move! You did not say which way." Pointing, he added, "That animal scared me. Make it go away."

The guard laughed at this and said, "Stay here, and you'll be more than scared. We'll feed you to that thing." Playing his role, Crooked Foot shrunk back at his words.

This made the guard laugh even more. "Get up. Get

out of here before the monster comes back," he said and pointed toward the gateway. "They're taking her to the pens because it's her feeding time. She will be hungry, and if you stay here I won't save you."

Hearing this, Crooked Foot grabbed his crutch, got to his feet, and hobbled to the gate. Reaching Bright Moon still in the alley, he said, "Grandmother, we must leave... soon! They're taking the beast that frightened me back to its pen for feeding, and it might eat me!"

Putting her hand on his shoulder, she let him guide her out of the alley and away from the construction. The guard stood and watched as they disappeared back down the trail. For a time, he listened as she tried to console the frightened boy. Tiring of that, he disappeared back inside shaking his head and muttering to himself.

### 

Through hand signals, Bright Moon had Crooked Foot guide her off the trail and into the brush. From their hidden place, this pair of Narwikin spies watched as the handlers and the guards guided Makata along the path to her pen. After studying the layout, Bright Moon said, "Come youngster, it'll be dark soon, so we should join the workers returning to the village." She got up and held out a hand.

Crooked Foot took it and placed it on his shoulder. "Where do we go?" he asked.

"Take the path toward the village until you get to where it splits. From there, take the branch that veers away from the village and follows along the river. About half way between the village and the forest there's a grove of trees where the river makes a bend. That's where we'll find our supper and a place to rest for the night."

Crooked Foot remembered seeing the grove when they first stood on the hill overlooking the village and the river. It stood out because the area between the village and the grove lay open, flat, and clear of obstruction, as did the area between the grove and the forest. Bordering the river, it was surrounded on three sides by a swamp, dry at this time of year and barren of trees except for this one cluster. Tall grasses and rushes were left to fill the void.

Beyond the bend, it was a different story. Grasses and reeds flowed back to meet a ridge, divider between the end of the swamp and the beginning of the forest. There, forest and undergrowth came right up to the river's edge.

Until the pair reached the grove, they'd be quite visible to anyone in the village who wished to keep an eye on them. Crooked Foot didn't know what Bright Moon had in mind, but he knew she didn't make any requests without a reason.

It was near sunset when they finally reached their goal. Before darkness fell, Crooked Foot cut tree boughs for their bedding, piling each one in Bright Moon's open arms.

When they had enough, she whispered, "Lead me over to that fallen tree and help me sit down facing the river." When she was seated, she added, "Cut a sharp stick to use as a fish-spear and then wade into the river. Don't forget to use your crutch. Our supper will be here soon. When it arrives, stay calm."

Her instructions puzzled him, but he'd be patient. The setting sun shone the last of its brilliant light over the rippled water. Crutch under his arm, a makeshift fish-spear at the ready in his other hand; Crooked Foot waded into the river. The cool water, not more than waist deep near the shore, covered a sandy river bottom that fell away to deeper water about a man-length or two further out. A fallen tree, long dead, marked the boundary between deeper and shallower water.

Swept down by spring floods, the tree had become

grounded and was now anchored in place by the remains of its root ball[39] with its barren limbs stretching toward the sky.

Ever mindful of his role, he limped slowly back and forth between sandy shore and deep water, crutch under one arm and his fish spear in his free hand. Head down, he watched the water as if he were actually fishing.

Time seemed to drag by before, in the fading light, Crooked Foot spotted a dark silhouette underwater. It approached him from the direction of the deeper water beyond the fallen tree. Was it something bent on doing him harm? Freezing in place, he tightened his grip on his spear. Nearing his feet, the silhouette reached up, a hand broke the surface, grabbed the tip of his spear, and jerked it sharply downward. Crooked Foot bent forward at this sudden action. As quickly as the event began, it was over. The hand released the spear and its owner made an underwater summersault, pushed off against Crooked Foot's legs, and swam back toward the tree.

Straightening up, Crooked Foot regained his footing. His makeshift spear, previously lifeless, now held a large silver-sided fish that throbbed with a rhythm familiar to him as it attempted to free itself. Turning toward shore, he held his catch in the air, smiled, and looked toward Bright Moon as he said, "I believe I have just speared our supper."

Without looking directly at him, Bright Moon said, "Good! I am hungry. Come fix a small cooking fire. Don't forget to use your crutch."

---

[39] root ball - The compact mass of roots and soil formed underground by plant roots. This mass of tangled roots and dirt is often seen attached to trees that are toppled over by a storm or flood.

# Chapter 41: Planning

Bright Moon stared at nothing as Crooked Foot struck flint to tinder to get a fire going, and then he found suitable branches for a make-shift spit. After trimming them to size, they would hold the fish as it was turned over the fire. Still playing the part of a blind woman, Bright Moon gave the fish, now lying quiet at her feet, a nudge with her foot and got it flopping again. Going by sound, she reached down and pawed the ground until she found it. Seizing it by the gills, she smacked it soundly against the timber she sat on, stunning the wounded creature. Crooked Foot took it from her and using his knife, he prepared it for cooking.

The dark night sky swallowed the last rays of the sun, making their meager cook fire the only light. A soft bird call sounded from somewhere in the undergrowth. Cautiously, Crooked Foot risked peering into the glade but saw nothing. He looked over at Bright Moon for explanation. She smiled, gave him a slight nod and he turned back to the task at hand.

While he went on with the cooking, Bright Moon sat with her head tilted downward to hide moving lips from possible on-lookers. She spoke in a low voice not to Crooked Foot but to an unseen listener. Crooked Foot continued to turn the spit, but paid careful attention to the conversation and didn't interrupt.

"Tigal's animals are here," Bright Moon said. "They are kept in a separate stockade. The drovers are kept in a different stockade nearby, but in the vicinity of the place Silver Fox and Little Fawn were kept as slaves. These sites are outside of the village, away from the ovens and the construction."

A voice in the bushes whispered, "Are there guards

there? How many did you see?" Even as a whisper, Crooked Foot could recognize Red Deer's voice. From somewhere beyond the grove, he had crept through the tall grasses to arrive here unseen.

"Guards, yes, but very few." Bright Moon answered quietly. "They work everyone, slaves and drovers alike, hard. It leaves them too exhausted to need more than a few guards."

Red Deer paused, apparently mulling this over, and then asked, "When will you be ready?"

Bright Moon smiled, "In their hospitable manner, they will allow us today and tomorrow. We are to be gone the day after or face death." She stood up, stretched, and then went on, "I would like to be rid of this place. We should go tonight, well, early in the morning when they all are asleep. Can you arrange it?"

"Howling Wolf, White Badger and the others have made arrangements along the trail. We are ready and can meet you back here tonight."

"Good. We will bed down here and wait."

There was a slight rustling in the bushes, hardly more than the breeze would make as it passed, and then all was quiet. If any of Magram's people were watching, they saw nothing.

Bright Moon sat back down, a contented smile on her face. "Is the fish ready?" She asked casually. "I am hungry!"

### 

Supper finished, Crooked Foot banked their campfire and spread their sleeping robes on the boughs. A casual observer, Bright Moon was sure there would be one, would see them settle in for the night and would report this to Magram. Because he did not see them as a threat, he would not bother passing word to those above him.

Excited, Crooked Foot thought it would take a long time to fall asleep, but he was wrong. The next thing he knew, a hand clamped over his mouth muffling his outcry. It was still dark, not even false dawn[40] yet. The red coals in the campfire smoldered.

To the lad's surprise Gray Wolf and Silver Fox's grinning faces were visible over Red Deer's shoulder. "It is time for us to get to work. Are you ready for some action?"

Crooked Foot nodded. Smiling, Red Deer released his grip across Crooked Foot's mouth.

Silver Fox handed out some pemmican. "I hope you enjoyed the fish I brought you last night. It was a long swim underwater, but I knew there will be no fire, no hot breakfast this morning, and I wanted you to eat well when you could."

Everyone gathered in a half-circle facing Bright Moon. "We'll go together," she said, "to the place where the path splits. Gray Wolf, Silver Fox and I will go to the village and find dugouts. We'll bring them back here and wait for you. We'll take the paddles from any we don't bring back."

Turning to Crooked Foot, she said, "You, my young ally, must show Red Deer and the others to the stockades. They'll take care of the guards and release the prisoners. You'll help with Makata. If Tigal is alive, he won't leave without her." Bright Moon paused and took a deep breath before she went on, "If he is not, I know he would want you to have her."

She looked at the faces of those before her. All of them belonged to young men she knew; men who were

---

[40] False Dawn - Also referred to as the Zodiacal Light, is a faint, roughly triangular diffused white glow seen in the night sky that appears to extend up from the vicinity of the Sun along an imaginary line called the ecliptic or zodiac. It is best seen just after sunset and before sunrise in spring and autumn when the zodiac is at a steep angle to the horizon. It is caused by sunlight scattered by space dust in the zodiacal cloud.

determined to succeed. Biting her lip, she raised her head and scanned the horizon. "It will be light soon. Stir up the coals and then throw a couple of small logs on the fire. When we are on the river, its glow will help us find this place." Leaning heavily on her walking stick, she got to her feet, "We had better get started."

### 

The group traveled the distance from the grove to the split without incident. There they broke into their separate sets. Bright Moon watched as Crooked Foot led Red Deer and the rest of his men up the path toward the stockades. Turning away, she found Gray Wolf and Silver Fox waiting patiently. Nodding to them, the threesome started toward their goal.

Moving soundlessly, Bright Moon's group reached a point where they could look over the beach and the dugouts. They spotted their first obstacle: a guard sat with his back against a rock. He was wrapped in a robe as protection from the damp night air. Her heart caught in her throat until the night breeze carried the rhythmic sound of his snoring. No one else was in sight. Gray Wolf tapped Bright Moon on the arm. She looked at him and he made a motion with his knife. She held his wrist and shook her head. "No," she whispered. "If the guard detail comes and finds a body they'll raise the alarm. If they find a sleeping man we'll be okay, even if he won't."

He put his knife away and looked at her. She motioned for them to follow. Getting up, they moved as quietly as smoke to the dugouts farthest from the guard. Noiselessly, they dragged three boats into the water. "Go back and bring the paddles from the other dugouts," she told her cohorts. "I will hold the dugouts here."

The pair made several quiet trips back and forth,

retrieving paddles and piling them in the bottom of the dugouts. Satisfied at last, she motioned for them to stop their work. Each took a separate dugout, climbed in and let the current carry them downstream. After putting some distance between them and the beach, they began paddling.

Bright Moon watched the shore and was relieved to see her small campfire. The first signs of dawn were beginning to show as they beached their vessels.

### 

The animals and the slaves were kept in the same area. Crooked Foot led the rescue party up the path toward the stockades. Red Deer and his men followed closely behind. The group proceeded quietly until it reached the outskirts of the pens. The air was ripe with the smell of fresh dung. If they got any closer without checking for guards, they'd risk ending up as prisoners. Crooked Foot called a halt.

The animal pens were built in the open. The camels were in a makeshift corral, but Makata's pen was made of heavy upright posts sunk into the ground. Rimming the perimeter, sharpened spear-like poles had been placed blunt end down and braced against the ground outside. The honed end of the shafts pointed inward to keep Makata back lest she push over the posts and escape. So far … it worked.

Drovers and slaves were kept in two separate cells carved into the side of the hill. At one time, these had probably been mine shafts. Now they were secured with posts and doors.

This close, Red Deer now took the lead and the group crept closer to the stockade area. He stopped when they reached a point where he could get a good view. There were two guards. One sat huddled over a small fire while the other lay wrapped in a robe sound asleep.

Picking the side of Makata's pen away from the

guards, Red Deer led the group closer to their goal. He pulled Crooked Foot aside, "Go out and do something—try to open the gate—to attract the guard's attention. When they come after you, duck back here. We'll do the rest. Okay?"

Crooked Foot rounded the corner and made his way to the gate. A heavy log, about chest height, was used to keep it closed. Large stones on the end of the log nearest the jamb acted as a counterbalance[41] allowing the bar to be easily raised or lowered by one person. Feeling along in the dark, he found the tip of the bar had a smaller weight attached. If he used his flint knife to cut through the bindings, he could lower the burden to the ground and drag it out of the way. This would let the bar slowly arch up, out-of-the-way, and the gate would be free to open.

He had not come to the guard's attention yet, and began to wonder what it would take, but Makata solved the problem. Having picked his scent out of the air, she moved forward as far as the makeshift spears would allow. From there, the great mastodon extended her trunk in an attempt at slipping it through an opening in the uprights. Crooked Foot could see that she would fall short of her goal and he stretched out a hand. The tip of her nose and his fingers found each other. Sniffing as she went, her snout slid over his fingers, quietly at first, then with noisy enthusiasm. This got the guard's attention. He poked his sleeping partner and they both jumped to their feet.

One of them yelled, "Hey you! Just what do you think you're doing?"

Startled out of his reverie, Crooked Foot jumped. Turning to see the two guards running his way, he gave

---

[41] Counterbalance/Counterweight - A weight that acts to balance another; a counterpoise or counterweight. A force or influence equally counteracting another.

Makata a final pat then ran back around the corner of the pen. The guards, not wanting to let him get away, quickly rounded the corner right after him. They were greeted by clubs and were laid out before they could raise an alarm.

Red Deer cautiously peered around the corner. No one was about. Moving from shadow to shadow, he quickly made his way over to the first cell. "Tigal," he called softly, "Tigal." There was no answer. "Tigal," he called louder.

In the back, someone stirred and sat up. From out of the darkness came a weak but familiar voice, "Who calls Tigal? Who calls my name?"

"It's Red Deer of the Narwikin. We're here for you."

"Red Deer, my friend ... I am glad to see you, but how are you going to free us?" Others, their sleep disturbed by this conversation, had started to talk and move around.

Red Deer smiled. "One thing at a time; everyone needs to remain quiet while we get the gate open." He motioned to his men. A couple ran up and, using their kop-covered knives, began cutting the ropes that held the barricade in place. Freed, it was easily removed, and the inmates started limping and staggering for the door.

Tigal was the last to exit. At the doorway, he was greeted by Red Deer's smiling face and threw his arms around the lad. "My son," Tigal said, "you don't know how happy I am ... we are ... to see you. I thought this day would never come!" He looked at Red Deer and then at the few men with him. "How many are with you? This is certainly not enough to fight off Kam Udo's army."

"We don't intend to fight them ... at least, not here." Red Deer explained. "We must move quickly and quietly. It'll be light soon, and I want to be out of here. Divide your men up into three groups: Those who cannot walk; those who can; and those who can run." Looking at Tigal, even in the dim light, he could see how much the ordeal had drained him.

"We will be safe soon. Divide up your men. I must go and free the others."

Tigal spoke with his men in low tones while Red Deer went to the cell holding the slaves. Many of them, awakened by the noise, were sitting up or crouched around the cell door, trying to see what was going on.

Red Deer peered through the bars into the dark interior. "Is there anyone here who cannot walk?" he asked.

The ones in front looked over their shoulders to those in back. Finally, one spoke, "No, we can all walk. Can you get us out of here?"

"Yes, but you have to follow my directions without question. It means your life. If you put my people at risk, I will kill you myself." Red Deer scanned their faces to see if there was any sign of disagreement. "Okay. When you come out, line up in two lines. If there is anyone who'll need help, you may have to carry them. Everyone understand?" He motioned and more men came out of the darkness. Drawing their kop-covered knives they began sawing at the ropes that held the barricade in place.

Red Deer went back to Tigal. There were two groups of men with him. "If it means getting away from here, they all say they can at least walk," Tigal explained.

Red Deer nodded. "Good, now I need some animal handlers. Get baskets on the camels. If we have to, we can carry people in them. Have your men act quickly. It'll be light soon."

By the time Red Deer returned to the slaves' pen, his men had their cell door open and were cutting their restraints. "As soon as you get everyone freed, get ready to herd them toward our meeting point. Do it quickly and quietly," he instructed.

The camels were milling about in the corral, snorting and calling softly. Drovers hurried about attaching baskets and harnesses. Red Deer caught one of the drovers by the arm asking, "Can you do anything to keep the animals quiet?"

"They will be okay when we get underway. They seem to take comfort in following Makata." A look of panic crossed his face, "You are taking her, aren't you?"

Red Deer, smiling at his concern, answered, "Yes, we are. Everybody is out of the cells, and we are starting to move them along. I will see about getting her out, and we can be rid of this place. Let me know when you are ready."

He watched as the drover went off to check on progress. Looking over at Makata's pen he spotted Crooked Foot stroking her outstretched trunk. The boy had a way with the animal. It would be a big help.

The drover returned. "We are ready. Do you want me to bring the camels out now?"

"No," Red Deer replied. "I don't know how many people your animals can carry, but get as many of the children and weaker adults loaded into the baskets as fast as you can. We have about a day's travel ahead of us." The drover nodded and went off.

Red Deer joined Crooked Foot at Makata's pen. "Glad to be together?" he asked. Crooked Foot, his eyes alight, nodded but said nothing. "We're ready to move out. I'll get the gate open. You're going to ride up top with Tigal. Keep her calm and quiet. I will have a couple of guides out front. You follow them. The camels will follow you. Everybody walking will follow behind. Understood?"

Wearing a big grin, Crooked Foot nodded acceptance. Red Deer opened the gate. Makata snorted and stepped cautiously forward to greet them. Red Deer watched as the mastodon's trunk seemed to pass all over the boy, as if it were making sure he was real. Then it curled around his waist, picked him up, and gently set him down just behind her head. Even from this distance Red Deer could see the smile on

Crooked Foot's face.

### 

False-dawn found the procession underway. For a big animal, Makata could move both quickly and quietly. They met Bright Moon, Silver Fox and Gray Wolf at the grove. Red Deer had most of the group continue their journey. They had a long way to go and needed to put some distance between themselves and the village before the alarm was sounded.

"You made good time," Bright Moon told Red Deer.

He nodded. "Better than I expected," he said. "I had the two guards bound, gagged and thrown into the cells. I also had all the gates and pens closed and placed a couple of fake bedrolls nearby to make everyone think the guards are sleeping. At first glance, it should look pretty normal which will delay things a bit, but they'll be on our trail soon."

Red Deer's words were greeted by turmoil coming from the village. "Well, I guess they found out we're gone. Take these people with you. They are too weak to walk far, but can paddle."

Once aboard the dugouts, the people started paddling down river. There was a light fog rising from the water. Red Deer watched as it swallowed them. *Fog is good; it'll help hide them from pursuers.* Then it hit him … *fog and the fact that Bright Moon has most of the paddles from the other dugouts with her, will certainly delay pursuit on the river.* He laughed to himself at the idea and then, satisfied this part of the plan went well, Red Deer turned and hurried up the trail after the rest of his charges.

### 

Kam Udo paced back and forth. He raged at the loss of the slaves and the animals. He raged at the delays in the building project. But mostly he raged at what he called the incompetence of those who reported to him.

Magram, Romnog, and Paxtald stood at attention and tried to look inconspicuous while wishing they were somewhere, anywhere else. Even Ogdun, the architect, stood quietly in nearby shadows with the same wish.

"Explain to me again," Kam Udo raged, "how the slaves and the animals are gone. What army came and took them?"

"Not an army ... well ... ahhh, not that we know of," Romnog stammered.

"The only strangers here were an old blind woman and a lame boy, her grandson," Magram volunteered.

"An old blind woman and her lame grandson? They were here, right here, under the noses of your army, and the two of them did all of this? Is this what you want me to believe?"

"Yes, Excellency," Romnog replied quickly. "The boy was seen at the animal pen. The guards gave chase but were knocked out. We found them tied up in the back of the slaves' cells. They didn't see anyone else and feel the old woman was some kind of witch who cast a spell on them." Thinking he could appease Kam Udo, Romnog added, "Not wanting to have their fears spread among the others, I've kept the pair locked away in the cell. I can have them executed before the rumor spreads."

"Fears? Rumors? Does your army have a problem?" Kam Udo gave him a piercing look.

"Well, rumors have been flying ever since the boy and girl escaped. It's said they used magic to trick their guards, and more magic to survive the falls. Then Gachald and his guards went after them and never returned." He paused knowing this next part wouldn't go over well, "And a few boats turned up missing this morning."

"More! Gone?" Kam Udo asked incredulously.

"Yes, Excellency, several dugouts are gone, along with most of the paddles from our other dugouts."

Kam Udo snorted in disgust, "I suppose the guard there saw nothing." One glance at Romnog gave him his answer, so he continued, "I don't think the animals took the dugouts, so it had to be somebody else, probably unrelated. You can take a nose-count of the remaining slaves later. Right now, I want you to put every man you have into the field. Track down these thieves and my animals and bring them back here. I'll deal with these upstarts myself." Kam Udo paused in his order-giving and looked at Romnog who stood immobile as if transfixed. "Well, what's the problem? Why aren't you moving?"

"How'll I find them?"

"Do I have to do everything? The big animal, the one called a mas ... mas ...."

"Mastodon," Romnog ventured.

"Yes, that one," he replied. "It is almost as big as the palace we've built. It should be easy to find. It leaves prints in soft ground and huge piles of dung wherever it travels, so if you cannot see it, maybe you can smell it." As an afterthought, Kam Udo added, "Leave me enough guards to keep the villagers in check."

Wanting to appear in command in front of his leader, Romnog turned to Paxtald and ordered, "Get the men ready to march. I believe the slaves are hiding in the swamp. We will start by sweeping that area to the forest."

Tired of them, their incompetence, their lack of imagination, Kam Udo waved them away.

Happy to be out of there, Magram, Romnog, and Paxtald turned and exited quickly. Kam Udo watched them leave, and then turned to Ogdun. "The cave behind the palace, is it still open?"

"Why yes, Excellency," Ogdun responded quickly, "it is as you instructed. There is a hidden door from your private quarters into the cave and the exit route through the caverns has been marked."

Kam Udo nodded. "Good! It pleases me that you, at least, can follow directions."

Ogdun nodded in gratitude for the compliment.

Kam Udo went on unruffled, "Make plans to abandon the city."

Raising an eyebrow, Ogdun questioned, "You're expecting trouble?"

"The reason I am leader and others are not is because I expect success." Giving Ogdun a long cold look, he added, "but I also have a plan when others fail to reach my expectations. Gachald was sent to retrieve two runaways and find the home of these mysterious Narwikin. It was a simple task. I expected him to succeed. He has yet to return, let alone return with the runaways. I believe this is because he failed. Now, I've given Romnog a simple task. I am expecting him to succeed. At the same time, I am not going to risk my life if he fails."

The meaning clear, Ogdun said, "I will make plans to abandon the city, Excellency."

### 

It didn't take Red Deer long to find the others. In this part of the swamp, the grasses stood taller than most men. To move faster, the escapees traveled single file in several lines, but even then the passage of people and animals left trails. With the exception of a few places, the marsh was dry this time of year. There were some wet, soft spots, as well as a few seemingly bottomless bogs. Not wanting to get trapped in these, their trail twisted and turned through the grasses. *This was good*, he thought, *it would help delay their pursuers when they tried to follow. I don't want the pursuers to find us too soon, but I don't want to lose them either.*

### ###

Romnog had his soldiers spread out in a long row as he and Paxtald led their march across the swamp. There would be no opening anyone could slip through. They banged their spears on their shields as they marched, hoping this drumming would make the slaves fearful and the animals panicky. The blind fear it would create would cause the quarry to abandon their hiding spots and run in terror.

At this early hour, the air in the swale[42] was still and humid. The soldiers, sweating in their heavy leather armor, struggled through the tangle of grass in their pursuit. They labored on knowing they would only have to give chase long enough to wear the escapees out. Their victims, overworked and underfed, could not last long. In time, the soldiers were sure the slaves would be either captured or killed.

### ###

From behind them came the sound of drumming. Kam Udo's army, on the move, was trying to close the gap between them. Red Deer was sure there exact location was unknown, but Romnog could see their zigzag path through the grass and reeds. The drumming was done to torment the slaves and instill fear.

Stalks of grass wavered in the light breeze that flowed out from the forest. It was hardly noticeable to the soldiers trudging through the bog that reached out from the forest to bathe the edges of the village.

---

[42] Swale - A low place in a tract of land, often forming a wetland. It is usually moister and often having ranker vegetation than the adjacent higher land. A valley-like intersection of two slopes in a piece of land.

The groups of fugitives exited the swamp at the ridge and immediately lost the protection the tall grasses provided. Red Deer's men ran along the ridge bordering the swamp. Pulling back hides, they exposed piles of wood kept dry and hidden. A man bent over each and began striking flint to make a fire.

Seeing the slaves run for the safety of the trees, the approaching guards let out a cheer and broke into a run. A difficult task in this heat with all their armor, weapons, and shields, was made easier by thoughts of a quick victory. The cool breeze in their faces picked up. It was a good sign, a welcome omen.

Red Deer put a couple of his men in charge of herding the fugitives and the animals along the trail through the forest. They would continue to put distance between themselves and their pursuers. Red Deer, and the few others who remained behind, set up a delaying action.

Before the caravan disappeared into the woods, Crooked Foot, from atop Makata, turned to watch events behind him unfold. With the campfires now blazing, the men grabbed burning logs and flung them into the swamp. Where each landed, a fire started.

Aided by the breeze, the flames spread through the tall grass growing as it spread. In a short time, it was a wall of flame rushing toward their pursuers. Watching for tripping hazards and bogs, the guards didn't see the flames racing their way. A howl went up when they did. Casting aside their equipment, they made a quick retreat.

Red Deer and his men, seeing they'd managed to turn Kam Udo's army back, at least for a short time, turned and ran up the path their people had taken.

# Chapter 42: On the Run

The fugitives followed their Narwikin guides up the forest trail. To put distance between their group, the swamp, and Kam Udo's army, the guides set a quick pace and forced everyone—men, women, children—to keep up. Breaking out of the forest, the party crossed a creek and entered a meadow where the guides called a halt. The escapees sprawled out on the cool grass to rest.

They had hardly hit the ground when a pair of strangers emerged from the shelter of the forest on the far side of the meadow. The fugitives scrambled to their feet ready to flee, but calmed down when their guides greeted the newcomers. A wave of the hand from the strangers brought another surprise: a small group of Narwikin women, holding baskets of food, emerged from the protection of the trees.

Tired from the activities of the morning, the fugitives ate and rested uneasily while they watched the smoke filled sky behind them.  Red Deer's small group caught up with this band of fugitives. They looked at him expectantly.

Red Deer smiled confidently as he told them, "Kam Udo's army has been turned back for the time, but they'll regroup and pursue us again. Because of their strength we have to use deception. We're going to split into two groups and take separate paths so I can lead Kam Udo's army away from you. You've had a short rest but there is a long way to go before you're safe. It's time to get moving."

### 

When Romnog's army advanced on the fleeing prisoners, he and Paxtald had been in the lead. Facing that wall of fire racing their way, the men bolted. When they made it safely out, Paxtald noticed that Romnog was the first one to greet his men.

Romnog's army stood before him, bruised, cut, weaponless, and covered with soot, a reflection of his own condition. "You cowards!" he scolded. "Had you pressed forward you would have captured the prisoners, but you chose to run in the face of valor. Now that the fire has died down, go and collect your weapons. Then we'll go after those insolent dogs." Recognizing the humiliation he had heaped on them, he raised his fist high in the air and shouted, "Retrieve your honor. Make them pay for this!"

Paxtald kept his thoughts to himself, but in his mind, he was torn. *He calls us cowards, but during the pursuit he was in the lead. When he faced the same danger we did, he made the same choice we did, and in doing so, he beat us out here. Now he stands before us and calls us cowards!* He thought this, but, valuing his life, he could not speak these words aloud. He did the next best thing. He encouraged the men to give Romnog a rousing cheer. Stirred by this zeal, the men turned and walked into the smoldering remnants of the marsh. Picking their way through hot embers, they searched for discarded weapons.

The sun was nearing mid-day by the time they could start. Everyone would have a shield and weapon of some kind, but none would have a full complement. What they lacked in equipment they made up for in rage.

### 

Red Deer watched his men herd most of the escapees and all but two camels down the creek. The water, not more than ankle deep, ran fast over a mix of sand, gravel, and rocks and ensured their tracks would be wiped clear before long. Someplace downstream, the group would leave the creek and be greeted by more supporters. If all went well, by late afternoon they'd be safe.

For Red Deer and his party, it was another story. They were the bait to lure Kam Udo's army into giving chase. To do that, he had to make good use of two men, two drovers, two camels, a boy with a mastodon—and all the cunning of the Narwikin.

His men had collected camel dung along their route from the swamp. He had the camels' remaining baskets loaded with stones. They would spread the camel dung as they traveled along the trail. The stones would give the impression the camels still carried the same weight.

They started up the trail, using branches to sweep away some of their tracks as they went. "Cover our tracks," Red Deer explained, "not so good that they'll lose the trail, but not so sloppy they'll realize we are trying to mislead them."

In doing this, he hoped their pursuers would believe the group had remained together. Only time would tell.

### 

Romnog listened as his scout interpreted the tracks.

"The fugitives rested here for a time. Then they crossed the creek and made off that way up the trail and into the forest," he said, and pointed confidently at the trail leading into the forest.

"You're sure?" Romnog questioned. "They didn't go down the stream?"

"It looks like they tried to make us think they used it but they'd never get all the animals, especially the big one, through the soft bed of the creek."

Romnog looked at the water as it played over the sand and gravel. No sign of tracks. Nothing seemed out of place. He remained silent as he considered his scout's words.

Uncomfortable with this silence, the scout continued his report. "They tried to hide their tracks, but got sloppy and forgot that it's hard to hide a beast that size. I followed the trail into the forest and found dung. Farther along, there's a tree ...."

Exasperated, Romnog interrupted, "You were in a forest! There are a lot of trees. What's so important about that one?"

Looking up the trail, hands on hips, the scout shot back, "Tree branches higher up were broken by the animal as it passed. The beast left prints in the hard earth. If it did that there, it would never get through the creek. Yes, that's the way they went, I'm sure.

As the scout finished, Romnog made a decision. "Okay, follow me." He started for the forest. The scout fell in behind him, smiling confidently at his success.

### 

It wasn't big enough to be called a mountain, but it was bigger than a mere hill. There were low, tree-covered hills running from the river to its base. The front of this escarpment was like the upturned edge of a table that had been crisscrossed with multiple goat tracks. The summit overlooked a sharp, rocky descent to the forest in the river valley, but its top provided a flat grassy meadow. To get to this meadow, Red Deer and his brood had to scurry up a trail that see-sawed back-and-forth across the escarpment's face.

From these heights, hidden behind some scrawny bushes that sporadically decorated the ridgeline, Red Deer kept watch over the path they just traveled. Behind him, out of view of anyone in the valley below, his group rested and waited for Kam Udo's army to emerge from the forest; waited for them to follow the switchbacks up the same steep trail; waited for them to fall into another trap.

His men finished the last of their food stock and

relaxed against the remains of the cairn[43] while the camels and Makata fed on grain and meadow grass. All of this had been stockpiled there by the Narwikin and their allies days earlier.

Crooked Foot crept over to lay by Red Deer's side. "Do you see anything?"

"Yes, the lead group just came out of the forest." He turned to look at the boy as he spoke. "They'll be looking around. If they don't see anything, the rest of the army will follow. We'll wait till they're part way up before we surprise them. Go back and check on Makata."

Staying low to remain out of sight, Crooked Foot backed away from the edge before getting to his feet. Moments later, Red Deer followed, first on his belly and then on his hands and knees before he too could stand without being seen. The pair hurried over to where the mastodon stood enjoying its meal. Seeing Red Deer approach, the drovers and scouts threw off their relaxed moods and got to their feet.

"Time to go?"

"Yes," Red Deer replied. "Go in the direction we talked about. We'll catch up in a little while."

Without further discussion, the men roused the camels and were off across the meadow, toward the base of the next set of hills.

### 

It was a long walk up the creek and through the trees, longer than most anticipated. To keep them moving, the Narwikin scouts had to alternate between coaxing and driving. Things changed when they saw the river. Someone in

---

[43] Cairn/Cache - A pile of stones used to mark a path for walkers and climbers. Also a place where food and other goods are stored temporarily.

the lead let out a yell as they emerged from the trees. Seeing this waterway gave them new vigor. Their steps automatically quickened. Another shout and the underbrush parted as a small group hurried out to escort stragglers. Rafts and food waited at the river's edge. Everyone boarded and the vessels shoved off, allowing the current to carry them downstream.

After a long trip on the water, a ram's horn sounded. People, carrying baskets of food, came across a raft-bridge and greeted them. Safety and friendly faces. They had finally arrived!

### ###

His scouts signaled an all clear, and Romnog motioned for his army to move forward. Emerging from the forest, they started climbing the steep path up the hillside. The scouts led the way up.

Romnog studied the terrain. *Something about this location bothers me. I don't want my uneasiness to show. My men would take it as a sign of weakness. After all, the fugitives were ahead of them, and my men would have caught them by now if it weren't for this string of bad luck we encountered. Maybe there is magic involved. In their haste to give chase, Paxtald had not told the men to carry rations. Now, signs of hunger were beginning to show. We will catch them, I am sure. If my men are hungry, the fugitives have to be hungrier. We did not feed them that well. They are running for their lives and should soon tire. They will make a mistake, and then we'll have them at our mercy!*

Halfway up the hill, he looked up to study the terrain again. It was then he saw it. The beast, the animal they call a mastodon, pushed something near the edge of the bluff. Frozen in his tracks, he was unable to yell a warning.

### ###

Earlier in the day, riding atop Makata, Crooked Foot had directed her actions just the way Red Deer described.

Lined up along the edge of the bluff were several large boulders. Just over the lip, spaced along the upper part of the route, were a few seemingly innocent piles of rubble. Small trees decorated each stack, camouflaging their true purpose.

Looking over his shoulder, Crooked Foot watched the camels tread their way across the meadow. Red Deer, laying on the edge of the bluff, let out a low bird call to get his attention. Turning to face forward, he spotted Red Deer's hand up in the air signaling, "Wait! Wait! Wait! Now! Move forward!"

"Hup, hup," Crooked Foot called to Makata as he nudged her with his heels. At his urging, the big animal moved forward to the first boulder. Putting her head down, she pressed against the rock surface, dug her feet in and began pushing. The boulder gave way under the steady pressure and rolled the last distance to the edge and over. Makata stopped short. The boulder didn't. Over the lip, it rolled noisily downhill, taking with it rubble—additional rocks and other debris—from a couple of their hidden piles.

Shocked at the approaching menace, Kam Udo's army stood open mouthed and watched the landslide thunder their way. From somewhere, a yell broke their trance, and men scrambled to get out of the way. In the meantime, Crooked Foot steered Makata to the next boulder … and then the next. When there were no more, Red Deer climbed aboard, and the trio turned and started across the meadow along the trail the camels followed.

### 

Angry, Romnog strode back and forth, enraged against yet another misfortune, until Paxtald presented himself.

"Sir, the scouts have reached the top. They report the escapees are crossing the meadow and nearing the hills."

Pounding a fist against his open palm, he demanded, "Casualties! Do we have any casualties?"

"There were only a few serious casualties. The men's biggest complaint is that they are hungry." Paxtald knew the men were hungry. Everyone thought this would be a short expedition. In their haste to depart, no one had taken extra rations. Even though he was considered slow witted by many, he knew enough not to make an issue of this to his leader, lest the blame be heaped on him.

Romnog dismissed the report with a grunt. "They can eat after they get the slaves back. Get the men on their feet and to the top of the bluff."

### 

Keeping a steady pace, Makata carried Crooked Foot and Red Deer along the trail. They closed the distance between themselves and the others, finally catching them near the base of the hills. Nearby, the Narwikin and their allies had made another cairn. The drovers brought the camels to a halt under some trees. Makata stopped there. Red Deer glanced over his shoulder. "Good, they're still coming. We can rest here awhile. There's some food for us and the animals." The men opened the cairn and handed out its contents.

Dismounting, Red Deer added, "I don't want to get too far ahead. I want them angry and tired so they aren't thinking clearly, but I also want them to think we're tired and slowing down so they will continue to give chase."

They ate and rested before starting out again. Romnog's army was approaching but wasn't close enough to give them problems. Red Deer wanted to stay ahead, but still keep within their sight as they moved along the base of the hills. At the mouth of the canyon, his group turned in, making sure Romnog saw them and could easily follow.

### ###

Hidden along the ridge, Howling Wolf and White Badger watched Red Deer's group turn into the pass. Romnog and his men approached the valley's entrance and came to a stop. He and a small group huddled there to confer while they watched the fugitives and animals disappear around the bend.

Finally, not wanting to have their prey escape, the huddle broke up and began to follow. Romnog led his army, now arranged in three-lines, shoulder-to-shoulder, as they moved up the canyon after the escapees. Believing they would finally succeed, the men began beating their weapons across their shields in rhythm with their steps as they closed the distance to the bend.

Looking at White Badger, Howling Wolf asked, "Did all the obstructions get removed?"

White Badger nodded. "Yes, there's nothing to hide behind and no one will think anything is out of place."

"Good. Now we wait." Together, they watched Romnog and his entire army move into the canyon.

### ###

From his perch atop Makata, Crooked Foot could see beyond the vine covered barricade to the wall of animals milling around.

Someone opened the barrier and the mastodon marched slowly through, scattering the menagerie of animals, but not panicking them as she made her way to the back of the herd. The camels paraded through behind her, and the opening closed once again.

Makata reached the back of the makeshift corral. Without coaching, she turned to face the direction she had just come. She stood there and waited ... waited as if she knew the next step.

### 

Romnog called his army to a halt and summoned Paxtald and his chief scout. "Look around and tell me what you see," he commanded. The men eyed the terrain.

"This is a box canyon," the scout finally concluded.

Romnog grunted, "If that's true, the only way out is the way we are going in."

"Looks like our fugitives may have finally made a mistake," the scout sneered.

Romnog nodded. Turning to his men he ordered, "Battle formation!"

His men, now arranged in three-lines, shoulder-to-shoulder, fire-scarred shields up, spears jutting out, began moving forward. As they rounded the bend they saw a few of the fugitives. They appeared to cower in front of a vine covered barricade. Behind it, Romnog could see a young boy atop the mastodon. Smiling, the men confidently marched forward. After all this, victory was at hand!

### 

Moving along the ridge, Howling Wolf and White Badger, kept an eye on the progress of Romnog and his army. They watched as the soldiers formed into a battle formation and began marching forward, lured deeper into the canyon. Turning to White Badger, Howling Wolf quietly said, "It's time."

White Badger nodded and signaled others. A ram's horn sounded. White Badger's men opened the barricade separating army and animals.

Musk-oxen stood, heads down, horns out. Shields and spears now faced horns and hooves.

Red Deer let out a triumphant yell and hollered,

"Now! Narwikin now!"

From behind the mass of animals, loud drumming began. Horns sounded. People let out whoops. A cacophony of sound filled the canyon. The animals stomped nervously, but held their ground. Makata, rose up on her hind legs, came down with a thump and then lifted her trunk and sounded a mighty blast. Agitated, the animals milled about, stomped their feet and pushed each other. Rising up again, Makata repeated her performance. That was all it took. Animals flooded out as the mastodon continued to trumpet. The ground shook under their pounding feet. Guards, now facing a stampeding herd, froze and then turned to run.

Bundles of burning twigs and straw flung from the canyon rim filled the path just traversed with blinding smoke. At ground level, the retreating army found it difficult to see. From hidden places, Narwikin tugged on ropes raising trip lines and the intruders went sprawling. Those who followed tripped over downed comrades. Though they tried to get to their feet before the herd caught up with them, they failed!

# Chapter 43: Council of War

Light from the campfire danced around the longhouse walls. Howling Wolf sat with council and other tribal members. No one spoke. It had been a long day, and the events had drained all of them.

Howling Wolf finally broke the silence, "It's not over yet."

Those around him stirred at the sound of his voice.

"What? Not over?" White Badger was aghast at the idea. "Kam Udo's army has been destroyed."

"Do you hunt the great bear only to leave it wounded in its cave?" Howling Wolf paused to let his words sink in, "Kam Udo still exists. His plans haven't changed. He has always been determined to succeed, and now, because of what we have done, he is enraged. He will raise another army. Then his people will be back here. We will have to go through this again. Perhaps the next time we face him, or the time after that, events will end differently."

White Badger could voice no arguments. Conceivably, others agreed too, but did not have the words … or the will to say them.

Turning to White Badger, Howling Wolf said, "See that the night watch is posted. Then we should all get some rest and take the matter up tomorrow."

Unintelligible noises, mostly grunts, signaling agreement at least with getting rest. Individuals and groups got up and began leaving. There was little discussion among them.

### 

When Red Deer returned to the village, Mamuta, the

sun in the sky, was beyond its zenith. White Badger watched him approach and then asked, "What did you find?"

"It looks like Kam Udo's army was completely destroyed. I don't know for sure, but I don't think anyone escaped the stampede. We buried the dead. We buried their weapons with them."

White Badger nodded, "It is best. Their weapons didn't serve them well. They carry a bad omen." Thinking about it a moment he added, "I can't see any of our people wanting to use them."

Red Deer changed the subject. "Our actions yesterday scattered the herd. Some animals have been rounded up, and others have returned on their own, but many are running free."

"We have some back? This is good!" White Badger said. "I will let Howling Wolf know you've returned and give him your news. Now you should get some rest. Little Fawn has prepared a place for you."

### 

Huddled around the fire in the long house, council members listened as Howling Wolf spoke. "Wawakin, the wind that comes from the Great Ice, is here now to remind us that the white rain will be on us soon. The time for action is limited," he said. "We have rescued our friends, some of the Sabala, and others who were held captives, but now there are more mouths to feed. What do we do?" He stopped momentarily to give his audience time to consider his words; to react to his question? Those present had nothing to offer so he continuing, "Kam Udo is another question. Do we pursue him? If this is our plan, do we enter Kam Udo's lair now or wait till spring? We must be wise in our decision. Who would wish to speak?" After looking around at the crowd, he sat down.

White Badger stood. All eyes focused on him. "It is as you said. The white rain will be here and we have many mouths to feed. We had gathered the herds as a food supply and they became our protection from the marauders. Now the herds are scattered. A few have returned, but not enough to feed us through the Long Cold. If we don't want to starve we should follow the herds. If we return here next spring and Kam Udo is a problem, we can deal with him then." There was a chorus of grunts as White Badger sat down.

"We've all hunted." Unnoticed by others, Red Deer had slipped into the meeting. As he spoke, all eyes turned to him. "Wounded, an animal seeks shelter, a safe place so it can recover. When they come out again, they are stronger … smarter … harder to defeat. Kam Udo is wounded. If we wait till spring, he will be stronger and wiser. We must track him right into his lair and destroy him there, now!"

Red Deer looked around. Murmurs arose. Harsh words, if any were to be spoken, were interrupted by a shuffling in the back. The crowd parted, and an old man came forward.

He looked around at the people—tribe members and council members—gathered here. Clearing his throat, he said, "I am Great Otter of the Sabala." Directing his attention toward Howling Wolf, he went on, "My people had been happy, but then the raiders came out of nowhere." His voice broke a little as he went on, "We were nothing to them. Those of us who survived were made their slaves, even our children." He paused and looked around. There was silence. All eyes were on him. "The caravan came. The one we had traded with for many seasons. Before we could warn them, the intruders had made them prisoners." The old man paused again. His audience sat in rapt attention. If they looked at him closely, they might detect the sheen of emotion in his eyes. "Your people came, first the young man and woman, and they were made slaves like us," he said, "but they escaped and that gave us hope." An admiring murmur of approval went up as the crowd honored the exploits of Silver Fox and Little Fawn.

Holding up his hands, he continued, "An old blind woman and a lame boy, her grandson, came. It was your Great Shaman in disguise. Because of her magic, your people freed us ... but not all of us. Others are still slaves and they can't wait till spring." His story finished, he moved to the side and sat down.

Tigal, still weak from his wounds, spoke without standing, "My men and I have suffered at the hands of this tyrant. Great Otter speaks the truth."

Pandemonium broke out as the whole assembly tried to speak at once. Howling Wolf let this go on for a time, then stood and raised his hands. When calm was restored, he said, "The council will discuss this." He sat down. Things were quiet for a moment and then chaos reigned again.

### 

Red Deer watched Silver Fox as he put the finishing touches on the instrument in his hands. "Making another spear, Fox?"

Silver Fox looked up from his work and asked, "How many do you think we'll need?"

Red Deer laughed. "Don't know. Maybe you should make some more."

Silver Fox leaned against the tree behind him and gazed across the river toward their island home. "Do you know how we're going to do this?"

"Other tribes are joining us. The biggest part of Kam Udo's army is gone. He's left with some household servants and personal guards." Red Deer wrinkled his nose, "They'll hide behind the walls, close the gate, and try to keep us from entering."

"From what I've seen, the walls are high and thick. Don't know how we'll get through." Thinking about the task, Silver Fox's shoulders slumped in despair.

"With luck, we should be able to go through the gate."

Silver Fox shot Red Deer a questioning glance. "Go through the gate? They'll have the gate closed and barred."

Smiling, Red Deer dropped his voice and leaned in close, "We'll be bringing our own gate opener …." Turning his head slightly, he looked toward where Crooked Foot exercised Makata.

Following his gaze, Silver Fox saw the boy atop the mastodon. A scaffold of branches crisscrossed the animal's body. Hides draped over this framework all but covered the beast.

Recognizing Red Deer's meaning, Silver Fox smiled, but still had a puzzled look. "What's with the costume?"

"We don't know if any of the guards left behind know one end of a spear from the other. Just in case somebody gets lucky, the hides are meant to protect Makata."

Silver Fox nodded and then asked, "So what's going to happen?"

It was Red Deer's turn to shrug. "Roughly speaking, we'll tie a big log to Makata. She'll use it to knock down the gate. We'll follow her inside. Once we're in, I think resistance will disappear. Sound okay?"

"That's it?"

Red Deer shrugged, "Hope so," then he added, "Oh, Little Fawn wants to lead a group in from behind, but I don't think anyone is happy with that idea."

Silver Fox looked startled. "Do you think Waving Grass will be able to talk her out of it?"

"Oh, she'll talk to her, but talk her out of it that's

another question."

"How about you, did you talk to her?"

Red Deer threw up his hands, "Not me. I'm staying out of this. Waving Grass can have that job. Little Fawn will have to persuade her and the council … I don't think that will happen. Even still, I expect to be inside and have everything over and done with before she arrives."

Satisfied that the problem was resolved, the pair relaxed, and the talk changed to other things. Eventually, they'd find out everyone had underestimated Little Fawn's determination.

### 

What once was a steep-walled shallow valley, this pass had previously provided an easy pathway between one side of the mountain range and the other, but now Kam Udo's stronghold blocked the way. It was there because he recognized the value of this strategic location. Control this pass and nothing would move without his blessing. He would require tribute be rendered for the privilege of crossing. He would succeed because his fortress was built not only at the pass's narrowest point, but also the place where the walls are the steepest.

Indeed, it was perfect. The canyon walls were as high as the pine trees dotting the landscape. Above the walls, the steep, overgrown terrain has the reputation of being a place where only wild goats are thought to venture.

When Silver Fox worked on the airshaft, Little Fawn had made many trips to the construction site. Under the guise of working, she inspected their design for flaws. They were built to withstand an attack from either end of the pass. The sides, however, were another thing. The builder expected the mountain ridges to protect them. This could be their weak point. This is why Little Fawn directed her group along this route.

Two of her men, forward guards, went ahead of Little Fawn's party as they moved single file through the tree covered hills. Everyone carried weapons and coils of rope. It was early morning, and everything was still quiet, even the men. Having heard of her exploits, they appeared to be in awe. She hoped they shared her confidence … and not her nervousness.

### 

Not everyone had agreed with her plan. Little Fawn recalled standing before the council to present her ideas, "Using the few forces the Narwikin possess, a frontal attack alone would be dangerous."

Council members nodded in agreement and waited for her to continue. "The fortress is built between the canyon walls and against the bluff because they believe no one would be able to cross mountains with a force big enough to mount an attack. I've been in their city and have seen this place myself. They are right."

Stone-faced, the council sat waiting for her to continue. "But a small group might go where no army could, work their way over the mountain, and create a diversion by attacking from there. It is as I said, I know their city. I've been there. I can do that. I can lead that group."

Finished, she looked at the council. They were still for a second while her words sank in, then mayhem. Everyone talking at once until Howling Wolf stood to get their attention. Respectful silence fell over the crowd.

Addressing her formally, Howling Wolf said, "Little Fawn, daughter of White Owl, it is true you've been captive in their city. It is also true you've shown strength in battle; great wisdom in protecting the little ones in your charge; as well as in escaping your captivity, but the task you describe provides great risk. Risk for yourself and for all those who join with you." As he concluded, respectful silence was broken as murmurs of ascent from the council and tribe members punctuated the still air.

Before speaking again, she waited for the chatter to die, then said, "Great leader, you, council, all of us here are concerned about the welfare of the Narwikin. You've spoken of those acts I performed. I did so, and would do so again, on behalf of our people. Though we try to remain at peace, Kam Udo and his people won't let us. They cross the countryside, raiding where they please, taking what they want. Enslaving those not killed. We gather here to talk of doing battle, to put an end to this menace once and for all. But, to go into battle fearing risk is to create greater risk and possibilities of failure. This will leave many Narwikin wives as widows, children as orphans. Who will look out for the Narwikin then? What would keep them from becoming slaves? We can't hold back. We can't fear risk."

Silence once again, followed by the noise of conversations as everyone tried to talk at once with council members leaning in to confer with each other and Howling Wolf. Finally, he rose and the conversations died out. "The council," he began, "will take your request under advisement."

Later she heard the council had been split on the decision, but they came to a favorable agreement in the end. They'd let her lead a small group, but there would be limitations. Both Waving Grass and Red Deer were unhappy with the decision. They spoke to her with great emphasis about the restrictions, which she agreed to and then promptly forgot.

### 

Little Fawn's group came to a halt. Trying to remain

calm, she went forward to check out the situation. Prepared to ask, *what's the holdup,* she found the problem in front of her. There was no need to voice a question.

# Chapter 44: Doing Battle

Crooked Foot sat atop Makata, his red spear, its point now covered in golden kop, honed to a razor-sharp edge, laid across his lap. Quietly, he watched as Red Deer studied the enemy stronghold looming in front of them. As expected, the Sabala village was empty, abandoned.

Bright Moon, her bag of medicines in hand, chose an empty hut closest to the fortress. From there she could see the action that was about to play out. The morning sun was on the horizon. From behind the walls, a flock of small birds rose into the air and circled around before heading for the village. Smiling, Bright Moon recalled seeing birds in crates near one of the huts. Leaving her things, she ran outside, gathered the nearest cage and set off to find Red Deer.

Under the cover of darkness, Narwikin braves had piled bundles of grasses near the bastion. When set afire, the smoke created would screen them from the defenders' shots. To further protect themselves, bundles of branches were lashed together making rolls as tall as a man. As they moved forward, the Narwikin planned on rolling these in front of them as added protection from spear and arrow. Red Deer climbed aboard the mastodon and looked around. The Narwikin and their allies waited for his signal. From the village, Bright Moon hurried toward him as fast as she could shuffle. "Wait!" she called.

Hearing her voice, Red Deer looked up and saw her coming his way. On her back, she lugged something big. "I'd better go see what's got Bright Moon moving this fast." Climbing down, Red Deer went to meet her.

As he approached, Bright Moon stopped and lowered the crate to the ground. The old woman spoke through gasps,

"Birds! I saw a bunch … above the fort … this morning."
She stopped long enough to swallow and take a deep breath
before continuing. "The villagers left … some behind. More
left … in the village. I remembered … Little Fawn said …
they roosted in the thatch roofs … at the fortress."

Red Deer looked at her questioningly.

"Tie a fire brand … to the bird's feet …." There was
a twinkle in her eye as she concluded, "Send them home."
Still panting, she leaned on her walking staff and smiled at
him as she waited for her words to sink in.

The idea, beautiful in its simplicity, finally registered.
Picking up the cage of birds, Red Deer smiled back at her. "It
should give them something to think about."

At intervals, his men had readied small campfires.
These would be used to light the bundles of grasses laid out
earlier. They waited for the signal to start.

Handing over the container of birds, Red Deer
pointed toward the fort as he said, "Our little friends roost in
the thatch roofs inside. Take cord and tie twigs and tinder
together and then dangle these packets from the birds' feet.
Set the bundles smoldering and then release them so they can
fly home."

He headed over to where Crooked Foot waited atop
Makata. By the time he was seated behind the boy, the first of
the birds flew overhead, trailing small clumps of smoking
brands beneath them.

Red Deer clasped Crooked Foot on the shoulder.
"Well, little brother, are you ready for this?"

Patting Makata, Crooked Foot nodded but said
nothing.

"Yeah, me too," Red Deer said. He looked from one
side to the other. Everyone was in ready. It was time! He
signaled his men. "Narwikin! We go forward to end this!"

Crooked Foot gave the mastodon a nudge.

Unexpectedly, she raised her trunk, trumpeted, and started ahead. The Narwikin and their allies followed. Runners, carrying torches, ran forward to set the piles of grasses afire. Smoke hung low in the damp morning air.

Noises—someone banging on a gong and hollering— came from within the fortress. There was no question, the attack had been discovered.

### 

At Little Fawn's feet lay a fissure, quite deep maybe two or three man-lengths wide. Twisting and turning, left and right, the fissure went on in either direction as far as the eye could see. All eyes were on her. What would she do?

Trying not to appear apprehensive, she made a slow turn, taking in the surrounding terrain. Large and small, boulders bordered both sides of the fissure. The ground seemed to be crisscrossed with ledges. In many ways it was just like the land they already crossed. From somewhere ahead, a muddle of voices rose in alarm, and a light whiff of smoke reached them. The Narwikin had started their assault. The realization created a greater sense of urgency. She had to come up with a plan and quickly.

"There!" she said, pointing. "Pick up that fallen tree and slide it across the chasm to make a bridge."

They found that the tree was bigger and heavier than it looked. The men were able to lift it off the ground—but just barely—and move it close to the edge. There would be no way they could slide it across that gaping mouth in front of them.

The fissure mocked Little Fawn's efforts. She leaned against a boulder behind her. The roar of battle grew louder; smoke grew thicker. At the fortress, the Narwikin were approaching the battlements. She knew Red Deer's men carried tree trunks, notched at intervals for footholds. They would lean these against the wall and begin their climb. The defenders would try to push the trunks away.

Suddenly it hit her. Pointing to a couple of men she said, "Hold that end! Keep it from sliding into the chasm!" Turning to the rest, she ordered, "Help me raise the other end! We'll walk it up this boulder. When it's upright, we can let it fall across the chasm and make a bridge."

Everyone bent to the task. Grunts, groans, and straining muscles raised the timber. Aiming carefully, they gave it a push and the tree toppled toward the far side, landing with a bang and raising a cloud of dust in the process. A broken limb protruding from the base pointed to the sky and provided a convenient handhold for Little Fawn to grab. Using it, she pulled herself up onto the trunk.

As a bridge, it looked a lot smaller, the chasm a lot deeper, than it had looked before, but if she showed any weakness about crossing, others might also. She couldn't afford to have anyone get nervous and back out, or fall during the crossing. Eyeing things, she commanded, "Get me a climbing hook."

Responding to her request, one of the men produced a set of antlers attached to a rope. She twirled the antlers overhead looking for a target on the far side. Aiming for a likely spot beyond some boulders, she let the hook fly. It landed in a clump of brush near the target area. Pulling back on the rope, Little Fawn was able to drag it back until the antlers became firmly lodged in the brush. Satisfied, she looped the rope around the limb that had been her handhold.

Turning to the others she explained, "I'll walk over our bridge first and make sure the other end is secure. When I signal, the rest of you can follow. We'll probably need the rope, so the last one over should bring it with them."

Without waiting, she turned and, one hand on the rope, she began to walk across the fissure. Recognizing her actions could either boost the men's spirits or weaken them, she made sure she neither rushed nor crept. She took comfort from the touch of the rope and the solid feel of her feet against the trunk. However, she did not to look down or even think about what she was doing and had to hide the fact that her legs were willowy by the time she reached the far side. On firm ground once again, Little Fawn silently rejoiced as she tied the rope to a tree. Knowing the men wouldn't let a mere girl outperform them, she confidently signaled those on the far side to start across.

### 

"Imperial Sir," a guard reported, "during the night, an enemy gathered and now occupies the village. They haven't sent an emissary or otherwise signaled their intentions, but I am sure they mean us no good."

Kam Udo nodded and waved the guard off. Bowing low, he backed away, and then made his exit. Turning his attention to Ogdun, Kam Udo gave him a cynical smirk saying, "Looks like your friend, Romnog failed at his task."

Ogdun cringed under his gaze. "There's been no word from Romnog?"

"No *word* from Romnog?" Kam Udo hissed. "Romnog's *word* is at our gate. I don't know what happened, but I don't expect we'll see him again."

"Majesty," Ogdun implored, "we are behind sturdy walls. Surely the rabble outside will never be able to enter."

Kam Udo shot him a cold stare. "Ask Romnog what this rabble is capable of; maybe he'll be able to assure you."

A long silence followed allowing Ogdun time to consider his future. *Gachald had hopes of moving up, maybe getting Romnog's position, but Gachald left and had not returned; probably will never return. Paxtald, the little yes-man, was too dim-witted to be a threat, and was probably lucky to rise as high as he did. Romnog was a threat, and I believe he had dreams of doing away with Kam Udo and seizing the leadership himself. In fact, I counted on him attempting to do just that. Romnog would take out Kam Udo and I would take out Romnog, but, alas, he too is gone, and his little flunky, Paxtald, with him. That leaves Magram and me to deal with Kam Udo. Magram is a petty, self-important, lackey. Take him aside and feed him a bone, like the dog he is, and he would do anything. Fortune could go my way yet!*

Unknowingly, Kam Udo interrupted Ogdun's thoughts with, "You've made the arrangements for departure I asked you to make?"

Ogdun nodded. *My answer is the same as the last three times you asked: Yes, I made the arrangements! It is obvious to everyone around you that what you believe is a calm exterior is a sham only you believe. The time will soon come when our relationship will be broken and we will part company.*

"Good. Load my household servants with everything we'll need. Have a few of the guards accompany them to the other end of the escape route."

"Do you think it'll go badly for us?" Ogdun raised an eyebrow. *Just for the fun of it, let me irritate you one more time!*

Exasperated, Kam Udo began enumerating events and the shortcomings of others on the fingers of one hand. "A simple task—bring back two escaped prisoners—appears to have not gone well for that incompetent, Gachald," Kam Udo snarled. "Another simple task–bring back those who stole my animals and my slaves–appears to have not gone well for those incompetents, Romnog and Paxtald; it was only out of kindness that I kept that useless pair around hoping they might learn from me. Now, my fate once again is in the hands of others. If my people succeed, nothing is lost. If they fail, then I'll be prepared. Now go and make the arrangements."

###

Smoke hung heavy in the air. The Narwikin aggressively pressed their attack and the defenders did their best to counter their efforts. Wherever scaling ladders were put in place, the defenders pushed them away. Watching the events, Red Deer spoke aloud, "They're pushing the ladders away but not throwing spears. Does this mean they've few weapons to spare or is it a trap?"

Crooked Foot, not knowing if Red Deer had spoken to him or just thought out loud, replied, "They seem to do everything by force, so a trap would seem to be beyond their thinking."

"This is where we find out. Have Makata move forward quickly. I want the log to hit the gate hard."

Crooked Foot nudged the beast with his heels, calling, "Hup, hup, hup" as he urged her forward.

Responding to his command, she lifted her trunk, blew another loud trumpet before turning to head for the gate at the end of the alley. Seeing this, a cheer rose from the Narwikin.

### 

On the hillside overlooking Kam Udo's city, Little Fawn and her men could see the inside of the fortress spread out in front of them. Sheltered by the parapet, the few defenders ran from place to place along the rampart as they pushed away ladders or hurled rocks. Their efforts were beginning to fail under the fierceness of the Narwikin's attack. Here and there, thatch roofed huts were on fire, but few paid attention. Through the smoke, Little Fawn could see a device mounted on a platform. It was the large bow Crooked Foot described. Men were getting ready to put it to use. She heard Makata's trumpet and the roar from the Narwikin that followed. She and her men had to get down there and put the bow out of action. The distance they needed to cover was too far to jump, but not too far for a quick descent by rope.

"Ropes," there was excitement in her voice, "fasten our ropes together. There is no one below us. We'll climb down and attack the bow in the courtyard."

The ropes were made up of leather strips, wound together, and knotted at intervals to make it easier to climb up or down. Tying one end to a tree, they dropped the coil to the parapet. A man started down almost as it hit. The next man started as soon as the previous man's feet touched the bottom. When a man cleared the rope, he drew his weapon and fanned out in a defensive position.

Defenders at the gate opened a porthole. Crack! The bow fired its projectile. The spear buried itself in the door at the edge of the opening. Their aim needed some work. Those operating the device weren't the trained marksmen Crooked Foot had watched. The men at the gate tried to close the porthole but couldn't because the spear blocked the way.

Bang! The door vibrated under the force of Makata's blow but still stood. Abandoning their work on the porthole, the men ran to the braces, hoping they remained secure.

Little Fawn led the way along the parapet till they reached an incline. Following it, they were able to descend to ground level and make their way between a maze of huts, some ablaze and others not. She and her little group arrived at the outskirts of the courtyard within striking distance of the platform.

### 

Under Crooked Foot's urging, Makata, trunk held high, moved noisily forward. The tree trunk she carried hit the gate a solid blow. The gate held, but the straps securing the tree to the mastodon didn't, and they had to cut it loose.

The gate was at the far end of an alleyway. Narrow at

the mouth, the alley widened out into a courtyard and then narrowed again as it neared the gateway. When they first entered, the layout had seemed odd. Now in the alley, the reason behind the design became evident. Defenders, hidden behind the walls overhead, rose up screaming their war-cries and throwing spears and rocks on the throng below.

The Narwikin warriors were forced to dodge and attack at the same time. In doing so they became part of the problem when some of their own spears, having missed targets, fell back on them.

"It's a trap," Red Deer yelled, "we can't stay here or retreat without being slaughtered. We must beat the door down."

Crooked Foot urged Makata forward. As she neared the door, the animal lowered her head butting the gate, the force of the impact nearly dislodging Crooked Foot from his seat. But the door stood, not as solid as before but it still blocked the way.

"Try again," Red Deer commanded.

Not sure the animal could take another such impact Crooked Foot looked around for another way. It was then he saw the solution.

# Chapter 45: Defense

Outnumbered, Little Fawn's group had the benefit of surprise on their side, little more.

A crash sounded from the area around the gate. The noise was followed by more shouts as both attackers and defenders stepped up their activities. The guards on the platform loaded a new spear. Under the sharp bite of their whips, slaves tugged at the lines, pulling the bowstring back. A guard stood to one side, ready to trigger the weapon. Little Fawn knew she must act now. Raising her war club high in the air, she yelled, "Narwikin! Let's go!"

Under the din and chaos of battle they reached the platform before they were spotted. "Intruders! Intruders!"

Alerted by the guards warning, his comrades turned—weapons drawn—to meet Little Fawn and her group. There was a crash followed by the roar of men doing battle from near the gate.

### ###

Crooked Foot patted Makata on the head as he called, "Down, down, down." In response, she lowered her head until her tusks touched the ground.

A timber across the top of the gate rested on the gatepost. A hole cut through the end of the timber allowed the gate to turn on a peg attached to the doorframe. A similar arrangement supported the bottom of the gate. Together, they formed hinges that allowed the gate to swing open or close. A gap existed between the gate and the ground allowing it room to clear obstacles. With Makata's tusks in the dirt, Crooked Foot continued, "Now ... Forward, slowly, slowly." Trusting his guidance, the big animal lumbered forward, leaving furrows in the ground as she moved. He smiled as he watched the tusks slide through the gap under the gate and wondered if anyone on the other side saw this. He would not give them time to react. Patting Makata's head, he commanded, "Now. Up! Up!" The beast raised her head. The gate slid up, clearing the pegs. Freed, it leaned back until it came to rest against her forehead. Crooked Foot nudged her with his heels, calling "Forward! Hup! Hup! Hup!"

Seeing the beast wearing the gate like a shield as it charged the platform, the trigger man yanked the firing cord, and then turned and ran.

### 

With the gate gone, Narwikin warriors flooded through the opening. Resistance melted quickly as the defenders, now outnumbered, threw down their weapons.

At the platform, those who Little Fawn had been fighting broke and ran toward the large edifice built into the ravine wall. She, weapon in hand, chased them through an open doorway. The room was dimly lit, and she needed time for her eyes to adjust.

From behind her came a slamming noise, the kind made by a heavy door closing. Too late, she realized her error. Turning to escape, she was greeted by a fist. The heavy blow knocked her off her feet. Hitting the floor, she lost her weapon. It was the last thing she remembered as she faded into blackness.

### 

Before she was fully conscious, Little Fawn felt someone's rough hands seize her. After being flipped on her belly, she was held down while her wrists were tied to a pole placed across her shoulders. A noose went around her neck, her feet tethered, and then she was turned over again.

Rough hands, probably the same man who had been handling her, began slapping her and a voice growled, "Come on you, wake up!" Changing his approach, her tormentor began shaking her. Not getting the response he wanted, he began alternating between slapping and shaking.

Little Fawn moaned, opened her eyes and demanded, "Stop! Stop doing that!"

Staring down at her were the beady eyes of a heavyset guard with features as rough as his hands. He looked familiar. Behind him, faces only vaguely recognizable, Magram, Ogdun and Kam Udo, peered at her.

"Ahhh, my dear, you've come back to us. How nice!" Magram's voice was sticky sweet ... and ominous. "When you left, there was work for you to do. Now that you're back, there's still work for you. This time we'll give you a big enough load you won't be able to run away. Get her to her feet, Sagarld. It's time for us to move."

*Sagarld! He was one of the pair that she and Waving Grass had to deal with right after their village was attacked. She could not let on she remembered him or the revenge he would seek would be worse than the treatment she was already getting.*

Sagarld, the rough handed guard, jerked her into a sitting position. Behind her, there was a scurrying sound, and an unseen burden was fastened to the pole that crossed her shoulders. The room spun. She squeezed her eyes shut then opened them again hoping this gave her enough time to size up her situation. Her head hurt. Her arms, stretched out to either side, were tied to a pole at her wrists and it had a heavy pack attached. She had been stubborn, arrogant, and careless and now was a prisoner once again. It was too much! Moaning, she tried to lay back but couldn't.

Sensing she had recovered, Sagarld broke out in a broken-tooth smile. Almost consoling, he said, "I was afraid I had hit you too hard." Then his gruff voice suddenly changed. "But you're okay, so get on your feet. It's time to go." He yanked her up. Little Fawn took a couple of staggering steps before collapsing to her knees. "Get up!" her tormentor roared.

Wobbly, she got back to her feet. Wrists roped to the pole across her shoulders, she staggered forward under the weight of her new burden. Looking around, Little Fawn saw others—servants, slaves, and guards—moving through a small doorway. "No," was her sullen answer, "I'm not going."

Kam Udo stepped forward making a threatening motion with a knife, "You, your people have caused me enough problems. Now move or die on the spot." Emphasizing Kam Udo's words, Sagarld yanked on her leash tightening the noose around her neck. She gasped for air and he gave her another broken-tooth grin.

Little Fawn's choices were to move or choke. Burdened by the weight, hampered by the cords hobbling her feet, she shuffled forward to join the rest of the departing group, her only comfort was the fact that Sagarld walked with a limp and she had given it to him.

### 

Smoke and cinders from dying fires wafted through the air. Red Deer watched as his Narwikin warriors rounded up the last of the defenders and herded them into a circle. Weaponless, their fighting spirit gone, they meekly faced this wall of spears and stern faces.

Addressing the prisoners, Red Deer said, "You were only following orders. I've no argument with you. It's Kam Udo, who brought this on you and the villagers. He is the one I seek. Tell me where he is, and I'll go easy on you."

Their shouts and gestures filled the air as everyone volunteered information at the same time. Red Deer held up his hands but couldn't silence the crowd. Crooked Foot, still mounted on Makata, came to his aid by having her face the crowd and trumpet. At that great sound, the horde fell back and was silent.

Singling out one man Red Deer pointed to him and asked, "Where is Kam Udo?"

"Sir," the man responded, "He is in the palace behind you, the place where the girl went."

"The girl? Little Fawn? Where is Little Fawn?" Looking around, Red Deer tried to remain calm but was secretly frantic. Turning to Crooked Foot, he ordered, "Take Makata and bring up the log we were using as a ram. They probably have the door to the palace barred, and we'll need it."

Searching the faces of his warriors, he found some of the men who had been with her. "Where is Little Fawn? When did you last see her?"

"We came to the platform together. Then fighting broke out. In the confusion, no one could be certain, but some thought they had seen her chasing a defender toward that big building."

Makata and Crooked Foot arrived with the timber. Leaving some warriors to guard the prisoners, Red Deer and his men went to the palace. Two volunteers ran forward and tried the doors. They opened inward without a problem showing a dimly lit interior. Torches were found, and men fanned out to search.

A long stone table stood in the middle of the room. On a dais beyond the table was a great stone chair. It was draped with animal hides and augmented with skulls. Embellishments around the room included bowls, baskets, and figurines. Here and there, animal hides and half-finished murals decorated walls. Multiple bowls of paint sat near each mural, but there was no one around.

Red Deer stood, stunned by the silence. Gray Wolf,

Crooked Foot, and Silver Fox stood at his elbow. They held their torches high as they searched the room.

"Where are the people? Where did they go?" Silver Fox puzzled.

Red Deer shrugged. "This seems to be the only way in and out." He shook his head in dismay. "We'll have to bring up some of the prisoners and question them. Either they were wrong about Kam Udo's whereabouts, or there is another way out." He turned to leave.

"Wait," cried Crooked Foot. "There," he said, pointing, "over there. I saw that hide move."

Red Deer motioned to his men who moved forward, torches and weapons in hand. Approaching the hide from the sides, weapons ready, a brave grabbed the covering and jerked it down. Behind it was another doorway. Cool air and darkness greeted the men.

"Torches!" Red Deer called. Several men, a torch in one hand and a weapon in the other, stepped forward, Silver Fox and Crooked Foot among them. Motioning for them to follow, Red Deer and Gray Wolf ducked through the doorway.

Finding themselves in a long passageway, they followed it until they came to another room. This one had larger doorways with more corridors. Some of the passageways lead back to the starting point; others were dead ends. Kam Udo's architect had created a maze and Little Fawn was lost somewhere in it.

Red Deer began his search by sending men down corridors. One-by-one dead ends and double backs were eliminated until they came to the last corridor, and this one led to a cavern. Red Deer and his men peered into the darkness. Almost lost in its far reaches, they could see the flicker of a torch just before it faded from view.

Red Deer continued to peer into the gloom. "In my

travels, I've been in this kind of place before. There are no animal tracks to follow."

Gray Wolf nodded. "We must mark the trail ourselves."

Singling out a man, Red Deer said, "Hurry back and get the bowls of paint and brushes. Come back here."

Selecting another man, he commanded, "You wait here with your torch. When he returns, follow us and mark the trail. We'll go ahead. The two of you can catch up as you mark." To a third man he instructed, "You wait here with your torch for our return. It'll give us a bearing and guide us back to this place."

The first man turned back for the paint while the other two stood waiting for him. Armed with torches, Red Deer led his group along the path toward where they had last seen the flickering light.

### 

How big was the cave they were crossing? Crooked Foot didn't know and couldn't even guess. He clutched his red spear and trailed along after Silver Fox, Gray Wolf, and the others. The torches his people carried barely pushed back the darkness that surrounded them.

Within this abyss, the path twisted and turned. At times, it skirted large, possibly bottomless caldera;[44] at other times, light of their passing torches was reflected by the dark surfaces of pools of water.

Now and then, Crooked Foot looked over his shoulder to see where the man they left behind stood. His torch marked the place where the group entered the cave. They were there to provide assurance to the rescue party that

---

[44] Caldera - In geology, a large, basin-like depression resulting from the explosion or collapse of the center of a volcano.

they could find their way out. Its light had become no greater than a glowing coal, and it was getting smaller with each step Red Deer's group took. These were Narwikin braves and they did not lose heart knowing that between that faint light and themselves, another torch flickered. The men with the paint were moving this way, marking the trail as they came.

The breeze in their faces, light when they started, had increased as they walked. Now, it carried the sound of voices. They slowed their pace and Red Deer had those carrying torches stay back, but motioned for Gray Wolf, Silver Fox, and Crooked Foot to follow.

Peering around the corner, Red Deer found the cave opened to the outside and fresh air. The terrain sloped downward to a sunlit flat shelf at the edge of a ravine. The area was strewn with rubble and boulders. A rope bridge crossed the gap between sides of the gorge.

Most of the guards and Magram—who had probably waited for the guards to cross to make sure it was safe for him—were already on the other side waiting on the boulder-strewn, grassy margin near the edge of the forest. The bridge swayed gently as slaves and servants, burdened by heavy packs, slowly edged their way across.

Kam Udo sprawled on a litter,[45] Ogdun stood nearby and the two were embroiled in conversation. A respectful distance away, a pair of Kam Udo's lackeys stood ready to carry his litter across. Just beyond, closer to the bridge, Little Fawn knelt resting her burden on the ground and waited her

---

[45] Litter - A type of couch with both feet and handles used to carry dignitaries. The feet were used to sit it on the ground when not being carried. The handles were used by porters to lift and carry the couch and its occupant. This vehicle was usually carried by two or more persons. Development in later years created many versions, one being the sedan chair. In more modern times, a litter is used to carry injured or wounded from battlefields to hospitals.

turn to cross. Nearby, her burly guard sat on a boulder and casually played with the leash fastened to the noose around young woman's neck. Believing they had made good their escape, no one rushed.

Red Deer whispered to Silver Fox, "Go back and bring the others. Tell them to come quietly; only use one torch to light the way; have the torchbearer hang back, I don't want its light to alert our prey. " Silently, Silver Fox disappeared into the darkness returning with the others almost as quickly as he left.

Dividing his people into two groups, Red Deer directed one to spread out to the left and the other to the right. He and Gray Wolf would approach from the center and create a distraction. With his people in place, the pair moved stealthily forward, taking advantage of any cover. The discussion between Kam Udo and Ogdun grew more heated, occupying their attention. Little Fawn's guard chose to ignore them and continued to bask in the warmth of the sun.

The slaves on the bridge completed their crossing, bringing the argument to an end. Kam Udo's lackeys lifted the sedan chair to begin the trek. Leaping out from behind a rock, Red Deer shouted, "Narwikin!" His men, spears at the ready, also jumped up.

Fear drained Kam Udo's face of any color it had. He sat up so fast it caused his porters to lose their balance. Stumbling over their feet, they ended up dumping him on the ground. Unceremoniously, their leader landed face down on a rock and received a bloody nose.

Undaunted, Kam Udo—blood flowing freely— jumped to his feet, and pushed passed the litter bearers as he scrambled to reach the bridge. The little man didn't stop running until he reached the other side. Over there, he insured his safety by having guards line up, ready to repel any attempts at crossing. Magram, seeing a chance to improve his position, directed a pair of husky guards to grab axes and position themselves near the anchor point on the left side.

Little Fawn's beefy guard jumped to his feet and drew his weapon forgetting about his charge in the process. Little Fawn also jumped to her feet, took careful aim, and swung around in a close circle. The end of the pole she shouldered caught her guard beside the head and he went down in a lump. Still restricted by the cords binding her feet, she shuffled toward Red Deer, but was caught short. Ogdun, having grabbed her leash, gave it a sharp jerk.

Choking, red-faced, she ground to a halt, and he yanked her back to him. Pulling her in front of him, he grabbed a handful of hair in his leash-hand while he pressed a sharp, golden-bladed knife to her throat. Glaring at Red Deer he hissed, "Give me no trouble ... and she lives."

Little Fawn squirmed in his grip, but trussed up as she was, couldn't free herself. The noose barely let her breathe. Behind her, Ogdun let her struggle for a moment and then whispered hoarsely in her ear, "Back up. We're crossing the bridge."

"No," she replied stubbornly.

Ogdun twisted her around so she could get a look at the depths of the chasm. Her knees went weak. "You choose. Which will it be: the bridge ... or the ravine?"

Caught between a bad choice and a worse one, Little Fawn nodded her acceptance and Ogdun, keeping her between him and the threat he faced, slowly began shuffling backwards toward the bridge.

The Narwikin formed a semicircle around the area, but none were able to get between the bridge and Ogdun. Red Deer started forward, but stopped as Ogdun made ominous motions with the knife at Little Fawn's throat.

Red Deer glared at him. "You won't get away."

Ogdun countered, "She's my safe passage ... I only

need her to get across the bridge."

As they spoke, Red Deer tried to edge closer, but Ogdun, realizing what he had in mind, shouted, "Stay back. I'll stab her and dump her over the edge," he warned, "and you're not close enough to stop me."

Her face streaked with tears, Little Fawn looked at Red Deer. Pleading, she spoke in a low voice, "Let him go."

"Well, I guess that's settled." Ogdun glowered. "When I am over there and feel safe, I'll release her." *Right after I have the ropes to the bridge cut ... for all the problems you caused me, she can be my trophy.*

The pair mounted the bridge and stumbled along backwards. It was difficult, but—still needing a shield—Ogdun continued to keep Little Fawn between himself and the Narwikin.

Edging backwards, the pair finally reached the middle of the bridge. At this point, Ogdun felt they were far enough out to be safe from attack. Not wanting to stumble, to end up going over the edge, this close to freedom, Ogdun pulled Little Fawn around to face the far side.

Atlatl and red spear in hand, Crooked Foot had watched every step the pair had taken. Until now, Ogdun had not presented much of a target. It was not much of an opening, but it was enough. The lad knew he would not get a better chance.

A flash of red cut through the air and buried itself in Ogdun's back. Surprised, he looked down at the kop-tipped shaft that had pushed through and now protruding from his chest. Still gripping her hair, he sank to his knees, pulling Little Fawn down with him.

"Go ahead, cut that one," Magram commanded. His words were followed by a steady thunk-thunk-thunk as axes chopped at a rope support. He stood back and smugly watched the guards carry out his orders. From the look on

Magram face, he enjoyed his new role.

The noise from the far side caught Ogdun's fading attention: Kam Udo no longer needed him. For Ogdun, the sight dissolved into darkness, his grip loosened and he toppled over. The bridge rolled under the impact. His body, now lifeless, slipped over the edge and into the chasm. His departure set the bridge swinging wildly. Shrieking hysterically, Little Fawn slid closer to the brink.

Red Deer leaped onto the bridge and pushed forward. Diving, he managed to cover the final distance and grab the pole across the girl's shoulders before she followed Ogdun over the edge. Putting an arm around her, he pulled her to a sitting position. Her face, red, she gasped for air. He wanted to get her back to firm ground, but knew he had to release the noose before he could get her to stand.

Kam Udo's guards cut through the first of the bridge's support lines. The bridge tilted, twisting and bouncing from the shock of release. With one hand, Red Deer seized a bridge rope and wrapped his free arm around the wheezing girl.

Silver Fox attempted to crawl to them but found it only made things worse. His friends were too far out for him to reach.

Everyone heard Magram's next command. "Good, now cut the other one." At his urging, Kam Udo's guards doubled their efforts on the second support.

Hearing this, Red Deer slipped both arms under Little Fawn's in order to get a better hold. The pole on Little Fawn's back rested across his arms and secured her there as long as he gripped the ropes.

There was a loud snap as the guards finished cutting the second bridge support. The bridge-remains, held in place now only at the Narwikin end, fell freely. As the bridge fell back, Red Deer could see himself speeding toward the ravine wall. Hoping that he could absorb the impact of the crash, he stretched his legs out to absorb the impact. They still suffered a bone-jarring crash. Red Deer felt the ropes sliding through his grip. He slipped further down before he was able to regain his hold. Little Fawn, her face changing from red to purple, eyes pleading for help, looked at him as she gasped for air.

The Narwikin's first indication the pair had survived was a string of curses from Kam Udo. He filled the air with rants of ill-luck and the failure of the incompetents that surrounded him. "Don't just stand there," he finally ordered, "slay them!"

Silver Fox was the first to react. Still on his belly, he lunged forward and looked over the edge. Red Deer and Little Fawn dangled from the ropes. "Hang on!" He yelled.

Red Deer looked up and shouted to his friends. "She's choking! Hurry and get us up!"

They had no rope, had not brought any with them. It was too far, and there was too little time left to fetch some.

"Quickly," Silver Fox yelled, "help me haul them up." He started tugging on the ropes that were the bridge-remains. Gray Wolf fell in beside him, and they began pulling together. Since there was not enough rope free for more than a couple of workers to pull, retrieving the pair dangling from the bridge-remains started slowly. With each tug, additional rope was made available and more hands could join in the task.

A spear hit the ravine wall near Silver Fox and bounced its way to the bottom grazing Red Deer as it passed. Before other guards could react, a few well-placed Narwikin arrows forced them to fall back.

Silver Fox and Gray Wolf continued pulling on the ropes. Sporadically, spears, arrows, rocks, continued to fly— sometimes aimed at the workers, sometimes at the pair being hauled up—most times, these were fired so quickly, it appeared that there was no thought of aiming.

"If anybody sticks their head up, take a shot." Gray Wolf instructed. This tactic drove Kam Udo's people back.

Two heads finally came level with the rim, and with the next tug the pair were hauled over the lip and onto solid ground. Her face, no longer red, or even purple, but blue, Little Fawn was limp as they lay her out.

"Get the noose off and get rid of that pack," Red Deer ordered.

A knife edge slipped under the cords cut her free and a crowd of eager hands disposed of her burden. A whooshing sound, followed by a fit of coughing, signaled the girl's first deep breaths. Color slowly returning to normal, Little Fawn rubbed her neck and throat and was suddenly aware that she was free to move her arms. Red Deer cradled her protectively in his arms.

From across the way Magram declared, "Narwikin, my leader, Kam Udo the Magnificent, orders you to surrender and plead for his mercy. If you don't, he will return to hunt you down. What is your answer?"

Near the remains of the bridge post, Magram stood next to his leader, a man who he not only towered over, but also outweighed. Flanked by two guards, the smug look on Magram's face showed how much he enjoyed issuing this challenge.

His anger at its zenith, Crooked Foot twirled his sling over his head. "Here's our answer," he barked as he launched the missile—a fist-sized rock. It was a greater distance then any he had previously attempted, but the blow caught Magram between the eyes. The blood it drew flowed down his face. Stunned and temporarily blinded, he stumbled around, arms flailing the air, as he attempted to grab something for support. The overseer tripped on the rocky terrain and collided with Kam Udo. The short tyrant tried to push him away. In the fracas, each man locked fingers in the other man's tunic.

Unable to support this sudden attack, the shorter man fell backwards and the pair hit the ground. Too close to the edge, the tangled duo slipped over the rim. An arm's length down, Kam Udo managed to grab a protruding bush growing from a crevasse. There were no other handholds.

"Help!" Kam Udo called to the guards peering down from above. The plant's roots started to pull loose from its stony perch. "Help me! I command you!" Panic clearly evident in his voice, his eyes bulging with fear, he clung to the bush and tried to pull himself higher.

The two guards looked at each other, but did nothing.

Coming to his senses, Magram reached up and grabbed at the bush. "Stop moving!" He commanded. "The bush is coming loose. You'll kill both of us!" Hoping to knock Kam Udo off and save himself, he gave his leader a sharp elbow. Stirred by the blow, Kam Udo stepped up his struggle.

There was a pop-pop-popping sound as the plant's roots ripped out. Plant roots staring them in the face, the pair floated downward. Magram choked out a wordless gasp. From the look on his face, he no longer enjoyed his new position. Each one gave a final scream as they joined Ogdun.

Crooked Foot watched as the guards looked at each other and then across the riff at the Narwikin. The pair raised their spears in the air and chorused, "Narwikin, we salute you!"

Following that surprise, the pair turned and walked away to join the rest of their party. After a short interval, an unknown voice was heard ordering everyone to proceed.

Gray Wolf and Silver Fox stood over Red Deer as he cradled Little Fawn. The Narwikin watched this odd procession march up the trail and disappear into the forest.

Tearfully, Little Fawn choked out a few words. "It's

over ...."

Crooked Foot, his anger still smoldering, issued one comment, "... for now!" He continued to stare at the place where the procession had disappeared into the forest.

— **The End** —

# ABOUT THE AUTHOR

The author's career spans 40 years in Information Technologies where providing documentation and training was a major part of developing applications. During this time, whether working on large-scale computers, PC's, or networked systems, the author found the success of any applications was highest when the materials were tailored to the audience to keep their attention.

The Ice Age Saga trilogy (The Shaman's Song, The Sojourner's Tale, and Crooked Foot) are all written as action-adventure stories meant to entertain readers of all ages. Notes are included to explain unfamiliar terms or expand on descriptions. These are not stories of what was, but more stories of possibilities, of what could have been.

The author and his wife, both retired, have been married 45 years. They have three adult children and live in a suburb of Detroit.

You can email the author at:
evansandrew50@yahoo.com

The author maintains a website, www.evansandrew50.weebly.com, where he writes about his books and ideas on the background he created.